A

CROWN

OF

DARKNESS

BOOKS BY JESSICA THORNE

A
CROWN
OF
DARKNESS

JESSICA THORNE

SECOND SKY

Published by Second Sky in 2024

An imprint of Storyfire Ltd.
Carmelite House
50 Victoria Embankment
London EC4Y 0DZ

www.secondskybooks.com

Storyfire Ltd's authorised representative in the EEA is Hachette Ireland
8 Castlecourt Centre
Castleknock Road
Castleknock
Dublin 15 D15 YF6A
Ireland

ISBN: 978-1-83790-930-8
eBook ISBN: 978-1-83790-929-2

For Pat, still my hero, always my hero.

GLOSSARY

Asteroth (country) [Ass-te-ROTH], Asterothian (adjective), capital Pelias – currently ruled by a regents' council in the absence of Aeryn, Queen of Asteroth, Chosen of the Aurum, 'The Lost Queen'

Aurum, the [Or-um] – one of two powers formed from old magic in the cataclysm, the Aurum represents light. It sits in opposition to the Nox and takes the form of flames. The centre of its power is held in the Sacrum in Pelias. In each generation it selects a woman from the royal family of Asteroth as its Chosen and she becomes the queen

Aurum-forged steel – metal forged with the power of the Aurum, the opposite of shadow-wrought but the same thing

Cellandre – forest in the northwest of Asteroth/southeast of Ilanthus

College of Winter, the – independent college for the study of all magic, located to the north, beyond the borders of Asteroth and Ilanthus, governed by an elected chancellor

Darkwoods – parts of wild forest infected with traces of the Nox where bargains can be struck and shadow kin roam

Hedge witch – a witch living in a rural setting, administering to the needs of a village or small local community, generally unaligned, regarded as lesser by the College of Winter, the maidens and the sisterhood

Ilanthus [Ill-AN-thus] (country), Ilanthian (adjective), capital Sidonia – currently ruled by Alessander of the line of Sidon, King of Ilanthus

Knightsford – fortified town on the edge of Cellandre with a garrison of knights

Knights of the Aurum – sworn warriors in the service of the Aurum. Once the power (or light) of the Aurum runs through them they become Paladins

Line of Sidon [Sid-ON] – bloodline of the royal family of Ilanthus. Spilling the blood of Sidon in a place of old magic is said to summon the Nox

Maidens of the Aurum – society of witches dedicated to serving the Aurum – currently led by Sister Maryn. By law in Asteroth all women with magic must submit to the Maidens of the Aurum and serve through them while all men must return their magic to the Aurum

Nightbreaker – Aurum-forged sword of the Grandmaster of the Knights of the Aurum

Nox, the [Noks] – one of two powers formed from old magic in the cataclysm, the Nox represents darkness. It sits in opposition to the Aurum and is said to take many forms, but it is worshipped as a goddess by the people of Ilanthus

Old magic – primal magic torn into two opposing forces by a magical cataclysm long ago, now passed into legend, but still lingering in some remote places, and used by some witchkind

Otherlight/Othersight the way Wren can see magic – not a magical thing as such but her term for the way she perceives it.

Othertongue – secret language of magic known primarily to witchkind

Pact, the – peace agreement between Asteroth and Ilanthus which ended the last war

Paladins – senior Knights of the Aurum, touched by its light and blessed, filled by the light when its power is invoked which makes them stronger, faster and lethal. Servants of the Aurum, and the queen of Asteroth, her protectors

Pelias [Pel-EE-ass] (city) – capital of Asteroth

Rebel witchkind of Garios – witches who have refused to serve either the Aurum or the Nox but seek independence, freedom and rights of their own

Sacrum, the [Sak-RUM] – a stone circle now enclosed by the temple in the palace at Pelias which houses the flames of the Aurum, the most holy site of the Aurum

Sanctum, the [Sank-TUM] – secure compound in the royal palace in Pelias housing the Maidens of the Aurum

Shadow kin – creatures formed from shadows which can beguile, infect and overpower humans, turning them into monsters serving the Nox. They use music, illusion and brute force to hunt and trap their prey. When a bargain is made, shadow kin often claim the price

Shadow-wrought steel – metal forged with the power of the Nox with the intention of containing or harnessing magic. The sisterhood are skilled in this art, forging the weapons to fight and capture others

Sidonia [Sid-ON-ee-ah] (city) – capital of Ilanthus

Sisterhood of the Nox – society of Ilanthian witches dedicated to serving the Nox

Witchfire – a magical spell which conjures flames, used primarily as a weapon as very difficult to control

Witchkind – people able to wield magic, able to command or cajole the powers of light and dark, or attuned to old magic in some way

PROPHECY OF AELYN THE FIRST

When the Nox is scattered across the land,
Sidon's walls come down.
When the Aurum sleeps in silent flames,
Pelias gives up its crown.
When shadows take the Aurum,
the Nox will take the throne.
When the Nox is crowned in the Sacrum,
the lost queen stands alone.

PROLOGUE
ELODIE

All Elodie's life had been mapped out for her, its course rigid, unwavering, absolute.

She knelt before the flames and bowed her head, trying to focus and run through everything exactly as she had been told. Reach out to the Aurum, offer up yourself, your heart, your soul.

'*All who walk this path walk upon a knife's edge.*'

The words of her ancestor Aelyn rang through her head and they were forever true.

This was the first step. She was Chosen, they said. But she was also fifteen years old. Just fifteen and already she had no future.

She thought of the boy in the kitchens. He was a year older than her and he was a newly made knight. His kit was old and clearly repurposed. It might have belonged to his father, or an uncle. Or even his grandfather. The light alone knew, the Knights of the Aurum never changed.

But he was kind. And gentle. And he had the loveliest eyes, dark and deep. And that smile, a rare and precious blessing. She might have chosen a man like that herself, if she was ever given a choice. But that, too, was impossible. Still, she could dream.

He hadn't known who she was and she had liked that. Roland, he said his name was. And he blushed.

'You've left it far too late,' Aunt Ylena sniped at her mother from just a little distance away, beyond the ring of white stones around the Aurum's flame, where they stood watching her, as still and austere as the unmoving statues of their ancestors encircling the chamber. 'This should have been done years ago and you know it.'

Elodie's mother laughed. 'She's just a child, Ylena. Don't wish her life away.'

'She should have already made her formal vows to the Aurum, not this playacting. She should be married. She's your only heir, and the line must continue. If you'd put aside—'

'Enough,' Aelenor snapped, and all the good humour was gone. They were forever at her to set Elodie's father aside and take another husband – because Jonquil had not given her another child – but Aelenor would never do that. It wouldn't make any difference, she had told him, when Elodie's beloved father had begged her to listen to her advisors. And that was that.

'She is to be queen. I would have thought you would understand that.'

'I want her to at least have what I have, Ylena.'

Love. She wanted her daughter to know love. And Elodie did, perhaps. Or the first stirring of it. She had looked at Roland and something in her mind had said, quite clearly, *He's mine.*

She would just have to persuade him of that. Because once her bodyguards had finally found her – safe and unharmed, of course, just talking to him in the kitchens by firelight – he had been horrified. He'd dropped to his knees, begging her forgiveness. And the spell of anonymity had been broken.

'She must marry. We need this alliance, or there will be a war.'

A cold shadow passed down Elodie's back, like a whisper of winter. Marry? Who did Aunt Ylena want her to marry?

'I notice you bring this up when your own child has taken the vows of a maiden.' Aelenor's tone was scathing.

'That was hardly my choice. Maryn is headstrong. Almost as bad as her.'

Her. Elodie smiled a little. They couldn't see anyway, and wouldn't be looking if they could. She was communing with the flames of the Aurum, or was meant to be, but the Aurum rarely responded to her anyway. They weren't exactly chatty at the best of times. The holy fire was distant and silent but one day she knew she would channel it and speak with its voice and divine its will. Like her mother did as queen and Chosen.

Maryn would have been so much better at this than she was. But Maryn was the daughter of the second-born princess royal, not the queen. A cousin, not an heir or an equal. Not Aelenor's daughter. Everyone was fond of reminding both of them of that. And Maryn knew her mother of old. She and Elodie were like sisters more than cousins. And now Maryn wasn't here. She'd joined the Maidens of the Aurum, where her magical abilities could be put to the best service of the kingdom. Mainly, Elodie thought, to escape the machinations of her own mother. Lady Ylena, princess royal of Asteroth.

Elodie tried to focus again. Maryn could do this. The flames danced for her, grew bright and blinding when she approached. Perhaps Maryn should have been chosen and not her. Perhaps...

There was no good in wishing for things which could not be. Like freedom. Like Roland.

Light and dark, flames and shadows, Elodie's whole life was divided into what was allowed and what was not allowed. She suspected the country knight in the kitchens fell very much into the not allowed category. Oh, but she wanted him.

'I'm not sure Evander of Ilanthus is...' her mother paused, picking her words carefully, 'an ideal match.'

'But he is the best hope of peace. And we can ensure his cooperation.'

Aelenor sighed. 'There's no need for that, surely. It's... distasteful. No, there's time yet. The Aurum will guide us. She'll know when she sees him.'

Oh, but she did know. Elodie knew she should say something, anything, but she was afraid as well. The light of the hearth had played on his face, in his eyes.

And he had been so kind. She longed for kindness, gentleness, for someone who would love her completely and never fail her.

There wasn't time. Within a year, Aelenor was dead and Elodie was engaged to be married to a prince of Ilanthus. And what a disaster that had proved to be...

The flames of the Aurum warmed her face and she looked up into the light. She was no longer a girl. Not in any way but in her heart. And everything had fallen apart.

What was your vow?

The voice echoed strangely. It sounded a little like her mother's voice, but it was something else as well. More than one voice. A chorus. It rang around the back of her mind, and came from every corner of the chamber. The white stones encircling her vibrated with its sound. Outside them, there was only darkness.

And that wasn't right either. She should have been able to see the whole Sanctum. There should have been maidens in attendance, and courtiers, Paladins to guard her... Roland... and Wren...

This wasn't right. She wasn't a fifteen-year-old girl hearing all the options of her future being closed off. She was a woman, a queen, a mother...

What was your vow?

The voice that was many voices came again, more insistent this time.

'To... to serve.' Her words were forced from her throat, whether she wanted to speak or not.

And have you?

The ground shook beneath her and Elodie stared into the fire, tears burning the corners of her eyes. Had she? She had tried to. That had to count for something, didn't it?

But the Aurum rarely bothered with intentions. Action was all.

And have you served us, Elodie?

Elodie closed her eyes but the light forced them to open again, forced her to look into its depth, and in the white-hot heart of the flames of the Aurum images formed. A man, strong, broad-shouldered, tall. Not the boy she had fallen in love with the moment she saw him, the man with whom she should have spent her life, but the man he became, the man she had deserted. Her every desire. The love of her life. He held a sword in front of him like a challenge, a sword which became a column of light, and his expression was both grave and heartbroken.

The last time she had seen him...

Beside him stood a girl, small and slight, with a mass of black hair which moved like ink in water around her, alive with enchantment and power. Her dark eyes looked huge in her pale, resolute face, and she spread her hands wide. Darkness and shadows tangled around her fingertips. But in that darkness Elodie could see stars. Light within the shadows. It should have been impossible, but not for her daughter.

Wren.

And Roland.

Elodie's heart ached. But they were lost to her now. They were gone. And she... she didn't know where she was.

We fight the Nox, they had sworn, all of them, Elodie, Roland, even Wren in her innocence, *with flame and sword.*

Well? the voice of the Aurum asked.

The flames roared through her, deafening her and blinding her as everything she was, everything she would have been and everything she wanted was burned away again.

CHAPTER 1

WREN

'That's enough, princess,' a voice called out behind her, in a kind of sing-song that was almost mockery. 'Come back quietly now. We don't want trouble.'

Wren froze in the middle of the sumptuous corridor, her heart threatening to tear itself out of the cage of her ribs. Her bare feet sank into the deep pile of the carpeting as if she might somehow root herself there.

Already. How had they found her already?

Three of them this time. They were all smiling, the bastards, like this was some kind of joke. And to them it was, she realised. They'd been charged with watching her. Maybe the door hadn't been left unmanned accidentally.

They did so like their games. That was an Ilanthian trait. Games of cat and mouse, games of life and death. Stupid, cruel and senseless games.

She bolted back up the corridor, away from them, heading past the door she had slipped out of and down the stairs at the far end, their entrance hidden behind a silken wall-hanging. She had been this way before, several times, on other thwarted escape attempts. She had no idea how many times. Or how long this game had been going on.

The guards passed by the door, cursing as they ran, and headed on towards the grand gallery. They had missed her. Wren let herself breathe again.

Perhaps they hadn't expected her to go this way. Maybe they had forgotten it existed.

The nobility of Ilanthus didn't take the servants' stairs, and only the nobleborn could guard the royal family and their belongings, a position of honour. They certainly didn't use the stairs to reach the servants' quarters below ground. They preferred to pretend such places didn't exist, that food and wine, and their many luxuries, appeared as if by magic when they needed them, that there weren't a thousand slaves toiling away beneath them.

They might not use the word slaves, but that was a moot point. Everyone served here, one way or the other, willingly or not. There were ways to ensure that and the royal court was very free about using them.

Finally, Wren stopped, listening hard, at the foot of the grey staircase. No one seemed to be following. She crept forward, intent on every noise around her, her eyes frantically looking for the next opportunity.

She had never made it this far before and knew she had to be careful. It wasn't like she had a map, not even of the little of the palace of Sidonia that she had managed to explore. She had to keep going but slowly now. Above stairs there were courtiers and guards everywhere, always someone watching. She didn't want to think about what would happen to whoever had left the door open.

Even if she made it outside, she wouldn't know which way to go. But it didn't matter. She had to try. That was all she had left.

Get out. Get the bracelet off. Find a way out of Ilanthus.

She had to get away.

The days flowed into each other and sometimes she was given things to eat and drink which twisted her world in on itself. She had no idea how long she had been here. Weeks perhaps. Weeks since Finn had brought her here and promptly betrayed her. Sidonia was a maze. And the palace was a maze within that maze. The royal court spent its time in revels and debauchery, laughing at her when she didn't join in, calling her names and mocking her. When they bothered to pay attention to her at all. She bored them. They had expected so much and she had not delivered. She didn't care. It didn't matter. She just had to get out of this place.

The Sisterhood of the Nox looked on, watching her the way someone might watch a mouse trying to wriggle out of a trap. In the absence of Hestia Rayden, they were led by a woman called Lady Oriole, who never took her cool judgemental eyes off Wren whenever she was paraded out in front of them. She didn't know what they were expecting to see or what they wanted her to do. They didn't claim her, or help her. They didn't do anything but watch. Same with the king.

It felt like they were waiting for something and she did not know what. And Finn... Finn was no help either.

There were racks of clothes in one of the rooms, whether in storage or awaiting repairs, she didn't know. Everything was Ilanthian in style, naturally, but nowhere near as grand as the garments the nobles of the court above wore. They were more substantial, for one thing. At the other end from the hallway, she could hear the clatter and roar of the kitchens. But beyond that... fresh air beckoned her. Her nostrils flared with the possibility.

Knotting her hair up at the back of her head, she grabbed a headscarf to tie around it and a shawl which she flung over her shoulders. She couldn't do anything about her own filmy clothes but try to cover them. Cover herself because the light alone knew the gown they had picked out for her did little of that. It plunged down her front and back, with little more than a twist of satin to keep it up at the nape of her neck. There were no shoes or boots so she just carried on, barefoot and desperate. She didn't have any choice.

She almost made it. Her hand pushed open the narrow door to a herb garden and for a moment she felt sunshine and fresh air on her face. For just a moment.

Strong arms seized her, hauling her up and off her feet.

'Got you!'

Wren didn't waste time screaming. There was no point and no one was coming to help her. Not now, not ever. She kicked back with all the strength she could muster, felt her foot connect with something soft and, with a gasp of pain, the guard holding her let her go.

But the other one was waiting. He grabbed her arms without pause, twisting them up behind her back in a fluid and brutal motion. She pitched forward, helpless, unable to break free.

'Little bitch,' the first one snarled, raising his fists.

'Stand down!' said his companion in patient tones. 'You don't want to mark her. You know what he'll do. We haven't seen Captain Elendris since he hit her.'

Of course they hadn't, Wren thought grimly. Elendris was dead, a smear on the courtyard far below the tower room where she was kept. And he had deserved it too. She could still feel the hand which had struck her face, the imprint of it on her cheek, the way her face had exploded in pain and white-hot blindness. And recalled everything else he'd sworn he'd do to her because no one would stop him.

That had just been the first time she had escaped.

It wasn't the last time and neither would this be. The trouble was, she wasn't able to get far. Not with the bracelet still on her arm, not with the eyes and ears of the whole court against her. But she had to keep trying.

She had tried to call on the light again, but in this place that didn't seem to be possible. The Aurum was not responding, not as it had back in Pelias when she had healed Leander and made her stupid deal with Finn. Coming here had broken that connection. And the Nox... she couldn't reach it even if she had wanted to.

And part of her very much wanted to.

There had to be a way to get the magic-dampening bracelet off her arm. Once she did... once she did, she would make them all pay. And they knew that.

'Here, pass the stinger,' the guard holding her said and Wren's struggles became frantic.

'No, please,' she gasped but they weren't listening to her. That got people killed as well. She'd tried befriending one of them, a younger man called Trin, in the hopes he would help her somehow. He had never even got the chance.

Trin was dead as well, strangled on orders of King Alessander, while she watched. They'd held her in place, right in front of him while he tried to babble out excuses and apologies. While he had begged for his life. They'd wound a silken cord around his neck like one of those collars they made the servants wear and then, slowly, tightened it, an inch at a time. His face had turned the most horrible shade of purple and he had wept. Or tried to. By the end he'd been unconscious so at least there was that small mercy, but he'd known all along what was happening. Guilt still ate through her at the thought of it and she woke from nightmares where he came to her and told her it was all her fault.

He wasn't wrong.

It was getting harder and harder to tell her nightmares from reality in this place. But still she tried. She couldn't give up.

Elodie wouldn't have given up. Neither would Roland. Nor Finn...

Wren swallowed hard and pushed the thought away as hard as she could. She had to.

'You bring this on yourself, you know,' said her captor, almost kindly. And then a sharp point of pain jabbed into her neck. The numbness that followed flowed through her like encroaching ice. Her body went limp, helpless, and she slumped forward. When the guard let her go she fell. 'You put more in that than usual,' he said to his companion.

'Serves her right. She got me right in the balls.'

Serves him right, Wren thought bitterly, as everything went black.

CHAPTER 2

WREN

A gentle hand woke Wren by tracing a line down the side of her face, along her jaw and down the column of her throat. It stopped in the dip between her clavicles, teasing the sensitive skin there. She drew in an involuntary breath and shivered. Lips brushed her shoulder, lips which smiled against her skin.

But for all that momentary pleasure, her head was pounding and her body was sore.

Blearily, she began to take in the room, and realised why. Her arms were drawn up high above her head and tied there securely. As her senses slowly returned to her, so too did reality and an understanding of where she was and what was happening. She jerked back, terrified.

But there was nowhere to go.

His hands caught her before she could hurt herself, pulling her forward against his body and holding her there. Weak and still fighting off the effects of the soporific drugs the stinger had delivered to her system, it was all she could do to open her eyes and look into his face.

Into his eyes. His beautiful blue eyes.

They were the eyes of another man now, cold and distant,

laughing at her. And yet, she longed for him, ached to feel his touch. Her body betrayed her, even now.

'Hush, little bird. How often are we going to play this game?'

It was Finn's voice, Finn's face and body and his touch. But by all the oldest magic, she knew it wasn't him. This was Prince Finnian of the line of Sidon, as cold and heartless as his famed ancestor of long ago, not the man she loved. He even sounded like Leander, using that pet name for her. A prince of Ilanthus and her beloved no more.

But she couldn't believe that. Not entirely. Somewhere, somehow, Finn had to still be in there.

'Let me go,' she told him as firmly as she could manage. Her voice shook and she hated herself for it.

He smiled again, a teasing, sultry smile which promised so many things she couldn't allow herself to think about. All the things she still wanted. All her hopes and dreams...

There was a laugh buried in his words that made her insides twist. 'I... don't think so, princess. And that is not an answer. Shall we try again?'

Wren forced herself to breathe as his hands continued to skim across her flesh, teasing her. The stinger had numbed her all over as it stole her consciousness but now, as it wore off, it heightened every sensation. That was part of its design, he had explained. Part of the fun.

And oh, how he liked to play this game.

She didn't want to think where he had learned it or how. It was a torment of pleasure.

Finn untied her hair and pulled it down from the knot she had made of it, threading his fingers through it. It fell to the small of her back now, black silken waves. He combed through it until he had worried out every tangle. Then he swept it to one side. His lips brushed against the nape of her neck, right at the top of her spine, his teeth grazing her skin, and she couldn't stop the groan of need which shuddered through her.

'Why deny yourself, Wren?' His breath played against her, still teasing her as much as his voice did. Desire thundered through her and she struggled to dampen it down. Tears stung in her eyes with the effort. 'Just say yes. I thought this was all you wanted. I'm yours, you know? I always will be. Just as you are mine.'

Not like this. Not now. Not here... He was different here.

'Let me go,' she said again. 'I won't give you what you want. You know that.'

He pulled back, releasing her so abruptly it was almost like a slap. 'I promised I wouldn't take anything from you that you didn't offer freely. But I want you to admit that you still want me. I want you to be happy. I could take you, you know. Nothing could stop me.'

She glared at him. Of course she knew that. She also knew what she'd do the moment she did have access to her magic again. Perhaps that was what was stopping him from forcing himself on her. What she had once given freely and with joy, he now held over her like a threat. What they had shared, and the memory of every exquisite moment, was a torment.

Or perhaps it was something else. He wanted her to give in, to beg him, to be his, body, mind and soul. That was the most important thing to him now, that she accept him as he was now, that she surrendered.

It was all part of his wretched game. He wanted her subservient, bound to him. He wanted the powers of the Nox.

'Let me go.' It was all she was going to say to him. She just had to be strong. But with his gentle caresses, his kisses, the strokes of his hands against her skin... it was so difficult. She wanted him still.

'My poor little Wren,' he said scornfully. 'That's never going to happen. You are far too precious. And you'll get yourself in such trouble outside my chambers. Don't you know that? In this court, you'd be fair game. A witch without her powers, a princess without a crown. They would fall on you like a rabid pack of hounds. You're lucky my guards are so loyal.'

He turned away from her, leaving her dangling there, and settled himself on the divan opposite her, where food and wine had been left on a low table. He'd been eating, she realised, waiting for her to wake up. Glancing around the room she saw a number of his servants, gifts from his father to welcome him home, women and men, all young and beautiful, obedient and devoted to him. Concubines, lovers, slaves. Whether that devotion was derived from magic or drugs or the sheer need to survive in this benighted city she didn't know. They wore soft leather collars around their throats, like pets.

And that was how he treated them. She loathed him for it. That was what he wanted to make of her now. A pet. A slave.

Shadows of old, part of her wanted that too. She didn't want to fight anymore. She just wanted Finn to touch her, to hold her and to love her.

Sometimes she wondered what Lynette would have said about that. Something scathing, with disgust rolling off it. Light, she missed Lynette's overprotective hovering now.

Wren would not let herself join them. So far he had not turned them on her, though sometimes he threatened to and they eyed her hungrily. He preferred to keep her to himself and drive her to distraction with soft touches and caresses, with the lies that he still loved her and that if she could only submit to him everything would be all right again. Sometimes she almost believed him. He sounded sincere.

But Finnian had been as good as his word, for all that was worth now. He wanted her to beg for him. He hadn't forced her and he had not allowed anyone else to lay hands on her without repercussions. She thought of Captain Elendris, loathsome little man that he was, the way the malice in his expression had turned to shock when Finn had thrown him from the window. Wren shuddered, turning her face away. No one dared touch her without their prince's permission.

Perhaps she could be grateful for that small mercy. But gratitude to him could lead to something more and she couldn't have that. She had to be strong.

Finn... no, Finnian. This was not her Finn, not a Knight of the Aurum, not her Paladin, not the ward of Asteroth who had loved her and cared for her and done all in his power to protect her from the first time they met. That man had vanished the moment he had broken the charm and released the spell which had brought the two of them here to Sidonia. This was Prince Finnian of Sidon, the Ilanthian crown prince and next in line to the throne, and she didn't know him at all. How could she? They were not the same man.

Except they were. He was. She only had to look at him to know that. Something had changed. Either he had been lying all along, or something had happened when that spell was cast to change him, or now, when faced with a future of ruling this kingdom and spending the rest of his life in this hedonistic court, he had decided to embrace it and all that it entailed. He was an Ilanthian to the core. She had been warned.

She hated him.

And a treacherous part of her still longed for him as well. Her memories were too vivid, too intoxicating, and the love they had shared...

... had been a lie.

Finn sank back in the cushions, lifted a glass of wine to his lips and watched her while a lithe young woman with long black hair settled herself between his splayed legs, running her hands up his breeches towards his belt. He never took his eyes off Wren, watching, waiting.

All the servants watched as well. Watched him hungrily. Watched her jealously, or in disbelief, or simply watched...

They would report back to the king, she knew that. So did Finn. So he generally let them fawn all over him. He had to, he told her in quieter moments; it was expected.

She didn't believe that either. He was enjoying it far too much. Enjoying them, enjoying tormenting her with them.

The woman between his legs moved eagerly, up and down, and Finn reached out to tangle his hand in her hair and pull her in closer. He let his head fall back, exposing the long line of his throat, and his breath quickened.

Wren closed her eyes, but that didn't stop the sounds reaching her. She kept her eyes closed, even though her tears leaked from the corners and she could do nothing to stop them.

Later, so much later, when he had finished with his lovers – his slaves, she reminded herself and detested him for it – Finnian dismissed them. He waited until the two of them were entirely alone before checking the room and locking the door. He paced the perimeter like a caged tiger and pulled the heavy curtains over the stained-glass windows. Then he untied her, releasing her arms at last.

She was too exhausted from standing in that awkward position to resist him, her aching body folding into his embrace. He lifted her in silence and carried her to their bed, where he settled her in that sea of luxurious material, pillows and cushions.

'Drink,' he said and lifted a glass to her lips.

What could she do? Her throat was parched and he knew it. So she drank.

He would do this, tending her, feeding her, caring for her, as if he still loved her. He would brush her hair until it shone. But Wren knew it for the trap it was, the trap it had to be.

How could he still love her and do everything else he did?

'Sleep now,' he told her and she realised he had drugged the wine again. Of course he had. It could hardly be a surprise at this stage. He needed her to be compliant. And whenever it wore off, she would try to escape again.

One day, she promised herself... One day she would make it out. No matter how long that took.

Her body grew heavy and sleep crept up around her like shadows. She curled into his arms and let it take her.

It was easier than fighting. That was all she did, every day, internally and externally. Fighting against him, against the court of Ilanthus and what it would make of her, of the terrible desire that rose within her and threatened to overwhelm her entirely. Against the power of the Nox which flowed in her veins. Against her memory of a love she had thought pure and true, and endless.

Because no matter what happened, she was not going to give in.

She couldn't give up hope, no matter how he tried to trick her, seduce her or steal it from her.

As her exhaustion took her, Finn buried his face in her hair, breathed in her scent and gathered her close. His voice was the faintest whisper on the edges of her dreams.

'You can't keep doing this to yourself, Wren. Sooner or later, you'll accept it, accept me, and become who you have to be here. Otherwise my father will lose his patience and when that happens, it will be so much worse. You realise that, don't you? You must accept it, willingly. Please, just give in, little bird. Let go.'

HEDGE WITCH PROVERB

When you are lost, look for us in birdsong.

CHAPTER 3

ROLAND

Roland dreamed of Elodie that night. Like every other night. She was reaching out to him from a tangle of twisted briars formed of shadows, her pale arms torn to shreds by their thorns. And though he hacked at the seething mass with his blazing sword, he couldn't free her. Even Nightbreaker had no effect on them. They kept growing, coiling around her and crushing her in their sharp embrace.

The earth of Asteroth drank down her blood and the land sang with its touch. Old magic hummed in the air, something far beyond either light or dark. And certainly beyond the two of them. It demanded more and more, sacrifice, blood, self-destruction.

He woke up swallowing down a scream of rage and loss before it could escape. They had camped last night in a patch of ragged woodland on the edge of the Great North Road. They had left Pelias and even Knightsford far behind them now. The land here was wild and uncaring, the mountains stooping over them. The road to the College of Winter should have been direct and easy but something kept turning them around, some-thing not quite natural. They were not lost. He knew that.

Olivier's maps showed them the way. But they couldn't find the path, or when they thought they had, it twisted in another way.

Olivier looked up from keeping watch, his back to the embers of their fire, but said nothing. Anselm slept on, a deep and dreamless sleep of a man with no regrets.

Boys, thought Roland wearily. They were just boys and he should never have allowed them to come with him.

But he had, and it was too late to send them back. Not to mention far too dangerous. Who knew what Lady Ylena and her pet councillors would do to them for freeing him.

If he tried, they would argue of course. They were good at that. Well, Anselm was. Quick and clever and oh so determined. And Olivier's loyalty was beyond question. Where Anselm would argue, Olivier would just carry on, stubbornly, doing what he thought was right. That had not changed. They were in their twenties now, far from actual boyhood. But to him, they were still boys. Still the squires he had taken under his wing along with Finn, grateful that his ward had friends. Each in their own way in need of his protection, he had given it with his full heart, sure then that he would never have children of his own so lavishing that care on them instead. In his own way. He was still the Grandmaster of the Knights of the Aurum then and they were sworn to serve.

He lay back again, trying to calm his breath and his erratic heart, staring at the stars peering through the high canopy of leaves overhead.

He'd left her behind. Left her lying there helpless. He hadn't even been able to say goodbye, not really. His Elodie, his love, his queen...

And if she did awaken would she call him a traitor as well? He'd stood against her when she had been consumed with the power of the Aurum, but he had done so in order to save Wren from her wrath. Surely she would understand that. The Aurum itself might not, but Elodie would. She had to.

If she understood anything at all anymore. If she ever awoke.

No, he couldn't think like that. He had given up on her once and she had come back to him. He had to keep believing. He would find a way to save her. Sister Maryn of the Maidens of the Aurum believed an answer could be found in the College of Winter, and that was where he would go. He'd find a solution. Elodie would awaken and they would be together again.

But something dark and foreboding in the back of his mind taunted him with the thought that his life had never been simple and he didn't deserve such blessings. He'd left her behind. Just as she had once left him.

He had to pray that the Aurum would protect her. He had to believe that. She had been locked deep in its power, and it was trapped inside her. It needed her to survive. At least that was what Maryn had implied. He only hoped the maiden was right. She knew secrets of magic and the mysteries of the flames. She had to be right.

Trying to sleep was pointless now. It would be dawn soon. He roused himself again and got up.

'Grandmaster?' Olivier asked. No more than that but it was his way. The query was unspoken. What did he need? Was something wrong? What could Olivier do to help?

There was no way to answer. Roland wasn't sure he even knew the answer anyway.

Nightbreaker, the great sword of the Grandmaster of the Knights of the Aurum, lay by his side, instead of the woman he loved, the queen to whom he had devoted his life even in her absence. He strapped it back against his body and felt the weight as something that belonged there. Part of him.

It was all he had of her. Once again. The sword had been his companion for more years than Elodie had.

Well, except in his dreams.

And now she lay locked in an enchanted sleep, miles away in Pelias, the power of the Aurum itself burning inside her.

At least, he thought bitterly, he knew where she was this time.

He made his way to the edge of their camp and into the bushes to relieve himself.

That was when he heard it: movement, all around them. He let out a low whistle to alert Olivier and backed up, bracing himself for attack.

The undergrowth came alive all around him, a wild rustling and groaning as the ground itself ripped open. Roots and vines rose like living things, tearing themselves up from the earth and down from the canopy, and Roland staggered back, drawing Nightbreaker. He wasn't fast enough, not against something like this. No one could be.

This was more than an enchantment. This was wild magic, old magic.

Behind him he heard Olivier cry out in alarm, shouting Anselm's name, but the other young knight wasn't even fully awake yet. The same roots surged up from the earth around his sleeping form and engulfed him in moments. Olivier was backing towards him, trying the impossible task of covering all angles alone.

Roland retreated, aware that Nightbreaker had not flamed to life in his hands. Perhaps the Aurum was not able to help him here. Perhaps it couldn't help at all anymore. Or perhaps this was not an attack of darkwoods or shadow kin, and therefore nothing to do with the Nox.

Then, abruptly, all went still. The leaves made soft murmurings in the breeze and the trees creaked softly. There was no birdsong, no sign of animal life around them. Just that eerie silence.

Some primal instinct in Roland would give almost anything to flee if he could. But that was not an option.

'Hold,' said a voice, young, soft and quiet, with a slight waver indicating it was not actually as confident as it was endeavouring to sound. 'Hold or the forest will tear him apart.'

The roots and vines tightened on Anselm, one coiling around his throat. His face was visible, eyes wide with fear, his jaw clenched tightly. He struggled all the same, even though there was no getting out of that trap.

'If that was your intention you would have done it already,' Roland replied to the leaves and the undergrowth. Still no sign of who he was talking to. The woodlands were still and so unnaturally quiet. 'Let him go. We mean you no harm. We're just passing through.'

'Knights of the Aurum just passing through?' said another voice, definitely a girl this time, high and sweet as birdsong. 'Now I've heard everything. Where's the trail of death and destruction?'

The first voice – a boy perhaps – hissed something at her. Their voices came from all around the clearing though, as if echoing back on themselves. A deliberate trick, Roland thought, but a clever one. A warrior with less discipline would be thrown off balance, trying to look for the source and not focusing on anything else. Such as his priorities.

'Let Anselm go, and we'll talk,' he told them.

'Why do you think we want to talk to you?' the girl snapped.

'Shut up, Lark.'

Roland glanced at Olivier, who cast him a confused glance. They sounded like children, young adolescents at most. Siblings too close in years to talk without argument. Twins perhaps.

'I mean it, Robin. We should just kill them and—'

Roland raised his hands and slowly lowered his sword until he could set it down at his feet. They weren't to know he could retrieve it in a heartbeat. He was trying to make a point. Olivier followed suit, though he didn't look happy about it.

'Talk to me,' Roland said. 'My name is Roland de Silvius. I'm listening. What do you want? Who are you?'

A vine slid forward cautiously to prod at the sword and then recoiled sharply, as if stung. It withdrew, back into the undergrowth. If they had thought to snatch the sword away they'd have to do better than that. Nightbreaker could look after itself. It had been forged in the Aurum and magic was an innate part of it.

A boy stepped out of the trees, his hair tangled with sticks and leaves, his face smeared with dirt and coloured oils, not yet even in his teen years. Behind him, there was a girl, roughly the same age, wearing the same sort of clothing decorated with leaves, bark and flowers.

Not children. Not quite. But not definitely adults either.

Roland drew in a breath. They looked feral and he was not sure what was going on here, who they were or what they wanted.

'We are witchkind,' said the boy in a steady voice, glaring at the knights. 'We live free or we die. And you're all our prisoners.'

CHAPTER 4

ROLAND

The two witchkind children watched the knights with eyes like hunters' as they led them deep into the forested valley in the foothills of the mountains. Not like children. That was unsettling. The forest realm seemed to leap and flow around them, easing their way and closing behind them in a disconcerting manner. The other disturbing thing was that the boy, Robin, had let them retrieve their weapons as if they were of no note. Lark, his sister, who had been rather too keen for comfort to just kill them, followed behind, as her brother led the way. The three knights led their strangely docile horses on foot.

Their otherness grated on Roland's senses. This wasn't magic in the way he knew it. It felt different, an old magic, and far stronger than it had any right to be.

'Where are we going?' he asked Robin.

The boy, no more than twelve, Roland thought, all long limbs with a coltish way of moving, cast him a scathing glance which seemed to belong to someone much older.

'Tobias asked us to get you. The paths here are twisting and only we can lead you. The College doesn't want to be found.'

Roland could believe that. There was nothing natural about

this passage through the trees. And nothing natural about the way they couldn't find the College either. But he had to admit, he was intrigued as well. How were they doing this? And why?

Elodie would know. Or at least Elodie would know what questions to ask. She'd have it worked out in seconds. Perhaps Wren would as well.

Oh, how he wished they were here now. Someone with a way to reach these wild little witches and make them understand he meant them no harm.

Except... except only a short time ago he would have ordered them hunted down and brought to the Aurum if they showed their faces in Asteroth. The boy would be forced to relinquish the magic he was born with, and given the option of joining the knights. Many had. The girl would join the maidens. Because that was what was done. Witchkind were dangerous.

Like whoever bespelled that maid to kill an Ilanthian princeling. The maidens had blamed rebel witchkind for that, hadn't they?

Who was Tobias? They could get no more than a name and once Robin said it Lark hissed something at him and he rapidly shut up. Clearly he had said far too much.

The chancellor of the College was called Tobias Vambray, but why would he be sending these wild children to find Roland? There were any number of skilled witchkind within its walls. Something didn't add up and Roland hated that feeling.

All he could do was follow in silence, keeping his wits about him as the forest moved and whispered around them. They could be heading into a trap, he knew that. But what choice did he have?

Roland wished he had word of Finn and Wren, that he could have some indication that they were safe somewhere. He knew Finn would look after her, and Wren could certainly look after herself when it came down to it. But there had been no news of them and Roland didn't like that at all.

When they took a rest, he watched Lark, her tangle of brown hair and furtive green eyes, and wondered what his daughter had looked like when she was that age. Another young girl named for a bird with far too much magic at her command.

Wren might not be his flesh and blood but she was his daughter. He was resolute on that and no matter what magics were involved he would not accept anything else. He'd seen the heartbreak in her eyes when she had realised differently, had felt it echo through his own body. Regardless of how it might appear, he knew she was his.

'Do you have family?' he asked Lark.

'I have Robin,' she snarled at him. Like being threatened by a kitten really, he thought and let his smile show. That didn't sit well with her either.

So just the two of them. And this Tobias. 'Is Tobias your father?' he tried again.

'No,' Robin cut in, his voice sharp. 'We don't have parents. Few witchkind do. We just have siblings, the ones who care for us and support us. Like the sisters in that story. We protect each other. What kind of parent would dump a child in a darkwood to die, call them cursed and a crime against the Aurum?'

So that was what had happened, was it, Roland thought, his heart sinking for them. No wonder there was such anger in them both.

Olivier stiffened, opened his mouth to protest and then stopped as the girl turned her glare on him instead, like a cat following prey. Her mouth was a hard, flat line. 'That's what you all think,' she said. 'Don't you? You Knights of the Aurum. And its people.'

Something heaved its way up through the ground, a vine covered in thorns. It wavered above Olivier threateningly.

'No,' he said, calmly enough, but something simmered

beneath the surface of his features. The Arrenden family were especially devout in their worship of the Aurum, Roland recalled, and Olivier was no different. He had always been that way, first to his devotions, never missing a day, as if trying to compensate for something. But he looked genuinely horrified at the thought of children being turned out into a darkwood because of an accident of birth. 'No one deserves that. What they did was wrong.' He paused, glaring at them. 'And against the law.'

'Once you get far enough away from any knights no one cares much about the law,' said Lark. 'None of you ever venture into the wilds. People do what they want and witchkind have to seek protection where they can. The College offers that to some. We—'

'Lark,' Robin said, his tone all warning.

She scowled at him.

'Where was it?' Anselm asked. He was eyeing the thorny vine nervously. He still bore the scratches of Lark's initial attack and wasn't keen to repeat the affair. 'Where were you born?'

'Here, there, everywhere,' she murmured as if recounting some kind of fairy tale. 'It doesn't matter anymore.'

Robin swatted at the vine irritably. 'Put it away, Lark,' he said. 'You aren't impressing anyone. And Tobias said not to hurt them. Or scare them. We promised.'

Tobias... that name again. That was something. Roland locked eyes with Anselm who nodded slightly in recognition of that fact.

'Who is Tobias?' Anselm asked.

'You're full of questions,' Lark said huffily and stood up. The vine snapped back into the undergrowth, vanishing from sight but somehow lingering in their awareness, a threat. 'We should move. We've still got a long way to go.'

'We could ride,' Roland offered. 'It would be faster.'

'Not where we're going. It's not fair on them,' was all Robin said, and set off again.

The horses, Roland realised. The boy seemed far more worried about the horses than he was about the knights, or himself and his sister. Which was another factor to consider. These children were powerful in old magic, and though they tried to hide it, they were afraid of him. That was not comforting. Scared creatures – people or animals – could do terrible things. Especially when they had such power.

'THE TALE OF THE THREE SISTERS', AUTHOR UNKNOWN

Once upon a time there were three sisters and from the day they were born it was clear that they were powerful witchkind. The people of their village shunned them and as the girls grew in power and beauty, so too did the hatred they engendered until the villagers would no longer suffer them to remain. The girls were driven out, into the wilds where dangerous creatures roamed and no one could survive the night. The village turned their backs on them and they were forgotten.

But the three witchkind sisters did not forget. They cried out for aid. They touched the flames of the Aurum and found its fire relentless and spiteful. They sought solace in the shadows of the Nox and found all its promises empty.

The Maidens of the Aurum tricked them into their strong-hold but the sisters gave themselves to the wind and escaped their high walls, returning to the safety of the trees.

The witch-hunters of Ilanthus came for them but the sisters escaped them, wily and cunning as the forest itself.

What place is there left for the likes of us, they cried out, we who will not submit to these powers and bend to their rules?

An answer came from a forgotten song that still flowed

through the roots of the world. The old magic came for them and offered them sanctuary. But the need for vengeance burned in their souls until all that was left was ashes.

And though the guardians of the old magic tried to comfort them, they would not listen. They did not want comfort or protection.

We will release the old magic, they said, and we will remake the world. As the Nox fell they saw their opportunity. As the Aurum grew quiet they laid their plans.

One went north to the College of Winter. One went west to the heart of Ilanthus. The last went south to Pelias, the stronghold of Asteroth.

Each of them found a place and made it their own. And they waited.

And they did not forget.

CHAPTER 5

FINN

Finn had been stabbed before. He'd been so close to death that even a whisper would have pushed him over. He had been beaten, and hurt, and bleeding out. He had burned with fever and screamed with broken bones.

But he had never known pain and weakness like this.

On the day he finally awoke with a clear head, he wasn't sure at first where he was. Not where he ought to be, that was certain. He groaned as he tried to move, almost falling off the narrow bed and onto the floor of the... cell?

'Your highness!'

Hestia's voice. She was with him.

But that was... impossible.

Hestia's hands caught him and stopped his fall, settled him back on the bed. She sank down to her knees beside him and studied his face.

'Hestia?' he tried to say, but his tongue felt a thousand times its normal size in his mouth. His cousin tried to smile, but her skin looked parchment-thin and pale. Dark circles smudged the skin underneath her too-large, tear-stained eyes.

'Yes, I'm here. I'm here. Thank the endless night. Just take it slowly.' She smoothed her hands down either side of his jaw, catching on a growth of beard and a knot of hair far longer than he would ever have chosen. How long had he been unconscious? How long had he been here, wherever here was? 'Hold on, I'll get help.'

And then she was gone.

Finn stared at the roof of the cell. Definitely a cell. Narrow, dark, the stonework exposed. He could hear Hestia shouting something through the whine in his head and his body felt strange. Yes there was pain, but also... wrong. He felt wrong.

Too tall, too thin, stretched out and...

He tried to pull himself up on his elbows and a sharp pain sent him back down with a gasp. It wrenched its way out of his throat and took with it all the air in his lungs.

Then Hestia was back, lifting a simple ceramic cup to his mouth. He drank deeply, the water fresh and cool, and oh so very welcome.

'Take it slowly, Leander,' she whispered. 'It's going to be all right.'

Leander?

Finn pushed her back in panic. The last thing he remembered was breaking the glass pendant and everything changing around him. He'd thought it was the spell to take him to Sidonia, but now...

He lifted hands that were not his hands and stared at them. Leander's rings, and his perfectly manicured nails and his long fingers... He was wearing the remains of Leander's clothes, all save the ones destroyed by blood and...

'What... what happened?' he whispered.

He had held his brother as he lay dying, tried to staunch the flow of blood, begged Wren to help. And Leander had spoken words of othertongue and...

He lifted those alien hands to his chest, to find the thick

bandages expertly wound about him. But it wasn't him. None of it was him.

'The girl stabbed you. We couldn't escape. They saved your life, Leander, at least there's that. Please, you've got to think. They want information, things I don't know. I don't even know if you know the truth of it. But we're in a terrible position. Wren is missing. The queen is enchanted. They...'

They... the Asterothians. They were still in Asteroth, in Pelias, and this cell lay far below the city, deep in the heart of the mountain. This was where people went when they were never going to be seen again.

'Hestia, it's me.' His voice shook. Leander's voice.

This couldn't be real. It had to be a nightmare.

She stroked his hair again. She wasn't doing much better herself, he thought, though she had been given some considerations as a lady and a member of a royal court. But still an enemy court. Had she been ministering to him? They wouldn't leave her in a cell with him, would they?

But who was in charge now? Roland would never do this. Not to her, and not to him either.

But to Leander... maybe...

'I know it's you. Sweet darkness, you haven't said a word in days, and that was the ravings of a fever. But it's going to be all right, Leander.'

'Not Leander, it's me. *Finn.* Hestia, I'm Finn. Finnian Ward. Where is Roland? Where's the queen?'

Hestia pulled back, staring at him now. 'But you...' Her eyes narrowed and peered in closer now. Her hands turned to iron against his head, holding him still so she could really study him. Whatever she saw turned her face even more pale and bloodless. 'Great shadows, how is that possible?'

A noise outside brought their attention to the door of the cell. She released him and turned as if to shield him from whatever was coming.

'Hestia? Where are we?'

'Say nothing, do you hear me?' she snapped. 'Nothing at all. Not yet. I need to figure this out. I need to—'

The door opened and a Maiden of the Aurum stood there, tall and imposing, wearing the expression of an executioner. Behind her were a dozen guards and two knights.

'So he is awake,' said Maryn. 'Very well. Bring him. Send word to the regent.'

The guards filled the room, encircling him and Hestia.

'No, please,' Hestia protested. 'He's weak and I think still delirious. Just give us time to—'

'Enough, Lady Hestia, or you can take his place.'

Hestia drew herself up to her full height. 'I will in a heartbeat. I'll tell you whatever I can.'

Maryn's eyes flicked over her face, tracked over to Finn, and then back to Hestia. 'Well, you've changed your tune. That's interesting. Bring them both.'

The body in which Finn found himself was still weak and he hurt everywhere, but that didn't matter to the guards who manhandled him up to his feet and dragged him from the cell.

Hestia followed, walking independently but entirely surrounded, and behind her Sister Maryn swept along like a ghost. Anger came off the woman in waves.

This was not good. Not at all. Maryn loved Elodie, he knew that. Apart from Lady Ylena she was the only blood relative the queen had left. She would do anything for her. And she was powerful, the most powerful of the Maidens of the Aurum.

Finn couldn't quite catch his breath or still his swirling mind. What had happened and how? He'd been all set to take Wren to Sidonia, for her own safety. Once there he'd thought he would be able to find time to think again, and work out what to do. But now... he was still in Pelias, in Leander's body. And presumably...

A jolt of pure rage and betrayal shot through him. He tore

himself free of the guards just for a moment and turned on Hestia – Maryn, the knights and their perilous situation forgotten.

'How is this possible? Did you do this?'

His cousin shied back from whatever she saw in his face. And then the knights stepped in between them – Hector Uderon and Vasilly Grey. Finn's mind filled in their names just before they closed on him, weapons raised. Finn ducked and rolled, moving instinctively in a body which protested every action. But it didn't matter. He had to stop this, whatever was happening. He twisted around, assessing the situation in lightning speed. The guards had drawn swords and it only took two blows to take one. Poor Vasilly didn't see him coming. The weight felt cool and familiar in his hand. It belonged there.

'Stop!' Hestia screamed, not at them, he realised, at him. But he couldn't stop, not now. He would not be marched off to die in his brother's stead. He would go down fighting first.

Because the only thing running through his mind was that, somewhere, Leander had Wren.

Light flared inside him, light so bright he felt it burning through him, acid in his veins and a migraine in his head. It brought him to his knees and when he was able to look up, Maryn was standing over him, her face fixed in a terrifying expression of interest.

'What has happened to you?' she asked. Her hands traced figures in the air around him, studying something he couldn't see, and she glanced at Hestia. 'Did you do this?'

'No. As if I'd have the power here. You know that, of all people you know that.'

Hector seized Finn's arm, hauling him to his feet, and this time Finn couldn't fight him. His body felt like jelly and he couldn't quite breathe.

'Bring him,' Maryn said. 'Fetch the regent. Now. And you, Leander of Sidon, don't try anything like that again.'

'I'm not Leander—' he began.

Maryn froze, staring at him in much the same way as Hestia had. 'Then who or what in the name of the great light are you?'

'I'm Finn,' he whispered and the light surged through him again. Light and fire and the body housing him screamed at its touch.

CHAPTER 6

FINN

The chamber of the Aurum was strangely cold and dark. Someone had lit lanterns all around the edge but their light didn't seem to penetrate as it should. In the centre, the bowl-like depression where the flames should have been was empty. Finn took all this in just before the knights let him go and he fell onto the marble. It was polished to a mirror sheen and in it he could see...

Long silvery hair, falling like silk around a thin, elegant face with high cheekbones, a strong jaw almost hidden by beard growth, and eyes so cold and heartless they looked like ice. He supported himself on his shaking arms, staring at Leander's face, with Leander's eyes, and knowing that it was him in there. Finally seeing the reality of it made the thunder of his heart drown out any other sounds at first. Nausea boiled in his stomach.

Hestia reached him first, her hand hooking under his chin to draw his attention up to her instead. She knelt in front of him like the mother he had never known.

'Don't look,' she whispered. 'I'll work this out. There has to be a way—'

'And I would very much like to hear the explanation,' Maryn cut in. 'Or is this another Ilanthian trick?'

'It's not a trick,' Finn said. The corners of his eyes stung but he would be damned if he would let tears fall at a time like this. Rage and fear and everything in between flooded him. 'How? How is it possible?'

Hestia helped him to his feet. 'The Paladin's light is still in you, a part of your soul, but Leander's body is rejecting it. Don't try to draw on it again, understand me? It might kill you.'

Maryn was still watching but everyone else had gone now. She'd sent them away, he realised, because whatever was going on here was against every principle she knew and clearly no one wanted word getting out. He stood between Hestia Rayden, servant of the Nox, and Sister Maryn, the foremost Maiden of the Aurum, and neither of them knew what had happened to him any more than he did.

Maryn approached carefully. 'Strange,' she murmured, making Finn feel like some kind of experiment. 'Do you see this?'

'Well of course I do. I'm not an idiot.'

'You didn't see it all this time, *sister*.' The word dripped with animosity.

'I am almost drained of my magic. He was unconscious. Anything I could do now would risk my life without help from another. It was all I could do to heal him. And you didn't notice either. You were too busy blaming us for everything. You and your regent.'

'Stop,' Finn told them wearily. It was too much and he felt like some kind of prize they were fighting over. 'Tell me what you do know, or what you can see. Please.'

Maryn huffed. 'Well, now I know for sure you aren't Leander, it makes more sense. As much as it can make sense. I see the Aurum's light in you, and also... not. Like an afterimage from staring at the sun. The othersight is confusing at the best of times but this... this makes no sense.'

'Leander always was unnaturally talented,' Hestia said softly. 'He studied magic by whatever means he could and stole what he couldn't master, even old magic. What did he say to you in that room before he...'

There had been light, the light of the Aurum. Wren had been trying to save him, even then. She couldn't work the magic herself but perhaps she had reached out through him. And Leander had held the pendant and...

'His blood was on my pendant, where he touched it. He was dying. The Aurum's light was alive in me, swamping me. Wren raised it, or it tried to use her, or...' Finn gave up. He didn't know anything helpful. 'He said something. Gibberish.'

'Othertongue,' Hestia finished for him. 'Not gibberish. It had to be. He tapped into the spell in the pendant and piggy-backed on it. That's not part of our magic.'

'Nor ours,' Maryn replied, thoughtfully. 'But some witchkind can slip between their own minds and those of familiars. How would your crown prince have learned that?'

No need to ask why he did it. Leander had wanted to live, had wanted Wren, and he'd wanted the crown which had been denied him. Now... now he had it all. Finn felt as if someone had punched him in the guts at the thought.

'He has friends in the College of Winter,' Hestia said bitterly. 'They still use old magic, those who can harness it. Although "friends" is probably too warm a term. Some of our sisters have relatives there, after all, men who fled the blade or those who didn't want to serve. Lady Oriole, for example, who had his training in her hands. Divine darkness, is this the meaning of my vision? The crown on Finn's head but not—' Finn couldn't miss her tortured expression.

'What vision?' Maryn snapped.

'Of Finn as the king of Ilanthus, a king who would save us

from this madness and unite our people, ushering in a period of peace and prosperity.'

'That certainly doesn't sound like Leander,' Maryn said bitterly. 'What did you see? What exactly?'

'A battle in the Sanctum, a boy's hand on a dark crown, Finn on the Ilanthian throne... The details are unimportant.'

'I've found that with visions the details are often the most important thing of all. And your sisterhood, do they agree with you? Could they have done this?'

'But I can't believe the sisterhood would have a hand in this. We were trying to build an alliance. The king saw no harm in my mission here.'

Maryn's hands knotted together as she kept studying Finn's face, like she was looking for a thread to unravel. She shook her head slowly. 'No harm at all. I never took Alessander for a fool. But then I never took the College for traitors either. Cold and distant, perhaps, and far too interested in taking magic apart to work out what makes it powerful, and obsessed with old magic. But we are all witchkind. Oh, this is not good. What are they up to?'

'They?' Hestia asked.

'The College. I thought they might have an answer about Elodie, something old magic could help with, or one of their healers... I sent word but they have not yet replied. The chancellor was always a helpful enough sort but there has been some political upheaval brewing of late so I just thought he was too busy to—'

Behind them a door banged open, making all three of them jump, and Lady Ylena entered, followed by her entire retinue. The lady regent looked like an incarnation of wrath and it was all Finn could do not to drop to his knees. It was purely an instinct of self-preservation.

'Have you discovered anything useful?' Ylena snapped without preamble.

Finn expected Maryn to instantly tell her all but the maiden turned to face her mother, her shoulders taut. 'He knows nothing, lady regent.'

'Or he refuses to speak of what he knows. He's an Ilanthian, Maryn. He lies as easily as breathing. They both do. I have indulged your bleeding heart long enough. Your courtesy to Lady Hestia is one thing but he's conscious now, recovered enough. Find out what he knows or I'll have others put him to the question in more definitive ways. It would be a shame to undo all your good work but needs must.'

Hestia's hand tightened on Finn's arm. There was a tremble buried in that grip and he wondered what they might have done to her while he was unconscious. Courtesy to Hestia, Ylena had said. That had to mean Maryn had protected her somehow.

'I'm not your torturer, Mother,' Maryn growled, distaste evident in her expression.

'You're whatever I tell you to be. Or I will replace you.'

The maiden let a slow smile spread over her face, a smile without any warmth at all. 'Sadly for you, my lady, only the Aurum can do that.' She glanced at the empty hollow where their holy flames should have burned. 'And it's not available right now.'

'Because of them! I tire of this. Take him to the dungeons and wring answers from him.'

'What you are suggesting is an act of war,' Hestia protested. 'He is a prince of Ilanthus. He was injured beneath your roof, under a truce, by one of your servants. Right here. This goes against every tenet of the Pact.'

But Ylena just tilted her head to one side as if looking at a recalcitrant child. 'You think we are not already at war, Lady Hestia? That witchkind chit was no servant of mine. More likely she belonged to your kind. I never took you for a fool, but you came here on a fool's errand so perhaps I misjudged. Know this, I will send that boy back to his father in pieces if needs be.

I will know what you did with the princess and I will know now.'

They could tell her, Finn thought, but she really wouldn't like it. And killing him would only...

'Then you do my father's work for him,' he said in what he hoped was the same arrogant tone Leander would use. He knew it far too well. 'You'll rid him of a failure of a son, clear the way for Finnian Ward to be his heir, and give them all the war of vengeance they have longed for. All in one go. Well done, Lady Ylena. How long do you think they have been planning this? Asteroth will be razed to the ground and the earth sown with salt. Look around you. You no longer have the Aurum to protect you. And my father has been gathering his forces for years, waiting for his moment. Do not hand it to him on a platter.'

Lady Ylena's eyes narrowed and he knew he'd scored a point or two there. Not that it truly mattered. Not to her. It was probably a mistake. He was good at them.

'Take him away,' she snarled.

Hestia cried out something, words in othertongue that made his skin crawl.

His gaze went unerringly to Maryn. The Maiden of the Aurum trembled, her hands clenched into fists at her sides as she struggled to channel what power she still could. With the Aurum asleep, she was also scraping away at her reserves. For him, for Hestia.

'Go,' she told him, her voice strained. 'Quickly. Both of you. Hestia, you know what to do. I give you the strength, by my vow, what magic I can. It's old magic but all I can offer.'

Before Finn knew what was happening Hestia seized him in her arms. Pain and exertion lined her face as she drew on those fragments of magic she could glean from the world around them, old magic of stone and silence, long forgotten and alien to her. Maryn had woken it and now Hestia used it, trying to transmute its poison into some kind of power. Shadows spilled out all around them, twisting around their bodies, and Finn felt the light inside him flicker wildly. Pain lanced in its wake as the dark magic threaded through Leander's body fought against it. This wasn't possible, he wanted to say, not here in the Sanctum, not here in the heart of Pelias.

A travelling spell, one woven of a magic both familiar and entirely different to the light or shadows Finn had felt before, coalesced through them.

Hestia screamed in pain as it burrowed through her, tearing at the shadows of her own power and pulling it apart. It was vicious and determined, and Finn felt it wind around them, the light in his mind and the darkness in Leander's body screaming at its touch. But it was strong, this old magic, stronger than it should ever be, choking the powers innate in him and in Hestia, as it swept the two of them away.

'CHOSEN PATHS', FROM GUIDANCE ON MAGIC BY LIVIA, MAIDEN OF THE AURUM

We know of magic of light and dark, and that of the wild which is all but lost to us. We study and align ourselves with one or the other and sink ourselves into its nature so that it becomes a part of us. We breathe it, and it nourishes us, the magic of our chosen path.

Attempting to use the other is like trying to breathe underwater, or a fish drowning in air. A Maiden of the Aurum reaching for the Nox, or a member of the sisterhood channelling the Aurum, is pouring a poison into her soul.

And using the magic of the wild, that old magic, if it can be found, that way lies madness. It may steal all that you are and leave a hollow shell. It may steal your heart and your mind and leave behind a wild beast. It may make you, briefly, stronger than ever before, until it leaves like the fickle creature it is, and takes all you are with it.

But in the end the result is always the same. Giving yourself over to old magic is folly.

CHAPTER 7

ELODIE

The light burned and blistered. It never wavered, but beat down on her, relentless and uncaring. Elodie had never been afraid of the Aurum before but now... now she barely knew it. It was everywhere, all-encompassing, her entire world, her whole existence and it would never stop.

That was what it told her.

Over and over again.

And she ought to be no more in that light. She ought to be burned away.

But something small and stubborn, something that was so fundamentally the core of Elodie, clung on.

Not Queen Aeryn of Asteroth. Nor yet the Chosen.

Just Elodie.

The woman who had loved Roland and given him up for the sake of her kingdom. The woman who had raised a child and seen past her origins to make her a good and strong person in her own right. A hedge witch. A healer.

Slowly, she tried to uncurl.

'I will not be destroyed. I will not give in. I still have a purpose.'

Something laughed. Something bright and terrible.

Foolish girl. I will fill you until there is nothing left of you. I will remake you as I see fit. We will burn this world until we find our enemy and then...

Enemy? Wren. It meant Wren.

'No,' said Elodie and her voice shook the world the Aurum had built around her. The prison in which it was keeping her.

She reached out blindly. In the past, she had always reached for the light, and that was her mantra, her creed. That was what she had always told Wren, time and again, always reach for the light.

But she couldn't do that now. The light was no longer on her side. It wanted to grind her down until she was no more than a mindless slave. And then it would use her to hunt Wren down and kill her.

No, she thought. There has to be another way. Some other way. Anything!

Something else responded, something deep in the mountain, something swirling through the air. It rippled through the water and it beat in every living heart.

The old magic coursed through her and somewhere, in that royal bedchamber, her body convulsed. She had not been made for magic like this. She was created for the light and it had always welcomed her as she welcomed it. But this... this was something other, alien, something ageless that had been waiting all along.

So be it, she thought wildly. If this is what I must do.

She had felt the old magic in the forest and had reached a kind of détente with it long ago, a bargain. There had been at least two spirits of old magic which had woven their lives around her and Wren, protecting them both. It had always been there, beneath the surface, sometimes aiding her, sometimes ignoring her requests. The light had always responded sooner and faster, so she had thought – fool that she was – she had thought the light was all. But the magic of the wild had not turned on her.

Magic was magic. She could use this. There would be a price but she could use it. Anyone witchkind could, but the destruction it could wreak on them was intense.

Something reached into her very heart, just as she reached deep into the heart of the land itself. Old magic roared around her.

Hedge witch, it said, and just that title alone was an exultant cry of joy.

She heard someone crying out in alarm, shouting for help. It took Elodie a moment to untangle where the cry came from. Was it the old magic? Another vision from the Aurum? But no, the voice was familiar. And real...

It was Lynette. Her friend shouted her name, trying to pin her down and contain her struggling form, and Elodie caught a glimpse of the bedchamber where she lay, just for a moment, a blinked sketch of her body thrashing about in that huge bed, burning with a fever, lost. Lynette of Goalais was watching over her, trying to care for her and help her along with the healers.

At least she had that.

And then she spun away, desperate and afraid. Old magic had her in its teeth and she was flying.

Maryn would know what to do. Where was Maryn?

In the chamber of the Aurum, she found her friend. She stood there talking intently to Lady Hestia Rayden and with Hestia...

That couldn't be right. He looked like Leander, and sounded like him but... the light in him was wrong, so wrong. The light of the Aurum. In place of his cold grey eyes, so like his uncle Evander's, she saw the blue of the ocean, its darkest depths. As if he was partly a reflection in a pool and partly a man, and the two were not the same anymore.

Old magic coursed around her, reaching out for her. It

burned along her veins like a poison. Not the magic of the Aurum this time. Something else, something older that was stirring. Because the Nox was scattered and the Aurum...

The Aurum was trapped. In her, in her body, pushing her out into the wider world, or the space between worlds. And in that liminal space something else gathered. They fought for her.

Old as the stones, old as the earth, old as the sky. Its sighs were the wind and its heartbeat shook the mountain.

It pulled Elodie deeper, like a child intrigued by a new plaything. It wanted answers. It wanted to know... It wanted everything, beyond reason or consideration for her.

'No,' Elodie said again, clinging to the scene before her, to Maryn and Hestia and...

Ylena arrived in a flurry of rage and Elodie could see that force sparking around her, inside her, winding through her body and around her old bones. Ylena didn't know it was there but Elodie saw it and saw the tendrils that spread out from her. Back to someone... someone else...

Hedge witch.

Old magic was loose in the world.

It would tear Asteroth apart. And not just Asteroth...

If she could reach it though, form some sort of agreement as she had with the powers in the forest long ago then maybe...

You serve me, the Aurum snarled. It would hear no argument, no debate. She was meant to obey. She had been born to serve this power of light and flames and absolute obedience.

But she didn't. Not now. She served her kingdom, her people. That was the truth of it. That was why she had taken Wren and run away in the first place. That was why she had given up Roland.

Roland... she had to find Roland...

Great light, she thought and stopped herself while the Aurum laughed, but the Aurum was not everything, no matter what it believed.

She felt Hestia seize on the magic carrying Elodie, a wild and desperate hope born out of fear. Ylena was threatening them, threatening... him...

But Hestia was depleted and weak. She had used all that she had to save the prince. Wren's prince, Elodie realised. Finn. Her daughter's beloved, just as Roland was hers. The power of the Nox rose briefly in response to Hestia's entreaties and started to fail almost at once. Maryn reached out, trying to lend her strength. Even Maryn instinctively understood the truth of it, the necessity. They had to get Hestia and Finn away from Ylena.

Ylena, or whatever was using Ylena to do its bidding, willing or no, wanted Finn. To bind him, control him, or perhaps just destroy him. If they could break him they could use him against Wren. It could not stand.

Hedge witch, let us help.

Elodie threw all that she had into the heart of that spell, all that remained of her, and watched the old magic rise to spirit Hestia and Finn far away.

After that, nothingness swallowed her whole.

WITCHKIND LORE

No one can truly understand old magic.
It is wild and wanton, it knows no rules.
It is like a child, forever young.
A bird in flight, it is a thing of joy.
Give yourself over to joy.
But to wield it, give yourself completely.
For if you hold back anything from its embrace,
Its tide may rip you apart.

CHAPTER 8

WREN

Finn woke Wren far earlier than he normally rose, his tone curt.

'We don't have a lot of time. Make yourself presentable.'

Confused, she pushed the fall of her dark hair out of her face and found the room full of servants. Not the usual ones either. Not the lithe, seductive and desperate souls he normally surrounded himself with since they had come to Sidonia. These people were older, with downcast eyes and impassive faces, wearing ornate livery or simple robes of pale colours. There were more women than men and they all busied themselves with various tasks. Several filled a large bath with steaming, fragrant water, while others laid out a selection of gowns the like of which Wren had not seen since coming here.

They reminded her of Lynette, if you took all her fire and independence from her. At the thought of anyone from Pelias, that same pang of loss and regret stabbed into her and Wren winced, trying to push the memories away.

She had taken it all for granted, hated it. And now... she only wanted to be back there. She wouldn't even argue with Lynette over the array of clothing the lady-in-waiting laid out before her. The outfits and the hairstyles could be as elaborate and ridiculous as her heart desired. Anything, aside from a crown. The thought of that and all it implied still chilled Wren to the bone. Now more than ever.

'What's happening?' she asked.

Finn paused in the doorway and cast a glance over his shoulder. 'The king wants to see us. Formally and in front of the whole court. Don't make trouble, Wren. It will not go well for you if you try anything.'

Try anything? What was she going to try? She was helpless here, his captive and by extension a captive of the royal court of Sidonia. All that had been made perfectly clear.

Wren felt listless and lost.

She had tried to reason with him, tried to work out what had happened and why he was behaving this way. The court was one reason, of course, and the excuse that he was protecting her had worn very thin. He wouldn't take the bracelet off her wrist and let her protect herself. Nor would he hear any thoughts of letting her go, or the two of them escaping together.

Part of her wished she could just curl up in the night and never wake again. If the Nox came to her now, she'd welcome it with open arms and a willing mind. Perhaps that was his intention.

True to his word, he hadn't forced himself on her. Oh, he teased and tormented, and indulged his own needs with various bedchamber companions whenever he wanted. And she hated him for that.

None of this was an act of love. He wasn't really trying to protect her. The emptiness in his eyes as he watched her told her that. He wanted her to want him, to beg for his touch.

And that just made her even more resolved. He had betrayed her. Whether it was in the act of protecting her, or in order to blend into this terrible place, it didn't matter. From the moment they had arrived, he had changed and she would not change with him or accept the man he was now.

The royal servants washed her and dressed her. They fussed over her hair as if it was a treasure, threading it with silver and jewels. It tumbled down her back, glimmering like the night's sky. No one was allowed to cut it and she was certainly not permitted near anything she might use as a blade. The king himself had forbidden that, she had been told.

The gown was in the Ilanthian style. It clung to the curves of her body, accentuating her form. It was black as well, and shot with sparkling threads. A silver sash cut a line from her shoulder to her hip, fixed in place with a brooch like a crescent moon.

She slipped her feet into the tiny slippers made of silk, and stood there, hardly recognising herself in the mirror. They had transformed her from a half-wild captive into something else.

A princess.

Or a goddess.

The thought sent a chill down her spine.

It had taken hours to prepare. The servants bowed, as one, and stepped back, gazing at her as if in adoration, and Wren frowned. She didn't like that one bit. And yet inside her something dark and hungry uncurled in pleasure.

'Good,' Finn said. He too had bathed and changed. He was dressed to match her, black breeches which moulded against his legs and hips where they rode low. He wore only a silver sash across his bare chest which gleamed with a perfumed oil. The muscles seemed even more defined than usual and Wren's gaze followed the dusting of dark hair which trailed down his chest, to his abdominal muscles until it vanished beneath his waistband. Slowly, carefully, she drew in a breath.

When she looked up again he had that insufferable, knowing grin on his face that she had never seen before they came here. Like he could read her mind. And her stray thoughts amused him greatly.

'What is happening?' she asked in as cold a voice as she could.

'My father wants to see us, to see what progress we have made. So unless you want to be handed over to him, you'll cooperate. Adore me, Wren. Show him that I've tamed you. Otherwise...' He shrugged, as if he didn't much care what happened to her.

It made the dark anger she was nurturing in her depths surge up and she drew in a breath as, for once, the bracelet didn't suck it all away in an instant. Anger, she realised. Anger she could use. She just had to hold onto it, control it.

'That isn't actually an answer,' she told him.

'It's a party,' he went on. 'For us, I imagine.'

'Why for us?'

'Oh,' and that cruel smile which didn't seem to fit on his face was back again, 'perhaps we'll announce our engagement. Wouldn't that be nice?'

No, she did not like the sound of that one bit, not that her opinion mattered. But when he offered her his arm, she took it. What else could she do? She was not going to be dragged out in front of the whole court kicking and screaming.

It was a ball. She heard the chatter of the assembled court long before they arrived and her first instinct was to pull back. She had no intention of letting him parade her around in there in front of the entire court, like a trophy or a pet. But Finn just clamped his arm on hers and carried on, until she had no choice.

They burst into a wall of sound and motion. Music was playing far too loudly as the two of them descended the curved staircase. It drowned out the conversation and the next thing she knew all eyes were on her. It was so much worse than the ball in Pelias. Here she felt helplessly exposed and alone. No one here was on her side.

'I... I don't want to,' she whispered, praying once again that he would listen to reason, and somehow be the man she loved once more.

'Don't make a scene,' he told her curtly. 'Smile.'

As if she knew how. Her stomach twisted.

'Why are you doing this?'

'Because I have to. Because I can. Now do as you're told.' She started to walk again, but he couldn't make her smile. Nothing in the world could do that now.

A young voice cut through the noise around them. 'Prince Finnian? Oh thank the sacred night, it's you. I've been trying to see you since we got back.'

A boy pushed his way towards them through the crowd, as finely dressed as any of the rest, wearing a tunic rather than being bare-chested like the Ilanthian men around them. His sash was a dark green and he looked exhausted. But his face was lit up with hero worship. She remembered him, she thought, from the Ilanthian embassy, Hestia's son.

'Laurence?' Finn said in a cool voice. 'This is not the time.'

'I know, but please, I need you to intercede. Gaius has tried. He's still trying. They have my mother captive.'

'Who do?'

'The Asterothians. She was left behind with Prince Leander and... please, my lord prince, the king can negotiate for her release along with that of his son's. She always spoke so highly of you, and you have connections at the court in Pelias. And with the princess here...'

He trailed off, staring at the two of them, so hopeful.

'Your mother,' Finn said softly and the words turned into a laugh. Laurence blanched and pulled back a step. Wren watched that hope die and wondered how many times that had happened to him already. He couldn't be more than fifteen. 'Your mother meddles far too much in things that don't concern her. It was only a matter of time before she landed herself in trouble. Asteroth will never make peace with Ilanthus. Now, if you please, this is no place for children.'

Finn swept by the devastated boy, dragging Wren behind her.

The Finn she had loved beyond reason was gone. Wren understood that now. This man, this Ilanthian prince, was someone else entirely. Cruel without need, heedless of anyone else. He couldn't even be kind to a boy seeking his aid.

With that realisation she felt something inside her crack open, leaving only a hollow emptiness, dark and frantic. The anger was there, but so was something far worse. She didn't know its name, but it felt like despair.

CHAPTER 9

WREN

As they approached, the king looked up from his seat on the raised dais, still cold and austere, his pale eyes raking over Wren's form. He beckoned her forward, but she couldn't move. Her feet felt like stone. Beside her, Finn had stiffened and that smug self-assuredness seemed to falter. Anyone would hesitate when faced with Alessander of Ilanthus. Anyone sane, anyway.

Finn took a determined step forward, ready to drag her up the steps to his father's feet.

'No,' said Alessander. 'Just the girl.'

'But Father—' Finn began, clearly annoyed.

'I may have named you my heir, boy, but that does not make you my equal. Stand down. Wren of Asteroth, come forward,' the king went on. She almost had to tear herself out of Finn's grip, but just one look at the man before her said that it wasn't going to end well if she didn't do as he said. Her eyes burned as she forced herself to walk towards him. Then she stood still, alone, waiting as he inspected her again.

'Well?' he said more softly.

'Oh yes,' said General Gaius. 'That's her.' He stood at the king's side, resplendent in dress uniform. 'Will you trade her?'

'This treasure?' the king replied. His smile was unbearably cruel. She could see Leander in him, with his white hair and icy eyes, and a shadow of this new Finn as well, but neither of his sons could ever have made her feel quite so alone and lost. She was an object, a thing, not a person at all. A *treasure*... 'What could they offer in return of a fraction of the value?'

'My lord king, your son and Lady Hestia are still captive in Pelias. We can negotiate for their return. The regent, Lady Ylena, will be reasonable—'

Alessander laughed. 'You have met Ylena, Gaius. Are you so very sure about that?' Then his humour died away and he fixed his attention on Wren again. She wished the ground would swallow her up, or that she still had the ability to draw the shadows around herself and hide. 'You, girl, are you content with the prince? What progress has been made?'

He was waiting for an answer. All Wren could do was stare at him.

'Speak,' he barked.

'I-I don't know what you want me to say.' The words were out before she considered them.

'The truth, lady. They told me you loved him, that it was the scandal of Pelias. Well?'

'I... I loved him. But...'

'But what?'

'He has changed.'

The king smiled a thin and nasty smile. 'Has he indeed?'

Gaius frowned at her, confused, but held his tongue. Had he noticed the difference in Finn as well? He didn't look pleased though. Not at all. But no one interrupted the king.

Except perhaps a prince.

'Father,' Finn began, the tone ready to cajole and charm. Funny she could hear the deceit in him now. 'You know how women are...'

Which was the kind of thing her Finn would never have

said. Wren closed her eyes, and felt the bleak emptiness grow larger again. With it came a brush of darkness that was almost a relief. She caught hold of it, those tendrils of night and shadow, and pulled them closer. The bracelet on her arm turned cold as ice but she didn't care. She could barely feel it anymore. What was the pain it could cause compared to everything unravelling inside her?

'Come closer, your highness,' the king said quietly. He was still maintaining the charade that Wren was a princess then, rather than a captive. Perhaps in his eyes she was both. Trade her, the general had said. Was that all she was now? A game-piece on a playing board? If she begged him, would they send her back? 'Lady Oriole, if you will.'

A woman dressed in a black gown as fine as Wren's stepped forward from the left-hand side of his throne. She had dark eyes and red hair, and her long fingers were threaded together in front of her. Around her neck she wore a silver necklace which pressed heavily against her pale skin. The sense of the Nox's magic came off her in waves. She was powerful, more so even than Hestia, and she carried with her an aura of otherness.

Wren took an involuntary step back but there was nowhere to go.

'No!' Finn shouted suddenly. 'This is not what we agreed!'

The king slammed his hand down on the arm of the throne, his fist clenched. The noise made Wren jump. 'And we have waited too long for your side of that bargain. Where is this willing queen you promised? Where is the obedience? I see nothing but a frightened child! Do it, Oriole. Now.'

Wren tried to back away but there were guards on the steps behind her. She glanced over her shoulder, but Finn was being restrained by more of his father's men. There was no way out of this.

Oriole approached her.

'I won't hurt you,' she said in a smooth and firm voice. 'But

63

first of all we need to be sure. We know what we have been told but the Asterothians have betrayed us too many times. Bow your head.'

Wren's throat tightened. There was nowhere to go, nothing she could do. And she didn't even need to bow her head because Oriole was far taller than she was and besides, she was standing on the step above her. There was nowhere Wren could go, no one to help her. She wanted Finn. Not Finn as he was now but Finn as he had been. She wanted him, needed him. But she was alone.

Oriole pressed her long fingers to either side of Wren's head and held her still. She closed her eyes, concentrating on something, words of othertongue drifting from her lips.

Shadows surged from every corner of the room, thick and black as smoke, and rushed towards Wren.

Wren threw back her head as the shadows swirled around her, lifting her hair to dance with them. The darkness filled her eyes and the voice of the Nox sang inside her blood. There was light bleeding from the stained-glass windows, the colours darkening. She tried to breathe and felt the night fill her lungs. Stars flashed in her eyes and when she lifted her shaking hands she saw swirls like ink moving beneath her skin.

The bracelet glowed with otherlight, blazing in her sight, desperately trying to absorb the magic coursing through her. But it couldn't. Power bled from her skin, and it hurt. Light and shades of old, it hurt. She tried to breathe evenly, tried to grapple with everything in her and reach for the light. That was what Elodie had always said. Always reach for the light.

But there was no light here. Not really. Any that fell on her was sucked away, driven from her. She tried to step back but felt her feet go from beneath her.

Oriole caught her hands, pulled her up and then stared into her face. The Sister's eyes widened, first in disbelief, then shock at what she saw there. Whatever she had expected of Wren, this wasn't it. A lie, perhaps, a trick, but not the Nox itself, not even the little of it Wren embodied. She sank to her knees, head bowed.

Others followed suit; all around the throne room, Ilanthians great and lowly fell to their knees before Wren until she was the only one standing. The king still sat on his throne, staring at her with an unreadable expression.

No, not the only one standing, she realised.

Finn's fingers bit into the flesh of her arm like a vice.

'Enough!' he snarled and she barely knew him. 'Don't give her power when you have no idea what she'll do with it, you stupid bitch. Do you want her to kill us all?'

He tried to drag Wren after him, but she didn't move and, despite his strength, he stopped. He couldn't move her. Not now.

The Nox whispered words of othertongue, words she couldn't use. Not yet. But that didn't stop her saying them. Just to see the reaction.

Finn abruptly released her, a look of fear and confusion sweeping over his handsome face, his face that... wasn't quite his face...

Maybe she could use this power after all. Maybe...

Othersight showed her the angles and planes of another man's features, silvery grey eyes, and a tight, arrogant mouth. Wren peered closer, peeling back the layers of whatever enchantment he had used, and saw him realise what she was doing.

'Stop this, Wren,' he told her. A warning. A threat.

But she didn't. She didn't have to. There was no need to obey him, and he could not protect her from anything here. He'd never intended to. He was a lie. Everything he said, everything he did, everything he was.

'You're not Finn,' she snarled softly, little more than a breath, but rippling with rage. The Nox growled in her words.

65

For a moment he held his ground, but his face paled a little and she smelled his fear. Oh, he knew what she could do, and what she was. And he knew she was angry.

Not just angry. Enraged.

'Leander? What did you do to him?'

CHAPTER 10

WREN

Leander drew a knife and stepped back from her at last, as if even being near her burned him. But before Wren could stop him, he pressed it to his own throat.

'Well?' he spat. 'Is this what you want, little bird? I don't know what it will do to me, but he'll definitely be dead if his body is dead. Is that what you want?'

She wanted answers. And tearing him apart with shadow kin, as the urge racing through her body was telling her to do, was not going to help.

All around them, weapons were drawn. Well, he had just pulled out a knife in the presence of the king, not to mention the dark magic now coiling around Wren. You'd imagine they'd be delighted, she thought. This was what they wanted, after all. Their dark goddess returned. But perhaps it wasn't quite the wonder they had envisaged. More like a nightmare.

And, night curse him, Leander was right. She couldn't risk any harm coming to Finn. She needed to find out what that spell was and disentangle the two of them. Only Leander knew what he had done. Whether he did it himself, or the guards fell on him, the outcome would be the same and she couldn't risk Finn. Not now. Not when she knew…

The spear of relief she felt was unexpected. It was Leander. It had been Leander all along, not Finn. Not her Finn. Mind racing, she turned back to the king and the sister of the Nox still kneeling on the edge of the dais. The general was directing his men and the guards were still moving, encircling the two of them. They were in mortal danger.

But she smiled. She couldn't help herself. The fierce and irrational surge of joy made the darkness around her and within her purr with delight.

'Come, oh divine darkness,' Oriole intoned softly, spreading her hands wide in supplication. 'Goddess, queen, endless night and sacred dark, hear us and accept our offering of service. We will bring you sacrifices and—'

Wren laughed, cutting her off. She had one chance. She had to take it. She could be what they expected, couldn't she? She could pretend.

'What do I want with sacrifices?' she asked. She held out her arm. 'You're supposed to serve me, then do it. Release me.'

The bracelet glimmered, still suppressing the magic flowing through her, still trying to hold her in check.

Oriole glanced at the king and, slowly, he shook his head. 'I think not, divine darkness,' Alessander murmured. 'We are not fools. You are angry. And rightly so. Perhaps in time, when you have calmed down. In the meantime, the sisterhood must give me their resolution, Oriole.'

Still trembling, Oriole rose to her feet. 'My lord king, the sisterhood recognises the princess as our lady and offers her a place within our halls.'

'No!' Leander shouted. 'I refuse to accept this. She is mine. Tell them, Wren. Tell them now!'

Or he'd hurt himself. Hurt Finn's body. The threat in his words was implicit. He still had the knife. No one else knew who he was or what he was doing. They didn't know it was Leander.

No. This was not happening. She would not allow it. The anger rose, the darkness with it, shadows crawling through her. And with them came power. More than power.

Give in, the Nox whispered. *You know you want to. I can help you. Together we can make them all beg for mercy. Let me in, little vestige. Be my vessel and let me fill you.*

But Wren couldn't do that either.

The bracelet wouldn't allow that and for once she was grateful. All the same her breath caught in her throat, and her heartbeat thundered.

'We can help you,' Oriole said. 'The voice of the Nox is powerful, but it cannot control you. It will threaten and it will entice. But without your agreement, it is but a voice. We can teach you control. Balance. Come with us. We will protect you and help you.'

'Hestia said...' Wren didn't know where the words came from and they failed almost as soon as she said them. Swallowing hard, she tried again. 'Hestia said it was about balance.'

'Hestia is wise,' Oriole said, her tone smoother now, more self-assured. 'The wisest of us. And should she return, she will be chief among your teachers. Until then, I humbly offer my guidance.'

Wren let the anger die down, just a little, released her rage and the shadows subsided with a sigh.

'Yes,' she whispered, desperate now. 'Please. Help me.'

Lady Oriole nodded, her expression calm again, radiating satisfaction. She had won.

'Father,' said Leander, still wearing Finn's face, still living this lie. 'You can't do this. She doesn't know what she's saying. She's mine. She promised. *You* promised.'

'I promised you nothing,' Wren told him, but Leander mounted the steps to the dais, approaching his father. Of course he ignored her. What interest did he have in anything she might have to say?

'Don't do this, Father. I warn you. I will not let it stand.'

The shadows rose again, swirling like leaves caught in a whirlwind. They tore through the chamber, throwing back the guards and forcing them away. For a moment Wren thought it might be Leander's doing but he stared around, wide-eyed, and his gaze locked on her in accusation.

But it wasn't her either. Not this time. Her anger might have stirred them but it couldn't call the shadows, not here, not while she wore that accursed bracelet.

The king pushed himself up to standing as the darkness deepened, centring on the middle of the chamber, a vortex of darkness coalescing in the middle. In its depths, she saw two figures, one standing tall and the other slumped in his arms.

And she knew them, knew them both.

Hestia, limp and pale, magic draining out of her as she spilled her power in a recklessness born of panic and desperation... her eyes almost entirely white as she sank to her knees. And trying to stop her falling, holding her so tenderly... white blond hair whipping around his razor-sharp face... Leander.

Only it wasn't Leander, was it? His grey eyes fixed on hers and in them was a warmth that had never been there before.

'Finn!' Wren shouted, and her voice cracked as she scrambled across the space between them on legs that would barely move.

He stumbled and almost fell as the darkness around them faded. Laurence reached the two of them before Wren could, grabbing Hestia and lowering her to the ground.

'Aunt Oriole!' he screamed. 'Aunt Oriole, please, help her! She's used all her magic. It's drained her. She's dying.'

But no one else was listening to the boy. Panic spread throughout the chamber, chaos breaking out all around them.

Old magic surged through the ground, through the air, a

power the likes of which Wren had never felt before. It was not just the Nox, or the Aurum. It was something else, wild and out of control, chasing the magic that had brought Finn and Hestia here. Lines of light and darkness wrapped around Leander's body and Finn struggled against them, but she watched them spread out, tangling around the two men.

'What is the meaning of this?' the king shouted. 'What is happening? Lady Oriole—'

With a snarl, Leander grabbed his father by the shoulder and plunged the knife into his throat.

Blood splattered across his face – Finn's face – bright and red, scarlet making his stolen blue eyes unbearably bright as they fixed on Wren's horrified gaze.

The king slid from his grasp, sprawling on the steps beneath his own throne, his eyes wide and glassy in death.

CHAPTER 11

FINN

Shadows swirled around Finn's borrowed body, and his stomach almost emptied itself as everything came to a juddering halt, as if he and Hestia had slammed into a wall of night. She gave a groan and slumped against him, all strength leaving her suddenly limp body. She slipped out of his arms as if lifeless. He tried to grab her, to hold onto her, but it was like trying to seize water.

The world twisted sickeningly, struggling to right itself, and he looked up. They were in the throne room in Sidonia, his father gazing down at him, and a man standing beside him, the man in Finn's own body...

And then he was standing in two places, both beneath and beside the throne.

Wren cried out, her eyes wide in horror, and something hot and wet splashed over his face. He was holding a knife and...

'He's killed the king!' Leander cried out. Leander, back in his own body, still wounded and exhausted, but seizing the moment and directing the panic of the assembled court against his enemy. And Finn had always been his enemy. Now his brother had made him the enemy of all of Ilanthus in a single moment. 'He's murdered our father. Seize him. Now!'

The pounding in Finn's head reached a crescendo and he staggered back. His father sprawled across the steps to the throne, no longer moving, blood drenching his chest. It wasn't possible. It wasn't...

He hadn't...

The knife fell from his numb hand. Wren's lips moved, as if trying to form his name. She was so close, just a few steps away. Beautiful, fragile, clothed as the dark goddess the Ilanthians saw in her. Her eyes were wide and dark, filled with tears. She wore a gown like the night itself and her hair curled around her in ever moving waves, alive with magic she couldn't use because of the bracelet they had trapped her with.

'No,' he whispered, unsure who he was trying to reason with. Who here was going to listen? Only Hestia knew what had truly happened and all Finn could hear was Laurence pleading for someone to save her. 'Please, listen.'

The guards fell on him like that same wall of night. The struggle was brief and brutal. His body didn't seem to work for him, like it belonged to a stranger into whom he had been dropped without warning.

Leander had reached the dais and grabbed Wren, pulling her back. Had she been trying to help him? Or had she been as horrified as everyone else? But the moment he laid hands on her, his fingers digging into the pale flesh of her arm as if to reach the bone, she tore herself away from him.

'Finn,' she gasped again, and her voice shook but she didn't seem to know who she was looking at or which of them was which.

Finn was hauled to his knees in front of his brother.

'Lock him up. We will deal with this treacherous murderer later. I will have such tortures for you, brother.' Leander smiled.

He actually smiled, though he hid it a moment later as he turned to the court. 'Bring healers, attend the king.'

Attend the king? Alessander was dead. Even a fool could see that.

And Finn was, he realised, very much the fool in this situation. He thought he'd been escaping, setting things to rights. Instead he had walked straight into another trap. Whether it had been planned this way from the start or whether Leander had seized the moment was impossible to say.

'Oriole, see to Lady Hestia,' Leander snapped. 'Take her to the caves and secure her. She has many questions to answer. General Gaius—'

'No!' Laurence cried out. He was kneeling by his mother, trying to help her. He was just a boy. Leander looked like he'd gladly kick him clear across the chamber if he could reach him now.

'Take young Rayden too. He can discover what it really means to be a son of Sidon. The princess and I' – he jerked Wren against him – 'have a lot to discuss.'

'Hold,' Gaius barked at his men. 'Your highness, you are not in command here. Lady Oriole, please see to Lady Hestia.'

'The king first,' one of the others argued.

'The king is dead,' Oriole said in a trembling voice.

A shocked ripple ran around the room and someone cried out, several people. Even Gaius seemed stunned and at a loss as to what to say. Alessander had been the soul of the kingdom. A cruel and vicious king, but still their king, their centre and their guide in the dark. Without him...

Finn locked eyes with his half-brother and knew this was the moment Leander had dreamed of. He had everything now. Everything.

All he needed to do was get rid of his father's newly chosen heir. And he had just managed that by barely lifting a finger.

Just sinking a blade into the king's body. And using Finn's hand to do it, in front of the entire court.

'Well actually,' Leander replied coolly as the noise subsided and all eyes turned to him, 'the chosen heir killed our beloved king and I claim the throne in his stead, so I very much am in command here, general. Finnian Ward is to be confined at our pleasure. His execution can mark my coronation and my marriage to the princess.' He almost shook Wren as if to prove a point but with that movement she tore herself free of him.

'I will never marry you.' Her voice rang out, clear and determined in the audience chamber, silencing everyone.

She staggered backwards, away from Leander, and it was Oriole who caught her before she could fall, the older Sister still trembling with outrage. She was trying to soothe Wren, to murmur words of help and comfort, but it was hopeless.

'You don't get a say in the matter, my dearest little bird,' Leander taunted her. 'I am king now. Ilanthus is mine. So are you. No more demurring. I tried to be nice. You need to learn your place.'

He lunged at her again but winced as his newly reclaimed body betrayed him. It was still injured, still recovering. Finn remembered the pain well enough and Leander hadn't accounted for it. He stumbled and two of the courtiers came to his aid. Leander gasped, snarling in rage, but he didn't let go of them, using them to support himself.

As Finn tried to right himself, to force his legs beneath him again and struggle free, the guards were taken unawares, too distracted by the injured new king and his reluctant bride. He only had a moment, seconds, no more than a heartbeat. In a practised move he tore a sword free of a guard's belt and turned on them, even as they were still trying to work out who was in control and why, which commands to obey and what side to take.

'Wren,' Finn shouted. 'Wren, we have to get out of here.'

But she didn't move, only stared at him as if she no longer knew who to trust. And how could she? He turned in a wide circle, holding the guards off, and held his free hand out to her. It shook far too much and there was blood covering it.

Wren just stared at him like she loathed him, or pitied him, and it made something tear inside him.

'Oriole,' she murmured, and he could hear the heartbreak in her voice. 'I claim sanctuary with the Sisters, as offered. Please.'

Oriole glared at Leander and something unspoken passed between them. There was no love lost there, clearly. Everything in Ilanthus was about power and, right now, Wren was the crux of all power in Sidonia. Didn't she see that? Couldn't she see that they were all using her?

'And it is granted,' Oriole replied with an obstinate kind of formality designed to infuriate another without giving them an excuse to attack. Not that Leander needed any excuses. 'Lady of Divine Darkness, the honour is ours.'

The other Sisters stepped out from among the courtiers, all dressed in black, their hands already moving in intricate patterns as they drew dark magic around them, weaving them together to shield Oriole, Hestia and Wren, surrounding them like a pack of shadow kin. Wren slumped in their midst, still staring at Finn as if she no longer knew what to believe.

No, he wanted to tell her. *It's really me. I promise it's me.*

But the only thing he managed to say was her name, before the guards swarmed over him once more and, this time, they beat him to unconsciousness.

CHAPTER 12

FINN

The shackles bit into his wrists and the chains weighed him down. Finn knelt on the dank floor of the cell because he no longer had the strength to stand. Nor the will.

Wren had chosen the sisterhood. She had chosen the Nox.

And, in truth, he hardly blamed her. He had no idea what Leander had done to her, all the things he might have put her through, all while wearing Finn's face. The thought churned his stomach and tormented him. It was far worse than any agonies the torturers of Sidonia or Pelias could inflict on him.

No wonder she had chosen the sanctuary offered by the sisterhood. It was the easiest escape. From everything.

He might have been able to fight their way out. He had to believe that. But it would have been a slim chance. He had already failed her in every way possible. He'd betrayed her, placing that bracelet on her arm. True, it had been intended to save her, to keep her from being lost to the Nox, and then he had brought her to Sidonia against her will. Or tried to. He couldn't even protect her from Leander when he had finally followed them here.

Who was he kidding? The royal guards would have slaughtered him before they reached the doors to the throne room. Just as they believed he had slaughtered his father.

Perhaps it was better this way. Finn could die in the darkness and join her in another life somehow. Wait for her beyond the veil.

There was no way out of this for him, not now.

He was going to die here, in the dark, beneath Sidonia. That had always been his fate, no matter what he might have hoped, no matter what dreams of salvation had been dangled in front of him for most of his life. All lies, as it turned out. Fate had a way of ensuring what was written would come to pass. It was only a matter of when and how.

Leander had managed to turn the whole court against him. Hardly a great feat, but he might have hoped for some sympathy once upon a time. Not anymore. He'd been parading around here in Finn's body, doing whatever he wanted, tormenting Wren and finally murdering their father. There was nothing Finn could do now to clear his name. Nothing.

He didn't even have a hope that Wren would forgive him. She might realise the truth, he prayed for that much. But he knew how trauma lingered.

And whenever she saw his face now...

He could tell that much just from her expression when she chose the protection of the Sisterhood of the Nox over him.

'This is a sorry state of affairs, your highness,' said a voice from beyond his cell. He lifted his head and tried to make out who had spoken. On the far side of the bars, he saw General Gaius. Just the general alone.

Finn let out a long breath. 'Is Hestia alive?' he asked. That had to be the first question. Hestia had drained herself of magic to bring him here. And even if everything had gone wrong after that, he owed her.

'Hestia? I thought you would be asking about the princess. Or your brother, perhaps.'

'What happened?'

'After you were... removed from the throne room, the sister-hood departed with the princess, and Lady Rayden. And the boy. The late king's body is being prepared for his funeral. King Leander was overcome by his injuries sustained in Pelias, but is stable now. We have him safely in the hands of the finest healers.' He was carefully skirting around something, Finn realised.

'There isn't going to be a trial, is there?' Finn asked.

Gaius shook his head. 'There doesn't seem to be any need, does there?'

'It wasn't me.'

'And yet we all have the evidence of our eyes. Your behaviour has been erratic of late. Everyone can attest to that.'

'Hestia will tell you—'

'Lady Rayden is unconscious. Her magic drained her and whatever spell she performed to bring the new king back to us, well... I'm not sure she will recover.'

He said that last part so quietly that Finn almost missed something in the tone. He cared about her. Deeply.

'I'm sorry for that. She... she's always been there for me.'

'Not this time. And for that, I too am sorry, Prince Finnian.'

'Are you here to execute me?'

That would be the quickest and most efficient thing, wouldn't it? A soldier's death wouldn't be so very bad, and Gaius would make sure it was quick. Roland would have done as much for him.

The general's hand fell to his sword, as if the thought had not actually occurred to him.

'I fear the king would be displeased if that was to happen. No, I am *not* here to kill you, Finnian. I'm here with a message.'

'A message?'

'Yes. And given the current state of affairs and the general unrest, I'm not exactly thrilled to be an errand boy.'

Finn just stared at him. What else could he do? The general

wasn't given to humour, dark or otherwise. He never had been. He was Alessander's man, and his strong right arm.

And now, Finn supposed, he was Leander's. Although Gaius didn't seem so very enamoured by that prospect.

'And who is this message from?' Finn asked at last.

But Gaius didn't say anything. He just tossed a piece of mangled metal onto the stone floor. It clattered to a stop in front of the cell bars and all Finn could do was stare.

It was twisted and broken, as if some force had torn through it like paper, but he couldn't mistake the delicate patterning or the sheen which marked it as shadow-wrought. It was half of the bracelet which Leander had once worn, the same one Finn himself had put on Wren's wrist to dampen her dark magic.

Slowly, Finn dragged his gaze from the remains of the bracelet back up to the cold steely eyes of the general.

'And the other half?' His voice sounded hollowed out and broken, like it belonged to someone else or he was hearing it from far away, echoing back on him.

'With the king.'

Half for him, half for Leander. There was no doubt who sent it. Who destroyed it the moment it was removed from her skin. And it was certainly a message.

'Just this?' Finn asked.

She had to know he was here, that he was a prisoner. She had to know what Leander would do to him.

But he had betrayed her. He had chained her and left her helpless. And he had done that long before he'd activated the spell to bring them here or fallen victim to Leander's enchantment to swap their bodies.

He had no excuse but that he had thought he was doing it for the best. Clearly he had been wrong.

Gaius just stared down at him, a grim expression, and Finn wondered if he had in fact changed his mind, and would draw that sword to put an end to him after all.

'The sisterhood is hers now. She serves no king, no crown, no one. She is the goddess incarnate and all of Ilanthus will bow to her. All of Asteroth too. There is nothing to stand in her way. Queen and goddess, embodiment of power, lady of the darkest night... Do I need to go on?'

Finn shook his head. 'Leander won't like that.'

'He does not. It is a call to civil war, Finnian. Religious war, in fact. And your princess is at the heart of it. She'll tear this kingdom to pieces with her demands.'

Finn sucked in a breath to still himself, to try to grasp equilibrium in a world that seemed intent on tearing him apart like that ragged bit of metal.

'She's not my princess,' he whispered at last.

Gaius just nodded. 'She doesn't belong to anyone now.'

'And where do you stand, general? With the king?'

'With Ilanthus,' he murmured softly. 'But who is to say what that means anymore? What have you and your brother done, Finnian? What have you created?'

'This isn't my doing.'

'Isn't it? We should never have gone to Pelias. I said that at the time. But Hestia was insistent and Alessander listened so I obeyed. Just as I will obey now. The princess...' He paused and then shook his head. 'The goddess incarnate has issued an ultimatum and Leander has no choice but to agree.'

Finn lifted his head, staring at the general. 'What are her demands?' he asked.

Gaius curled his lip. It was not a comforting expression but, then again, it wasn't meant to be. He was not like Roland. There was a cruel streak to him, especially when it came to those beneath him.

'As the Nox, she holds the crown in her gift. She knows it and so does the realm as a whole. Many will choose her over the king and why wouldn't they? She is a living power, magic itself in human form. Without her agreement to his rule – her signature on it, as it were – your brother will never be secure. She has a price.'

A chill crept up Finn's spine as he guessed where this was going.

A price...

'And what's that?'

'The sacrifice promised to her twenty years ago. You.' He nodded to the guards behind him. 'Bring him.'

PROPHECY OF VARIANA OF ILANTHUS

In the darkest realm a light will grow,
In the flames a shadow lies,
The forsaken shall be restored to us,
And the dark queen shall rise.

CHAPTER 13

ELODIE

The world shook and trembled. Flames leaped up around her and Elodie shied back, raising her hands to protect herself.

She had never needed to protect herself before. Not from the Aurum.

But here, here in this place of dreams and nightmares, everything was different.

What have you done?

The voice boomed through the Sanctum, shaking the stones themselves.

Done? She had done nothing. She could do nothing. The power she had managed to steal in order to help Finnian and Hestia escape had vanished now and she was lost again. Flames surrounded her and light beat down on her relentlessly, and she was helpless before it.

For a moment she had been free, and part of her had been everywhere, in the wind and the water, in the earth itself. She had sensed them – Finn and Hestia hurtling through the shadows as they travelled by the dark ways of magic, just as she had once travelled through the light; Roland, travelling through a tangle of ancient forest, his sombre mood tearing at her heart;

and Wren... terrified and confused, with the darkness closing in all around her.

But then the flames surrounded Elodie again, dragging her back into this prison between the worlds of life and death.

The Aurum was furious.

'Why are you doing this?' Elodie asked, her voice shaking. If it was really her voice. Her mind needed to create a reality around her, to keep the fragile threads of her sanity intact. Or so she believed. So she saw the chamber of the Aurum, the Sacrum, and she felt herself there in body as well as mind, even if she knew her body lay still and silent in a bedchamber, as helpless there as she was here.

If anyone had a mind to do away with her now, she wouldn't be able to defend herself. She would be lost.

She was lost.

Rage ripped through her again and she forced herself up from her knees. This was not happening. She would not allow it to happen. The Aurum was powerful and determined, she knew that of old, but so was she.

'Who has done this?' she yelled. 'Who is behind it all? You have to know. You're meant to know everything!'

That was what she had always been told. That was what the Aurum wanted her and everyone else to believe.

A figure formed before her, one made of flickering light, candle flames and stars, reflections on glass and polished silver. There were no features to be discerned, not really. They were fleeting and quick, moments caught in the light.

The Aurum. She was looking directly at the Aurum and it was trying to take a form with which to... what, communicate? Fight?

Elodie, it said and the voice was a sigh of regret and loss, echoes of her mother, and her grandmother perhaps. *Elodie, what have you done? Why do you still defy us?*

Another trick, another ploy. It had to be. This sympathy was nothing like she had faced so far.

'I have to,' she replied. 'You can't just demand—'

Of course we can. There was a sigh which made the world around her shake. Or maybe it was just her. The sound rattled through her body. *Perhaps we were mistaken. Perhaps you were not the one after all. I should find another to be my sword, my Chosen. My champion.*

The figure shimmered and changed. Not her mother this time, not a woman at all.

Roland.

But not Roland either. His dark eyes were alive with fire and light. He smiled, but that was not his smile.

'Stop this,' Elodie told it. 'You can't.'

There is nothing to stop me. He has vowed to serve me, and he has not broken his vows.

Not like she had, it meant.

'He stood against you to defend Wren. He will always stand against—'

A blast of light lashed out, striking her in the stomach and sending her folding back on herself. She didn't even see where it came from but that hardly mattered. She knew the source. Roland's image dissolved again and for that brief respite she was grateful. She couldn't look at him like that. It wasn't real, she had to remind herself. None of that was real.

Except it felt real. Far too real.

With a snarl of frustration, Elodie tried to drag herself back to her feet again, to take control of her emotions and find something real to cling to.

Roland, she thought. There was still Roland. And he still loved her.

Just as she still loved him.

The Aurum laughed, reading her thoughts. A horrible, mocking laughter and, for the first time, great light and shades of old, she hated it. It had tried to control her all her life. It had dictated what she did and when. She had given up everything to protect it and now... now it laughed. Laughed at her emotions, her love. How dare it? Perhaps him, perhaps... not?

The child of the Nox is weak, it told her and her anger faltered at this change of tack. *She falters. Perhaps she will serve me instead. That is what you told her to do, is it not?*

Her own voice rang out in this bright and empty place, rebounding off the edges and coming back to taunt her. '*Always reach for the light, Wren. Promise me.*'

No, Wren was her own person and always would be. Elodie had to believe that. Wren would hold true and would not give in to these petty, jealous powers.

Because that was all they were. She could see it now. Warring factions, like children fighting over a toy. The Nox and the Aurum had been made from old magic but they didn't have a fraction of its power or its patience.

'Wren is stronger than you know.'

So you hope. She is already failing. Better she serve me than the Nox, surely? If you tell her to obey, to submit, she will and what a queen she will be in your stead, a creature of glory and power, ruling both these mortal kingdoms, all magic bending to obey her. The old magic has taken an interest in her as well. It is seeking her out. As our incarnation she will be worthy of worship. That's what mortals really want, Elodie. Someone to love, to serve, to adore. They will follow her.

'The Nox created her,' Elodie tried to argue, hoping that the very idea would protect Wren from the Aurum, that it would be too disgusted to be truly tempted.

Even my enemy's tool can be of use in my hands. She is susceptible, and vulnerable. Now more than ever. She has lost everything. Yes, I think perhaps she will do. If not, if she prefers to burn, there are others. You are not special. Not anymore. You made your choice, hedge witch.

Those last two words were a curse.

The light swirled like a storm before her, and Elodie felt it growing, expanding, reaching out of this prison. For a moment the light was everywhere, burning through her and scourging her flesh. She cried out, her voice echoing here and somewhere else, somewhere beyond her own world. Into the ways beyond, where she had flung the Nox, and into the paths of light that she used to travel.

And then the Aurum was gone.

We live in the light of the Aurum, she had always been taught. Now the Aurum itself had abandoned her.

Elodie sank down, her body without strength, without hope, lost in the emptiness.

ON OLD MAGIC BY PALIGINAUS

When we consider old magic we think of it as something long ago broken and dispersed, but it still lingers. It finds its way through the world, sometimes in familiar faces, sometimes in new ones. Sometimes in the wind, the rocks and the water, seeping through cracks and empty crevices in our world. It is an unknowable thing.

Some may claim to understand it. They lie.

CHAPTER 14
ROLAND

The College of Winter lay deep in the harsh mountains of the north, and could only be approached by certain roads, many of them secret. With Robin and Lark accompanying them, the three knights made their way through the forest leading their horses. Light slanted through the tall pines which towered over them. Snow began to fall and by the time they left the cover of the trees, it was coming thick and fast, and Roland feared it would slow them down further. Robin was right. It was like the College didn't want to be found.

Neither of their witchkind guides talked much, but then nor did Roland. Anselm tried to engage the children in conversation while they ate and sometimes while they travelled.

'We should reach the College tomorrow,' Olivier said as they camped for the night. Mercifully the snow had stopped but the wind still bitterly cold as they set up shelters and huddled together by the fire. He was studying the maps he had brought with him, his expression still grave, as if they defied him somehow. He was trying not to make eye contact with Robin or Lark, Roland noticed, and never addressed them directly.

Lark seemed to find this intriguing. In fact Olivier was the one person she seemed drawn to, the one she wanted to talk to. It was clearly starting to get on Anselm's nerves but then the young Lord Tarryn had always been protective of Arrenden.

Robin clapped his hands together and blew on them. Neither of the siblings were equipped with the heavy cloaks the knights had brought in their packs but the cold didn't seem to affect them quite as much. Robin was quicksilver, always moving, always watchful. His long brown hair tumbled over his green eyes and he had wound a scarf around his neck as he hunkered close to the fire.

'Is there a history of craft in your family?' Lark asked Olivier.

Olivier just glared at her. 'I don't know what you mean.'

'A hedge witch, perhaps?' Robin asked. They were like a pair of magpies harrying their prey. 'Healers? Or even Maidens of the Aurum? You have the instincts for it, and you're clearly sensitive to the tides of power in this world. Your sense of direction alone—'

'I know how to read maps, nothing more.' Olivier got to his feet and stalked away to the edge of the clearing, the conversation finished. Roland frowned at Robin who just shrugged, entirely unrepentant.

'Must you?' Roland asked.

'A man should be true to himself. Your knight is not.'

'There is no knight more true,' Anselm snapped, his voice unusually sharp. 'You just delight in causing trouble. All witchkind do.'

He got to his feet and followed Olivier, muttering darkly under his breath.

'Perhaps not all witchkind,' Roland said. 'But he isn't wrong about you, is he? What do you want? Really?'

Lark rolled her shoulders back. 'At the moment, something warm to eat and perhaps a steaming bath. As if...' Robin laughed at her but gave no reply of his own.

Roland sighed, took off his own cloak and held it out. 'I'll thank you to stop needling my knights. They are tired and they have given up everything to this cause.'

Robin wrapped the two of them in the cloak and nodded his thanks, managing to look a little chastened at least. Meanwhile, Lark's eyes alighted on the sword, strapped to Roland's back.

'Is that it? Nightbreaker?' she asked. When Roland nodded she smiled, an expression both knowing and mischievous. 'I always thought that was an interesting name for the sword of a Grandmaster of your order. How many knights has it broken, do you think?'

Roland shrugged. 'Every Grandmaster who has carried it, I imagine. The name is no joke and the double meaning is intentional. Our role is not something to be taken on lightly. They say it carries part of the Aurum in it, like a Paladin. Chosen and blessed.'

'And those two are both Paladins like you?'

'Yes, I believe so.'

There was still a seed of light in each of them, but something else as well. Something Roland didn't want to consider. Wren had put it there. It wasn't darkness. Not quite. But he didn't have a word for what it was.

Robin hummed to himself, warming his hands again. 'What would they give to serve the light, do you think? What would you give?'

'I've given everything,' Roland told him bluntly.

But Robin shook his head, his eyes gleaming in the firelight like emeralds, giving him a trickster cast, something just a little too other about him, as if something far older was looking out at Roland through those eyes. Lark snuggled in against her brother, watching in silence, just as keenly. 'I don't think so. Not yet anyway.'

They were witchkind, this strange pair. They lived free or died. Roland rather suspected more died than anyone knew.

Some went to the College of Winter and that was that. And others...

He was suddenly ashamed to realise he had never questioned what happened to the others.

It felt like the edges of his world were slowly being chipped away and he did not like it one bit, the way the twins watched him, the things they said, and he felt a savage surge of shame and remorse.

'Your queen was like us, for a while, when she was Elodie of Cellandre, a hedge witch. We knew of her. It gave us hope.' Robin poked the fire with a stick, staring into it. After a moment it grew brighter, flames burning more merrily than before, and Roland narrowed his eyes, glaring at it.

He ought to ask about that, he thought, but the subject of Elodie was still heavy on his mind and he didn't want to discuss it. Or that same shame and remorse. Perhaps they had turned from needling his knights to needling him. Testing him. Seeing what threads they could pull until he unravelled.

He laid his hand on the sheath holding Nightbreaker and forced his mind to calm. When he opened his eyes again, they were both watching him with that strange predatory intensity.

'What is it?' he asked.

'The sword... tell us its story?'

Like children again. And yet, not quite. 'It's the sword of the Grandmaster of the Knights of the Aurum, forged in its flames by Aelyn the First. No blade had ever been Aurum-forged before. They say it has never failed a knight of true heart, and never will, that the Aurum goes with it and that the men who carry it will always be true.'

Robin nodded slowly to himself but Lark didn't look so convinced. 'There's light in it, that's true. But it can't decide if someone is true, or dictate who they are. That's up to the men themselves, isn't it? Are you true, Roland?'

Was he? He'd failed Elodie, left her behind, lost in that

endless sleep. He was trying to find a way to help her, and Ylena wouldn't have let him near her if he had stayed but...

Enough, Roland thought. This strange pair knew nothing about any of them. They were just prodding at weak points to get a reaction. He didn't know why. For their own amusement, it seemed. He rose to his feet, intent on finding Olivier and Anselm. They should have been back already and the mountains were not safe to wander in. He'd tell them to ignore the witchkind and keep their own counsel from now on. Perhaps agreeing to have the twins as guides was a mistake but he couldn't deny that they had taken a much quicker path to the College of Winter with them leading the way. A witchkind path, they had called it, but to Roland it looked like any other road through the forest. That said, he wasn't so sure it was entirely natural. He wasn't sure of anything anymore.

The trees pressed close around him as he passed, but up ahead he saw another clearing, one bathed in moonlight, where Anselm bent over Olivier, his face all concern.

'It doesn't matter,' Olivier was saying. He sat on the ground, his legs drawn up against his chest. 'It was years ago.'

'Of course it matters. He has no right to make such insinuations. If we didn't need him I'd—'

But Olivier looked up at Anselm, and his face held anguish. 'He isn't wrong though. And he's just a boy and he's had a hard life. He can't help but be blunt. My family might have treated me like those children. And if I had not pledged myself to the Aurum, what would have become of me? They wouldn't have kept me, not knowing that about me. It was the only way. Otherwise—'

'There is no otherwise. You gave up a birthright to the Aurum. You are where you're meant to be, Olivier.' Anselm dropped to his knees in front of his friend and pressed his gloved hand against Olivier's face. 'The two of us are.'

Olivier tried to smile, but the expression didn't really take hold. 'My parents would have something to say about that as well. Shameful, Anselm. That's what we are.'

Anselm just shrugged. 'So be it then. They can think what they want. But you and I? We're *not* shameful. There is nothing wrong with this.' He leaned in closer, his lips brushing Olivier's, his fingers burying themselves in the other man's hair.

It was a private moment, far too private. Roland withdrew, careful not to make a noise.

Olivier had a secret and Lark had come very close to the mark. Many of the knights said they gave something when they took their vows to the Aurum. Roland had never felt it himself but then Elodie had long ago told him he had the magical sensitivity of a large rock. But Dain had, so had Yvain. His fellow Paladins had felt the power of the Aurum in all things. Perhaps it was something they should have discussed more, but it always seemed to him a personal choice, like who to love, and none of his business. It didn't make them less of a knight. But clearly Olivier was concerned.

Family expectations, and judgemental beliefs, could be damaging.

Men called to knighthood had to give up anything magical to the Aurum. Was that what Olivier meant? It had clearly not been an easy choice, and he felt he had been given no choice at all. Which was wrong.

Tomorrow, Roland thought, he would find some way to reassure the young knight, hopefully without revealing what he had seen and heard here. But Lark had been right in one thing.

It was up to a man, or a woman, to decide who they were, and whether they were true.

Snow began to fall again and the wind was rising. Roland returned to their camp to find the witchkind twins on their feet, on the far side of the fire, facing the darkness beyond. They were watching something, something Roland could not yet see.

'Roland?' Lark whispered, and all the bravado was gone

from her. She was focused, but not afraid, intense. 'Draw your sword. Quietly, carefully.'

There was an edge to her voice that made Roland obey, slowly and smoothly slipping Nightbreaker free. A soft glow illuminated the blade, neither firelight nor moonlight, but something else entirely. The horses stirred nervously, whinnying in growing alarm, and Roland felt the skin tighten across the back of his shoulders, the hairs rising. He knew this feeling. Knew it far too well.

Shadow kin threaded through the trees towards him, like sharks scenting blood.

CHAPTER 15
ROLAND

Roland's instincts kicked in before he even raised his voice in warning. He was already moving, bearing down on Robin who stood directly in the line of attack. Shadow kin rose before him in a wave but, before Roland could reach him, the boy raised his hand and said something in a musical form of othertongue that Roland didn't recognise.

The snow changed direction, like a living thing, a blizzard swirling towards their attackers. An enchantment, it had to be. Icicles formed on the branches overhead, long and sharp as knives, before breaking free and slicing through the air. The nearest shadow kin reared back, baring its teeth and then plunging towards the witch.

Roland got there first. Whether Robin had slowed it or adrenaline made him faster, he didn't know. It didn't matter. He was defending children. The outcome was all that was important now. He pushed them both behind him and felt the surge of frozen air wash over him. That didn't matter either. Couldn't matter. He put it from his mind and thrust Nightbreaker up into the creature of the Nox. The sword blazed with light and a terrible scream tore through the night.

That brought Anselm and Olivier running, instincts as honed as his. They were knights through and through and he had trained them well. In seconds they had formed up a defensive shield around the camp and, with Robin hurling snow and ice at their enemy, they held their ground. The forest around them raged, thrashing like a wild beast, attacking their attackers, as Lark used it as an extension of her will.

But there were more shadow kin coming. Far too many.

'Don't let them get to the horses,' Roland warned and Olivier backed up to defend their mounts, who were now panicking, their cries loud as they thrashed against the ropes securing them.

Roland turned to say something, even as Anselm called out a warning, and shadows rushed towards him, barrelling into him with a force which almost took him off his feet. But at the last moment, Robin was there, hands up, ice screaming forward. The shadow kin crashed into the boy. The snow stilled, the wind dying, and Robin slammed down onto the hard ground, a shadow tangled around his length, shining teeth bared. Lark screamed and the woods convulsed with her fury.

Olivier was there, plunging his sword through the creature, ripping it away from the witchkind boy.

Another lunged towards them and Anselm sliced it out of the air, his sword a line of light. Roland turned back to face another, this one intent on cutting him off from the others. Not just one, he realised, but three, all coming from different directions. The creatures were huge, the largest he had seen since the battle at Knightsford, and focused on him just like the ones which had attacked him in his office in Pelias, and this time there was no Wren or Elodie to turn the tide.

'They're too many,' Anselm warned. 'If we can get to the horses, make a break for it...' He already sounded exhausted.

'I'll hold them here,' Roland told them. If they were after

him alone he could use that, give the others a chance to escape. 'Make for the College and—'

'No, Grandmaster,' Anselm said. 'You have to go. We can hold them until you escape.'

Damn it, no. Roland refused to desert his men or the children. Not here, not like this. He gritted his teeth, ready to argue with them, ready to command them if he had to.

The shadow kin seemed focused on him alone, as if another force directed them, as if they were after him in particular. No, he was imagining things. Shadow kin were normally mindless and indeterminate. They didn't pick out one person, not like this. But when he moved left, Nightbreaker blazing before him, that was where they went. If he could lead them away from the others...

It would be suicide. But there was no choice left. He wasn't about to let them take the children or his men. Not when they wanted him.

But why did they want him?

The sound of horses thundered through the pass ahead of them, echoing off the mountainside. Before Roland could say anything, to warn his companions or give another order, an unearthly voice, sweet and high, broke through the noise of attack. Music filled the air and the creatures of the Nox shied back, screaming. More voices joined it, three of them, four, singing in harmonies that rippled through the snowy night. As the song reached a crescendo, the shadow kin fled.

Five figures emerged from the trees on horseback, swathed in heavy jewel-coloured robes with fur-lined hoods pulled up to hide faces. Their song fell away to silence as they circled the camp. The leader and two others swung down from their mounts, landing elegantly in the snow.

The leader brought his hands up to show he was unarmed. Roland nodded to the others who stood down, as he slowly lowered Nightbreaker.

'Well met, Grandmaster,' the new arrival said in a deep melodic voice. 'We sensed the attack and came as quickly as we could. We represent the College of Winter.'

Roland nodded cautiously, but he didn't sheathe the sword, not yet. 'And you are?' he asked as gracefully as he could manage.

'Tobias Vambray of the College of Winter, Grandmaster.'

This was good. It had to be, and yet something tugged at the back of Roland's mind, something that unsettled him. Vambray was the chancellor of the College of Winter and though Roland had never met him his name and reputation were well known. He remembered Ylena mentioning him with a sort of respect, which was rare enough.

What was the chancellor doing out here and why didn't he introduce himself as such?

'Well met, Master Vambray,' said Roland, as a sickening wash of relief ran through him, still mingling with that dread uncertainty. 'We come seeking your help. Queen Aeryn of Asteroth is lost in the Aurum and the maidens bid us find a solution within your halls.'

Vambray studied him for a long moment. Well, it was mostly true. Maryn had told him to find an answer in the College.

'We have had word from Pelias of all that befell her and, of course, we will do all that we can to help. But we had to cut ourselves off from the world at large. For our own protection, you understand. The chancellor will explain all.'

As he spoke Roland saw the young woman standing to his left glance at him and frown as if she wanted to argue. She cleared her throat and Vambray turned his attention on her, his smile a little strained. 'It's fine, Vivienne. Don't fret. All will be well.'

But though she said nothing else Vivienne didn't look comforted. She withdrew a little, watching them closely.

'I don't understand,' Roland replied. 'Did you enchant the paths here to hide the College?'

Vambray smiled, as if that was the most natural thing in the world, the strain vanishing like morning mist in the sun. 'It was necessary, Grandmaster. These are dangerous times. We have been waiting for you to come for some time now.'

Roland frowned. Vambray seemed so certain, adamant in that assertion, but much in this made no sense to Roland. 'But if you had word from Pelias and you were waiting for us, why hide the roads? How could we find our way?'

'And yet here you are. Or almost. We sent Robin and Lark to guide you, did we not? Come, we can be at the College within an hour. However,' he paused and Roland felt that uncomfortable stutter in his chest again, 'we have secret paths to speed us there, and we will need to blindfold you all so that you can come with us.'

At this, the chill suspicion that had nothing to do with the snow and the frigid air returned. Roland glared at him but there was nothing obviously deceptive in the man's face.

'Blindfolded?' Anselm asked sharply. 'Why? We are Knights of the Aurum. Our word should suffice if you wish us to remain silent about your paths.'

Vambray spread his hands wide. 'Secrets are not to be shared lightly. The chancellor demands it. Besides, it is for your protection.'

Their own protection? Roland doubted that.

'Are you not the chancellor? I thought—'

Tobias shook his head. 'No, I am no longer chancellor. I stepped aside. It was... it was necessary.'

'Tobias,' said Vivienne again, her voice a little more plaintive, but the man ignored her. His eyes darted away, as if loath to make contact with any of them. 'Really, we should make haste.'

'I see,' Roland said, despite his own misgivings. He really

didn't see. But they didn't have a choice. They needed to reach the College and find something – anything – that might help Elodie. If there was knowledge to be found, someone who could help, it would be there. 'We agree to be blindfolded if that must be.'

So long as they had their weapons, all would be well, he told himself.

'Chancellor Vambray – I mean, Tobias,' the woman beside him said. The slip over the man's title was interesting though. He might deny his title, but others still used it. What was going on here? 'Please, reason with the children. They won't come with us.'

Vambray shook his head, fondly, his earlier discomfort forgotten. 'Lark and Robin are free to come and go as they wish.'

Roland frowned at the two witchkind children who had already backed up to the treeline. They had that stubborn look about them he was already beginning to dread.

'We brought them here, as you asked,' said Lark. 'But we aren't going in there. Not yet. There's no place for us in there. And we like the open air.'

This suspicion was almost as bad as what they had displayed towards the knights. Olivier shifted uncomfortably, unwilling to let them go.

'Come now,' said Vambray. 'We should be going before the shadow kin regroup and attack again. We should not even be out here. Their number grows all the time.'

'The shadow kin?' Roland asked. There shouldn't be any shadow kin in this area, not the number they had encountered and certainly not enough to cut the College off completely. He needed to know the truth. Or as much of the truth as these witchkind might tell him. 'What has been happening here? You were the chancellor.'

Vambray cast him a look of dismay.

'Not anymore. I was honoured to step aside just two weeks

ago, as my people required. The new chancellor has ordered us all to remain with the walls but...' He shrugged. 'Well, we still watch the paths in case anyone is in need of help, as is our way. And just as well, it seems. Now, we should move on, all of us.'

'You sent the children out to find us?' Roland asked. He liked this less and less.

'We did as asked,' Robin said. 'But the College are not in charge of us. Now we're leaving.' Lark threw her arms around him, holding him close. The forest seethed again, and suddenly plants surged up around them, hiding them from view. By the time they receded the children were gone.

'Find them,' Roland barked at the others. 'Quickly.'

But Vambray shook his head. 'No need. They are safer than we are, I promise you. They are not children, Grandmaster. Not really. They are wild creatures and will not thank us for trying to control them. And they are right, they shouldn't be in the College, not now.'

Roland exchanged a worried glance with Olivier and Anselm, but what could they do? The children were gone as if they had never been there. Wild creatures? What did that mean?

But had his own instincts not told him that they were not quite... normal either?

Tobias Vambray cleared his throat. 'I swear to you, Grandmaster, no harm will befall them. They go as they will in this world. We know them of old. *Old* magic, you see? Now, if you please, let us get you to safety.'

SECRET PLACES OF ILANTHUS
BY ANOTH TRINITAS

There are many sacred places beneath the city of Sidonia, all governed by the Sisterhood of the Nox. To pass through these caves is to encounter the Nox in all her forms and to lay oneself bare before her. The goddess sees all in this total darkness. No one can enter and return unchanged. Secrets lie there that cannot be revealed.

And as always, such a journey must end in blood.

Blood spilled, blood sacrificed, blood which creates something new, or brings forth something so very old.

CHAPTER 16

WREN

'Do you think it will work?' Wren asked again, pacing across the floor with her hands knotting together in front of her. The light from the stained-glass windows fell in a blur of colours on the flagstones beneath her feet, and shadows danced with firelight on the walls, but otherwise the room was dark. Lady Oriole sat by the fire, her eyes fixed on the flames as if to burn them from her head. She clearly did not approve of Hestia's plan, but now she was restored to them, Hestia Rayden outranked her. And perhaps Oriole was not so terribly overjoyed about that, though she tried to hide it. They were part of a hierarchy, after all.

'It's all we can hope for at the moment,' Hestia replied. She still looked washed out and exhausted, dark circles staining the skin beneath her eyes. She sat in the chair opposite Oriole, wrapped in furs but she still shivered though the room was sweltering. 'If not, we'll have to try something else. Leander has to believe that you have fully embraced the Nox.'

'And perhaps she should,' Oriole interrupted. 'It does not do to make mockery of such powers, Hestia. Not even for you. Either of you. No good will come of it. You are asking her to walk the sacred path. The Nox will demand a price for that.'

'I understand, Oriole, and I promise we are not taking any of this for granted. The Nox will have her due. Isn't that right, Wren?'

Wren swallowed hard on her suddenly tight throat. That was another thing she didn't want to consider.

'And we will make Leander king of Ilanthus?' she asked, hoping to change the subject.

'So long as we save Finnian, that's all that matters,' Hestia replied coldly. 'If Leander wears the crown it won't be for long. I have seen—'

'I know what you've seen,' Oriole snapped irritably. 'We all know. But this is not the way of our people. The Nox chooses the king. We do not trade the crown away for our own ends.'

Hestia waved an elegant hand at Wren. 'And she is the Nox. And that crown he would wear is a mere trinket. He wants the Crown of the Nox, doesn't he? To place on *her* head and make her his.'

'Would that be a bad thing? Having a channel for its power, focusing it? The Nox is not... not entirely sane, Hestia. Not anymore. That makes her dangerous. Not this girl, the Nox. You know that to be true.'

'The Crown of the Nox was put out of their reach long ago,' Hestia countered. 'And for good reason. The line of Sidon abused the power of our goddess for their own ends. With it they can control her, perhaps even make her little more than a slave. It's a blasphemy. We act as intermediaries between the king and the goddess. That's the way it should be. Would you inflict that on Wren?'

'Better it be inflicted on one than on us all, Hestia. Surely you can see that if we do not do something, the Nox will only become more volatile?'

But seeing Hestia was unaffected by this prospect, Oriole changed tack, glancing at Wren, a dismissive look which cut her to the core. 'Much good it would do if we could use it anyway.

The crown is lost and she is not the Nox. Not yet. She's just a girl. She begged my help. Mine, Hestia, and I gave it. Now she is denying her own fate, as well as ours. This will all come to ruin.'

Wren shifted uncomfortably. Oriole spoke about her as if she wasn't here and Wren didn't like that, or the way she talked about controlling the Nox. She sounded almost eager. She sounded afraid of the goddess they all claimed to love. And, from what Wren had experienced of the Nox, maybe she was right to be afraid.

Hestia sighed and her hands trembled against the black fabric she wore. At the doorway to her cosy little study, lined with books and warmed by the open hearth, Laurence stirred, his eyes fixed on his mother, his mouth a hard line. Whenever she looked for anything he was there in an instant and Hestia invariably waved him away. He ignored that as well, which Wren admired. This apple had not fallen far from the tree, it seemed.

'What kind of ruin?' he asked in that gentle voice.

Oriole's expression softened. All the sisterhood had a soft spot for Hestia's son. He was of the line of Sidon as well, or so they said. Cousin to kings and princes, and the son of a sorceress. There was far more to Laurence than being a mere boy.

'So far,' Oriole continued, 'Wren has withstood the Nox and held herself apart, whole and stable. This is admirable and shows her strength of will.'

Wren frowned. 'But I thought you wanted – the sisterhood, I mean, and the Ilanthians – I thought you wanted her back, possessing me.'

Oriole gave a dismissive snort. 'We serve the Nox in all things but these past twenty years… well, let's just say it is somewhat easier when she is distanced from our world. A lot less death and sacrifice for one thing. Politically speaking, though we worship and adore the queen of the darkest night—'

'Oriole,' Hestia said with a note of warning in her voice. She had been the one to bring up blasphemy. It was a dangerous charge in a world such as theirs.

'Oh hush, the girl has a right to know.' She fixed Wren with her darkest glare. 'The Nox unbound is a terror for a tale of the darkest night. Some say our royal family wronged her, and others that she simply went mad with power. Or that she was ever thus. We had ways to control her, mitigate her powers and keep her controlled, happy.'

'The sacrifices?'

'Among others. There are artefacts of power hidden in the deepest caves with good reason. If you touch the wrong treasure, or walk the wrong path, or make the slightest misstep... Once, all men with magic died for the Nox, and not so long ago either. Far too many. Perhaps Leander should have been the one to be sacrificed but Alessander adored him, so much so that he sired another to take his place. And look where that got him. The blood of Sidon is eternally drawn to kill each other, thanks to the Nox's own curse on them. And if Leander has his way, she will answer only to him. However, I don't think he has the strength. The Nox must be controlled and brought to heel, but it will take more than just brute force. I for one do not want to go back to the days of blood and death. Neither does she.' Oriole gave Hestia a brief nod. 'Not with a young son of the blood royal.'

All three of them glanced at Laurence, who turned grey and pressed back against the door. 'What?'

This clearly had never occurred to him, or they had kept it from him. Poor boy. But there was no keeping secrets now. It was time to be honest at last.

'Quite,' Oriole replied. 'But if you enter the caves of the Nox, Wren, being who and what you are, you'll strip away such protections as the light has afforded you in the past. You will expose everything you are to the Nox. A greater portion of the fragments of her power are gathered there. She may seem more convincing. She may even seem sane. But she is still dangerous. Our lady of the darkest night is powerful in these caves, even broken and scattered. This is where her heart lies. I fear...'

'You're afraid I won't be able to withstand the Nox if I go into the caves alone,' Wren finished for her. 'That'll she persuade me to let her in. And that if I give into her there...'

'There is a reason that the caves were sealed,' said Hestia. 'And that the artefacts of power were hidden. But it is the only chance to get Finn back. To demand he be brought anywhere else but the caves of sacrifice is folly. Leander would see right through it. Yet, by entering that holy place, by walking the path which will take you there, you may lose yourself entirely, bringing into being the very thing you fear.'

It was a risk she had lived with for so long now, it almost seemed normal to her. A foregone conclusion that one day it would happen. Something she just kept pushing further down the line. She looked directly at Hestia now, Hestia who she almost trusted.

'What if I do become the Nox and kill Finn anyway?'

'It is... a possibility,' Hestia admitted.

'Not just Prince Finnian,' Oriole muttered. 'Any number of us. Even the sisterhood. The Nox is vengeful. Dangerous. Possibly insane still. And powerful here. Too powerful.'

No possibly about it, Wren thought but said nothing. She couldn't help but glance at the boy again. He was listening closely now, intently. 'Then maybe Laurence should have a say as well.'

'I—' At first he seemed so confused at that idea, he didn't manage more than that syllable. 'I don't think you'd kill me, princess.'

Wren smiled, tears stinging her eyes. She hadn't expected that, nor to feel so grateful for his belief in her. Though she didn't share his confidence.

'But she would no longer be *her*,' Oriole told him.

'Then give me another solution,' Hestia exclaimed. 'One which protects the prince and extracts him from his brother's clutches soon because Leander is going to torture him and kill him. You know he will and we need Finn if any of us are to survive. He is the king who will set all to right in this kingdom and usher in a period of peace and prosperity. He is the son forsaken by his father, and he will crown our future.' A flicker of despair crossed Hestia's face before a different thought seemed to strike her. 'That wretched body-swapping spell gave Leander every excuse he will ever need. Where did he even learn how to do something like that? You were his teacher, Oriole.'

'He was always too bright for his own good,' Oriole sighed. 'There are factions within our own sisterhood with sympathies there. They would follow Leander if it meant more power for themselves, no matter where it came from. They would take that crown and use it. They would try to harness all magic, break everything apart to get to it.'

A crown, buried deep in the darkest caves of the Nox, one which could control a goddess... no wonder Wren had always recoiled at the thought of wearing one.

'There would be nothing to take power of if the old magic rages free,' Hestia warned the other sister.

'And if Leander can crown Wren as our lost queen? What then? He will control her and the sisterhood. If we could but reach a compromise with him...'

'No,' Wren said with an assuredness she wished she felt. She knew one thing though – there was no compromise that would save Finn. And besides, she had thrown down her gauntlet to Leander already. She locked eyes with Laurence who was still frowning. Slowly he nodded, his jaw firming. He was as brave as Finn, she thought, and her heart twisted a little.

'The risk is mine to take,' she said, cutting across the two of them. 'And the caves can be sealed, can't they?' They nodded, slowly and thoughtfully. 'Then you seal us in there. If anything goes wrong, if I lose control... Then it's just Finn and I. Leander won't be able to reach us.'

That had to be enough. Because if she did fail she was leaving them all to Leander's mercy.

CHAPTER 17
WREN

Word came far sooner than Wren had expected. Leander had agreed. Still expecting some kind of betrayal, Wren tried to make herself ready when really there was nothing she could do to prepare for this. The caves lay beneath the city, deep in the earth. The way was lit by flickering lanterns and the sisterhood would accompany her there. She didn't like the way they watched her, these women who served the great darkness. Their eyes were far too knowing, hungry, and she didn't like the feeling that she was missing something or being used in some way. She had no reason to trust them, not even Hestia or Oriole who had come to her rescue in the throne room.

There were those among them ravenous for power, Oriole had said. And Hestia had not denied it either. Those who would use the Nox or release old magic to get it.

A small treacherous voice inside her said she'd made a mistake. She should have trusted Finn then, should have tried to escape with him. But she hadn't. Her mind had not known what to think or which way to go. She had looked into the face that had tormented her since they'd arrived here and hesitated. That had been Leander's gift then, forcing a wedge in the trust between her and Finn. He must have loved that, mustn't he? She had handed him his second victory of the day, more so when she saw the betrayal in Finn's face.

What must he be thinking now?

He'd seen her choose the sisterhood instead of him, and now she was demanding him as sacrifice.

And she was risking herself to do it. If anything she feared Hestia was downplaying the danger. She could feel the power in the air and in the earth, waiting for her, a sense of the Nox just biding its time.

Once more she wore the gown Leander had forced her into for the presentation to the king; much as she wanted to tear it from her body, it fitted the role she needed to play now. Her hair glittered with gems, and flowed down her back, the longest and most powerful she had ever allowed it to grow. Given the amount of magic in the air around her, she feared that if she tried to cut it off it would just grow back again in moments. And there was dark magic everywhere here, in the air, in the rocks, in the water coalescing on the ground, even in the lantern flames. She could feel it crawling over her skin and tracing invisible fingertips across her scalp. It prickled at the back of her neck and whispered sweet promises just on the edge of hearing.

All she had to do was reach out and take it.

Elodie's voice haunted her, lingering just out of reach, telling her not to be a fool, to reach for the light, to cling to it, to deny the shadows and push away the empty promises of the shadow kin.

When she was a girl in Cellandre, she had danced with the forest itself more than once and its song had almost swept her away. Elodie had pulled her back and kept her safe and made her promise never to put herself in such a position again. All magic was dangerous.

All the same, what else could Wren do? This was for Finn. She couldn't abandon him.

She could do this, she promised herself. She had to. She would be strong and resolute and she would make it through this some way. Even if she had to sacrifice herself for him... so be it.

The mouth of the first cave opened above her, stalactites like teeth overhead, glistening. The Sisters accompanying her stopped, waiting with their lanterns as she stood there, looking up at the opening.

'He will already be waiting,' Hestia said. 'That was the agreement. But to reach the cave of sacrifice you must pass through the rest – the deepest dark, the emptiness, the longing and the despair...' Four caves, each with a name more desolate than the last. That was the path Wren had to follow to reach the place where the royal family would leave their sons to die for their goddess.

'No deeper, Wren.' Hestia stroked her hair gently. 'There are places where the deepest secrets are buried, where the Nox herself would fear to tread. There are things that would break your will and twist your mind. The kings of old used them to try to constrain the Nox, or enslave her. Their use cost the line of Sidon everything. They were taken and hidden. For everyone's safety. You must keep hold of yourself. Here, this may help.' She pressed something cold and hard into Wren's hand. It was a glass pendant, like the one she had given Finn. The one he had broken to bring them here, which Leander had used to swap their bodies and escape Pelias. It wasn't black though. This one looked like someone had captured gold dust in a ray of light.

'What is it?' Wren whispered. The other Sisters had drawn back and only Hestia remained, giving her this parting gift as quietly and secretly as she could.

'The last of my magic, I fear,' said the other woman with a brief, brittle smile. 'A travelling spell, like the other. If all else fails, it will carry you and whoever you touch to safety. Just break it to activate it.'

'How will it know where is safe?'

Hestia hugged her. 'It will know.' She stepped back then and bowed to Wren. 'I fear I've made a terrible mess of this. I should never have underestimated the lengths Leander would go to. He makes plans within plans, and will not settle for anything less than total control. And the Nox... my goddess can be rational here, sane, but only here, I think. Close to the heart of her power, the place she made her own. She may try to beguile you or persuade you to help her. And she may be convincing. But once she leaves this place, so too goes what remains of her sanity. It is just a fleeting thing and not to be trusted. Be careful, my dear girl. If I fail... if something happens to me...' She glanced over her shoulder briefly and then fixed Wren with a look of such determination that it stole her breath. 'Protect my boy, and my true king, please, my lady. I beg you. Protect them for me. Keep them safe. And do not let Leander win.'

Wren nodded slowly and it felt like a kind of bargain made in the darkwoods, something which bound the two of them together. She wanted to say 'But nothing will happen to you' or something like that, but the words failed even as she thought of them. Her eyes burned as Hestia turned away and vanished, leaving her alone.

I can do this.

But another part of her doubted that. There was no light down here. And how could she reach for the light if there was no light anymore?

Finn was waiting. She didn't have a choice. If she didn't go, Leander would surely kill him. Or just leave him there to a slow and torturous death.

Steeling herself, gathering such magic around her as she still could, Wren stepped into the shadows.

CHAPTER 18

FINN

They dragged Finn from the cell. Not unkindly, but more as if the men involved didn't want to have to touch him for too long, as if he had some sort of terrible infection which could be passed on just by touch, or association. No one spoke directly to him after Gaius and no one made eye contact if they could avoid it. Whether this was because they all thought he had murdered his father, their king, or because they knew what his fate was to be, he couldn't say.

A jug was held up to his face but, desperate for water as he was, he jerked his head back. Finn knew what this entailed. They wanted him pliable, biddable. It would wear off far too soon for him but for now...

Someone grabbed the back of his neck in a grip like iron, squeezing. He gasped without thought and his mouth filled with the sickly sweet liquid. It choked him, and he tried to spit it out but still they kept pouring until he thought he'd drown in it. He swallowed down far too much of it, far more than he should, but they didn't stop. Why would they? The more he took now the easier their job would be.

'Don't damage him,' someone murmured, a soft and delicate voice. He jerked his head to one side, which made everything twist and blur as if he was underwater. A woman dressed all in black stood there, beside the general. One of the sisterhood. He didn't recognise her. Not Hestia or Oriole, but someone who served them. She sounded younger, though her tone was implacable. 'My lady will not be pleased if he is hurt in any way.'

She was just here to oversee matters.

Don't damage him. As if he was nothing more than some kind of delicacy, a gift...

Which, in fact, he was...

This was always your fate. The voice whispered at the back of his mind, a laugh rippling through its soft tones. *You are mine, Finnian. Just as you were always meant to be. A prize... and bait...*

What little strength he had flowed away with his breath. Conscious thought became a chore, something he couldn't quite grasp. He knew what was happening, but not what to do about it, or how to stop it. There didn't seem to be any way to resist. Not anymore.

He was stripped and washed, the water bitingly cold on his skin. And then scrubbed clean. The women who came in to do that took their time, revelling in their power over him while all the time the black-clad sister watched, like she was supervising the preparation of a feast. Warm oils came next, worked hard into his muscles, numbing his flesh at first and then, as they took effect, making him unbearably sensitive. His skin felt every breeze, every sigh and every laugh. And there was nothing he could do.

When his cock started to stir under their ministering hands, one of the women made a comment which was met with a sea of soft, knowing chuckles.

The woman in black hissed a command he didn't understand, an admonition of some kind, and they all fell silent. When they released him, he sank down to his knees, waiting.

There was something else he should be doing, he thought vaguely. Running, fighting, breaking free... maybe? But he didn't have the strength and his body betrayed him. Besides, there was nowhere to go. The drugs in his system had stolen any rational thought.

The woman stood over him now, leaning in close, her long black veil brushing against him. 'You are blessed,' she told him. 'And beautiful. You will serve as you were always meant to serve. We witness this, son of Sidon. Your blood is chosen. Bring our goddess back to us. Lead us to the crown.'

Her words flowed around him like music and Finn felt his mouth lift into a smile. Her hand cupped his face.

'Fear not,' she said in formal tones. 'Our lady will come for you and your life will be hers. There will be no more fear.'

His life was already hers, Finn thought absently. It always would be. It had been since he had first seen her. He thought of the forest, of the lush green leaves pressing close, wrapping themselves around him and tightening their grip. They had drawn him into the darkwood and he could smell the same fragrances now, the ones that had beguiled him, and stolen all his wits.

Memories of Wren filled his head, dizzying, intoxicating. Her touch, her kiss, the way she opened to him and wrapped herself around him. The way her hair moved against his skin, tangling him in her power. She was everything, all he longed for, and that had been the case all along. Like he had always been meant for her and her alone.

Wren, not the Nox. He had to remember that. The difference.

It was like a spear of agony running through him. Wren

thought he had betrayed her. And Wren would be the one to take his life.

And perhaps that was fitting too. He couldn't fight it, not anymore.

The Sister peered into his face. 'Yes, he's ready,' she said. 'Time to go.'

Gaius nodded to the guards who seized him again, but this time they had to carry him rather than drag him. And that didn't matter either.

'Wait,' an unwelcome voice cut in. Leander. Of course it was Leander. Even now he couldn't resist having the last word. One final dig.

Finn tried to focus on him, but his head flopped forward and his eyes closed.

'Look at me, you pathetic bastard.'

Leander grabbed his chin and wrenched his face up. Finn forced his eyelids open again, fighting against whatever seemed to be gluing them together. The sickening swirl of drugs in his system wanted him to comply. It didn't seem to matter who was asking, and even Leander could command him now.

Whatever Leander saw in his face as he studied Finn, a slow and vicious smile spread over his fine features in response. 'So that's all, is it? This is what you've come to? Great darkness, I hope she tears you apart. I hope you're looking into those pretty eyes while she does it. And I hope she knows what she's doing to you.'

'Leander,' Finn tried to say, as if naming him might help.

'Your majesty to you,' his brother sneered. 'You thought that Hestia would save you? Make you king in my stead? No, this is what they always wanted for you, all the sisterhood. And I'm glad it's going to be your precious little bird who finally destroys you. Maybe she'll be more amenable after she's torn you apart, brother, when she comes into her power.' He leaned in close to Finn's ear and whispered, breath playing on his tormented skin.

'I'm going to have her, Finn, one way or another. Have no doubt about that. I'll make her forget you ever existed. You aren't a sacrifice, little brother. All you are is bait.'

Something in him rebelled at that, something which reared back in rage. He didn't know where it came from or how it broke free, only that Leander said those things, and he shouldn't. No one should.

Finn jerked his head back and then slammed his forehead into his brother's face. There was a satisfying crunch.

Cursing, Leander reeled away from him, clutching his nose. Blood splattered Finn's eyes and he smiled as he felt it drip towards his mouth. All around him weapons were drawn and people were shouting. A laugh burst out of him and then Leander's foot slammed into his stomach, sending him back in a sprawling heap. It knocked the air out of him and he thought he heard something crunch inside him but he didn't care. There was no pain.

'Enough!' the Sister snapped and a ripple of shadowy power filled the room. It sang to him, laughed at him, and lapped at the blood on his skin. Finn sank beneath its spell without a struggle. 'Someone help the king and remove him. He shouldn't even be here. You, we need to get this over with. Now. Bring him.'

Finn didn't fight. He couldn't. He just let them draw him into the darkness. The walls of the dungeon gave way to the walls of a tunnel and the walls of the tunnel gave way to a cavern. It arched high about him, and all he could think of was the warmth of the air and the fragrance of the forest and how those things shouldn't go together.

They bound him in the middle of the chamber, on his knees, his arms dragged behind him and tethered to his ankles. Shadow kin coiled around him, guarding him or restraining him, he didn't know, but their touch was soft and seductive, an impossibility. They sang to him, lullabies and songs of long ago.

As the darkness that had always lingered deep inside him finally took hold, he had one final desperate thought.

You're bait, Leander had said. So had the Nox.

Bait for Wren.

Bring our goddess back to us. Lead us to the crown.

They had plans of their own. This wasn't so much a sacrifice as a trap.

CHAPTER 19

WREN

The darkness wasn't quite complete. That was the one thing saving her, the sprinkling of lights and soft glows that spread out before her. But the tunnels were long and winding, and the caverns Wren entered vast. Her footsteps echoed around her. Even her breath seemed to haunt her.

What makes you think you can do this?

The voice came out of nowhere, and something slid around her ankles, almost tripping her. Just a shadow. Or shadow kin.

They were here then. Of course they were. And so was the spirit of the Nox.

Of course it was. It had been waiting for her.

The names for the different caves lingered in her memory.

The deepest dark, the emptiness, the longing and the despair.

The first one opened out above her, like a cathedral to the darkness. The light in the rock face glittered coldly, no longer a comfort.

In the centre, where the path dipped down, it was lightless. The deepest darkness she had ever seen.

Wren stopped, her chest tightening.

Well, little vestige? There was almost a laugh in the voice of the Nox which teased the back of her mind. Not a pleasant laugh either.

But Wren couldn't move. She wrapped her arms around her body, holding herself tight as if she might have to stop herself falling to pieces, and forced herself to breathe.

Balance, Hestia had told her. It was all about balance. That was the secret to magic. Or at least to dealing with the power of the Nox. When it came to the Aurum, Wren had no idea. The only way she had been able to channel the light was to push away the darkness, or to lose herself to it completely. And it hurt. Every time.

Except... she paused. Back in Pelias, when Finn had put the bracelet on her, with the Aurum running wild, devouring Elodie, it had reached out to her and tried to fill her.

Each of the powers sought to control, to dominate those who would serve it. They expected devotion, and obedience in all things.

I've never been good at obedience, she thought, and that dark laugh rippled around her again.

You'll learn...

That almost sounded like Leander. She felt her whole body recoil.

The Nox was playing with her now, tormenting her. If she couldn't go any further there was no way she could find Finn and rescue him. They'd say she rejected him and who knew what Leander would do with him then? No, she had to go on.

Balance. Like making her way along the edge of a cliff, or the blade of a knife. What had Elodie said about the queens of Asteroth? Some old saying about walking a knife's edge in order to rule. That was balance as well. Push darkness away to let in the light. It worked both ways.

The deepest dark was just the first step. She took it, forcing herself onwards. The deepest dark closed around her and all the little stars of light went out.

Wren kept walking, slowly, one step at a time. She couldn't see anything now, only feel her way in the darkness, listening to each footfall on the cold stone. But nothing blocked her path, nothing hindered her.

She just had to keep going.

Abruptly the shadows peeled back in front of her once more. It felt like pressing on the edge of a bubble and then passing through. Deep in her chest there was a painful tug as if something hooked inside her for a moment, holding onto her, and was dragged out. It left a hollow behind, a void.

But a glow of faint light started up again before her, leading her onwards. It was the same blue as the eyes of shadow kin, aglow from within, and it ringed a tunnel entrance.

I can do this, Wren told herself, almost dizzy with relief at having passed through the first cave. She drew in another breath and stepped into the cave known as the emptiness.

That small space inside her, that void she had felt, suddenly exploded in her chest. It surged through her, making her drop to her knees in shock. It was everywhere, in her mind, in her heart, even in her soul, hollowing her out and showing her...

There was nothing. She was nothing. She was a creature formed from darkness and created with the sole purpose of preserving its power on this earth. And now she was in its place of power, daring to defy it, to walk through its chambers and think herself... what? Autonomous?

No. She was nothing. She was just a shell waiting for the Nox to fill her. She had no power of her own, no purpose of her own, nothing. She had come here as she'd always been fated to come here and she should just fall to the ground and let it take her. She should just give up and...

Wren sucked in a breath, painful and wretched. Blood trickled from her nose in a hot wet line. Her blood. Real blood. She could taste its coppery tang on her lips.

'I'm... I'm not your thing,' she said and her voice rasped

against her tight throat as she forced out the words. 'I'm real. I'm my own person.'

Laughter rang around her this time, bouncing off the walls and ceiling of the cavern, and the emptiness shook with its mirth.

This was worse than she had imagined. The Nox had always been a distant thing, trapped in a far-off realm beyond her world. But now... now, here, it was real and dangerous. It could win this. She realised now that she was not necessarily going to walk out of this as she was.

They had known, Oriole and Hestia. They had warned her...

Tears stung Wren's eyes. The sisterhood had sent her in here knowing she would fail. Of course they had. For all their pretty words, they wanted the Nox back as much as any other Ilanthian.

'Oh Elodie,' she whispered. 'What am I going to do?'

Her voice echoed back to her, twisted into something pathetic and plaintive, cut with sobs.

She was helpless, worthless, nothing. She had been created rather than born. She had been made for a purpose which had nothing to do with her desires and needs.

Another voice came to mind. She didn't know how but it was Roland, the soft baritone of his voice which rippled over her senses.

Elodie said that the Nox formed you based on her dreams, her wishes, on what the two of us once had. It reached into her heart and took what it found there. So I am your father in every way that counts. Just as she is your mother. Always remember that.

Those words... those precious words he had said to her in the chamber of the Aurum when she had almost lost hope. That acceptance. That love...

My little bird, Elodie had called her, and never in the mocking way Leander had used those words after he had plucked them from her mind and manipulated them to taunt her. No, Elodie said them with love. And she always had done.

The emptiness pushed in on Wren again, trying to force her submission. It would hollow her out and make her ready for the Nox. That was what it was trying to do, but she couldn't let it succeed. She wouldn't. There was more to her than a shell, a vessel. She was the woman Elodie had made, the woman Roland saw, and that was who she wanted to be.

The woman Finn loved. Who loved him in return.

She drew in a breath and power filled her. Not a power from beyond, or scraped from the remains of the shadows. Her own power. Bright and terrible.

She threw back her head and screamed defiance.

The magic of the emptiness recoiled and the cave system shook as if an earthquake tore through it. Wren forced herself back onto her feet and staggered onwards. It hurt. Everything hurt, but she had to do it.

The next cave loomed over her. It wasn't as large as the last two, but the moment she entered, she felt its touch. And with it came a new kind of need. What was empty was replaced with a hunger, a terrible, desperate want. It almost brought her to her knees again.

In the soft firelight glow ahead, she saw a figure, a man. Just standing there, waiting for her.

Finn.

CHAPTER 20

WREN

Finn didn't look like the prince Wren had grown used to in Sidonia. He didn't wear fine clothes or have that arrogant cast to his eyes. Instead, he wore the simple leathers and travelling cloak in which she had first seen him. His hair even looked like it still had briars tangled in it. He smiled, that half-hopeful, half-defeated expression, all confusion and self-deprecation, which made her pause.

The Finn she loved stood before her. The knight who had tried to save her in Thirbridge and got himself hopelessly entangled in the darkwood. Her Finn. The one she had longed for ever since they had fled Pelias.

No, before that. Ever since they had arrived in Pelias.

'Finn?' she whispered, hardly daring to believe it. She had found him. 'Finn, is it really you?'

Her voice shook but she didn't care if he heard that. Not him.

His smile widened and he opened his arms to her. His blue eyes softened with relief and in them she saw the flame of his desire for her.

The relief stole her breath and she started forward, ready to throw herself into his arms, after all this time. But something still wasn't right. His eyes...

Blue, yes, but not the blue she remembered. His eyes were the eyes of a shadow kin, the bright blue of flames on a marsh, flickering with the intent to lead her astray. Will-o'-the-wisp eyes that could only be seen in the deepest darkness, luring the unwary into danger.

She skidded to a halt, her arms coming up to defend herself. All she wanted was her Finn. But it wasn't him. This was just another trap.

'*And why can't it be him?*' a new voice asked. His voice. And yet, at the same time not his voice at all. It was empty, a whisper, an echo. It was almost perfect but the things it said... '*It can be whatever you want, Wren. The shadows can fulfil your dreams. You only have to command them. They'll obey you. You can have the Finnian Ward you want. Just say so.*'

No, this wasn't fair. This wasn't him and it was a trick. But the temptation was so strong...

He took a step towards her and held out his hand. And they looked so like his hands. The long fingers, elegant but strong, callused from using the sword, hands that were not afraid of hard work or dirt, hands that were beautiful to her. Her gaze ran from them up and across his skin as he reached out. The muscles of his upper arms were finely toned and so strong. His shoulders were broad and she could bury her face in the curve where they met his neck. If she pressed her lips to the skin there, so sensitive beneath her kiss, he would shiver with pleasure. Her stomach tightened with need, with desire, with longing. Because he was everything. He always had been.

'*Come to me, Wren. Please.*' His voice was a soft rumble against her, rippling through her.

Great light and shadows of old, she wanted to. She wanted Finn. He was all she wanted and all she needed, but it wasn't him. It couldn't be.

Oriole had warned her about this cave, known as the cave of longing. She knew it was playing with her mind.

But it felt like something was tearing her apart from inside, that terrible emptiness swelling and growing and sinking its claws into her, ripping its way out of her chest. Her longing was so strong she was certain it would destroy her.

'Finn...' His name was like a talisman, a charm, to wind her will around and to cling to. For a moment this shade before her smiled, encouragement and triumph warring on his beautiful face. 'I want Finn. But you aren't him. You can never be him.'

'No,' he agreed. It agreed. And even as she watched it melted into the swirl of shadows. *'But we would have been for you. We would have given you joy instead of the agony he offers. Now you'll never know.'* With a hollow ringing sound, something fell to the stones at her feet and Wren bent to pick it up. Her body seemed to move automatically, as if she didn't have a choice in the matter.

It was a knife, like a sliver of moonlight, as long as her forearm, curving into a vicious tip. It filled her hand as if it had been made to nestle there.

'Go on then, go forward, and let the despair take you, little vestige.'

There was a doorway behind the shadows and they parted for her. But even as she tried to walk, they wound themselves around her, and their whispers promised anything. Everything.

But Wren pushed onwards, staggering through the cave, into a new kind of darkness. Not just of the world around her, not just the deep seductive night. This was a darkness of the mind, and it devoured her without a struggle. Part of her was already there, and she knew it was where she belonged.

She understood what she truly was. The need she had felt bled away into emptiness, into that sucking void of nothing in her heart. Now there was only despair.

There wasn't time. She didn't have time and neither did

Finn. She was going to lose him, she knew that. Nothing could stop that now. Perhaps he was already gone, dead or lost to her. She had taken so long to get through the caves and she needed to find him. She needed him and she had already failed him.

She had failed everyone.

There was no way to escape her fate.

After so much effort to choose her own path, she would meet her dark future here.

So, knife in hand, all she could do was let the darkness swallow her.

'SONG OF SUMMONING',
ILANTHIAN RITES

Come, oh divine darkness,
    and be made whole once again.

Come to your servant,
    supplicant before you here,

Where the veil is thin
    and your prison walls are weakest.

Come take the crown
    that once was yours.

Come and be mine,
    and let me be your servant forever.

CHAPTER 21

FINN

Shadows swam around Finn's body. They burrowed through his blood and coiled, squeezing, around his heart. The drug they had given him appeared to be wearing off at last but that just left him weak, cold and shivering in the darkness. There was no light here. It was a place of death and nightmares, one he remembered all too well. He'd always thought that his memories were an exaggeration, those of a child, where everything seemed bigger and darker and far more threatening than they should to a man.

He had been wrong.

Every terror of that memory was a faint echo of what engulfed him now. Or perhaps that was part of the nightmare that was this place.

His body ached, shoulders, knees, even down to his toes digging into the freezing stone.

They had left him kneeling, arms bound behind him and tethered to his ankles, unable to get up or move, his body entirely exposed. There was nowhere to go. Not really. He was lost, helpless.

No, not helpless, some distant part of him tried to argue.

There were still ways to fight. He was a knight. He had trained all his life for combat. He didn't need weapons. He was one.

And yet he just knelt there. And waited. He couldn't fight this. He was a fool to even think such thoughts.

When she appeared, he wasn't even sure that it was Wren and not some figment of his imagination, his childhood terrors. For months after Roland took him away from Sidonia, Finn had woken up screaming in the night. No one could convince him that the Nox would not come for him.

And here she was, taking the form he feared the most, the woman he loved and the goddess he was fated to die for, all in one beautiful shape.

Wren stepped from the shadows as if made from them. Her hair was long now, longer than he had ever seen it. It swirled around her with a life of its own, always in motion, curling and drifting on currents only it could know. Her face looked so pale, and there were shadows under her dark eyes which made his heart lurch inside him. What had happened to her here? What had Leander done to her? He could only imagine and he didn't want to. All he wanted to do was tear the bastard apart before falling at her feet, abasing himself and begging her forgiveness for ever putting her in such a position.

And she would never give it. He knew that now. The girl he loved, the one who would always forgive another, who had the most open and giving true heart he had ever met... she was gone.

Her mouth was a thin, hard line and still he longed to kiss those lips, to drink her down and lose himself in her.

She wore a gown, black as night and threaded with shimmering strands, which left nothing to his imagination. Ilanthian in style, it framed her body, highlighting the soft luminescence of her skin and the darkness of her hair and eyes. There were gems scattered through her hair and they caught the light like the stars in the night's sky.

Wait... the light... there was some kind of light. She

reflected it back at him. It gleamed in her eyes, and on the edge of the sacrificial knife she carried.

Another thing about this place he would never forget. That very same knife, in the hands of his father, pressing like a line of ice against his skin.

But his father was dead now. Dead by Finn's own hand, even if his will had not been behind it. Leander had used him and now Leander was king. And Finn...

Finn was back where he was always meant to be. A sacrifice. Her sacrifice.

After twenty years, she was coming to collect.

It wasn't Wren. It couldn't be Wren. Had it been like this for her, he wondered vaguely, looking at his face and knowing it wasn't him but someone else for all that time? Were all the tortures Leander had put her through as painful as this?

She must have known.

But in the throne room she hadn't come to him, she hadn't moved. She had chosen the sisterhood instead and found her safety there.

He still liked to believe that in that moment they could have escaped, even if that was the hope and dream of a child.

He had failed her so completely.

He deserved this.

The sisterhood had removed the bracelet that he himself had put on her, limiting her magic. Containing her. And now she was free. And so was the Nox. It was too late.

There was no use in fighting, not now. Nothing he could do but surrender to the inevitable and show her that, by this action alone, he was sorry.

With a sigh, he tilted back his head, exposing his throat to her, and she hesitated, her footsteps stilling in their advance.

'What are you waiting for?' he asked, horrified to hear the trembling in his own voice and the way it bounced back, mocking him from every corner of the chamber. 'I'm here. This is what you want. What you always wanted.'

'What I wanted?' she murmured, her voice dreamlike. 'What would you know about what I wanted?'

He laughed. He couldn't help himself. It wasn't joyful or mocking or anything like that. It was a broken sound wrenched out of his chest, out of his heart, because Wren was gone. And the being standing in front of him was still so beautiful that it was almost a relief that she would be the one to kill him.

'You're right,' he conceded. 'I don't know what you want, apart from my life. Or rather my death. Wren... Wren wanted her forest. She wanted to go back there and live there in peace and quiet. She wanted me to go with her and I should have. I should never have let them take her to Pelias. I should have listened but I was a fool. So I'll pay for that now. It seems fair, doesn't it? To die for her. Does she...' A wild hope seized him. Not a hope of salvation or anything so stupid as that. But a small hope, which was, at the same time, the greatest tragedy. 'Is there any of her left in you? Will she know? If I tell you how I love her, will she know?'

The woman shook her head, more in dismay than denial, but that hardly mattered. The Nox was just playing with him now.

'This is a lie,' she hissed. 'You aren't real.'

'I'm more real than you are.'

When she didn't come any closer he dropped his head again and stared at her. She seemed to swim in and out of focus, or was that his eyes filling with tears? What did it matter anyway? He was as good as dead here.

He shivered, his skin heating beneath her gaze. Desire surged back through him, unwelcome and strange. Just because she wore Wren's face and body, just because she still looked like the woman he loved... worshipped... adored...

But then she was a goddess now. Of course he adored her.

This wasn't right. That one thought managed to penetrate the tangled confusion of everything else. None of this was right.

'Wren?' he whispered, his voice a rusted knife in his throat.

'Finn...' she murmured in response and stepped towards him again until the knife was pointed at his throat. He couldn't tear his gaze away from her eyes, from the tears silvering her cheeks.

'Do it then,' he told her, making his voice harsh in order to force the words out. 'Do it and have done with me. Release me.'

Her hand shook and the point of the blade scraped against skin and stubble, a rasping noise which sent another shudder of fear and despair through him.

The Nox would never release him, he knew that. Not even in death. He was her creature and his soul would be hers. What that meant he wasn't sure. Would the dark power she embodied consume him for eternity or reanimate him as some kind of mindless slave? Once his blood spilled for her... again, he reminded himself because he had bled so many times for Wren, he had died for her and still she had refused to let him go...

'This isn't real,' she told him.

No, she was asking... begging... She didn't want this to be real. Did she?

But that didn't sound like the Nox at all.

Finn drew in a breath and leaned forward towards the knife, and to his surprise, Wren pulled back.

'It is real,' he replied. 'All too real. And if you have to kill me, I understand, my love.'

She bared her teeth, so fierce and angry. 'You aren't my love. You aren't real.'

Great light, he thought, she was beautiful. And powerful. And his...

And it *was* real. All too real.

'Wren...' Her name was an entire psalm and his heart sang the harmony. 'This is real and you are everything to me. You have to know that. You always will be whether I live or die. Whether you kill me or not.'

For another agonising moment, she froze. Then her hand spasmed and she dropped the knife. It clattered to the floor between them and she closed her hand around his throat instead, nails digging into the skin. He stretched up into her grip, because he couldn't rise, not bound as he was like a beast for slaughter. He was reaching out to a wild animal, half mad with grief, pain and betrayal. Her hold on his throat never moved, her slender hand like a collar holding him. Her dark eyes were wide and bewildered, but he saw hope there.

Finally he saw hope again. And knew it.

'Wren...' he whispered. She was here for him. To kill him or claim him, it didn't matter which. He was hers.

Wren bent forward, her lips brushing his softly for a moment. Finn groaned, a deep and endless sound of submission, and she kissed him.

What could he do but kiss her back?

CHAPTER 22

WREN

His kiss robbed Wren of all rational thought. Apart from one.

Finn... it was really Finn...

Finn who loved her, who had always come to her rescue, who had been there for her, Finn who she loved in return, beyond reason, beyond everything.

He was still tied up, his wrists bound together with a coarse rope, and then lashed to his ankles, a demeaning and uncomfortable position. He couldn't touch her or caress her but that didn't seem to matter. He kissed her, his mouth capturing hers and casting that spell it always did, lips moving as if he was trying to speak but couldn't form words, his tongue dancing against hers. She whimpered in recognition but couldn't do anything more but kiss him back. Slowly, she lifted her hands to frame his face, almost collapsing on top of him with relief.

His poor bruised and beaten face. What had they done to him? Light, was she hurting him?

There was no doubt in her mind now that this was Finn and not the shadow of him that had tormented her since they had arrived here. No trace of Leander remained in him, none of that cruel arrogance.

Just Finn. It was just Finn.

Her blood surged in recognition of the light in him and she felt it fill her veins. Darkness and shadows might coil around her but that didn't matter now. Her hair wrapped itself around his body, pulling him closer, binding him to her, and he gasped in raw pleasure, a desperate gleam in his dark blue eyes, hungry and ready for her.

His body was naked and there was no disguising his need for her, the ache in his flesh. His cock was a hard length, like iron wrapped in velvet, displayed like an offering. Wren longed to drop to her knees and take him in her mouth, or to push him down and wrap her legs around him, taking him deep inside her, letting him fill her. But there wasn't time. There couldn't be.

Common sense didn't matter. She couldn't tear herself away from him. Couldn't stop touching him and feeling him respond. Her Finn, her love, her everything.

'We have to get out of here,' she told him, her lips fumbling against his.

He jerked on the ropes, but couldn't free himself. 'This is a trap,' he said. 'You know it is. Leave me here. I'll work something out.'

'I'm not leaving you anywhere,' she replied. 'Not again. Not ever.'

'I'm nothing but bait to bring you here. That was what Leander said. I'm her sacrifice. They want you to give in to your power, to become *her*. And this is her place. He thinks once the Nox is in control, he can control her.'

The thought was laughable. And the laughter ringing around the back of her mind was not Wren's own. Even the Nox found Leander's machinations mockable. He knew nothing. Not about magic, not about her, and certainly not about the goddess he claimed to serve but desired to control.

This was the Nox's place of power, Wren knew that. She

could feel it. Blood had soaked so deeply into the stone all around them, ancient and ageless, so many deaths for her. Wren should have been helpless here. But at the same time... she had made it this far, faced the other caves and come through them. She was still herself.

And also she wasn't. She was something more. Darkness swirled along her veins and threaded through her hair.

I was their queen once, and they stole that from me. They stole my blood and made it their own. They bound me when they crowned me.

Wren released Finn as the voice rang through her mind, plaintive and still so angry. But there was loss and longing tangled in it. The Nox was remembering something, something old and heartbreaking. Just by dint of Wren being here.

Finn slumped down before her, confusion and resolve warring with the desire in his face, and she tried to smile for him, to reassure him.

This was her place. *Hers.*

'Don't be afraid,' she told him and her voice hardly sounded like her own anymore. Perhaps it wasn't.

The colour fled from him and his eyes glistened, but he still stared up at her in a combination of adoration and trepidation.

Leander would have kept Finn from her if he thought that would serve him better. And he might have been right. But now Finn was here and she was never letting him go again. The light in him drew her and she was like a moth attracted to that flame. Not just her. The Nox as well.

The Nox might hate the Aurum, but it needed it as well.

Balance, she thought, remembering what Hestia had told her, what Elodie had said. It's all about balance.

Join with him, the Nox said. *In life or in death, it matters not. Join with him here, in my place. Make him yours and I will protect him. We will protect him. I will show you how.*

Could it be a trick? Of course it could. But right now Wren didn't have any choices left.

I will lead you both out of here. I will lead you to everything you need. If you let me. But...

But there will be a price, Wren thought. And I will be that price.

I will not be controlled and commanded again. I will not be made into a monster.

But the Nox was a monster. Wren knew that. Perhaps they both were now. She wasn't a fool.

Leander was no fool either. And he had told Finn that he was no more than bait. They would be coming for her. They would find another way to bind her power and use her.

Never, the Nox hissed, the bloodlust rising again. *I will never allow that again. Sidon betrayed me. I was his queen and he stole my power. I will protect you. Let me help.*

Wren's consciousness spread out, testing the limits of the chamber, and she found them, soldiers, closing in. She almost smiled. They weren't even stealthy about it.

And with the Nox coiling around her, all it took was a thought.

Shadow kin swarmed around the entrances. There were some brief screams, cut off far too quickly, and then that deep and endless silence again.

'No one can touch us here,' she told Finn. 'No one can enter until I allow it. Do you trust me?'

He nodded firmly, though his teeth worried at his lower lip.

She pressed her hands to his head and sent a pulse of healing energy through him, wiping away pain. He cried out softly, more in surprise than anything else, a groan, and the sound sent a jolt of need through her.

'You're safe,' she told him firmly. 'I will always keep you safe, Finn, just as you tried to do for me. But I've changed. I had to. I needed to embrace what I am. Do you understand?'

Again, he nodded, just a simple dip of his head. A tear slid from his left eye and she felt the wave of grief as if it was her own. Did he think he had lost her?

Wren brushed her mouth against his again, trying to reassure him, her lips taking his gently but with determination.

She shrugged off the gown, letting it fall to the floor, and stripped off her undergarments until she stood before him as naked as he was.

'My lady,' he tried to say but she just kissed him again, until his reason seemed to slip away to whatever place she had relegated hers.

'We belong together, my love. We always will. And here, in this place, we will seal that promise. I'm not going to kill you, Finn. Never. But there are other sacrifices. So I need you to trust me. I need you to make love to me, here and now. I need you to be mine and to swear it, and I need you to mean it.'

She ran her lips along his jaw, biting the skin softly as she did so, grazing against flesh and stubble, and he gave another of those bewitching groans, rising up on his aching knees as she poured more strength into him. He leaned back, his whole body exposed to her.

'Wren...' Her name was a prayer on his lips and she lived to hear it there. 'I am yours. Body and soul. Yours to command. I always have been, from the first moment I saw you.'

Wren slid her arms around his neck and settled herself astride his hips until she could sheathe his cock with her body, sinking down on him with a moan of desperate want. Finn didn't pause to let her adjust this time. He thrust, fast and desperate, but that was what she needed. Just him, just his body and his will. He leaned back to give himself leverage, drawing her with him, his mouth seeking hers. They devoured each other and she moaned deep into his kiss as all control slipped away.

Nothing mattered. Nothing but this, nothing but the two of

them in the darkness, his fullness inside her and the growing wave of light and dark combined which engulfed her. Her body tightened, ready for release, and for a moment she felt herself changing, pulsing with darkness and light, until she hardly knew what she was anymore. Magic. It was magic, old and powerful. She had never felt anything like this. It was in her, threaded through her, and in him as well. Like called to like. They had always been meant to be together. Balanced on the edge of a heedless orgasm she suddenly understood, just for that moment, understood everything, before tipping over the edge, crying out words of othertongue and his name, weaving the two of them together in some deep and fundamental way. It was the voice of the Nox speaking through her, she understood that in a distant part of herself. She wouldn't have been able to dredge up any words right now, let alone magical ones.

The chamber was illuminated in a kaleidoscope of light, bouncing off minerals threaded through the rock face and revealing the countless intricate carvings all around them. It was beautiful, more than beautiful. This chamber of sacrifice transformed as she cried out, her back arching, her head thrown back, until she couldn't keep her eyes open anymore.

'Stay with me, Wren,' he begged. 'Please, stay with me, my love, my heart. Don't change... don't vanish... don't... don't...'

His voice twisted to an inarticulate gasp and he thrust up into her in a helpless rhythm, so deeply she felt like he was making himself part of her forever. Her conscious mind swam with relief and Finn's head fell back, his throat exposed to her teeth if she wanted to tear it open. He would let her. He would let her do anything.

Slowly, light and shadows eddied around them, drifting in elegant swirls, and she felt that pulsing magic still rippling through her. Different, this was different. And so much more powerful in its willingness.

Dark and light, deity and sacrifice, her and Finn...

She barely knew which was which anymore. She just clung to him, wrapping herself around him in the hopes this moment wouldn't end.

Whispered words of release in othertongue echoed around them and the ropes unravelled at his wrists and ankles.

He surged forward and she couldn't move in time to stop him. He caught the back of her head in one hand and wrapped the other around her waist, sweeping her up and then lowering her to the ground beneath him. So there he was, hanging over her, still inside her. Slowly, he lifted his head, his expression dazed and wondering as it rose to take in the transformation of the chamber of sacrifice, and finally came to rest on her once more.

He smiled. Actually smiled. The tenderness of that look almost destroyed her.

'Wren, what have you done?'

Slowly he withdrew and then took her hands, raising her to her feet. As they touched, she let her magic sweep through him to heal him and strengthen him. He almost dropped to his knees before her again, this time in deference, but she pressed her hand to his chest, stopping him.

'That was both of us,' she told him. 'Not just me. And now, I think, it's time to leave.'

'They'll be waiting for us. I can't defend you like this.'

As if she needed defence. But she knew he would try all the same. He was her Paladin and there was nothing else he could do.

'Not that way,' she replied. 'We aren't going that way. Not now.'

Don't go any deeper, Hestia had said. But that was then. And that was something she had told just Wren. Now, everything had changed. The Nox drew her deeper into the caves, to the dark and secret places long forgotten by anyone else. It would protect them, help them. That was what it had promised. And now she had nothing else to trust.

Without another word of explanation, Wren took his hands. Darkness closed around them as silent and as complete as the night itself and they vanished.

'THE BALLAD OF THE LOST QUEEN'

He whispered words of love to her,
She took him to her bed.
But he it was who wore the crown.
Though he placed it on her head.

In the shadows still she weeps.
In the darkness she must wait.
The lost queen who was forsaken,
Is bound by Sidon's fate.

CHAPTER 23
ROLAND

Roland watched their new companions. Something wasn't right, there was something that didn't ring true. There was no darkwood here, nothing to call the shadow kin in such numbers. They had seemed to focus entirely on him and the more he thought about it the more convinced he was. And this was before addressing all his other questions, about Vambray, Robin and Lark and whatever was going on at the College of Winter.

Reason argued that he was on edge and exhausted, that he was jumping at shadows – a thought which amused his bitter humour far more than it should really – that all would be explained once they had reached safety.

But Roland rarely put his trust in reason alone.

Elodie would know what to do, what to say to these people. She would charm them, or astound them with her abilities and her intellect. She would set the sky alight and they would beg to follow her.

Instead, there was just him. And he needed their help.

Led by the party from the College, the Paladins reached a ravine in the hillside and from there entered a tunnel. At least they were protected from the driving snow in here, though it didn't seem to be any warmer than outside. The blindfolds were removed. The witches held up their hands and flames formed above their palms, lighting the way. Whether they were captives or guests was a moot point, Roland thought. They had no choice but to follow.

The College of Winter was a fortress embedded in the mountains and from the moment they stepped within its walls, Roland felt the itch of unchecked magic worrying at the back of his neck. It was everywhere, in everything. They used magic like breathing here.

That sense of wrongness persisted. It was in the way the witchkind looked at him as he passed. From every wall, from the corners of the courtyard where the horses were stabled, from windows and walkways overhead, they studied him.

Roland was used to drawing attention wherever he went. This was different.

He wasn't the only one to notice. Anselm and Olivier took up position as close to him as possible, perfect bodyguards should he need them. 'Grandmaster, I believe we have a problem,' Anselm said in a low voice.

'Agreed.' Roland was loath to admit it but there was no doubt. 'Your assessment?'

'I'm not sure. Not yet. But we can't trust them. Olivier?'

'This entire place...' was all the other knight would say. 'Something is wrong. The children wouldn't even consider coming inside the walls.'

'And yet they brought us here,' Roland replied. 'There must have been a reason.'

'They weren't just children, were they?' Anselm asked.

'They *were* children,' Olivier said. 'Maybe they've been children for a very long time. I don't know. It doesn't matter. They have more sense than we do, I think.'

That wasn't exactly helpful, but Roland couldn't find the words to express it himself. And Olivier was not mistaken.

'Stay alert,' Roland told them. 'All is not as it appears here.'

They were witchkind and he was certain that the rebel witchkind of Garios they had heard so much about were ultimately centred here. He'd never be able to prove it, but somehow, he knew it.

Roland felt an undercurrent of fear running through this place. It didn't help that there was magic everywhere, spilling up through the ground. It wasn't the thrumming of the Aurum as it ran through the Sanctum. He felt that like his own heartbeat but this... it felt wild.

He watched the way Tobias moved through the College, the way his people looked to him. Some of them anyway, far more than Roland would have expected given he was no longer their leader. How had he lost power as chancellor? What had happened?

Tobias might be offering to help and might have saved him from the shadow kin attack but Roland still felt there were many things the witchkind were not eager to share with him. Nor did he blame them. Not really. Tobias had that furtive, almost feral edge to him. Perhaps they all did, each and every one. This was their place, their haven. They had been hunted, and coerced all their lives.

Usually by people like him.

And now he was intruding here as well.

It was the way of the Aurum, to draw people to that light, to demand service. He knew that better than anyone. It had called him and he had knelt and swore his vows gladly. But now he wondered what might have happened had he not been so willing.

No true knight would turn away from the Aurum. They were called and some men did not have the calling at all. Others felt it but had other priorities and duties, and some born with magic couldn't bear to give it up, to surrender that part of themselves. Maidens were trained from a very young age to serve and

Roland had never questioned that. But other women were not powerful enough, or preferred exile.

Some went to the College of Winter and that was that. And others...

He was suddenly ashamed to realise he had never questioned what happened to the others. Or how much choice was really presented to the children brought before those flames. They were young, very young. Did they even have the capacity to make an informed choice?

It felt like the edges of his world were slowly being chipped away and he did not like it one bit. He thought of the way the twins had watched him, the things they had said, and felt a savage surge of shame and remorse.

The people of Pelias spoke of rebel witchkind as a great threat, but there'd never been many who caused trouble. They were easily dealt with, the dangerous ones, and others of their own kind often turned them in. A threat was always a threat when it came to magic running wild. Now Roland wondered if they really were no more than hedge witches and wanderers, exiles, the lost.

And he had been complicit in driving them into the wilds. As much as the families who abandoned them, or the good people of their towns and villages who drove them away. He hoped enough of them made it here, to the small safety this place offered. Where else was there?

If he ever made it home, if Asteroth was ever safe again, it would have to change. He would see it change.

'We had word of the attack upon your queen,' said Tobias. 'We feared retribution. We have heard what happened to the Earl of Sassone as well. How he kidnapped and tried to execute the queen? And how there was another assassination attempt, a maid used as a puppet in the attack? News like that spreads fast, and Carlotta was witchkind.'

Carlotta, Roland thought. He knew her name and used it with familiarity.

'You sent her? As what, a spy?' He didn't say assassin. One step at a time.

Tobias grinned, such an innocent expression, and Roland didn't like it. 'No. Not to spy. Those of our kind who live and work in Pelias send us news from time to time, tales of their lives, their days, those they meet. Nothing more sinister than that. That's the way of families, isn't it?'

Roland had absolutely no idea. His family had dumped him with the knights as a boy and never actually bothered to get in touch again. 'You have a calling,' they had said. And that was that. He had never questioned it. There was so much he had never questioned. He felt like a fool.

'She was just a girl. She befriended my daughter.'

The grin fell away from Tobias's face. 'Yes. She was. Just a girl indeed. She was only here briefly, visiting friends and family I believe. Magic was involved in whatever happened to her, puppeting and coercing her. It is a forbidden kind, one which we do not practise. We would like answers as to what happened to her. She was murdered.'

At least they agreed on that.

'What does your chancellor say?'

For a moment Tobias's eyes seemed to cloud and Roland couldn't quite read what he saw there. Dismay, or disdain, or...

'Master Vambray?' It was Vivienne again. Her hand closed on his shoulder. 'Are you all right?' She took his hand, pressed something into it. Roland couldn't see what but it looked like straw.

The man swallowed hard and a shudder ran through him. 'Yes, I... I will be. Thank you, Vivienne. Perhaps we should see to the needs of our guests, find them quarters and some refreshments? Were any of you injured? Vivienne is one of our foremost healers. Truly gifted in that regard. She has charms of protection that are unmatched.'

Though she only looked a few years younger than him, Vivienne blushed like a girl at his words. 'Chancell— I mean, Master Vambray is too kind, but if I can be of help, I will.'

Anselm frowned and seemed about to say something, but the doors ahead of them opened and they were ushered into a reception chamber that rivalled anything Pelias could offer.

The far-off ceiling was painted dark blue and spotted with gilt stars, while on either side of them marble columns rose like saplings towards that ersatz sky. Gleaming bookshelves lined the long length of the wide-open space, with a central mosaic depicting fantastic beasts and elemental creatures, some of which Roland couldn't even name.

Elodie would be able to, he thought sombrely. She'd know all about this place. She would have made it her business to find out. Roland had never really given the College much thought beyond 'ally' and 'not a threat' and he was beginning to regret that now.

Beyond the reception hall, there was a long refectory with fireplaces at either end. The polished tables stretched its length, and in places people were already eating, while others gathered around to talk and laugh. A silence spread through the groups as they entered, all eyes turning on them. Once more they were reminded that witchkind didn't take kindly to knights. Perhaps they never would and who could blame them? Another thing for Roland to try to fix one day. His list was getting far too long. Vambray spoke softly to one of the attendants, whose eyes widened for a moment but who then bowed and hurried off to arrange a meal for them.

Food was served quickly, roast meats and fresh bread with a sweet wine which rivalled that offered at the royal table. The three knights ate sparingly, watching their host with some care, and didn't touch the wine. It couldn't hurt to be careful, no matter how warm their welcome. Or chill, as the case was here. If their caution was noticed, or deemed an insult, no one commented. People came and went with messages for Tobias and Roland thought absently that even if he wasn't chancellor anymore, people still seemed to be treating him as such. Some of them, anyway. And perhaps he was still fulfilling much of the role. It begged the question of what had happened and why the new chancellor was not doing their job.

'Your people still look to you for wisdom,' he said, carefully. Not a question. Not quite. A comment to be dismissed as a compliment, he hoped.

Tobias looked up from what was obviously some kind of accounts of stores and he smiled. 'Experience, I'm afraid, that's all. I did this part of the job too well perhaps, and the College must be provisioned still, especially with more witchkind finding their way here.'

'More witchkind?' asked Anselm.

'Oh yes, every day. Old magic is stirring in the land, wakening in people who were only sensitive to it before. They don't know what else to do and their family and neighbours... well... You must have noticed.'

'We had other things on our minds,' Olivier muttered darkly, and clenched his hands into fists. Beside him Vivienne gave him an odd look.

'Were you hurt?' she asked.

'No, it's nothing.' He flexed his hands again. 'Since coming inside your walls, I... it's nothing. Really.'

'Let me see.' Her voice was calm and determined, the kind of voice Elodie used with patients, and Roland knew Olivier would lose the fight. Anselm drew nearer to them, speaking in hushed tones. He saw Vivienne examine Olivier's hands and then she fished about in the pouch at her belt, handing each of them another of those little twists of straw.

She turned to Roland, her eyes nervous all of a sudden. He

thought of the way Carlotta had looked at him, on the rare occasions she tried to make eye contact. Vivienne's hand extended, with one of those charms in it, trembling against her skin.

Tobias was still talking and Roland hesitated to reach out.

'Whatever happened in Pelias has echoed through the land itself, I think.' Tobias put down the papers and leaned forward as if to impart some kind of confidence. 'And the witchkind have always been attuned to the land, to old magic. It grows stronger. Lark and Robin are evidence of that. These are just for basic protection and Vivienne makes them stronger than most. I have a hypothesis—'

'Vambray, what is the meaning of this!' A voice echoed from the far end of the refectory hall. Vivienne snatched her hand back, the charm vanishing with it. 'You bring our noble guests within our walls, and then don't inform me? For goodness' sake, man! What are you thinking?'

CHAPTER 24

ROLAND

A woman in a deep purple robe swept down the room towards him, accompanied by a flock of attendants. For a moment Roland sat as still as possible, just staring, because next to his queen and beloved, this figure was frankly the most beautiful creature he had ever set eyes on. His own age, perhaps, but certainly no older, she had an ageless quality to her face and movement, her dark brown hair swept up to accentuate her long neck and her soft golden skin. She wore academic robes of office, he realised, but on her they looked like something someone might wear to a ball.

She stole his breath. And his common sense as well. For a moment he couldn't think.

What kind of old goat have you turned into? Elodie laughed in the back of his mind and he almost flinched, as if she had whispered it from right behind him, as if he could feel her breath on the skin of his neck. Roland shook himself back to sense.

Tobias shifted uncomfortably as the woman approached and Roland thought for a moment he'd hoped to avoid her. Or feared she had overheard whatever he had been about to say.

All around them ripples of conflict seemed to flow out from their table. Vivienne and Tobias suddenly seemed uniquely vulnerable here, as other eyes turned on them, hostile.

Vivienne shrank back in her seat, whatever she had been offering Roland hidden now, and Olivier bristled with sudden concern as well. Anselm just stared, his expression positively hostile, which... which was not like him at all.

Knights operated on instincts more often than not. Roland had taught them to trust them. Clearly their instincts were saying something very different from his.

They didn't know any more than what Tobias had told them. He could have been lying, Roland knew that. And Vivienne was handing out witchkind-made charms like favours. Those could do all sorts of strange things to a man. Were his men already compromised?

No, not the two of them. Roland took a deep breath, steadying himself. He needed to be calm, he needed to think.

'Chancellor,' Tobias murmured, and rose to his feet before bowing low. Roland could see the tightening of his shoulders as he indicated Roland. So Roland fell back on generations of chivalric tradition and rose to his feet too. The knights followed suit. Training always won out. 'My lady, I have the honour to present Roland de Silvius, Grandmaster of the Knights of the Aurum. Grandmaster, I present our chancellor, Lady Alouette Butlier.'

The woman raised one perfect eyebrow and pursed her lips. 'I'm sure we know who each other are, Tobias,' she murmured with a voice like music.

Tobias spluttered out an apology of some kind but Roland wasn't listening to him. How could he when looking at her? She captured his attention and held it like a falconer with the jesses. A fascinating woman, one of power and nobility, strength radiating from her, along with her beauty. He almost felt dizzy just looking at her.

'By reputation alone,' he replied, as graciously as he could. It was a lie, but he prayed she wouldn't see through it. He didn't know her name. He'd never heard it before and yet knew that had to be some kind of dreadful oversight on his part. How could he have never heard of her? He couldn't let her know. He couldn't bear to disappoint her like that. 'And I regret that we have not had the opportunity to meet before now.'

Alouette smiled, her eyes sparkling like amber catching the light. 'Indeed, and would that it was under more pleasant circumstances. Our College is not what once it was and our hospitality lacking. But all that will be amended soon.'

'We've had nothing but the finest hospitality and much needed aid,' he told her. He wanted to compliment Vambray but somehow the words just seemed to die on his lips.

'From Tobias?' she laughed and all around them others joined in. It was cruel, mocking, and Roland straightened with a flash of indignation. 'Oh I'm sure he meant well but he's so caught up in his old books, aren't you, Tobias? And he has many duties to attend to. No, I will show you our true hospitality, Grandmaster.'

Vivienne flinched as Roland stepped forward, grateful for the chancellor's welcome. He heard her whisper something to Anselm, but couldn't make it out.

Alouette heard it too and glared at the younger woman as her hand snaked around Roland's arm, almost daring her to intervene.

'Come, Grandmaster, join me. We have much to discuss, you and I. Your companions may take their ease. Our hospitality is theirs to enjoy. Vivienne, you can take care of that, can't you? Or should I have someone else do it? You have to be useful for something.'

Vivienne nodded, defeated. 'Yes, chancellor. As you wish.'

Anselm cleared his throat meaningfully and Roland

glanced at him, more than a little irritated by the interruption. What did the boy want?

But Anselm wore an expression like stone and there was concern in the depths of his eyes. Even Roland could read that. Instincts, something in the back of his mind reminded him again. Trust their instincts as your own.

'Speak, Anselm,' he rumbled, letting his own voice be the warning. If this was some whim of his...

But Anselm never acted on whims. Roland knew that and the thought gave him pause.

'I should stay with you, Grandmaster. It is my duty and my vow as knight-at-arms.'

Again something niggled at the edges of Roland's conscious mind, something uncomfortable. He waved a dismissive hand. Better to let Anselm have his way. Otherwise he'd just find some means to sneak in and eavesdrop. Roland knew that all too well. 'Very well.'

If Alouette was unhappy with that she didn't show it, although there was some murmuring among her many attendants. A mixture of men and women, Roland realised, and a mixture of ages, though they all gazed at her with a kind of rapt adoration which was unsettling. He studied a few of the faces, and then glanced back to Anselm who had his jaw set in concerned concentration.

'Please, join me, Grandmaster,' Alouette said softly. She tightened her delicate hand on his arm and Roland instantly forgot about anyone else in that vast chamber.

CHAPTER 25
ROLAND

Roland could not for the life of him say what they discussed. Not in any detail. He knew they were welcome in the College and that all would be done to help them. Alouette already had her many experts searching for the information needed to help Elodie. He had been assured of that. He sat watching her speak, and lingered beside her as she turned her attention to other things and found himself living for those moments when she smiled at him, for him, alone.

Once or twice, she suggested he should relieve himself of weapons and armour, and possibly his clothes as well 'to get more comfortable'. It was only when Anselm made another noise of barely disguised alarm that Roland remembered the Grandmaster should never lay aside Nightbreaker, not least the rest of it. That was part of his vow and he had never failed in keeping that. He had only offered it to Yvain because he had been dismissed and Yvain named Grandmaster in his place. The horror on the man's face had said everything about his ambitions on that front, though his wife would have been happy, Roland thought. From lady-in-waiting to the highest station in the land to which she could aspire, not being of noble birth. Not that it mattered. Yvain had refused to take it, which he supposed, in the eyes of his knights, meant Roland was still the Grandmaster, even if he was currently in exile.

'She must be very beautiful, your queen,' Alouette said absently as she poured a fresh glass of the deep red wine. 'You have been so devoted to her for so long.'

'I have,' Roland replied warily. 'But it is not just a matter of beauty, chancellor.' Better to use formal titles and try to keep his honour in mind. He was here on a diplomatic mission really, even if it was without the blessing of the crown.

He turned the goblet around, staring into the liquid, aware that there were things he should be doing rather than sitting here in the chancellor's solar, with her guards and Anselm by the door. Just the two of them together, if they would only dismiss their attendants. He'd need to order Anselm out of the door and even now Roland wasn't sure the young knight would obey.

Alouette touched his arm again and soft warmth suffused his skin, as thoughts of Anselm drifted away. He almost lifted the goblet to his lips this time but paused just in time. He needed his head clear, something that was increasingly difficult to maintain. This place, he realised, ever since they had stepped within its walls, was interfering with their minds, their common sense. Or perhaps, he realised, just his own.

Anselm was on edge. Olivier was acting strangely. It had taken far too long to get here, guided by two children who were not entirely children, and they'd only managed the last part with Tobias's help. The shadow kin had come out of nowhere and they had been vastly outnumbered.

Vivienne had given Anselm one of those charms. One of the sort the witchkind used.

And now... now this woman he had never heard of before was in charge of the whole College of Winter. And he couldn't think straight...

He feigned drinking, without letting the liquid actually touch his lips, and watched her more closely, looking past that dazzling beauty and the charm and...

A charm... that was it. She was like a tapestry of charms, all woven around her to make her irresistible. They weren't made of straw, but of silver and gold, woven in her jewellery and through her clothes in shimmering threads. They were tangled in the length of her hair and slid against her skin. Everything about her was a charm. A look of smug satisfaction passed over her beautiful features, unmistakable. Roland took in another breath and thought of Elodie, of what she would say about all this. Something scathing, no doubt... And in that moment, Alouette's beauty faded to something nearer that of a mortal woman's.

Roland swallowed hard on a suddenly dry throat. He wanted that wine now, wanted it badly, but he also knew that if this strange enchantress he had never heard of before wanted him to drink... well, that was the last thing he should do.

The woman rolled her shoulders languorously, clearly aware of the effect it had on her cleavage, and almost purred with delight.

'And now, my dearest Roland, perhaps you should send your man away and we can have a more frank... discussion...'

The implication could not have been clearer, and she didn't expect to be countered. The spell she had wound about him should have worked by now, it seemed. He clung to his thought of Elodie as if it was a lifeline.

'Anselm,' Roland murmured, in what he hoped was a good imitation of what she expected. 'Perhaps you should check on Olivier. Make sure nothing untoward has...'

Anselm started to argue and Alouette glared his way which offered Roland the moment he needed.

He flung the wine at her and she rose with a shriek of alarm. It was as if some kind of cloying scent fell away from his body.

He could breathe again, think again. Which was just as well because her guards surged towards him, but Roland was ready, and Nightbreaker was at her chest in an instant.

'Drop your weapons,' Anselm barked at the armed men approaching them and Roland heard a note of relief in his voice now. Later, much later, they were going to have a frank discussion of their own about trusting your superiors. Right after Roland thanked him for not allowing him to fall into this trap alone.

Because it was a trap. He didn't know what was true, not anymore.

Anselm herded the three guards to a small antechamber. Luckily their reputations as Knights of the Aurum was doing most of the work for the moment and the guards complied with his instructions to the letter. He shut the door on them and wedged it closed with a chair.

'What exactly is going on here?' Roland asked the woman and she had the nerve to smile at him as if he didn't have her at sword-point.

'You appear to be intent on murdering the chancellor of the College of Winter, de Silvius. That won't go down well in the fortress full of witches, will it? All you have to do is give me the sword. I promise, no harm will come to you or your men. In fact, we'll make sure you're blissfully happy here, willing to serve.' Her smile became a smirk. 'Eager, even.'

'Who are you?'

'They told you. I'm the chancellor of the College of Winter. As of... oh, two weeks ago. It was an overwhelming popular vote, you know? Eventually.'

'You worked an enchantment on all these people.'

'Enough of them,' she admitted. 'You only ever need enough people to comply, you know. The others quickly fall into line. Or their own will take care of them for you.' She shrugged. 'That one has a remarkable ability to resist. So stubborn.' She flicked her hand to Anselm again, and a dark shadow passed through her eyes. They were not vibrant and beautiful now, but rather a flat brown and full of hatred. 'Or did you have help? Vivienne and her little charms, I suppose. I'll need to deal with her again, it seems. Stubborn girl. And you... You'll need to deal with *him*, Grandmaster.'

Before he knew what was happening, she pushed Night-breaker aside and flung her arms around his neck, pressing her lips to his.

The world blurred and slid sideways, as she slipped away from him. He turned, head whirling, to see Anselm just standing there, undefended, as if he hadn't thrown his lot in with a dark witch and betrayed the Aurum, as if he hadn't just attacked them both, as if he hadn't threatened her life.

The rage that filled Roland was more than he could name. He had never felt anger like this, an incandescent fire in his blood. What could you expect from the son of a traitor? His father, the Earl of Sassone, had almost killed the queen. The boy needed to be taught a lesson. He needed to beg for her forgiveness.

Which her? The voice was still trying to reach him from far away. *Elodie or Alouette? Think, Roland, think...*

No, this wasn't the time to think. Anselm needed to be punished. More than punished.

He needed to die.

CHAPTER 26

ROLAND

Roland roared as he attacked but Anselm seemed to dance out of the way, defending himself with an agility which did him credit. Not attacking, Roland realised. He retreated to the door, performed some kind of artful pivot and suddenly he was on the other side of Roland, with the chancellor behind him.

She sank back into her seat by the window, watching the two of them as if their battle was some kind of spectacle put on for her amusement.

'Grandmaster,' Anselm pleaded. And well he should plead. He'd plead until Nightbreaker was buried in his heart. 'Roland, please, listen to me. This is a trick, an enchantment. She isn't whatever you think she is... she isn't Elodie!'

The name was like a slap to the face with a wet cloth.

Her name.

Roland shied back, pulling a blow that should have taken Anselm's head off if it had fallen true.

Elodie. He was here for *Elodie*. And this woman... this *enchantress*...

That same fuzzy-edged reality pressed in on him again. But

at least Alouette wasn't touching him this time. He struggled to find balance again, to bring himself back to truth.

'Kill him, Roland. Kill him and then kneel at my feet and give me that sword,' Alouette snarled, all the music in her voice twisted now into rage and command.

Roland locked his gaze on Anselm, begging him to understand. He had to understand.

Three steps. That was all it took. He lunged at Anselm and with one arm lashed the knight's weapon from his hands. Anselm wouldn't attack him, that was his problem. Not even when Roland was trying to kill him and that was the weakness the Grandmaster needed. Always exploit a weakness. Who had told him that? Old Pykeman, or Lavendyss maybe? Years ago. When your enemy shows you their weakness, you use it.

He grabbed Anselm by the throat and drove him back to the foot of Alouette's chair, flinging him down onto his knees.

'Beg her forgiveness,' he told Anselm.

But Anselm, never one to beg for anything, didn't say a word. He bowed his head only because he didn't have any choice. Roland raised Nightbreaker on high, ready to bring its edge down on his neck and end him.

Behind them the door flew open so hard it almost twisted off the hinges. No doubt that magic was behind it but Olivier rushed in first. He faltered when he saw the scene before him. A host of witches and guards followed but Roland was still armed and dangerous. No one wanted to make a move or disturb the tableau before them.

'Time's up,' said Alouette in a sing-song voice. 'This entertainment is over and that sword is mine. The rest of you,' she raised her voice to the people crowding in the doorway behind Olivier, 'be about your business.'

No one moved.

'Why?' Anselm asked, his voice broken. 'What good will Nightbreaker do you?'

She laughed, a merry, ringing sound. 'You knights and your arrogance. You don't even know your own history. There is a fragment of the Aurum locked in that sword. And now, as it all falls apart, as your queen slowly dies and the Aurum with her, it will be all that remains. It might even have been enough to draw her back if you hadn't been rash enough to bring it here. You are so easily led, do you know that? The right words, from the right lips, at just the crucial moment.'

'This is all part of a plot?' Olivier gasped.

'Well done, little witchkind knight. Oh, don't think I can't see it in you. You deny it and offer it up to your great light but the traces still show. Marked forever as witchkind. You can feel it, can't you, coming back to you. As the Aurum fails the old magic stirs. You may have woken some of my devotees from their slumber, you and Vivienne, but it won't last. I made this College mine, and we almost took Pelias. We would have if that stupid man had just done what he was told, and burned the queen.'

'You were working with my father?' Anselm murmured, still trying to tamp down helpless rage.

'Your father?' She laughed and Roland realised that she hadn't even known who Anselm was before. She simply didn't care. 'Oh that is too amusing. Yes, the Earl of Sassone. He promised so much and delivered nothing. Only to be expected of a man, I suppose. Not that the girl was much better.'

'Carlotta,' Anselm growled. 'Her name was Carlotta. And she was a friend.'

Alouette laughed at him, a vindictive, cruel laugh. 'Well, you do have the strangest connections, Lord Tarryn. Or are you the Earl of Sassone now? Can Roland here strip you of your title as easily as he stripped you of knighthood?' She sneered at him, and though Anselm gave no response, his shoulders were taut as a bow string. 'The girl was a mistake, but she was no more than a tool. My sister should have been more direct from the start and she will pay for her shoddy craft. She was far too desperate to bring the Nox and the Aurum into conflict and thought killing one of the Ilanthian princelings would do that. Perhaps it should have, but oh, she does complicate matters.'

'Were you behind all of it?' Anselm asked.

'Not just me.'

'So you're a traitor.'

'A traitor? I swore no vows to your Aurum or your queen. No, nor to the Nox either. I never will. I live free. I will make the powers of the world my own, just as I have made the College mine.'

Anselm moved as if to rise, as if to attack, and Roland forced himself to press the blade against his neck until a line of blood appeared and Anselm froze.

'You tried to kill Roland,' Anselm said. 'You sent the shadow kin after him. On the way here, and in Pelias too.'

'I thought I needed him out of the way. Oh, but I am so pleased that they didn't succeed now. Look at him. What a servant he will make for me. Together, we will deal with Pelias and Sidonia. We will release the ancient powers and make them ours, with that sword and the Sidonian crown. And when your bitch queen dies, you'll all fall into line.'

Anselm sucked in a breath but didn't seem to have a response. Roland held himself still as stone.

'You have no place here,' shouted one of the other witchkind.

Another voice joined them, and more. 'Tobias showed us the truth.'

'You tricked us all, seduced and bewitched—'

'Do you hear yourselves? Bewitched? Of course I did. It is our power. We should use it. That was the way of old magic and the right of the witchkind kings and queens of old. Of all of us.

Grind these mundane fools into the dirt and rule, not hide and run or submit and be chained up in miserable holes like this.'

'You are not going to entrap us again,' Vivienne yelled. 'We can see through you now. Enough of us—'

Alouette snarled a few words of othertongue and Vivienne gave a cry, desperate and afraid. Roland heard her crumple to the ground but didn't dare turn to see what had happened to her. 'You need to learn your place too, it seems. Sneaking around behind my back, you and your co-conspirators. Little hedge witch charms and sly words... oh, I'll be happy to teach you, Vivienne, and tear their names from your mind, but first...' Suddenly all her attention was back on Roland like a crushing weight. 'Roland de Silvius,' her voice rippled with power and though he knew she was speaking othertongue to control him, he understood every word, 'kill that worthless knight and give me Nightbreaker.'

'I hope you've heard enough now,' Anselm muttered darkly.

'More than enough,' Roland agreed.

Anselm rolled to one side and Roland swung the great sword of the Knights of the Aurum in a wide arc, a blur of light and death itself, burying it in Alouette's body.

She slid to the ground, dead before she hit it.

Something shook the air, like a thread stretched too far until it snapped, and the whole College trembled, just for a moment. Then came gasps of alarm, dismay and bewilderment as Alouette's remaining spells shattered.

Roland wiped the blade clean on one of the sumptuous throws and flung the fabric over her body. Then he reached out a hand to help a somewhat shaken Anselm to his feet. The knight held his hand for a moment too long, studying his face as if to ask a question Roland didn't want to answer. Would he have killed him?

Light, he hoped not. Anselm clearly wasn't sure, but granted Roland the benefit of the doubt. Anselm was as much like a son to him as Finn was. So he had to hope the boy was right.

'You realise we could have asked her some questions?' Olivier said as he reached them.

Roland shrugged. 'But could we have trusted any of the answers?'

REPORT ON THE BUTLIER
INCIDENT, ANNALS OF THE
COLLEGE OF WINTER,
VOL. 4522

Few members of the College were unaffected. It was through the intervention of the Grandmaster of the Knights of the Aurum and his men that the spell was broken and the College freed, his judgement being swift and complete. Chancellor Vambray regained his position, and Lady Vivienne de Sullaine, who was to become First Healer, set about repairing the damage but it was to be a long ordeal.

Please see Vol. 4523 for the background and wider repercussions of the Butlier conspiracy.

CHAPTER 27
WREN

It felt like something else was guiding them, not the Nox. Something unseen and unheard but almost tangible in the air. There was something like a sigh or a song, a whisper that never quite made itself heard or a melody half remembered on waking from a forgotten dream. Wren followed, and so did Finn, because there was nothing else either of them could do.

Leander would be coming, Wren knew that.

The Nox's anger fizzed against the back of Wren's consciousness. This outrage would not be borne, this betrayal. It would not be controlled by a king of Ilanthus again. The power beyond was beside itself with a need for retribution and that was possibly all that was keeping it in check right now and stopping it from taking control.

It... her... Wren wasn't even sure anymore. The more the power of darkness tried to wrap itself around her, the more it felt like part of her, its outrage, her outrage, its desire so closely twined with hers that there might never be a chance of separating them again. It was part of her now and she was flowing back into it, changing it, both of them transformed by the proximity of the other.

And then there was Finn.

He was Finn again. That was her one relief. And Finn had always protected her and followed her lead when it mattered, unless she was putting herself at risk. Finn was hers.

Claiming him seemed to have transformed him. Her servant, her champion, her beloved... The look he gave her was one of devotion but also tangled with a wildness she hadn't seen since he had fought for her in the stone circle, subsumed in the power of the Nox, its creature rather than hers.

Now she thought it was both.

Was he even aware of it? Guilt washed through her and she had to push that away. Together, they would have to work it out, to find a way to save both their souls. But not now. There wasn't time for that now.

The throb of need was rising in her again which really wasn't helping. Every second she glanced his way, she wanted him. She could feel his warmth in the air, his scent tangling with hers, the need that fired up between the two of them at risk of boiling over in a moment.

And yes, the nakedness was not helping.

She forced herself to think of icy cold water, of plunging into the depths of a pool in Cellandre, but whenever she did, the image of him doing the same thing appeared and that was almost worse.

His hand touched her shoulder and she shivered, her stomach tightening with need.

'You feel it too, don't you?' His voice was a deep rumble in the darkness and did interesting things in her chest.

She nodded carefully. 'The Nox is strong. Only to be expected here, Hestia said, and the more I lose myself in you the more—'

'The more we risk losing our selves forever. I know.'

It was a new kind of torture, she thought, chipping away at her resistance. Need, desire, desperation... But all they could do was journey deeper into the dark caves, where she suspected none of the current sisterhood had ever ventured. There were no names for these places.

The air turned warm, heavy with intoxicating scents. The half-heard song grew stronger and she picked out the way with her othersight, a soft glow of blue-black in the darkness. Deeper they went, and deeper still, Finn's hand in hers. He let her lead – of course he did – and she hated herself for it. She didn't know what being here would do to him.

She didn't know what it would do to her either but that was beside the point. She couldn't leave him behind. Shadow kin still trailed them both, guard dogs or hunters. She would be as good as abandoning him to them and they were still hungry for him. Perhaps they always would be.

She could almost understand. A taste of Finnian Ward was addictive.

'Can you hear them?' she asked.

'Yes,' he replied, his fingers tightening on hers. 'They want us to go on. If we don't...'

'They'll kill us.'

'No, not that. They'd never dare hurt you. Me... they want me to join them. That's all they've wanted since Cellandre. I realise that now. To serve the Nox and be part of them. To lead them. They thought I had, when Leander—' He stopped abruptly, both speech and footsteps, pulling her to a halt. Wren turned and found herself in his arms, though they didn't tighten around her. He didn't pull her into his embrace. Rather he framed her, cautious and wary. 'I don't know how to—' Finn swallowed hard, and she was aware of the way his throat worked, of the tightness in his muscles, the fear. 'Wren, did he – did he hurt you?'

This was not a place for lies. Not between them. But she had dreaded this question. She wasn't sure how to answer.

There was only truth in this darkness. There couldn't be

anything else. She could see his face, just pick out his features, etched in otherlight, and the pain bleeding through them. She knew what he thought, what he feared.

'Yes,' she replied solemnly. She had to pick her words with care. 'But not how you think. He didn't force me to do anything.' Finn let out a breath, a rush of relief which was only half-deserved, she thought. 'He wanted me to be his willingly. He wanted to wear me down. He enjoyed it, enjoyed himself, took lovers – if you could call them that – and tried all kinds of means to break my will.'

'And you thought it was me.' That wasn't a question. He knew the truth. He'd seen it on her face in the throne room.

'At first,' she admitted. Finn started to pull away and she wrapped her arms around him, stopping him. Their bodies brushed together, a torture she had to just endure. He needed to know this. 'I didn't realise until just before you arrived and the spell broke. And then it was too late. I'm sorry, Finn. I should have—'

'Don't you dare apologise,' he growled. 'None of it was your fault.'

Oh, if only she believed that. If she hadn't tried to control him back in Pelias... if she had just trusted him... so many ifs.

And ultimately everything led them here, to the deepest darkness she had ever known, where only magic could guide them, and behind them lay death or enslavement.

No turning back then.

'We have to go on, see where this leads,' she told him. The words *I'm sorry* were on her lips again but she didn't say them this time. He wouldn't hear them.

He kissed her softly, his lips on hers the only comfort he could offer. 'And I'll follow you. You know that.'

What else could they do? They descended into the final darkness.

CHAPTER 28
WREN

Ahead of them, the tunnel opened up into another cavern, not as high or as wide as the previous ones. Veins of crystals ran through the stone, catching a meagre light from somewhere and reflecting it. No, Wren realised, not actually light, but that strange otherlight that indicated the presence of magic, magic of any kind, the magic of the world, sunken deep in the stones and the earth, feeding the Nox. Wren could feel it trembling in the air around them and, as they stepped into it, Finn hesitated, every muscle going rigid.

'Wren, please,' he said and he sounded like a knight again, her knight. 'Step back, behind me. It isn't safe here.'

Of course it wasn't. Nothing was safe. Not now. Not ever.

That same ripple of heat made her shiver, the presence of the Nox swirling around her and through her. It was hungry, angry, desperate... Wren forced herself to breathe, and took a step back beside him rather than behind him. What he thought he would be able to do here, she wasn't sure, but she still appreciated the gesture. The air was thick with enchantment, with raw and unfettered power.

In the middle of the cave, they could see a mound of treasure, like the hoard of some long-dead dragon. Gems, gold and a variety of artefacts had been gathered together and left there, some ancient storehouse or vault. The glimmer of dark magic from each and every item made Wren's head swim.

But there were clothes, and armour, she realised. And weapons.

And on top of it all, there was a crown, dark and gleaming with malice. Wren stared at it while everything else seemed to fade away. She didn't want to touch it. Her skin crawled with the thought.

She remembered it, somehow, but the way she remembered nightmares. No wonder she hated the thought of a crown, she realised now. No wonder the thought of something like that on her head had always produced such a visceral, horrified response. She knew why now. That crown. The Crown of the Nox.

Take what you need, said the voice of the Nox with a gentleness that surprised her, and this time it was not in Wren's mind. It was everywhere. *But touch not the crown.*

On that, at least, they agreed. She looked at everything else, trying to put the crown from her mind. There was so much, endless treasure, of all kinds.

'Where did it all come from?' she asked.

Offerings of many lifetimes, from the great and the lesser, from kings and priestesses, from my people, my servants and devotees...

'And at what cost?' Finn asked, his voice not so much full of wonder as doubt. She might even say dread.

All given willingly, son of Sidon. Just as you have given. Like the blood and seed of your line. It has ever been thus. I only take what is offered.

'Blood and seed?' The words came out in a rush of shock and Wren put out a hand to stop him retreating. Or attacking. But she need not have feared. Finn wasn't going anywhere.

The sacrifices of your line, the voice said. It almost sounded sorrowful, and entirely sane now, here in its heart of hearts. *Have they never explained?*

How could they? When would they? She saw the denial and confusion on Finn's face and felt her heart aching for him.

'It didn't have to be death,' she murmured, as realisation stole over him as well. 'It never had to be death.'

A flicker of disgust took the place of that confusion. 'No, they just chose to kill. My family. My father and his... my brothers...'

Generations of them... the Nox murmured, and it sounded almost in pain.

Only one brother remained. The one still trying to kill him. The one consumed with hatred.

Once it was a sacrifice made with love...

The voice was softer now, the harsh and twisted madness leaking away to leave...

Peace in darkness, Wren thought. Relief, and comfort, safety. Just as Hestia had told her when Wren had found her in the sacred space at the heart of the embassy.

The Nox was different here. At its heart. At its centre. Where its core still lingered, where long ago the people who loved it had left treasures and made their devotions, where they had poured out their love for the darkness. It wasn't insane here, or dangerous. It was heartbroken.

'They lied,' Wren said. 'Or... or forgot. They've all been wrong for so many years, and so has Asteroth.'

'Why?' Finn asked.

But Wren didn't have an answer for that. She stepped forward, approaching the treasury of gifts. She ran her hand over shadow-wrought armour, lines of iridescent blue shimmering in the black metal. She found leather and fine woollen clothes, soft linens all neatly folded and untouched by age. There was silk too, soft and delicate, the finest quality. Beside the clothes lay a vast array of jewellery. Anything that could be imagined was here, offered up to the Nox, the greatest craftsmanship and artistry, all given to the darkness.

The sword was mounted on blocks. It reminded her of Nightbreaker, of Roland. She lifted it, finding it strangely light and easy to wield, and passed it to Finn, who took it from her hesitantly. Better in his hands, hands trained to wield a weapon for years, than in hers. But nothing happened. The sky didn't fall, and his eyes retained their own colour and the same confused caution.

You may take whatever you need, the Nox told them. *I offer it to you freely and without conditions. My gift to you, my children. Your inheritance. All but the crown.*

'Inheritance,' Wren murmured. She couldn't stop staring at the crown – an elaborate thing with spikes like knives on top of it, made of shadow-wrought steel as well, inlaid with gold and jewels, the chill power coming off it in waves.

It unnerved her. And yet, she couldn't take her eyes off it. Someone had made that thing and left it here, the crown of a goddess, a thing of nightmares. Other items, especially the older ones, were beautiful, practical. But that...

Her skin crawled with the thought of wearing it. No, never, she couldn't.

'Clothes first,' said Finn, ever the pragmatist. 'Weapons and armour. We don't need anything else.' He hesitated. 'Unless, Wren...' He'd seen her staring at the crown. Wren cursed and turned away. She didn't want it. She had never wanted a crown.

And something instinctive told her that she especially didn't want that one, even if the Nox would have allowed it. Hestia had warned her. Even Oriole had said it would control the Nox. Which made her pause. She'd said the Nox was ungovernable, wild. She'd said it as if the Nox needed to be controlled.

'Is this a test?' she asked, half of him, half of herself. Not that it mattered. The Nox was the one to answer.

It calls to you, said the Nox. *It called to me once. Such power. The ability to rule. It promises the absolute submission of an entire world if you but have the nerve...* The words came like a song again, swirling around her and pressing in on her body and mind. Her own heartbeat sounded too loud in her ears and Wren felt a force far stronger than she was wrap itself around her like a suffocating blanket. *But it lies. It will bring you no joy, no peace. Only pain.*

'No...' she whispered, but she knew it was more through habit than anything else. And the Nox knew it too. It saw into her heart, recognised her desires, dark and determined. She could seize power here. Take control. She could become the goddess they wanted her to be and the sisterhood would obey her without question. She could stop Leander, take away the throne he had seized, and put an end to this war before it ever began. She could use that power to wake Elodie, to set her free of the Aurum.

Forever.

Let me show you...

She tried to take a step back, but she came up against a hard body, unyielding, as if it had been carved from the rock of the caverns around them. Finn didn't move, didn't help her. Perhaps he couldn't or perhaps he didn't want to.

He wanted her to trust him, she reminded herself, but was that really possible here?

He was born for the Nox, that was what everyone had always said. To die for his goddess, to serve her in all things. Even now.

But his hand on her shoulder was gentle, a comfort, a strength.

Darkness rose in a wave and this time there was nothing Wren could do to stop it. It crashed over the two of them, a tsunami which swept them away.

Into the darkness, into the void, into another place and time.

CHAPTER 29
WREN

There was a world of magic. Everywhere, all around them. Wren could feel it like her own body, like her heartbeat, her skin, the blood in her veins. There was freedom and joy and a vast intertwining of powers forever ancient and eternally new. In that kaleidoscope of energies, she found herself filled with power. Old magic, she realised. This was the chaos and joy of old magic. There was no dark and no light, just everything, all tangled together. Freedom.

Two children ran through the forest, eyes bright as the leaves, alive with light. She heard their laughter and remembered it. Powers, ancient and terrible, but so filled with joy. She knew them, somehow, remembered them. Echoes of them anyway. Once they had wandered wherever they would, danced in starlight. Afterwards, they were just dreams. In Cellandre, she thought, she had heard them calling her, when she was younger than they appeared. They had protected her, she thought. They had kept her safe. She had never told anyone that. When she had walked out into the storm of shadows, they had taken her hands and led her back to safety until Elodie could find her. She had danced with them so long ago, and sung along with their songs. She had known them.

But the greed of humankind tore it all apart, leaving those children like echoes in the land, just like Elodie's old stories had always said, when they tried to control magic and make it conform to their rules. Old magic could not be contained. And when humans tried to use it, it tended to use them in return, drain them, kill them. It would take back what it had granted them on a whim. They died in swathes.

Perhaps it was always meant to happen, because that much chaos couldn't continue without destroying the world.

When the cataclysm struck it felt like she was ripped apart. Her scream was silent, or drowned out in the screams of the old magic. She was torn away from it, the darkness dragged out into the light, and then pulled apart again, two things that should have been in balance separated for eternity. Nothing would ever put them back together.

The agony running through her almost made her lose her mind.

Finn held her close, cradled her. 'I'm here,' he whispered and his voice was lost in the disaster. But he still held her in his shaking arms. Was he seeing this too? Could he feel it? He couldn't. Not and still hold her. The Nox was relentless. She would see its creation, she would see and understand even if it killed her.

And then there was just darkness. After the destruction, it was peaceful and safe, a comfort. The quiet of the dark, the calm after the storm.

Like his embrace.

She was safe, for a time. She rested there and while the light raged through the land she offered safety to the other beings tossed in this tempest of destruction. She welcomed them, protected them. They thanked her, and that thanks turned to worship and she became their goddess and their only hope.

This isn't me, she wanted to say, but she couldn't find her own voice. Not anymore. She could only watch as this unfolded, a mute witness. Wren tried to struggle free but there was no getting out of this. And still Finn held her, his voice a soothing murmur. Somewhere, he was still holding her, in the darkness, still protecting her. And she would find her way back to him. She had to.

At first the Nox had no name, but they named her. She had no form but they imagined one for her. Where the Aurum became all-powerful flames, she was a woman clothed in night and stars.

No one started it. Not really. She could see that. But Ilanthus and Asteroth edged their way to war, and there was no reasoning with anyone. The Aurum wanted to protect those it loved and so did she. It was perhaps inevitable.

But the Nox did not allow herself to be drawn into the fray.

The kings of Ilanthus brought her offerings, gifts. She blessed them and their line. She took them as lovers and gave them strength and power and...

When they loved her, it worked. They protected her people and she was pleased.

But they grew jealous, and they wanted more power. More power than anyone should be allowed to have.

They wanted her power. To defend the kingdom, they said. They needed her to protect them. In the end, they resolved to make her comply and they found a way. Through the remnants of old magic which still lingered.

She had never killed anyone until the king – she didn't even remember his name at first – put that crown on her head. Such a beautiful thing, cunningly wrought and wreathed with magic that even she did not understand. That was her first mistake, to let him do that.

He flattered her, this silver-haired man with deep blue eyes.

He said he loved her and promised to serve her, and offered her his body.

She bore him a child.

Cold dread squeezed at the back of Wren's mind, even as she held that child in her arms, even as she knew that love and felt that all she had wanted was now given form, given flesh.

And one night, while she was sleeping, the king took the child and killed it. He drenched her in its blood and took that crown and bound her to it.

Sidon, she recalled at last. His name was Sidon.

Hatred was hot and white and terrible. Rage made her scream through gritted teeth. Hot tears splashed on her face. Finn's tears. He was seeing this too. He had to be. This was as much his story as anyone else's. That monster was his ancestor. And this was his origin too. His blood, his bond, his sacrifice...

She was bound to obey him, to serve him. No longer a goddess, not even a queen. Just a slave, a weapon. There was no choice left to her. He was powerful and mighty. He took many wives and lovers, sired a legion of sons and bound her to their blood and them to her. He warred on their enemies and... so much death followed but only the first one mattered to her.

When the Nox finally managed to tear herself free, when Sidon finally succumbed to death, she took a terrible revenge on his line, all of them, all those sons. She flung the crown here into the darkness where they could never touch it again, never use it against her. She cursed anyone who would try to wear it, or make her wear it again.

And from that time on the line of Sidon would serve her, die for her, be hers... without any choice in the matter. It was vengeance of a sort, a spell created in grief and rage, but it trapped the Nox as much as the descendants of that long ago king. At any time, they could have chosen the other path, but they all chose blood. Better to kill all of their line than to submit to her.

No wonder she had been helpless against Finn. No wonder he had been helpless against her. They had never had any chance at all. Everything felt empty and cold, like a lie. A destiny they could never have hoped to avoid. It wasn't fair.

'*But you love him,*' the Nox said. '*Is that not true?*'

Wren didn't know how to answer that. She did love him. But could she have done anything else? And did Finn have any choice at all?

'Wren?' he whispered, and his voice sounded like his own again. The world retreated, back to the darkness of the chamber with its flickering glow of blue-black light. The vision had slipped away from her and Wren was huddled on the ground, sobbing. She was wrapped in an Ilanthian sheath-like dress, the colour of ravens' wings, black shot with iridescent blue and threads of silver. And Finn wore the armour of a king.

He knelt before her, his head bowed, the sword on the ground between them.

Slowly Wren pulled herself back together as best she could.

I can give him a choice, the Nox whispered and the air trembled around them. *There is always a choice.*

'What do you mean?' Wren asked bitterly. She might have seen the truth of this being, its origins and its tragedies, but all the same, she wasn't so much of a fool as to trust it. 'What possible choice remains?'

'Whether to live,' Finn said. It was him, through and through. 'Whether to die. Or simply, whether to let you decide.'

'What are you talking about?'

'I will protect you, Wren. With anything I have. I always will and I will give everything to do it.' He bowed his head and his voice seemed to change, becoming formal and grave. 'I offer you my life, Lady of the Divine Darkness. To do with as you please. That is all I have ever had to offer and—'

'Stop this,' she told him. She didn't know if he was talking to her or the Nox and she didn't like either option. 'Stop it, Finn. Don't you dare—'

'I am yours, now and always. I make this offer freely, without coercion. You are everything to me, Wren. Everything.'

'You can't know that.'

He raised his head, his eyes fixed unerringly on hers. 'But I do. I always have. From the first moment I met you.'

'Really?' she asked, her tone scathing. 'When I was dressed like a boy and running from a pack of mindless bullies?'

A smile flickered over his lips, a soft and human expression which made her heart turn itself inside out. He gave a soft, self-deprecating laugh. 'All right, maybe not exactly then. But in the forest, in the darkwood... Wren... I say this freely, honestly. There's nothing making me say this, no enchantment, only the truth. And the truth is, I have always been yours.'

'Mine,' she echoed. 'Not... not the Nox's?'

'Yours,' he confirmed. 'I renounce my heritage, my vows and my blood for you. I am yours.'

Around them the air seemed to laugh and the darkness smiled against their skin. *Yours,* the voice of the Nox murmured. *And thus mine. Freely, not through blood and death. Through free choice and love.*

Wren stared into his eyes, trying to fix their colour in her mind, their softness in her heart, but even as she did so, they turned dark, as if filling with ink and Finn... Finn was gone.

Something else stood in his place, a warrior made of darkness.

And then she heard footsteps. They came from all around her and torches lit up the cavern as the guards arrived.

Far too many, all armed to the teeth.

With them came Oriole in her black robes, and Hestia too, the sisterhood gathering behind them. And if Hestia looked pale and ashamed, Oriole bore an expression of absolute triumph.

This was not good. Not good at all.

'Well, my queen,' said Leander, as he stepped from the midst of his men. 'A merry dance you've led us, but now you've come to your power the game is over.'

CHAPTER 30
WREN

'Hestia?' Wren asked, amazed that her voice didn't shake as she spoke.

'Lady Hestia no longer commands the Sisterhood of the Nox,' said Oriole coldly.

There was no doubt who now did, Wren thought, and any sense of nascent friendship she had felt for this woman dissolved.

If I fail... if something happens to me... Hestia had said. And something had definitely happened. She had no more power left, her magic broken, and clearly the sisterhood had discovered as much. And they had sided with Leander.

Perhaps that had been Oriole's plan all along.

'Why let me come here?' Wren asked.

Oriole spread her hands wide. 'This treasure house was closed to us, sealed away by the Nox herself because of that crown. And now it is ours again. You opened the way.'

And with the dark crown they could control the Nox. Wren recalled what Oriole had said about the Nox and the death and destruction their goddess had wrought.

Wren glanced at the crown briefly. It glimmered in the darkness, waiting.

No, she thought. Absolutely not. She had never wanted a crown, not in Cellandre, not in Pelias, and definitely not here.

'I don't think so,' she replied. 'Hestia—'

'Divine darkness...' Hestia murmured the words, but her gaze was fixed on the boy beside her, Laurence. And the armed men flanking the two of them. 'If I could help you I would.'

'Still defiant?' Leander actually had the nerve to laugh. 'I've explained how this goes, my dearest cousin. If you defy me, Laurence will suffer for it. And Laurence will do whatever I say, won't you, Laurence?'

The strange glassy expression that passed over Laurence's open features made a chill of premonition wriggle up through Wren's spine. He looked like Carlotta. And he didn't have a scrap of magic in him to stand against such a spell.

'Yes, your majesty.' He sounded like someone in a dream. 'Whatever you want. I am your servant.' He sounded dazed. Beside Wren, Finn stiffened and brought the shadow-wrought sword up to a defensive position. He sensed it too then. Of course he did. And Wren knew he cared about Laurence as well. About both Hestia and her son.

Wren remembered a spell Elodie had once used against her to make her obey. At least her mind had still been her own. Not so here. Laurence was little more than a puppet right now and Leander was revelling in it. Who had taught him this?

'Please, Leander,' Hestia snapped. 'I've promised I will not interfere. I've sworn fealty and I've done what you wanted. I brought you here. I led you to them. *Please.*'

Leander rolled his shoulders and tilted his head back, letting out a bored sigh. 'Enough of the mewling. Dear goddess —' His eyes locked with Wren's and he smirked at her, a slow and deliberate expression designed to mock her. 'Laurence, get the crown.'

Finn stepped forward to block any approach, knowing at once that the Nox would not have them use that crown again. Hestia flinched, a soft cry smothered by her hand on her mouth. Finn would defend the Nox. And Wren. He had no more choice in that than Laurence did right now.

Protect them for me, Hestia had begged Wren.

Wren's hands tightened into fists. Leander's magic wound about the boy, puppeting him, and there was nothing Hestia could do about it now. Nothing at all.

'Give the boy a weapon, Gaius,' Leander snarled. 'You can't ask him to go up against a Knight of the Aurum unarmed. Not even one as pathetic and fallen as Finn.' When Gaius didn't move, Leander drew his own blade and forced it into Laurence's numb hands.

He was going to get the boy killed. Perhaps he was doing it deliberately, to torture Hestia, to punish her for binding his powers, for standing against him. To punish Finn, to make him kill an innocent. To punish her.

No, she couldn't allow this. She simply couldn't.

I can stop it, said the Nox. *I can unbind the boy and destroy them all. I can—*

But when Wren reached out to seize the power it offered, something blocked her. It was like a static shock running over her flesh. Even Finn froze and Laurence moved like a sleep-walker to the treasure, took the crown in one hand and made his way slowly back towards Leander.

Wren jerked back, catching sight of Oriole and the other Sisters, their hands weaving shadows, using the power Wren had felt in the stones against her now. Not the power of the Nox, but something else. Something old...

What is this heresy? The voice of the dark goddess made the air tremble and Wren saw several of the sisterhood blanch, their hands falling still for a moment. They heard it too and it gave them pause.

'Don't listen to her,' Oriole snapped. 'This is our moment, the one I promised. The old magic will help us all. We can weave it and bind her. Do not lose heart.'

'Heart?' Wren asked, and her voice hardly sounded like her own anymore. The Nox wasn't just outraged now. It was furious. They were its servants... her servants and they defied her. Betrayed her. They were using old magic against her. 'I'll show you *hearts*.'

She didn't know where the surge of magic that filled her came from but it tore through her body, racing across the ground. She reached out and snatched those threads of power the sisterhood was using. One of the Sisters cried out, a terrible scream, and then another joined it. Wren twisted her hands in an abrupt gesture of rage that hardly felt like herself. Because it wasn't. They fell like wheat at harvest time, ribcages wrenched open in a spray of blood and viscera.

'Wren, no!' Hestia cried out in dismay. 'Don't do this. Please!'

She was far too late. Wren wasn't in control anymore.

Oriole snarled something, othertongue which grated against all of Wren's senses, undercutting the siren song of the Nox. It married with the magic of Leander's spell, piggybacking on it and then commandeering it. Hestia broke free, trying to block her son from reaching the king. Laurence turned, the sword still in his hands, and ran his mother through.

Everything seemed to freeze, the power, the anger, the air itself, as Hestia stared into the face of her young son and then slid to her knees. Blood bubbled from her open mouth.

A scream of rage filled the air, not from Laurence, or Hestia, but from Leander.

'What have you done, Oriole? She was my family, my blood. She was mine!'

Oriole cast him no more than a scathing glance.

'She was weak and useless, tied to dogma and tradition. The sisterhood is better off without her.'

With a sharp crack, Leander struck Oriole across the face and she spat a curse at him, lunging forward. Guards stepped in before she could do anything more, and their truce, such as it was, unravelled.

The spell on Laurence snapped. Perhaps their own spat meant they weren't paying attention, or perhaps they released him on purpose. Wren would put nothing past the vindictive self-centredness of the pair of them. The sword fell from his numb hand with a crash as he realised what had happened.

'No,' he whispered, voice numb in shock. 'Please, no.'

Enough, Wren thought, her consciousness only just clinging to reality. Hestia's blood, the blood of Sidon, was pooling beneath her. And the power in her was spiralling out of control.

Protect them for me, Hestia had begged.

'Finn, hold him,' Wren barked, sounding more like Elodie or Roland than she would have ever imagined possible. Finn didn't argue. Perhaps Finn would never argue with her again. He grabbed Laurence by the scruff of the neck and reached out his arm, still holding the sword, to Wren as if he knew what she was planning. Perhaps he did. He was a servant of the Nox now. That was what she had seen in his eyes.

And she was the Nox.

A moment of clarity shook her to the core. She had torn those women open without a moment's pause. Without a qualm. Not some distant power operating through her. She had known what she was doing.

Oriole shouted more othertongue and the tenuous grip Wren still had on the shadows faltered for a moment. The treacherous sister gave her hands another vicious twist and pain lanced through Wren this time. The same spell perhaps, reflected back on her.

Perhaps she deserved it. It wasn't enough to stop her, not now, but it shook her to the core.

'I'm coming after you wherever you go,' Leander shouted. 'Every warrior of Ilanthus stands ready and Asteroth has lost the Aurum. The knights are in disarray. Pelias will fall. Do you hear me, little bird? At dawn we attack. Everything is ready, troops, ships, weapons, men. I'm going to raze its walls to the ground, reduce the mountain to dust. I'm going to—'

Wren embraced the full force of the Nox, turned it on the sisterhood who ranged themselves against her – her servants, sworn to her, tied by vows and service, traitors all of them – and she ripped apart those who remained like wet rags. Oriole screamed, anger and pain twisting her voice as she felt her body wrenched open, her blood joining Hestia's.

Wren's eyes fixed on Leander, but she couldn't touch him. Her magic slid past him. He'd made no vows to break, it seemed, or had greater protection than she could tear through. He was the king of Ilanthus and that meant something when it came to the Nox. He had protections of his own. His guards started forward, steel ready.

Later, she promised herself. She would deal with him later.

With her free hand, Wren broke the pendant.

Safety, she thought as Hestia's last spell uncoiled around them, not a spell of shadows but one of blinding light. It would take them to safety – her, Finn and Laurence.

The problem was, she didn't know where that was anymore.

CHAPTER 31
ROLAND

There was mayhem as Alouette's death unwove the countless spells with which she had entangled the College of Winter. As Tobias Vambray reclaimed his position as chancellor, Roland watched with care as he interviewed those with whom Alouette had spent most of her time, but it soon seemed clear that they were just as baffled as he had been. Or excellent actors. That was something for the College to sort out by itself.

Roland had retreated to the chamber they had assigned to him, because it was easier that way. He couldn't solve their problems. And perhaps brooding in here was not his greatest idea but he needed his own space now, to think through what had happened. And what could have happened.

Roland had been lucky. More than lucky. Only the loyalty of Anselm and Olivier, coupled with Vivienne's charms of protection, had saved him. He knew that.

It was a bitter pill to swallow. He had never thought such a thing would be possible, that he would so easily succumb to an enchantment like that. He loved Elodie and always had. His heart was bound to her, he had thought, then, now and forever.

How had the witch blinded him to that? How had she wormed so easily past his defences?

He had been arrogant, that was how. He had been so certain of himself and his strength that he had never needed to guard himself against someone in that way. He was used to Pelias with its wards and defences, to his position as Grandmaster of the Knights and all the protections that offered.

He was a fool.

What would Elodie say? He tried to imagine her laughing at him but he very much feared she would not laugh at all.

But then he remembered those moments when he had almost heard her, warning him, and perhaps he had not been quite so lost as he had feared. He had to believe that. He trusted in his love. It had seen him through everything and it would again.

But it was hard to trust in so intangible a thing.

He mulled over Alouette's words more than he would have wished to. She had been behind the attacks on them in Pelias, behind the shadow kin and behind Sassone…

Could it be that the threat she posed was truly gone now? She had mentioned her sister…

A knock at the door to his chamber brought him out of his thoughts.

'Grandmaster?' It was Olivier, his whole demeanour furtive and unsure. 'If I may have a moment of your time? I have… I have a confession…'

'You do?' Roland frowned. Of all people, Olivier was the last person he would have thought had anything worth confessing. 'You may have to take it elsewhere, Olivier. I am no longer the Grandmaster, remember? And as for confessions… I have too many of my own to make right now.'

The young man's dark eyes flicked to the sword and back to Roland's face. He wore an expression which said that he had never been so unconvinced by any statement in his life. Roland was still the Grandmaster and that was that. He opened his mouth to speak, shut it again and dropped his gaze to the floor. He was ashamed of something.

Before he could say another word the door to the antechamber opened and Anselm slipped inside. Of course he did. He was never going to be far away and he and Olivier...

Oh, Roland thought, was that it? But there was no need for them to confess that to him. Even if he had not already guessed, there was simply no need.

'Olivier—' he began.

Olivier held up both his hands and they glowed, bright and remarkable, flames on his skin. The air shivered around them as the magic flowed through him. Not quite witchfire but something like it. In truth, Roland didn't have a clue what it was or what it might mean.

'I tried...' Olivier began and his voice failed. Swallowing hard, he tried again. 'I tried to stop it. But ever since we left Pelias, if we're in danger especially... The witchkind knew as soon as they saw me. The children...they said as much. Tried to make me admit it.'

Roland swallowed hard. Knights of the Aurum did not work magic. They were filled with the Aurum's light, fought in its name, defended it. But they gave all to the Aurum and held back nothing. This was not normal.

But what was normal anymore? The Aurum was gone.

'You are a knight and a Paladin,' Roland said. 'Touched by the Aurum, blessed by...'

By Wren. Not actually by the Aurum. And that had to have ramifications too. Suddenly he couldn't finish whatever he had been trying to say.

Olivier shook his head. 'I was born with it. Mostly it showed itself in small ways, cuts and grazes that healed quickly, headaches that cleared when I touched someone. Vivienne says that it has marked me again, that I'm a healer, but I'm not. I can't be. I gave it up when I took my vows,' he protested. 'I gave it back to the Aurum. What does it mean? If it's come back, what does it mean?'

Roland had no idea. As he watched, Anselm came to Olivier's side and wrapped his arms around his torso, pulling the other man into an embrace, holding him close. The flames guttered and went out and finally Olivier dropped his hands to rest against the other man's arm.

'All will be well,' Anselm said. 'It has to be. Healing is a noble calling, Olivier.'

'We could ask the chancellor,' Roland said, though he couldn't hide the doubt in his voice. 'The College is meant to have answers.'

'Are they?' Anselm asked, with more than a touch of bitterness. 'They haven't been very impressive so far. Only Vivienne managed to hold onto her own will, I think. Maybe Tobias but I think that was down to her. The rest of them... Gullible fools and pompous—'

Olivier cast him a look which reduced his complaints to a grumble.

Light, Roland wished Elodie was here. She'd know what to say, and what to do. And she... she was back in Pelias, trapped in an enchanted sleep with the Aurum and...

With a groan, he buried his face in his hands. 'The Aurum...' he growled. 'It has to be because of the Aurum. Tobias said the old magic was rising, even in people only slightly sensitive to it before, filling the resulting void, but what that means... I don't know.'

The answers were meant to be here, at the College, the solution to all their problems, a cure for Elodie... Instead, all that seemed to be cascading down upon them were even more problems.

He looked up, at the two men who served him and obeyed

him, who had given up almost everything to follow him. He couldn't let them down.

'We will find an answer,' he said at last. But even he didn't believe it. 'You should get some rest. And talk to the healer Vivienne, or Tobias. They may be able to guide you, Olivier.' Because the light knew, he didn't have the first idea how to help.

'Knights don't work magic,' Olivier said, his voice wavering when he tried to make it strong. 'How can I do this and still—'

'You are still a knight,' Roland snapped. 'That will not change. You made vows. You protected Wren. You are more than a knight. A Paladin. Remember that.'

Olivier looked stunned, his eyes wide, but Anselm just nodded. 'You see?' he said. 'I told you.'

At least they had each other. They were lucky in that.

A moment of peace would have been nice, but Roland knew that such wishes were far more than he deserved. Something trembled in the air, something new and unsettling. He looked up, over the heads of his knights, sensing the change. Something was coming, something else, something which made those old instincts for danger stir yet again.

An unnatural wind ripped through the room, even though the doors and windows were closed, bringing Roland to his feet, his hand already on the hilt of Nightbreaker. The two knights broke apart, drawing their weapons as well, the same sense of alarm firing through them. Instincts like flames in each of them, like those rippling over the length of Olivier's fingers again.

They were Knights of the Aurum, all three of them.

'Outside,' said Roland. 'Something's happening. Another attack or—' Or something worse.

Screams echoed through the College corridors and the three men ran towards them, out into the formal gardens where a ring of witchkind were trying to hold back something which came swirling through the clustering shadows. Something huge, powerful, something that rose in a wave and tossed them aside as if they were no more than flowers before a storm.

But the witchkind of the College were failing. They had never encountered anything like this before. Several had already collapsed, and Tobias was barely holding the ring of witches together around the threat.

'Our wards failed,' he yelled at Roland. 'It was like they were nothing but paper. What is it?'

Nightbreaker glowed with inner light, recognising the power of the Nox as it coalesced before him. Roland ducked through the failing lines of witchkind, and charged at the darkness.

Another blade met his, one black as night, iridescent with those blue shadows of shadow-forged steel. The force of it sent a shudder all the way up his arm and down his spine, but he held it there as a knight in armour of the same metal stepped from the darkness.

Roland took a step back as he recognised Finn. Or rather, didn't recognise him. His eyes were too dark, just black and endless, and his mouth formed a thin, hard line.

Finn moved like a blur, a piece of shadow himself, and the swords clashed again. Roland found himself on the defensive. Finn was faster than before, stronger, and he fought without any hesitation or regrets. No quarter given.

Perhaps he had always fought like this when faced with an enemy. Roland had never been on the other end of it before. But there was no doubt now that he was seen as an enemy.

'Stop!' Wren shouted.

Because of course she was here as well. Where else would she be but spinning night to her will, at the heart of any trouble?

His daughter. No matter whatever else she might be, she was his daughter.

Her voice did it, her command.

Finn stepped back, still eyeing Roland, Olivier and Anselm

as if he didn't know them at all. Wren, dressed in a black Ilanthian gown shot with silver and midnight blue strands, her hair wild and untamed, spread her arms wide and the shadows fell away. She looked so small and slender, frail, and yet the magical power obeyed her in an instant. Not a girl, he realised, not in the slightest. Not anymore.

No, she was still his daughter. That was the end of it.

The witchkind were staring at her with a mixture of wonder and terror. They didn't know what to do, not when faced with her. Few would.

'You shouldn't have been able to do that,' Vambray said in a far firmer voice than Roland would have expected.

'I'm sorry,' Wren replied, her voice shaking. 'It was... it was an emergency.' She glanced down at the boy huddled at her feet, his body splattered in blood, clutching something in his hands. He bent over it, frozen in shock and horror. No danger there, Roland decided. But Finn...

The danger came from Finn.

He didn't look like the boy Roland had taken in and raised. He didn't even look like a Knight of the Aurum anymore. A knight of something quite the opposite, in fact. A figure from old stories, from nightmares, forsaken and forgotten...

Long ago, stories said that the Nox had also had a champion.

What had happened to him?

'Wren?' Roland asked, in calm, measured tones. 'What have you done?'

And to his absolute shock, she burst into tears and threw herself into his arms.

CHAPTER 32

WREN

For a moment everything had been darkness and chaos, flashes of blue otherlight like lightning in the storm of shadow kin which carried them away. Wren heard screams and wondered where they were coming from. Not from her, and not from Laurence, though she wouldn't blame him.

And definitely not from Finn. He didn't make a single sound, just gazed through the shadows with eyes that reflected the darkness and those blue flashes of otherlight. It almost made his eyes blue again, for brief agonising moments. But not the dark blue she knew and loved. This was alien and dangerous.

Just wrong.

She stumbled as the shadows released them and then felt the surge of magic, neither light nor dark, Aurum nor Nox, rising around them. Old magic again, the same thing the sisterhood had tried to bind her with. Panic made her lash out and, worse, made Finn come to her defence.

Beyond the magical force which fell beneath her, she saw Roland.

Thank the light that Finn obeyed her cry to stop, standing there like a statue now as she fell into her father's arms.

Not your father, not really, a vicious whisper told her. The Nox didn't want to lose its grip on her. She pushed it away ruthlessly. *You're part of me, little vestige. And I am part of you. In the end, we will be one. That is how it will always end.*

The Nox was already unravelling again away from the caves. It didn't matter, the things it said. It was nothing. She had to remember that. The further it got from the caves, from the centre of its remaining power, the worse it would be. The less sanity it would cling to until its bloodlust overwhelmed it again.

And her.

The sobs came before she could stop them and she hardly heard what Roland was saying as he led her to the edge of the garden, finding a stone bench which she sank onto without releasing him.

Safe. Hestia had told her the spell would bring her somewhere safe. There was nowhere safer than with Roland. Nowhere in the world. She realised that now.

What a fool she had been to ever doubt him.

People scrambled out of Finn's way as he moved soundlessly to her side, his eyes scanning all around. And poor Laurence trailed behind him, clutching the crown so tightly that blood ran from his palms. His hands were shaking and his face was pale.

'Laurence,' Wren managed to say. She wanted to apologise, to tell him it would be all right, that nothing bad would happen.

But it already had, and he had done it.

'I... I didn't... I couldn't... they made me do it, my... my lady.' The words spilled out, halting at first and then in a rush of emotion. He dropped to his knees in front of her, as if he didn't have the strength to stand, and she tried to catch him.

Finn watched without comment or reaction. It was so unlike him to see another in obvious pain and do nothing. Roland saw it too and she noticed him nod to Anselm and

Olivier, who took up positions where they could intercept Finn in a moment.

This was not good.

'It wasn't your fault,' she murmured to the boy and reached out her hand in an effort to comfort him. Instead, he handed her the crown and she recoiled, almost dropping it. The cursed thing vibrated in her hands, recognising her. She pushed it back into Laurence's grip.

'What happened?' Roland asked. 'Wren, I need to know everything.'

'Leander happened,' she said bitterly. 'Hasn't he always happened? He killed Alessander and framed Finn. He's king now and he...' She glanced down at Laurence again. He was staring at the ground, broken. 'He bespelled Laurence and killed Hestia.'

Roland sucked in a breath. Inexorably, his gaze fell onto the boy and he saw everything. Because Roland always knew.

'This young man needs food and rest,' he said softly. 'And we need—'

'We need to get back to Pelias,' Wren said. 'Now. He's going to attack. He's probably already unleashing his army and he knows the city is undefended. He said the knights can't stand without the Aurum. What does that mean, Roland? What happened to Elodie? They said she was sleeping, that she was enchanted.'

'And the Aurum sleeps with her,' said Finn in that soft monotone. 'You are the queen now, my lady. You should take this.' He scooped the crown out of Laurence's unresisting grip and offered it to her again.

'No.' Her hair whispered around her shoulders as she shook her head, the sound like the laughter of the Nox, and Wren wanted to cry again.

But she couldn't. Not just because it would not help. There were no tears left.

Finn seemed unmoved. 'Then Pelias will fall. Who else can stop my brother now?'

The silence was bitter and awful. Everyone was looking at them. No, at her.

Anselm laid his hand on Finn's armoured shoulder, pushing slightly and yet gently to get his attention. Finn's lips curled back as if he might snarl.

'We can, Finn. All of us. Don't make her destroy herself and you. Come back to yourself, my friend.'

For a moment Finn's expression stayed as still as stone, but then he frowned. Just a little, just a crack in the unyielding mask. He lowered the crown, and as he did so the confusion grew more clear. The Nox's spell peeled back just a little. Enough.

'Wren?' he whispered. 'I... I don't know what...'

Wren rose to her feet and wrapped her arms around his neck, pulling him against her and holding him close. It was like embracing stone.

'You need to rest, all of you,' Roland told them, the tone of command unmistakable. 'I will look after Laurence. Chancellor, can one of your people find us all rooms and a change of clothes for my daughter and my ward.'

His daughter, his ward. He was claiming them both again, making sure everyone knew they belonged to him. And not just the people of the College of Winter. Wren and Finn as well.

'This is most irregular,' said the Chancellor. Shadows ringed his eyes and he had the haunted look of a witchkind whose magic was close to depleted.

'I know,' Roland replied cautiously. 'We have so much to untangle here, your people as well as mine. You and I must talk. There is a conspiracy which goes beyond the College and beyond Asteroth. Wren will do no harm here. Neither will Finn. They have just escaped the darkness at great risk to themselves.'

He nodded to them and Wren, fuelled by instinct, sank into a curtsy. Finn didn't move, not to bow, not to do anything. For a moment she had thought he had come back but now he was like iron again. Perhaps he sensed a threat. Perhaps he was just... gone...

'Chancellor,' she said, turning what she hoped was a pleading look on him. 'You must have a healer here skilled in magical ailments... please, we have need of your help.'

Vambray studied her face for a moment and then glanced at Roland, the obvious connection only now striking him. They must have heard the news... or rather the gossip...

'Your royal highness,' he said in a gentler, more formal tone. 'We will do what we can. Vivienne is our finest. She will attend you shortly once she has attended those who...' Awkwardness stole whatever he had been about to say but Wren knew anyway. Those who had been trying to stop her arrival, those she had already hurt just by coming here. The shard of guilt wedged in her chest cracked it open another notch. 'Rooms will be made ready. Please, accept our hospitality. Grandmaster, you are right. You and I have much to discuss.'

'Roland.' Finn held out the crown. 'You need to guard this. It's the crown of Sidon. The ancient crown of the Nox. Leander wants it more than anything, apart from the princess. We need to keep them both safe.'

Safe for what, Wren worried, but couldn't say a word as Roland took it from Finn, studied it with some evident distaste, and then left.

Only when it was out of her sight did she feel able to draw breath again.

It wasn't much of a room, not compared to the palatial chambers of Pelias and Sidonia. But it wasn't a prison cell either and for that Wren was grateful.

The healer, Vivienne, had listened to their story before she ordered Finn out of his armour and examined him carefully, everything from peering into his eyes, to listening to his heart-beat and testing his reflexes. She conjured up a spell which seemed to rely more on scent than anything else, and as she pressed her fingertips to his forehead, the aroma of lavender surrounded them. But in the end she just frowned at him, and then at Wren.

'He's full of shadows,' she said. 'As if he has been taken by shadow kin and remade, but not in their image. He hasn't physi-cally changed otherwise?'

'Only his eyes,' Wren replied, unable to stop looking at him, waiting for something terrible to happen.

'His eyes,' the healer murmured thoughtfully, staring into them as if looking for answers.

'But he sounded like himself for a moment back in the courtyard. When Anselm talked to him. As if he remembered. And when he gave Roland the crown.'

'Maybe that's the key then, his memories? Our emotions are intricately tied up with them. And your Grandmaster is correct; rest would do wonders for both of you. I'll have hot water sent up. Bathe, rest and talk to him. Maybe you can reach him. If not, we will have Anselm try again. But I think...' She gave a brief smile. 'I think you would have more luck. Those we love, those for whom we would give everything, they are the ones who can reach us when we are lost.'

'It's my fault he's like this,' Wren told her.

But to her surprise Vivienne shook her head. 'He brought this on himself. One can only be this consumed by the Nox if one allows it in. It is squatting in him, using him, and I think it is doing so as a means to protect you, which is the greatest wish of anyone who truly loves another. He agreed to this, that's the problem. You need to remind him that you are safe now, and that he can let go. Show him that. You have more magic in one finger than I have ever had, my lady.'

Wren felt her face heat. 'But no training.'

'No one has training for something like this. Now, I must see to the boy who came with you. He's in a state of shock. What happened to him?'

Wren told her, as briefly and clearly as she could, and the poor woman's face paled with horror and compassion.

'I couldn't leave him there,' Wren said.

'To be used in such a way again?' The anger simmering in Vivienne's eyes was just as plain. 'No, you did the right thing. Don't worry. I'll look after him now. If you will excuse me?'

She left them alone. Servants bustled in and out for a little while, bringing a platter of cheeses and cold meats, a jug which she hoped was wine, and hot water and a pile of clean clothes. Wren sat on the edge of the bed, watching, while Finn stood grimly, guarding her against people who were clearly no threat at all. He never said a word and that crack she had seen, when he had almost seemed himself again, seemed like a wish or a dream.

And then, finally, the door closed and they were alone.

Wren pursed her lips, trying to work out what to do, how to reach him. Elodie would have known. Elodie was a healer, but a hedge witch too. She had tended all kinds of ailments in her time living in Cellandre, those of the body and the mind, both physical and magical. She would have had a solution and it would be practical and perfect in every way.

But Elodie was in Pelias and she couldn't even help herself.

No, this wouldn't do. Wren imagined the look of absolute scorn her sometimes mother would have cast at her for thinking this way. It would not do at all. She wasn't some helpless girl to sit here and pine away while shadow kin or the Nox or whatever it was destroyed the man she loved. Not even if he had welcomed it in, and offered himself up.

To protect her from Leander.

'He isn't worth this, you know,' she said to Finn. 'And if we don't do something about you he will have won anyway. He will have destroyed you.'

Finn's head turned sharply, his dark gaze fixing on her. A reaction then. That was good, wasn't it?

'Come here,' she said. 'I want you to do something.'

He obeyed without questioning, because that was what he did now – obeyed her, worshipped her, killed for her – and came to a halt, towering over her. She reached out and touched his face, running her fingers along his jaw and feeling it tense beneath her touch. He let out a breath, a single, juddering breath that spoke of desire and fear and a thousand emotions all tangled together.

'What would you do with me, Finn? Your will is your own, do you understand? I release you.'

For a moment she thought he wouldn't move, wouldn't answer. Everything was so still she was sure she could hear his heart thudding against his chest. Or maybe that was hers.

Then he pulled her into his arms and his mouth closed on hers, devouring her.

CHAPTER 33
FINN

The darkness was everywhere, within him, shrouding his mind and clogging his veins, crushing his heart. And Finn didn't care. How could he care? He belonged here. He had always belonged here. The shadows of the Nox were all there was and his life with anything or anyone else was over. Any dreams he might have clung to, any hopes he might have cherished – they were nothing now. They had petrified and crumbled in that treasure-filled cave, where the Nox had showed him his lineage, and their past, and all the terrible things they had done.

The blood of the Nox's child was on his hands as surely as it had stained those of his ancestors. That was how it worked. No generation was untainted by that action. It had bound them to power and they had all benefited, becoming stronger, faster, chosen and blessed by the shadows. But it was the revenge of the Nox as well. She was hungry, and determined, and oh so cunning, his goddess.

And now she had him. There was no choice, no free will. All that he lived for was to defend her. And... and Wren... somehow.

But she was still Wren. Or would be. Her soft, seductive

voice told him that, promised him. Shadow kin whispered in his ears, keeping him still and quiet until the need for violence presented itself again. He had only to obey. His body was theirs, his mind just a toy really, a plaything to torment. The armour enclosed him, locked him away, and made him stronger and faster, and so much more deadly. Nothing could harm her when he wore that armour and stood at her side. That was the key thing. He would allow nothing and no one to harm her.

Not even if they wore the face of a friend. Not even if they looked like Roland.

Or Anselm. Or Olivier...

Come back to yourself, my friend...

For a moment, that brief moment, a light had touched him. He'd seen it so far overhead that it was like a star in the night's sky. But it was distant and unreachable. And he was lost.

He had to accept that, the shadow whispered and the Nox murmured sweet reassurances. This was right. This was his place, where he belonged, and he believed it.

He had failed in every other way. Here he could keep her safe. He owed her everything and had so much he needed to make amends for.

The Nox... Wren...

'What would you do with me, Finn?'

It was her voice, reaching out to him. Her touch against his skin. He breathed in her scent and his mind spun. What would he do with her?

Whatever she wanted...

The Nox purred with the idea and part of him recoiled again.

'Your will is your own, do you understand?'

No. That wasn't right. It couldn't be right. And yet, she was saying it. Wren was saying it, and whatever his lady said, that was his only desire. Except... except...

A growl rippled through him. It didn't come from him, but

from the Nox. It knew what she was trying to do and it didn't like it.

'I release you,' Wren said.

What did he want? What would he do with her? Protect her, cherish her. Love her.

He would love her. That was what he wanted. That was all he wanted.

She was in his arms, her body pressed to his and he kissed her like a drowning man seeking air.

And Wren kissed him back, returned his passion in equal measure, just as she had always done. Right from the start, right from the first time he held her and kissed her and had lost his mind with desire for her. This was what he wanted. Her in his arms, his lips on her skin.

The gown tore under his hands, the fabric ripping with a noise that was drowned out a moment later by her moan of need, which tangled with his name. Her head fell back, exposing the long line of her throat and he kissed her there, his mouth exploring her, his tongue on her flesh until she writhed against him.

She surrendered to him.

It wasn't meant to be this way. Something deeply ingrained in him told him that. He belonged to her, hers to command, hers to do with as she wished. He had given himself to her body and soul, to the Nox and to Wren and...

But Wren was not the Nox. Not really.

She was his beloved, his light, his dream. She was the one thing that kept him sane. She was his everything.

His hands cupped her breasts, thumbs caressing the nipples until they hardened to peaks, which he captured in his mouth. She arched, her hips pressing to his as if urging him onwards. Lowering her back onto the bed, he tormented her body, every noise she made spearing through him, making his desire climb higher.

He wanted to hear her pleasure, to make her cry out. He wanted her shaking and desperate against him. He wanted her body to ache for him until she couldn't stand it any longer. That was the way he felt all the time.

'What would you do with me?'

He would love her. He would protect her. He would try in every way to make her happy, to make her fulfilled, to keep her safe and let her be... let her be whoever she would be. Not the Nox, not a queen, not a princess or a goddess.

She was Wren. Just Wren.

And she was everything.

Wren opened to him, her body his, his name on her lips. He sank into her, filling her, and stilled, just marvelling.

She lay beneath him, her hair spilling all around them on the bedclothes, her eyes wide with need, pupils huge as her desire consumed her. One hand gripped his shoulder, and then fell back beside her head, the long elegant fingers curling. Strands of her hair wound about her wrist and her palm. Finn felt her fingertips trace patterns along his side, where the scars of the shadow kin bite still marked him, and then she released him entirely.

Wren arched her hips to him and he began to thrust into her, each movement a torture of the utmost pleasure.

His. She was his.

Completely.

He wanted to savour this, to cherish each and every moment, to fix it eternally in his memory, that she was his, that she gave herself to him without any conditions or complications. That he didn't have to obey her, or worship her.

That it was something he wanted. She was what he wanted. It wasn't an obligation but a wonder.

The dark and endless shades tangled in her hair moved, drawing the shadows around them into its lengths, absorbing the magic of the Nox and making it part of her. Wren opened her mouth, his name the only sound she could make.

His body tightened, a tingling in the base of his spine warning him that any moment now he'd lose that control he clung to and then—

He didn't know where the light came from. There shouldn't have been any light left in him. The Aurum was trapped and he'd given himself over to the Nox.

But suddenly everything was made of light. It roared through his body like a firestorm, blinding him, light which came from everywhere, bright and brilliant, every colour and every hue, all of it sparking along his nerves and rippling beneath his skin.

Finn threw back his head and cried out.

All around them the ground shook, the walls trembling. Lightning arced in the air and Finn knew none of that. He knew only that all-consuming, blazing glory.

CHAPTER 34

WREN

Finn's touch was different. Determined and knowing, but still so gentle it felt like he was going to drive her out of her mind. But this time he took what she offered and Wren let him. She wanted him to know that she was his, as much as he was hers. That this went both ways.

The greatest pleasure lay in giving him everything he could desire. She had tasted his submission and it was sweet indeed, but it wasn't everything. Her lover was strong and skilled, he knew how to make her cry out or sigh, and he knew every nuance of sound in between. There was no restraint this time. He held back nothing in deference to her.

It was more than she had ever imagined. Finn filled her, surrounded her. The weight of his body moving against hers stimulated every part of her. Somewhere deep inside her he touched some place of pleasure which robbed her of sanity and she cried out his name. Light grew inside her, light which could not be contained. The shadows too, all that darkness that was part of her, reached out for him. She held it back, denied it the control it so craved. She pulled the shadows from him, back into herself. Her hair coiled around her limbs, holding her back from reaching for him, the Nox inside her howling with need. It didn't matter. She didn't care. She wouldn't let it take Finn again. Not her Finn.

The pulse of need beat stronger and stronger. Finn kissed her exposed neck as she arched against him, as he thrust into her again and again. The power in her blossomed like night-flowering jasmine, winding through her with greedy tendrils and drawing still more of the shadows from him.

Finn shuddered, his body stiffening, and he buried his face in the crook of her neck, his mouth opening wide, his teeth grazing her skin. Wren cried out, opening to him, falling with him as he came.

And all the darkness in the world filled her.

Her eyes snapped open, as, dizzy and delirious, she beheld the man entwined with her.

He was made of light, of fire, of the rays of the sun itself. She had to close her eyes again lest he blind her.

She came with a cry of ecstasy, her body no longer her own, and she didn't care. He was all she wanted, and all her inner darkness desired. All those shadows, all those corners of the night, ached for the light that blazed through him now.

The Aurum, she thought, but it was a far-off and distant realisation. It was the Aurum inside him, filling him, scourging him until not a trace of the Nox remained. It was making him whole again, purifying him, filling him with the fire of a Paladin.

No, she was doing it. She was calling the Aurum somehow, just as she had in battle, and it was answering, freed at last from the long confinement it had endured. She could hear it singing to her, exalting in its liberation and the sheer pleasure it took from their joining.

Finn's voice cried out and broke, her name, she was sure it was her name, but it was a song as well. Her name was a psalm on his lips once again, the Aurum echoing through it.

For a moment neither of them could move. They were caught there, lost in their union and their ecstasy.

He moved first, awkwardly, as if it was a great effort, but as he came back to himself he seemed aware that he might be crushing her. He wasn't. She wanted to tell him that but couldn't find the words.

She couldn't find any words.

'Did I... did I hurt you?' he whispered. His voice was hoarse, but sated. And that warmth... light, she had missed that warmth, and the ache of affection.

Wren shook her head and felt her smile lift her face.

'You glowed,' she told him.

Finn gave a soft, almost-laugh. 'I burned.' His breath came out in a deep rush. 'You are a wonder, my love. How did you do that?'

'I just called on what was there. The Aurum loves you, Finn. It always has done. I knew it would save you.'

He bent his head again, kissing her lips first, then her jawline, then her neck. He was still inside her, and his cock seemed to stir again as he moved.

'I am still yours, you know,' he whispered. 'Body and soul.'

She swallowed hard on the knot of emotion rising in her throat. 'And I'm yours. That's the secret, isn't it? It isn't about one or the other of us, but about both of us. Together.'

'Together,' he agreed, and turned his attention to her pleasure again.

Later, much later, as dawn stained the window, Wren woke with Finn's arms still wrapped around her, and his long legs tangled with hers. She lay there, watching the play of light on the ceiling above her.

Not just the light of sunrise, she realised, nor the early rays coming through the branches of the trees outside the window. The glow was too warm, and it held more colours in its depths than sunlight.

What have you done? the Nox whispered, resentment threading through her mind.

She had saved him, that was what. Freed him from its control. She had done what she had to do to save him from a lifetime enslaved to a dark goddess. She might not be able to resist it forever, but she would not let it take him as well.

You fool. The loathing in the voice was unmistakable. *You've just handed him over to another form of subjugation. At least we would have let him live.*

Wren's immediate answer – that she was glad he was free, that it was just trying to trick her again – stumbled before she could fully give it form. Something was wrong. The Nox didn't sound angry, not really. It sounded... bitter, defeated, and heart-broken with it.

It sounded regretful.

'What do you mean?' she whispered as softly as she could. She didn't want to wake Finn, not yet. He was exhausted. After everything he had been through, she wanted to let him rest while he could. Turning her face, she studied his, soft in sleep, the tight lines around his eyes from stress and constant suffering barely visible now. Peaceful. He looked peaceful and that was good, wasn't it?

But the glow she had seen reflected on the ceiling came from beneath his skin. It ran like flames on the surface of oil, shimmering and bright, illuminating him from within, turning him to gold.

He belongs to the Aurum now, the Nox went on. *It fills him. Oh, child, what have you done? He is lost to us.*

That had been what he had always wanted, Wren reminded herself. He was a Knight of the Aurum, a Paladin, touched by its light. She had led him to the Nox and back onto a path he had fought against all his life.

You think the Aurum will treat him better than it has treated any other of its chosen? It will burn him until there is nothing left. It needs a champion. It needs a home. And you have given it both...

'Wren?' Finn's voice was blurred with sleep, but he had opened his eyes and was gazing back at her now.

They were so bright, like the sky on a summer morning, like sunlight seen through deep water, aglow from within. The light in his skin may have faded, but it had coalesced in his eyes instead.

'Yes,' she managed. The word almost lodged in her throat.

What had she done? She never thought things through, that was what Elodie had always said. She acted on instinct and that led to disasters. It always had done.

Reach for the light, Elodie had always said that. But what if Elodie was wrong?

Finn brought a hand up to stroke her hair and he smiled. Like he hadn't a care in the world.

'How did you do that?' he asked, and then gave his soft, self-deprecating laugh. 'Magic, I know. Everything about you is magic. And every time I think I am lost, you're there to save me, heart.'

He sounded so happy, so at peace.

This was what he had wanted, she reminded herself. This was what he had always wanted. To be safe in the light. To serve the Aurum.

And now it filled him. Spilled out of him. Suffused every part of him. She could feel it radiating through him.

A frown flickered over his brow as he watched her. 'Are you all right? Is something wrong?'

'Don't you feel it?' she asked.

'Feel what?'

How could he not know?

They were two opposite powers, light and dark, Aurum and Nox. And there was nothing she could do now to keep him. She had given him up, given him everything he wanted to save him.

But she couldn't tell him that. Not when she had to look right at him and see the love and the hope die in his beautiful blue eyes.

'Nothing,' she said. 'It's nothing. Just a dream. A bad dream.'

Finn smiled, his fingers playing with the strands of her hair. 'Let me chase that away?'

CHAPTER 35
ROLAND

Roland had dreamed about Elodie the previous night, in the brief hours he tossed and turned in a guest bedroom of the College of Winter. She was lost in the darkness, heartbroken, and try as he might, he couldn't reach her. He threw himself against invisible walls, like impregnable glass, but to no avail. The flames that danced around her guttered as if in a wind, and she looked so wan and helpless.

Elodie had never looked helpless. She was fierce and wonderful, his beloved queen.

But not in his nightmare. Here she was helpless and he was powerless, and they were eternally apart.

It was a relief to be on the road, after another brief conference with Vambray that morning.

The enchantments on the College seemed to have vanished with Alouette's influence, and the relief among the inhabitants was palpable. Roland heard them talking, the people of the College, these witchkind who had never faced such danger, ascribing it by turns to the arrival of the knights and their Grandmaster, and some who even whispered that it was the princess. What Wren would make of that he didn't know. She didn't seem anything like the girl he had known in Pelias and Roland didn't know how to even broach the subject of what she had endured in Sidonia. Or what changes had transformed her.

Because she was transformed. The dark power came off her in waves, so strong even Roland could feel it, and the effect she had on Finn was unsettling. More than unsettling. Her hair was long and rippling with shadows, her skin like moonlight and her eyes wide and dark, but ringed as if bruised. Previously, he had not seen the Nox in her, no matter how many times everyone had told him she was the dark goddess incarnate. She was a child, a girl, his daughter...

But he saw it now.

She looked exhausted this morning, her nerves on edge, and she kept glancing at Finn as if she expected him to go berserk. The Ilanthian gown was gone, which was just as well. She wore a simple travelling outfit, a leather jerkin over breeches, with a long green cloak, and looked far more comfortable in it than she had since he had first brought her to Pelias. But her eyes were darker than ever, deep and endless, and full of doubts.

Finn was transformed as well. He was the young man Roland knew and loved again, his eyes aglow, that darkness they had seen in him when he arrived banished. That was Wren's doing, because Roland understood now that, while she could call the shadow kin and bend them to her will, she could banish them as well.

Finn bowed to Roland, still decked in that dark mail of the armour he had arrived wearing. And though it was shadow-wrought steel and clearly of great age, made with the skill of a master, it didn't smother him as it had on his arrival here. Rather it shone with a blue-black light, and the sword strapped to his back remained sheathed. An ominous threat, no doubt, but not an overt one. Not yet. Just like Finn. Prince Finnian... He was controlled, careful in every movement, but when he smiled it was as if the sun came out from behind clouds.

'Grandmaster,' Finn said and Roland just pulled him into a hug before he could say one more formal word.

'Not anymore,' Roland told him. Finn pulled back with a look of shock and Roland gave him a rueful smile. 'The Lady Regent Ylena relieved me of that duty.' Finn frowned and looked ready to argue – of course he did – but Roland shook his head. 'It is done, Finn. Yvain is Grandmaster.'

'In name anyway,' Anselm muttered under his breath but when Roland glanced his way he had the nerve to look completely innocent.

'Enough,' he said. 'We must go back to Pelias and inform them of this plot. We must protect the queen, above all else. Vambray believes that we can wake her. He has told me how. Nightbreaker is the key. That was why Alouette was so keen to take it. If I had not brought it with me...'

'They would never have known to use it,' Olivier interrupted. 'It has never been known for magic. Yvain would have carried it as you did, as a sword.'

'Perhaps. He might have worked it out, or Maryn would have perhaps. Whatever the odds, we must return it. It represents the Aurum now.'

'And the crown we brought from Ilanthus represents the Nox,' Wren added. 'We must keep it from Leander at all costs. He can use it to gain control of the Nox. And of me.' She swallowed hard. 'I think the safest place is in Pelias, don't you? Perhaps the only safe place.'

A fortress city which Roland knew how to defend... he only hoped that was true.

And now, the main thing was to get there as quickly as they could. The southern road was clear and straight, but too exposed. If there were Ilanthian troops on the move, Roland's party could be in grave danger and he would not allow any harm to come to Wren. He would not allow Leander to take her. Not now when she had escaped him again.

But they needed to move fast. Covertly. And now.

He glanced back at Wren as they finally set off from the College of Winter and a chill crept down his spine.

⁂

They made much better time than Roland expected, stopping only briefly to rest the horses more than themselves. It was a hurried race for home and they didn't have time to talk. That was what he told himself anyway.

So when he kept watch in the darkest hours of the night, he was surprised when Wren came to join him.

'You should sleep,' he told her.

'I can't.'

Everyone else was asleep. Roland pursed his lips and pondered on how to deal with wayward daughters. He'd heard of such things, of course. Too many of the Paladins with daughters complained about it.

Roland didn't know what on earth they were going on about. Having a daughter…

He put out an arm and she nestled in against him. 'I'm scared,' she said after an age.

'Understandable,' he replied, unsure what else to say. She was right to be scared. There was a lot to be scared of. 'We will be back in Pelias soon, just another couple of days.'

'That's part of what I'm afraid of, Roland.'

He smiled at the sound of his name on her lips, the tone so like her mother's. But this was no time for humour. He knew that.

'We will make it. We will face it together. I won't let anything happen to you, Wren. I promised, didn't I? And Finn—'

'I tried to help him, tried to rid him of the shadow-touch but…' Her eyes glistened with unshed tears. 'I don't know. I may have made it worse, the other way. The light of the Aurum took him, filled him and it... it...'

'It's in Finn now? Not Elodie?'

She shook her head, helplessly. 'I don't know. Not really. Part of it maybe? But I fear it. If he's the Aurum, and I'm the Nox—'

'But you aren't,' he told her. 'He's Finn and you're Wren and that's the end of it.'

'No it isn't. I wish it was all. They want him to be king in Ilanthus. Well, before Leander killed Alessander and claimed the throne. And he wants to marry me – Leander, I mean – and... and...'

What a tangle, he thought. It was worthy of a mummers' play.

'Enough,' Roland sighed. 'We'll see it through. We will work it out. But first we need to reach Elodie and wake her. She'll know what to do, Wren. She always does. You know that.'

And in this he only hoped he was right.

CHAPTER 36

WREN

Roland was grim and everyone else picked up their mood from him. It was inevitable. And of course he wasn't wrong. It was dangerous, this flight south. On horseback, Wren took her place in the centre of the group, knights before and behind her, Laurence and Finn at her side. They rode in silence, leaving the College of Winter far behind them. All the time she expected an attack. Leander wanted her and the crown. He'd be waiting.

And then there was Finn.

The light in him shimmered under the surface, just out of reach, just out of sight. But she could feel it. Crawling through him, aware of her, watching her, when he was distracted or focused on the road. And it hated her. The Aurum.

Perhaps the armour kept it at bay. Perhaps it was Finn himself fighting it, but even he couldn't keep that up forever. She remembered the Aurum from Pelias, the way it had taken control of Elodie.

If Elodie, who had trained and studied and lived a life ready to be the Chosen of the Aurum, hadn't been able to withstand it, how could Finn?

The Nox was still broken. Wren might have access to some

of its power but so much was banished beyond the veil and it couldn't reach her. Not unless Leander had his way.

The crown was buried in a pack on the back of Roland's horse. Hestia's son followed the Grandmaster like a puppy, desperate for some kind of safety, and Wren felt the same way. Perhaps he reminded the boy of Gaius, or perhaps he just sensed that Roland was someone who could help him.

It was impossible to be in the Grandmaster's presence without feeling that he could still make everything all right. Even Finn seemed to fall under that spell without a moment of doubt.

Roland would make everything better. He always did. He always had.

Light, she wished with all her heart that he would now. Just with a wave of his hand, or a sweep of his sword.

They were still two days north of Pelias when the attack came, on a desolate stretch of road which offered little by way of refuge.

It was too quiet. She noticed that first. Far too quiet. No birdsong, nothing moving in the fields and hedgerows on either side of them.

'Smoke,' said Olivier. 'In the air, can you smell it?'

'Keep your wits,' Roland replied. 'Anselm? Ride ahead.'

Wren's skin tightened around her frame and she shivered as if a cloud had passed over the sun, stealing all the warmth of the day. Shadows stirred eagerly in the bushes on either side of the road.

Too eagerly.

They whispered, just on the edge of her hearing, and Wren stiffened in the saddle. Her horse almost bucked, dancing back instead of forward, and Olivier and Finn both turned to help her. Distracted, all of them. By her. Just when that was the last thing they needed.

'Look out!' she shouted.

They came out of the trees, and up from beneath the stones, shadow kin larger than any she had ever seen, and behind them Ilanthian soldiers. Wren tried to control her mount but the poor beast gave a crazed whinny and tore the reins from her hands, bolting ahead. All she could do was cling to the saddle, scrabbling to get the leather back into her grip.

The noise in her head became a high-pitched whine and behind her she heard the clash of steel. Anselm shouted something and the thunder of the horses' hooves drowned it out.

She reached out to the shadow kin, trying to focus, to command them, to turn them against their Ilanthian masters. They were her creatures, weren't they? Or the Nox's anyway. They had to obey her. They always had before.

But not this time. Even as she reached out, she felt the promised control snatched away, the magic wrenched out of her hands.

He laughed. She heard him laugh. Leander...

Oh little bird, it's not so easy. Did you really think I'd let you go just like that? They miss you. They want you back and I've promised to help. They won't obey you now.

His voice was almost like a caress. It chilled her to her heart.

He was already here. He was waiting for her. He must have known, used magic to track her or had someone else trailing them. Could word have been sent from the College of Winter the moment they arrived?

She would put nothing past Leander. The new king of Ilanthus wanted her back and he was not going to take no for an answer.

'Wren! Ride!' It was Anselm. He wheeled his horse around in front of her and the soldiers swarming towards them. The road ahead was blocked as well. 'Make for the trees!'

The trees? They were at the very edge of Cellandre. She'd be safe there. She had to be.

Cellandre had always been home. She knew it. Knew parts of it anyway.

It listened to her.

She didn't quite know how she did it. Seizing the reins again she turned the horse's head for the treeline and plunged into the forest.

The darkness rose like a wave before her. Fixing her attention on that, she focused her will and commanded it to part. For a moment it resisted, or rather something held the shadows firm. Someone.

Leander. It had to be. It had that familiar feeling of the last time she had fled through Cellandre, the way he manipulated her and tried to coerce her.

But she knew him now. She knew him far too well.

The shadows weren't responding but she could still reach for the light.

Always reach for the light, Elodie had said.

When she did, however, there was nothing there, her will sliding away from it as if it was oil.

No, this could not be happening.

The horse screamed and reared up. She grabbed hold of its mane, clung to it and tried to calm the creature, trying to reassure it even though she was very lacking in reassurance herself. The horse staggered forward and suddenly the air stilled.

She felt the surge of triumph surround her, something not her own. Stones, she realised. She was in a circle of stones, a thin place, hidden among the trees and the undergrowth. She didn't need to see the ring. She could feel it in the earth and in the air.

The Nox knew it. Leander knew it.

It was yet another trap.

The horse bucked and screamed as the magic of the shadows closed in on them, and she finally lost control of it completely. Wren tried to hold on, but she couldn't.

The next thing she knew, she was falling and the shadows rushed in to catch her and swallow her up.

And all she could hear was Leander's voice ringing through her ears.

At last.

CHAPTER 37
FINN

The thrill of battle fired his blood and the sword sang in his hand. Finn charged into the fray, and the faces that rose before him fell away just as quickly. Light filled him, the light of the Aurum, the light Wren had gifted to him. Part of him wanted to shout for joy, for triumph.

He was saved. She had saved him. This was where he was meant to be and what he was meant to do. This was what had always been intended.

He felt free at last. More free than he had ever been. The shadows inside him had been wiped away, every last one. His enemies were helpless before him. Mere soldiers of Ilanthus were nothing before him. He let the Aurum loose and turned the attack back on them.

Anselm and Olivier flanked him, charging alongside him, and the light filled them as well. It overflowed from him and they were sworn knights as well, touched by Wren's power and made Paladins in protecting him. She had saved them too. All of them. They were her men, and she had made them so effortlessly. Not in the same way he was, perhaps, but no less true. She accepted them as they were.

He looked for Roland and there he was, in the thick of the fight, in the middle of the road, Nightbreaker blazing in his hands. The Grandmaster was as skilled in battle as any of his men and the powers of the Aurum were as at home within him as anyone else. He was illuminated with it and Finn could feel his guardian's every movement, his rage, his determination to protect his daughter. He could feel everything and the zeal with which Roland fought only fuelled the fire inside Finn's soul. The Aurum blazed and sang inside him, racing along his veins and shooting up his spine to set his mind alight.

The shadows were a tide, sucking at the world, draining the tattered remains of old magic in order to strengthen itself. It crowed at him, that he was a fool, gullible and stupid, that it had already won.

'Anselm?' he shouted. 'Where's Wren?'

'She took cover in the trees.'

The trees were wreathed in shadows, dark and terrible. And Wren...

Wren. They had Wren.

He wheeled away from the fight without thought and five men encircled him moments later. But Finn didn't hesitate. All his life he had fought, and all his life he had reached for the light. Now it blazed inside him just as he had always wanted it to, and the sword moved like an extension not just of his arm, but his mind as well.

We fight the Nox, with flame and sword.

And now he embodied both.

He tore his way through them and urged his horse into a gallop, heading after her.

'Finn! They've taken the boy!' he heard Olivier call after him and the horse went from underneath him, screaming and kicking. Finn rolled and came up fighting as shadow kin tried to overwhelm him. The horse was away, thank the light. It didn't share poor Dancer's fate, not this time, and he celebrated that small victory.

Now all he could think of was Wren. He needed to find her, to save her.

She is our enemy. She is tainted to the core.

The voice almost brought him to his knees, knocking the breath from his chest. If he had been in any other place and time, he would have collapsed, but he was in the middle of a fight and didn't have the time to let anything of the sort happen.

You are blessed. You are purified. The refining fire rushes through you and makes you perfected. No longer forsaken, you have been made anew. Be grateful for you are chosen.

And he was grateful. Of course he was grateful.

But it was Wren.

Finn gripped the sword harder and started forward again, his legs moving as if through knee-deep mud. The Aurum railed in the back of his mind but he pushed it away.

And then he saw her.

Wren was on her hands and knees in the darkness, jet black vines coiling around her, thorns cutting her skin, her eyes so wide and terrified, so very, very dark.

She was not their enemy. The Nox might be. But not her.

'Wren!' She was in danger, and whenever she was in danger he would come to her aid. He had vowed it long ago. It was engraved on every secret place of his heart. 'Wren, I'm coming.'

She tried to speak but couldn't. There was a twist of shadow coiled around her throat, and though her mouth opened, no sound came out. Nothing.

Finn hacked at the darkness around her but it just dissolved and reformed. That was when he realised his mistake. They were in a stone circle, a thin place, where the Nox could reach out to her and take her. Where it could make itself whole and make Wren its own for once and for all. And even with everything she had endured, everything she had suffered and fought her way through, it would take her.

Which was exactly what his brother had planned.

'Wren,' he tried again.

But the being held in the twisted knots of shadow wasn't just Wren. The Aurum saw her, recognised the Nox, and a wave of pure unadulterated hatred stabbed its way through him and stole his breath.

The shadow kin snarled at him, but they couldn't touch him. Not now. They didn't need to.

The one holding her, its bright blue eyes flaming with malice, bared its shining teeth, gleaming with saliva, now made whole and so very dangerous. With a movement so fast he almost missed it, the shadow kin sank its teeth into Wren's shoulder. This time she screamed out loud, a high and wavering sound which shook him to the core.

'Finn, down!' Roland yelled from behind him and Finn ducked instinctively, his training too deeply ingrained in him to ignore. Nightbreaker's edge swept over his head, the wind caused by the air it sliced through cold on his skin, flattening his hair on his scalp.

The sword glowed, bright and beautiful, full of power and light, the same light he held inside him now.

It cut through the creature bearing down on him – the thing he had not even seen, so consumed had he been with worry for Wren – cutting a huge shadow kin clean in two. Roland stepped in front of him.

'Let her go!' he shouted. 'Let my daughter go!'

'Roland, look out,' Finn tried to say, but too late. Shadow kin struck Roland from every angle, tearing into his body with teeth and claws. His head fell back, his eyes glassy with agony, his mouth stretched wide.

Finn didn't think, couldn't think. All he knew was that his guardian was dying and he was just standing there. He snatched up Nightbreaker and rage filled him, blinding and wild, the type of rage that had only ever taken him when Wren was in danger. He barely saw anything, and yet he saw everything. Every movement, every shadow, every weapon. His body was that of the Paladin he had always wanted to be, possessed of the white-hot fury of the Aurum as he laid into them, a blade in each hand, one light and one dark.

The shadows fell before him and Roland landed in a heap at his feet. He heard Anselm and Olivier fighting their way to him.

And just like that, all went still.

Wren was gone. There was no sign of Laurence either. The Ilanthian soldiers were dead and all traces of the Nox had vanished. Everything. Shadow kin, the dark crown, Laurence, Wren...

Everything was still and quiet but for the sound of his heaving breath and his fellow knights racing to his side. Finn dropped to his knees, his hands turning Roland over and checking him for injuries.

And there were many. So many.

This was Roland, his guardian, the only man who had ever acted like a father to him in all his pitiful life. Roland, who had always been the strongest, the epitome of the greatest of knights, a kind and caring man who Finn had completely failed to appreciate...

'Grandmaster,' he gasped, as the strength the Aurum had imbued him with bled away in shock and horror. 'Talk to me, Roland, please...'

CHAPTER 38
ELODIE

A cry of anguish brought Elodie up from the haze of nothingness that had claimed her, jolting her as if she awoke from a dream of falling, seconds before she hit the ground. Her breath caught in her throat like a ball of ice and all she could feel was the thundering of her heart. And then... then a terrible wrench as that same heart tore itself apart.

A cold wind blew through her and she tried to look around.

Everything felt different.

Something was wrong. Terribly wrong. Not just here, not just in this place between worlds which served as her prison. Because that's what it was, she realised. She had failed the Aurum, and it did not take failure lightly.

But this was a place of the Aurum and right now the Aurum felt...

A loss?

The mist that surrounded her stirred, rising and falling like something vast and endless was breathing, something in pain. Elodie searched through it, not even sure what she sought until she saw it.

A figure knelt in the mist, half a dream and half a mirage.

For a moment, she thought it was the Aurum back again to torment her, but the blazing light was no more than a flickering candle flame now. Fading. Dying.

She still knew him. How could she not?

'Roland?' Elodie whispered.

He lifted his head like a flower seeking the sun, following only the sound of her shaking voice. The pain etched on his handsome features made her heart lurch.

'Elodie?' he murmured. 'Where... where are we?'

She scrambled across the vast and empty space between them and flung her arms around him.

Which when she knew for sure that this was not another trick of the Aurum. He didn't vanish like smoke, or change into something else. There was no laughter, no sneer.

He felt real and warm...

Great light and shadows of old, how was he here?

'Roland? What happened to you?' Something stabbed at her eyes and she blinked back tears made of acid which needled their corners. This couldn't be happening. He couldn't be here, not like this. It made no sense at all.

When he spoke, he almost sounded distracted, like a child waking from a nightmare.

'There was an attack... There were shadow kin. They took Wren, and Hestia's boy, I think. They would have killed Finn. He was... Where... where are we, El? Tell me.'

She tried to soothe him, her palm against his face. He leaned into her touch like a cat.

'It's just a place, a between place. Don't be scared.'

He shook his head and smiled against her touch. 'Not scared, my love... just... what does that mean? Between what?'

How to explain it? The concept was old and witchkind knew it well. There were tomes about it in the College of Winter. Elodie had studied copies of them, half a dozen of the finest, once upon a time, made specially for her and brought south.

'It lies outside of our realm,' she said, trying to be clear for him. 'Like the place where the Nox was banished. But not there. I promise, not there. It's between dreams and wakefulness, between thought and instinct, between life and—'

And then she realised the whole, dreadful truth of it, the horror her mind had been trying to shy away from the instant she saw him here.

He looked so confused, her beautiful Roland. So lost. But slowly, surely, he was already working it out. She could see it in his dark eyes, the dawning realisation. He had always been meticulous, methodical...

'Ah,' he said, and nothing else. When he glanced down at his side, blood seemed to blossom in the gash which had been torn clean through his mail and tunic, a wound which only seemed to appear as he remembered it existed.

It looked bad. Really bad. The healer in her mind was already assessing the possible damage, calculating the outcomes. None of it was good. The rest of her...

'No,' she told him, firmly, a command. 'No, don't you dare!'

As if she could actually command him in this. In anything really.

A smile tugged at his lips. Rueful, almost teasing. He was thinking the same thing, wasn't he? Their minds had always been in tune like that.

'I don't think I can obey this time, my love,' he sighed with regret.

Elodie tugged him closer, her splayed right hand closing on the wound. If it was the real world, that would have hurt him more than she could bear. But if it was the real world, she could have poured magic into him in order to heal him. Or failing that, she could have used her herbs, her knowledge of healing and everything else at her disposal.

But this was just a place of memories and raw will. And it was not her place.

'Don't you dare leave me, Roland de Silvius,' she snapped. Suddenly, she was furious. With him for getting into this position, with herself for being powerless, with this cursed place, with fate, with everything. 'You were meant to rescue me. You promised.'

He almost smiled and it tore at her heart with talons. 'Since when did you ever need rescuing?'

'Now!' She couldn't keep her voice from breaking. 'I need you now. And always. I can't lose you, Roland. Not again. Never again.'

He was fading, turning to mist in her arms, but she still saw that heartbroken smile.

'You never lost me, El. But your people need you. That's more important, love.'

'No it isn't. Don't be so... so... *stupid!*'

But Roland just kissed her. He smiled and kissed her.

For a moment his lips lingered on hers again, their touch too cold. She sobbed his name.

'Please, Roland... please don't go...'

But she couldn't stop him. Not this time. Perhaps not ever. This time, he left her.

❦

'Roland!' Elodie screamed his name out loud as she sat up in bed, her skin frozen, her whole body shaking with effort. Suddenly, very much awake.

Maryn started out of the chair opposite, her face worn and pale, her eyes ringed with shadows. She looked like she hadn't slept in weeks.

'Elodie? Oh thank the Aurum! Elodie!'

Her hands were firm and assured as she tried to assess

Elodie's health, taking her temperature and pulse. Always the professional, a consummate healer.

Elodie swatted her away. Her hand hit against a metal bracelet on her cousin's wrist, hard and cold as iron. Elodie's eyes grew round with alarm.

'Roland! Where's Roland?'

Maryn just frowned, hesitating to answer, and Elodie somehow knew that everything was so much worse than she had feared. Endlessly worse. 'Maryn? What has happened?'

Her cousin winced and then swallowed hard as she considered her possible answers.

'Majesty,' she replied in formal tones that warned Elodie that her fears were well founded. The Maiden of the Aurum wore a shadow-wrought steel bracelet which smothered her magic. How could anything be good in any of this? 'I regret to inform you that Pelias has fallen. The regents' council surrendered the city to the forces of Ilanthus. We are prisoners, you and I. King Leander of Ilanthus has taken Asteroth.'

'Through what right?' Elodie snarled. Leander? King? Not while she lived.

'Through right of conquest, and through right of marriage. He has claimed Wren as his bride.'

CHAPTER 39

FINN

Pelias had fallen. That was the first problem and not what Finn had expected. It had taken them two days' hard riding from the scene of the ambush to reach the outskirts of the city to find everywhere was quiet, terrified. The whole land seemed to have fallen under a spell of fear. The closer they got the more devastation they met. The land was ravaged, just as Leander had promised.

They had lost Wren, and Laurence too. And the crown. Now it appeared they had lost everything.

Roland rode like a man in a stupor, consumed by fever and the darkest of magic. Finn had done everything he could to bind him to life with the magic of the Aurum. He was not going to lose the Grandmaster. The wounds had been bad but somehow he had managed to stop the bleeding, and while Olivier had dressed them, Finn had poured as much light into Roland's body that it ought to have lit him up like the sun. But the injuries weren't healing and it felt like part of Roland was gone forever, had slipped over the edge into death and not come back.

And wherever that part of him had gone ahead, it was pulling the rest of him after it.

'We need to rest,' Anselm told him. 'He needs to rest. And we need some reconnaissance before we go any further. I don't like this, Finn. It's too quiet.'

At least that was something they could agree on.

'Make camp then, and see to Roland. I'll ride ahead and—'

'No,' Anselm said. 'You're not yourself and you might be all that's keeping Roland with us right now.' Anselm was never one to sugar-coat things. 'I'll go. I know secret ways through the city and who to talk to. I'll be quick. You stay here. Olivier can help tend Roland and you...' That look again, suspicion and concern twisted together. It wasn't that Anselm didn't trust him, Finn knew that instinctively, but he was wary.

The reports that had greeted them on the road, when they met fleeing refugees, were not good. Leander had arrived by sea with half his army and the others had poured south along the coast and through the forests. The city guards had died in their droves trying to hold back the onslaught. Rather than submit to siege, a completely unprepared Pelias had opened the gates on the orders of the regents' council.

That didn't seem possible. Finn tried to imagine Lady Ylena giving up like that. And what had happened to the Knights of the Aurum?

If anyone could find out it would be Anselm. Finn had to trust in that.

Olivier helped set up a camp in a small copse of trees and they waited. The night stretched out in silence. Roland slept soundly and Finn kept watch until Olivier relieved him.

'Will he return to us?' he asked. Of Roland, not Anselm. Finn knew to his core that Olivier had no doubts whatsoever about Anselm. Before long, their friend would be back with the information they needed.

Roland, however, was another matter entirely.

'He needs a proper healer,' said Finn. 'I don't know what I'm doing. Elodie would. And Wren. But I...'

The Aurum might be blazing inside him constantly, just like the holy flame in the Sacrum, but it shouldn't be. In battle it had felt like music, sweeping over him and through him in a wave he couldn't control. He was lost in it and his body fought with a will of its own, with a fury he had never possessed. He had never felt so much like a Paladin, consumed in the power of the light, so powerful and yet so helpless at the same time.

The Aurum would destroy him. And he would let it. Gladly.

A sound in the trees brought the two of them to alertness in an instant. Finn nodded to Olivier, who rose slowly and backed towards Roland, intent on defending him.

'What happened to him?' a young voice said from the depths of the foliage.

'Robin?' Olivier gasped and Finn recalled the two witchkind children who Roland had said brought them to the College of Winter.

'And me,' Lark chimed in, pushing her way out into the open without a trace of fear. 'You have need of us. This is a right mess.'

'Shh, Lark.' Robin came forward to join her. 'Don't make them feel bad. They can't help it. They don't know anything.' Lark shrugged, and scurried over to Roland to get a better look at him. She sucked on her lower lip and Finn was reminded of a weaponsmaster looking at damaged equipment.

'Can you help him?' he asked. They were witchkind, and perhaps something more than human, and Anselm had thought they were powerful indeed.

They both looked at him in unison as if he had grown an extra head. 'We aren't healers. Why didn't you get him to do it?' They both nodded at Olivier with a frightening synchronicity.

'Me?' Olivier said, his face pale. He took a step back. He

had always been jumpy about magic – all the Arrendens were – but the past weeks had made him even worse.

'Well that's what you do, isn't it?' Robin said.

Olivier's face took on a mulish expression. 'I'm a knight.'

Lark wrinkled her nose. 'Well you shouldn't be. You had a gift – a gift of old magic no less – from the moment you were born. Why would you want to go giving that up for? To be a knight?'

She said 'knight' the way someone else might say 'pig herder'.

Finn frowned, finally understanding. 'You were a healer?'

'No,' Olivier insisted. 'I was a *boy*. I wanted to be a knight anyway, and you can't use magic and do that, can you? My family said it was for the best. We serve the Aurum.'

'Well that's just stupid,' Robin sneered. The two of them were really not helping matters. Finn had barely believed Roland's tales about them, but now he was rapidly reassessing. 'I wouldn't want to be anything that badly. Especially not a *knight*.'

Finn needed to get a hold on this situation quickly. The scorn in the boy's voice stung more than he would like to say. Olivier had been born a healer, into a devout family, and he had given up the magic that made him so because that was what was expected of him. 'There's a law. It wasn't his choice.'

'There's always a choice. He could've run away. Joined us. Rebel witchkind live free or die.'

Olivier let out a low growl of a breath. 'And awful lot of them just *die*, you know?'

The two children – and for all their worldliness and precocious ways, they were just children – returned blank stares of hostility. Something else seemed to pass between them and suddenly Finn wondered just how young they were. And just *what* they were.

Finn took Olivier's arm, pulling him to one side and lowering his voice. 'Can you heal? Do you know what to do?'

'It was fifteen years ago, Finn. I barely remember what I could do. I tried very hard to forget, in fact. And until recently I didn't have the power in me anymore. Whatever happened at the College of Winter... whatever they said about it... I gave magic up to the Aurum when I vowed to serve. I—'

There wasn't time for this. 'And if the Aurum could give that back?' Finn asked. Olivier's mouth opened but for a moment he seemed to have lost the ability to form words. 'We need Roland, Olivier. He's the Grandmaster. If there's even a chance...'

Olivier glanced at the two witchkind children again, then at Roland, and finally dragged his gaze back to Finn. 'Maybe? But —' He swallowed hard, his expression troubled. 'If it's even possible, if it even works... What will that make me, Finn?'

Finn pulled him into a hug because he knew that feeling of being lost and so far out of his depth. But what else could they do?

'You'll still be Olivier, and you'll still serve the Aurum. You're still a knight. You always will be. The laws—'

'The *stupid* laws,' Lark corrected him, like some kind of exasperated teacher.

Finn almost laughed. If the situation wasn't so dire he might have. If he wasn't asking Olivier to give up everything he ever believed to be right... 'The laws are old, and to be honest, I think they've gone beyond their time. If any of us survive this, I'm not sure people are going to care. Right now, Ilanthus has Pelias and Leander has Wren. It may not matter anymore. But we swore to obey Roland, didn't we? To serve him? And to risk our lives for him?'

'Is that what I'm doing? Risking my life?'

Finn shrugged. 'Maybe?'

Olivier sighed and shook his head wearily. 'You and Anselm

were always his brightest students. I just struggled after you. I always knew that. And I always knew you'd lead me astray too. Now look where we are.'

'The last free knights,' said Robin, his voice strangely resonant. There was a glow in his eyes that was all too familiar. Finn felt an answering pulse in his chest and he stared. That felt like a title being bestowed on them by something ancient and wise. 'The old magic reaches out. Even the Aurum realises the danger we all face. The Nox has all but lost itself and it will take its creature with it.'

'Wren? You're talking about Wren? She isn't a creature.'

'The lost queen of Ilanthus... If she is crowned in Pelias...' His eyes seemed to roll up in his head and that weird resonance grew stronger. 'When she is lost enough in her power, and her will is almost gone, she will wear the crown and the Nox and Aurum will battle to destruction. The magic in the land will tear itself asunder. The lines which feed our lives, light our way and cool us in the shadows will be broken. Chaos will devour us. Magic will be no more.'

He swayed back and Lark caught him before he could fall. Witchkind indeed, both of them.

'He sees things that will happen,' she informed the knights solemnly. 'It may not be clear but it's always right.'

A seer, Finn thought. Dear light, what would the maidens make of a seer like that?

Nothing, because Robin was a boy. They'd make him give up his magic and send him on his way. It could have been worse. In Ilanthus they would have killed him in honour of the Nox. How had it all become so wildly twisted and wrong? How did anyone even start to go about setting it right?

He tried to focus again. 'They're going to crown Wren in the Sacrum with that Ilanthian crown and break magic apart, that's what you mean? Perhaps they think it will release the old magic, perhaps they just want it all gone. But who is doing this? Oriole in Sidonia said she had sisters.'

'Alouette in the College of Winter said the same thing,' said Olivier.

'So they have someone in Pelias as well. Another sister. Someone who persuaded the council to give the city up to Ilanthus. But who would do that? Not Lady Ylena, surely? Who else would have the power?'

'If Leander already had Wren, that might have been all the leverage he needed,' Olivier reminded him. 'But the knights, Finn, our brothers-in-arms... what happened to them? You're right. We need Roland. Our people will follow him in Elodie's name and he may be the last chance we have.' He drew in a deep breath and then his eyes widened as Lark took his hand and squeezed it in her own. Olivier seemed to shiver for a moment and then cast her a reluctant smile. 'All right. I'll do it.'

CHAPTER 40

WREN

Metal pressed against her throat, cold and sharp. It bound her wrists as well. Shadow-wrought steel. Wren knew that without looking. She could feel it, seeping through her, dragging her will and her magic from her. It was worse than the bracelet. So much worse.

But that wasn't the most terrible part of it.

Her shoulder burned as if acid was dripping down onto her from on high, creeping through her veins. Her skin felt hot and tight and when she moved, a spear of pain shot through her.

The shadow kin had subdued her and taken her somewhere, far from the forest, but she didn't know where.

The room was dark, and cold. So cold. It ate into her bones and left her shivering.

Wren tried to breathe calmly, tried to still her racing heart and focus on where she was and what she knew.

But it was dark and everything hurt and in the back of her mind all she could hear was the Nox howling.

It was over. It was all over. She had lost.

She felt another great spasm of pain tear through her exhausted body as the poison of the shadow kin took another bite from her soul. If they couldn't make her into the Nox will-ingly, they would do it this way, with poison and malice.

A gentle hand fell on her forehead, soothing and caring, like Elodie's hand long ago when she'd fallen sick with a fever or hurt herself in some way. Wren couldn't even open her eyes properly or focus on the figure beside her. It didn't matter. Hot tears leaked from her eyes, burning and blinding.

'Hush, my dear girl,' her attendant murmured. She knew that voice. Remembered it. Somehow. But the world was twisting and unsafe and she couldn't let herself go back to it. Here in the darkness she could still fight. If she concentrated hard enough she could cling to some last part of herself.

Couldn't she?

'It will be over soon, child. Just let go. Then it will all stop.'

No. Never. She couldn't let that happen. The Nox was rabid with need and hunger, ready to be unleashed on the world again and she couldn't let that happen. She dug in with the tattered remains of her own sanity to keep it on the other side of reality. She had to.

Oh but it hurt. Everything hurt.

She just wanted to give up. To sleep. To make it all go away.

'Wren,' the woman's voice, so familiar, so soothing, so calm. 'Wren, my love, let go.'

Somewhere a door banged open and Wren felt it rever-berate through her whole body. She jerked against the sound and tried to fight even harder.

'What's taking so long?'

Leander's voice. Sharp and needy, bitter. Light, she despised him.

'She's strong,' the woman replied, with not a little pride in her voice. 'But she can't fight it forever. The shadow kin poison in her and the bindings will wear her down.'

'I need my queen at my side. You promised you could do it.'

'And I will, your majesty. You have the crown and you will

have your queen. When you face the Aurum together, everything will be as you wish. Just a little longer. She is still too
strong. She will fight it.'

'Don't fail me like Oriole did. Whatever sad little ritual you
need to perform needs to happen soon. We can't hold this
wretched city for long without her. Your council may be abject
cowards but there are others with more fight in them. We need
to stamp out their hope and she's the key. I have the crown. I
just need the head to put it on. Make her cooperate. He's almost
here.'

And then he was gone again. He didn't even bother to
address Wren directly. She didn't matter anymore. She was just
a piece in a game, a queen, but queens were only there to be
used in service of a king.

I have the crown...

But Laurence had the crown, Wren thought with a sob.
What had happened back there? How long had it been? She'd
seen Roland fall but Finn had been there, Finn like a blazing
fire in human form, so unbearably beautiful to look on that it
made her heart break to see what she had made of him. But at
least he had been there. He would save Roland, wouldn't he?
He had to.

Laurence was just a boy, thrust into an impossible quest. He
wouldn't have stood a chance in a shadow kin attack, or an
ambush. With the knights distracted, shadow kin could have
taken him and the crown as easily as they took her.

She'd got this all so wrong.

The woman tending her lifted a goblet to Wren's parched
lips. 'There now, take a drink, my dear. You need to stop fighting. It's too late anyway. This will help. Just drink deeply and
forget, Wren. Become the queen you were always meant to be
and it will all be over soon.' She leaned in closer, her whisper
turning conspiratorial, the whisper of a friend, one she desperately needed to hear. But the words were no comfort. 'Once

you're crowned, we'll teach them all. Especially that upstart king. You and I, my dear, we will make him beg forgiveness.'

The liquid burned like molten metal down her throat and Wren swallowed reflexively before she even realised what she was doing.

Too late, the world started sliding into darkness again, a darkness which rose like a tide around her, and this time she couldn't fight it. She had no strength left.

And now we come to the end of it, said the Nox, its voice like a breeze, blowing away the cobwebs of hesitation and doubt in her mind. *Those who would make us slaves will learn. Once we are crowned, we will teach them all. We will show them the queen they forsook, the goddess they trapped, and then they will pay.*

Wren tried to hold on, tried to burrow down deep inside herself to hide, but the darkness followed her and found her there.

Finn would come for her, she tried to tell herself. He would always come. Her Finn, her love, he would rescue her. He would come.

She didn't know if she said it out loud or just screamed it in the depths of her own failing consciousness. It didn't seem to matter.

'Of course he will,' said Lynette.

Lynette? How was Lynette here? And what was she doing?

Wren's eyes snapped open to look into the face of the woman caring for her, the woman who had always been there from the moment she had been taken to Knightsford, who had tried to take Elodie's place in her life.

'Shh,' Lynette cooed. 'All will be well. It's the only way, Wren. Just a little longer, my love, and you'll free us all.'

Was this some kind of trick? Some kind of ruse to stop Leander? It had to be. Lynette was her friend. She'd always been on Wren's side.

'Lynette? What's happening? What are you doing?' The words wouldn't form properly. Her lips felt parched and swollen at the same time. Her throat closed as she tried to speak. Her body was no longer her own. Whether she succumbed to the potion or the poison or something else entirely, something inevitable that had just been waiting all this time, she couldn't fight any more.

Instead, she felt the Nox fill her, pushing her back into that tiny knot of a place deep inside her, into the darkness and the cold where she could do nothing at all.

'Don't fight,' Lynette urged her, lifting Wren's fingers to her lips and kissing them. 'Let go. It has to be this way. For witchkind. You'll understand soon enough. You can do this, Wren. I believe in you. Trust me.'

HERANDAL'S THE FALL OF
THE HOUSE OF SIDON

There are conflicting reports of the fall of Pelias to this day. In some, the knights were taken unawares. In others the regents' council ordered the gates to be opened. Yvain of Goalais, sometimes named traitor and sometimes named the Scapegoat, is often blamed for the failure of the knights to defend the city. Whatever happened on that fateful day, one thing is clear, Pelias was betrayed from within, at the highest level. The city guard could not defend against such a force and hundreds died in the attempt.

It should have been King Leander's moment of triumph.

CHAPTER 41

FINN

Finn was keenly aware that Robin and Lark were still watching them like a pair of wild animals sensing danger. He couldn't tell if they were afraid or all too eager. The forest seemed to stir around them and when Robin hissed at his sister to stop, it stilled again. A seer and a witch who could affect the natural world, running wild and unschooled... that was what had come of rejecting witchkind. The short-sightedness of it rankled.

And they were powerful. He'd never seen witchkind this powerful. Apart from Wren.

If he survived this – if any of them survived this – things would have to change. But that was for another day. It would have to be.

A more realistic part of his mind told him that the chances of surviving were perilously small anyway. But he fixed his mind on Wren, on finding her again, on bringing her back to herself, whole and unharmed. Anything else was a bonus.

He was no longer expecting anything more. Once he'd dreamed of a future with her. Now... now he just wanted her to live. To still be his Wren and not some kind of avatar of a dark goddess.

He pushed those thoughts aside as well. He didn't have time for them, not now.

'Roland first,' he said firmly. One step at a time. That was the only way to get over insurmountable odds. Roland de Silvius had taught him that.

'I don't know what to do,' Olivier confessed. 'When I was a boy I would just...' He rubbed his hands together and stretched them out. Light flared under his skin and he stared at it as it rippled and moved like reflections of water. 'Like... like that, I suppose.'

Robin was grinning, almost gleeful. He had that ageless look again, as if something else was peering out from behind his eyes. 'It's because the Aurum is here. In him. Help him, Prince Finnian.'

Olivier knelt down by Roland's feverish body and carefully peeled back the tunic where they had bandaged the shadow kin wounds. Dark lines spread out from the worst of them, across his sweat-streaked skin, and the Grandmaster shifted uncomfortably, muttering something they didn't understand.

Olivier sighed, and raised his eyes to the sky as if in prayer. Then he pressed his hands to Roland's skin. For a moment nothing happened but then, inch by slow and torturous inch, the lines of poison started to retract.

'He needs your strength, chosen knight,' Robin told Finn. Lark shuffled forward, peering at Olivier as if to get a better view. 'You need to give him back the magic the Aurum took. Now.'

Well, he was already in this up to his neck...

Finn moved carefully, reaching out to lay his hands on Olivier's head as the Grandmaster and one of the maidens had when taking their vows so long ago. But this time he wasn't taking anything away. He focused on Olivier, on his kindness, his diligence, his devotion. If anyone deserved such magical power, it was someone like him.

Blessed, he thought absently. Olivier was blessed. And loved. So very loved.

He thought of Anselm and half-smiled.

The rush of light took all of them by surprise. Olivier cried out in shock and joy, his back arching as he threw back his head. Light burst from his pores, golden and brilliant. For a moment he shook as if struck by lightning but then he drew in a deep breath and bent his will to the stricken man lying before him.

Because duty had always come first. And always would.

The Aurum sang in Finn's veins, filling his mind with its triumph. It chose this. Chose Olivier as a servant. Chose Finn as its embodiment. Chose Roland as Grandmaster. Chose to be here for this fight.

It was, Finn realised, in its own focused way, just as insane as the Nox seemed to be. Uncontrollable. Wild. Dangerous.

Olivier gave a sob and Finn snatched his hands back, cutting off the flood of power.

'What are you—? Olivier?' It was Anselm's voice, desperate with shock and fear. 'What did you do to him?'

He ran towards them, sword out, though whether he meant to turn it on Finn was anyone's guess.

And if he did, Finn knew, the Aurum would defend him. Even against his beloved friend. It would turn Anselm to ashes if he so much as...

No, Finn told it. The force within him pulled back sullenly, but was still ready to attack.

Just as dangerous. Just as mad. Great light and shadows of old... they were all playing with a fire that couldn't really be controlled. He realised that now. Perhaps he had always recognised it.

This was what he had wanted for so long. To be a Paladin. To serve the Aurum. To have its light fill him and serve its will.

And now... now he knew the real danger. He had been blind. A fool.

'Olivier, what did you do?' Anselm gasped as he reached them and pulled Olivier to his feet, studying his face, concern making his feelings evident. 'Are you all right? Tell me you're all right?' Olivier looked like he'd taken a blow to the head. He swayed where he stood, trying to speak but failing. Slowly, he smiled, as youthful a smile as Finn had ever seen on his face, filled with relief and joy.

Then Roland moved, blinking as if waking up from a nightmare.

'Knights,' he said in that low, gravelly rumble. 'Report.'

They were too well trained to disobey a direct order from the Grandmaster. Roland listened calmly as they told him about Wren's capture, about finding Laurence and the crown gone and about his injury. He remembered the two witchkind children and took the news of their help calmly enough. The argument of 'They're just children' was never said aloud. Roland didn't seem even faintly surprised at Robin's prediction, but nodded slowly and his frown deepened. He eyed the two of them carefully, but didn't shoo them away as they nestled in against him.

Olivier made his report like a confession and it was Roland who absolved him. Perhaps the only one he would ever accept it from.

'You did what you had to,' the Grandmaster said. 'It's all an act of service, Olivier. The Aurum wouldn't have allowed it otherwise.'

Inside Finn, he felt the Aurum purr in agreement but he didn't want to share that. It felt far too strange.

'But what am I now?'

'You?' Roland gave one of his rare smiles. It was bleak and brief, but it was a smile. 'I don't believe you've broken your vows. You are a Knight of the Aurum, and the queen would agree. We'll ask her, when we free her. Let her decide.'

Then he turned his attention to Anselm who reported that Pelias had surrendered, that the knights had been ordered to stand down by the regents' council and the Grandmaster.

'Yvain?' Roland said, and Anselm nodded solemnly. 'Why would he do such a thing?'

'I don't know. Leander had Wren, I suppose. It's the only reason I can think of but it doesn't make sense. He won't kill her. He can't. He needs her as the Nox. And he wants her as his queen. He always has done. Yvain would surely know that.'

The thought of that sent a chill of alarm through Finn. He had failed her again, hadn't he?

'Where are the knights?' he asked.

'In the prisons beneath the mountain with half the city guard. The rest are... there were some who fought back of course. He had one in ten put to the sword and... well, that stopped any more thoughts of resistance for now, I suppose. He plans to marry Wren and rule both kingdoms. She has apparently consented. No one appears to have seen her though. Or the queen.'

'Then we need to get into the palace first,' Roland said firmly. 'Finn, you're with me. Anselm and Olivier, you'll rouse the knights, set them free and get that resistance back into force. And you two?' He addressed Robin and Lark who tilted their heads to listen in that unnerving way of theirs. 'I need you to take word to the witchkind. To anyone who will listen. Bring help. Can you do that?'

Robin grinned.

'That,' said Lark as if speaking to an idiot, 'is why we're here in the first place.'

CHAPTER 42

ROLAND

What had happened to Yvain? He would never have surrendered the city, surely? Roland had trusted his old friend in that one thing above all else, his loyalty to the Aurum, to their duty, their people. But Pelias had been given over to Leander...

Roland couldn't focus on the shock of the news which was only part of what was making his head swim. He still felt as if only part of him belonged in the world, as if he had been dragged back by the scruff of his neck. Olivier looked wrung out, and these newfound powers didn't seem to have done him any favours. And yet, he was aglow from within, as if something which had been integral to him had not just been restored but amplified. The thought that for all these years knights had been forced to give up something so vital in service of the Aurum, despite the strategic advantage it might have given them, made no sense at all. Roland didn't know why, that was the worst thing. He was supposed to be the Grandmaster of the Knights of the Aurum and even he didn't know.

The change in Finn was no more comforting. The Aurum filled him like a Paladin under an Aurum-raised beacon all the time. It glowed beneath his skin, illuminating him like a lantern, bright and beautiful.

With nightfall, they armoured themselves – Finn wearing that black armour once more despite the light now coursing through him – and followed Anselm through the secret ways of House Tarryn into the city. Roland had always known that the Tarryn family had their own paths they could use, that they had ruled the lower city for generations and made it their own. Now, he realised it had gone much further than anyone had known. It was only a grace that until Anselm's father they had been loyal to the crown and that Anselm had rejected such treachery.

Anger simmered beneath Anselm's skin like the light beneath Olivier's. Roland supposed that he was the Earl of Sassone now, but no one had said it out loud except for Alouette and that had been a taunt. Sassone had betrayed them all and no one would want to take on that title, especially not now. Roland would have to watch Anselm, he realised. The young knight still wanted to prove himself loyal and that could drive him to anything.

But as Earl of Sassone, he was bound to defend Pelias. And Pelias, his city, was devastated.

His concern for Olivier's transformation was only part of it.

As they moved to part ways, Roland held his shoulders and fixed him with a stern look. 'Nothing stupid, Anselm. Find the knights, and free them. We will need every man we can get.'

Anselm frowned but then nodded slowly. 'Yes, Grandmaster.'

He really ought to correct him. That wasn't his title, not anymore.

He wasn't sure what he was now. But his people needed him. And so did Elodie and Wren.

'Finn?' he prompted as the other two left. 'We're heading for the palace. Are you going to be—' He wasn't sure what he was asking. All right? Himself? Able to control the Aurum inside him? Perhaps all of it. His brother was in Sacrum and surely the need to revenge himself on Leander was powerful. And the magic in his body would want to attack the Nox. When the Aurum descended on the knights in battle, Roland knew there was no control available, barely any conscious thought. It was the need for battle, the desire to destroy their enemies. The Aurum was all.

It had brought them all to their knees when Elodie last wielded it, and when she lost control of it he had thought they would burn.

And Finn had not been raised as its chosen. The Aurum had picked him because of Wren. And it might destroy him just to get to her, especially if Wren had lost her battle with the Nox.

'We must find the queen and Wren,' said Finn solemnly. 'Get them to safety. Everything else is secondary. I know my duty, Roland. My brother can wait.'

Roland only hoped that the Aurum agreed.

❧

The lower city was eerily quiet, far worse than when Sassone had kidnapped Elodie and the knights had ridden to her rescue. Now there was no sign of anyone, and nothing moved. If there was still anyone hiding here, they were hiding well and not planning on stirring abroad if they could help it. The city gates had been shattered. Houses along the main road were little more than blackened ruins now. But there was a sense of being watched as they passed, even while making their way to the palace along secret ways. While Olivier and Anselm headed for the prisons where Anselm had learned the knights were being kept, Roland and Finn found themselves alone in the square where the palace deliveries were normally inspected.

There were bodies scattered everywhere. Roland stopped, taking in the scene, assessing it with caution. Some were his knights, some city guards, but far more of them were civilians. Mostly men, but a number of women as well. Far too many. Makeshift weapons lay scattered about, alongside swords, axes and pikes. They had tried to defend their homes.

'How long ago?' Finn asked, his voice unexpectedly shaken.

'Four or five days, perhaps. Not long after we left the College.'

'And no one moved the bodies? No one came for their dead?' He sounded startled, and it made Roland wonder again who he was talking to. Finn knew things like this happened in war. He knew the methods the Ilanthians used, but perhaps the Aurum did not. It was all about the glory of battle. The aftermath... it had nothing to do with that, did it? So how much of the man with him was still Finnian Ward?

Roland winced. 'It's a message to everyone else. And trying to take the bodies would just mean more death. Come, we can't do anything else here.'

Elodie and Wren. They were all that mattered right now. Without the two of them, Leander had no leverage here. That was what the logical part of his brain was saying anyway.

They accessed the narrow passageway which led them through the cellars and up towards the kitchens, encountering no one on the way. The echoing silence continued, the people scarce. There were no servants and no guards and everything felt wrong.

So very wrong.

Pelias had never been this quiet. It grated on his every nerve.

It didn't last and when they heard the approaching patrol it was almost a relief. Swords in hand, they waited.

The Ilanthians were laughing about something that had

happened with a servant, their tone cruel and mocking. Roland steeled himself.

'Should have just let us have their bitch queen,' the first one scoffed. 'But they had to be all noble. Not so noble now, are they?'

'Maybe, but the king said no. Everyone else is fair game but not her. Said he owes her.'

That produced a filthy-sounding chuckle. 'Oh really? Owes her what?'

Roland glanced at Finn, whose eyes were blazing again, his mouth the same hard line as Roland's. He nodded.

Everything became a blur of movement as the Aurum roared through Roland's veins. With Finn so close, opening himself to its power was effortless. Not that the Ilanthians would have stood a chance anyway. They were just grunts really, half drunk on the power of conquest and stupid with it. Roland grabbed the leader by the throat and slammed him back against the wall, while Finn took care of the rest. He moved like a dancer, his sword a line of light. Moments later, six bodies lay sprawled on the floor of the corridor.

And when they were all dead, Finn still moved, looking for someone else to fight, someone else to kill. He lunged towards the last Ilanthian who shrank back from him in horror, almost ready to hide behind Roland.

'Your highness! Prince Finnian!'

Finn froze, staring at the man, his expression a hostile mask.

'Stand down, Finn,' Roland barked, and training won out, for which there were not enough prayers of thanks in the world.

'What... what happened to him?' the guard stammered.

Roland lifted his eyebrow. 'You invaded his home.'

'But he... he's one of us.'

'I'm really not. I never was,' Finn snarled. 'You all made sure of that.'

Roland turned on their prisoner. 'Where are they keeping the queen?'

CHAPTER 43
ELODIE

The door remained firmly locked. Once upon a time she and Maryn could have made short work of that. Light, they could have just blasted their way through the door itself. Or the wall. But the power that had once come to them so easily was no more than a flicker now. It felt like being left hollow and empty. Broken.

Elodie worked on the bracelet on Maryn's arm, trying to open it every way she knew how, but the Aurum would not answer her now. She tried to force it, cajole it, even threaten it. Until finally, in desperation, she spat out a hedge witch charm of opening and the wretched thing twisted open as if made of straw. Elodie stared at it for the longest time, unsure of what to make of that.

Worse still, it didn't help Maryn. Oh, at first she was relieved but the moment she reached for the light that had always been part of her, nothing answered and she sank back onto her chair, devastated.

'What are we going to do?' Maryn asked. And, in truth, Elodie didn't have an answer.

They had spent enough time pretending she was still asleep

now. It had not gained them anything. No one had come save a few guards and they didn't linger. No one seemed in any way interested in them. Perhaps Leander was planning to leave Elodie to die in here after all. Perhaps he'd wall the two of them up, let thirst and starvation take them and that would be that.

The kings of Ilanthus had done far more savage things to their prisoners in the past.

Enough. She was done waiting. The element of surprise was all very well, but not if there was no one to surprise.

Elodie made herself push that thought aside as she dressed herself as a queen should dress, and Maryn helped her prepare as if for a battle.

Which it was. And this was a kind of armour as well.

She was Queen Aeryn of Asteroth and this was still her kingdom. She had not allowed Evander of Ilanthus to take it from her and she was certainly not going to allow his nephew to do it instead.

The rest of the maidens had been confined to the Sanctum, guarded by Leander's personal troops. He had promised that if anyone interfered, they would be the next to be slaughtered. No one doubted it. Elodie took Maryn's hands in her own.

'Your majesty,' said the maiden, and curtsied. For the first time, Elodie felt that title rest on her shoulders as if it actually belonged there. She had run so far and so fast from this responsibility in order to protect Wren but now... now the only way to do that was to embrace it.

So she made Maryn tell the guard that the queen had awoken. And then they waited.

The door unlocked and Elodie turned to face this new threat, head held high and glare ready to destroy whoever crossed her.

But it was just Lynette.

The lady-in-waiting stared at them for a stunned moment, her eyes wide as they fell on Elodie.

'El—' Maryn began, in a tone of warning.

Lynette threw up a hand and a blast of wind ripped through the room, hurling Maryn back against the wall. It buffeted against Elodie as well but she held her ground, the assault not directed at her.

'You said you'd keep her quiet, Maryn,' Lynette said. 'Keep her asleep. That was our arrangement. That she could stay alive as long as she stayed out of it all. She's witchkind in the end, you said, more hedge witch than queen. You promised you'd handle it. It seems like you couldn't even manage that.'

'Lynette, don't hurt her,' Maryn gasped. 'Please...'

So Maryn had known. And Maryn had cooperated...

The surge of betrayal and anger was pointless. Elodie swallowed it down. Her explanations and pointless reasons could wait.

'Lynette, what do you think you're doing?' Elodie used the calmest, steadiest tones she could manage. Inside, her heart raced and her stomach churned in shock and betrayal but she couldn't let that show. Whatever deal Maryn had made, it had been to save her life. But it still hurt that her cousin hadn't seen fit to warn her that Lynette of all people was involved in all this.

This wasn't about Lynette, or Maryn, but Leander. He was the enemy here. Whatever the women had needed to do in order to survive, to protect her, Elodie hoped it had been worth it.

But where had Lynette come by that magic? Not from him, surely?

'I didn't want to hurt you, your majesty.' Lynette said the title with complete disdain. 'You were never meant to wake up and so you would have kept the Aurum trapped and helpless. King Leander agreed to that, because you saved his life. He doesn't want to hurt you. But you being awake changes everything.'

'Except the Aurum didn't stay with me.' There was no point in pretending. If she knew magic, she'd sense it.

The breeze moving around them both intensified, but still Elodie held firm. It seemed that Lynette's abilities weren't having the effect she expected. Or at least not on Elodie. 'Then where is it?'

'Why? So you can try and trap it again? Why would you want to do that?'

'I don't want to trap it. I want to destroy it.'

'In service to the Nox?'

'The Nox? No. I want them both broken. They have enslaved us all for too long. I'm letting the old magic free again, Elodie. My sisters may be dead, but I will finish our work. I promised. We all did.'

'You're witchkind?' Elodie had never known that. She suspected no one did until it was far too late.

'Yes, I'm witchkind.'

Several things slotted into place now. Who else would have had unfettered access to Wren's poor maid, Carlotta, to weave that puppeting spell around her?

'And... Carlotta? Did you do that to her? Lynette?'

'I had to. You don't understand. You're so entrenched in the duality of Aurum and Nox, Elodie.'

'You tried to kill Leander and now you're siding with him?'

Lynette threw her head back and gave a guttural cry of frustration. 'This isn't about him. Great powers of old, he's loathsome. He's a spoilt child who thinks everything is his due. But he's a means to an end.'

'I don't understand.' She had to keep the woman talking. She had to work out what was happening and find some way to reach her. But Elodie could already sense the fragile threads of control on Lynette's sanity slipping. She was drenched in old magic and it had a way of unravelling the minds of those who suppressed it for too long.

'Of course you don't. You don't understand any of it. I thought you might. You were a hedge witch. You lived in Cellandre and I hoped, when you came back here, you and Wren... I hoped... you could set us free.'

Elodie shook her head. 'Set... set who free?'

'Witchkind. All of us. But no. You just settled back into being queen and Chosen, letting the Aurum consume you. I had to act. My sisters failed but I will not.' Lynette drew herself up to her full height, a wild and dangerous light in her eyes. 'I will break both Nox and Aurum, and restore the old magic, and witchkind will be free again. The College of Winter will be ours and the Maidens of the Aurum and the Sisterhood of the Nox will bend their knees. Without the magic they have syphoned away from our world, the wild and natural power innate in witchkind twisted to serve them, they'll have no choice. This is how it was always meant to be. But you and your line seized magic and made it the preserve of a few. You sought to control it through channels of light and dark alone. But there is so much more.'

'What more? What are you talking about?' Oh but Elodie feared that she knew.

'Old magic! The oldest! Promised to us all!' She screamed the words, and a wild light of madness entered her eyes. The demure and polished woman was hardly discernible any more. How long had Lynette been hiding, waiting, manoeuvring herself into the right position? Not to mention the effects of old magic on those who used it unwisely and without guidance from its guardians...

A broad figure filled the doorway behind her. Yvain. 'Lynette?' he said. 'My love? I heard raised voices.'

Lynette flinched and Elodie could see the shame, the regret, the guilt.

'Oh Lynette,' Elodie gasped, realising the full horror of it. 'Lynette, what have you done to him?'

The knight had a blank look to his face, and a grim cast about him. Another spell was tangled around him. Elodie could almost see it now, like threads cutting into his skin. Not just one spell. Layers and layers of them, a lifetime of enchantments. Dear light, what had she done?

'All is well, my love. Wait outside. I'll be with you in moments.' Lynette's voice shook far too much for that to be convincing but Yvain didn't seem concerned.

'Of course,' he murmured as if lost in a dream. 'But the king sent word. He has need of the princess. The Ilanthian guards are here to take her to the Sacrum.'

Wren. Leander had Wren or soon would.

'Just a moment, love,' Lynette said, her eyes fixed on Elodie, reading the horror there. 'I will deal with him. First, I need to help the queen go back to sleep. She needs her rest.'

She raised her hand, magic swirling around it like an oil slick. Not the crisp feeling of the light of the Aurum or the dark embrace of the Nox's shadows. This was almost as out of control as the woman wielding it. Old magic, Elodie realised, wrenched from the air itself and twisted into something sickening, reflecting the mind that tried to control it. Elodie had woven old magic in the forest and since, in fragments. It had been fresh and clear and made her think of misty mornings or a sea breeze. It had never felt like this to her.

Old magic was all around them, as it had been in Cellandre, in the air and in the stones, in the water, in each of them. Where once it had slept, now it was awake but in Lynette's hands it was twisted with hatred.

'Don't do this, Lynette,' she warned. Although what she could do to stop her, Elodie had no idea. But there had to be something. Anything. She couldn't match Lynette force for force.

'Why not, your majesty? You don't have access to the Aurum anymore, neither of you. And that's all you've ever—'

Except it wasn't. She was more than just the Chosen of the Aurum. And as Lynette said, she had been a hedge witch. Perhaps she still was.

Elodie worked her fingers in the dance of an old hedge witch charm of protection, her muscles remembering the movements better than her mind. She wrapped it in othertongue and released it like a stone from a sling.

The force slammed into Lynette's face, knocking her head back as if punched. She slid to the ground at Yvain's feet.

Snarling, she wiped her bloody nose and clawed her way up his leg. Elodie began to spin another defence, waiting for Lynette to turn that magic on her.

'Yvain, kill them both,' she commanded instead.

And Yvain of Goalais, poor, faithful, loyal Yvain, the perfect husband and perfect knight, shuddered, all emotion wiping from his features as he stepped forward, sword raised, a living, moving and deadly statue.

CHAPTER 44
ELODIE

Maryn tried to put herself between Elodie and the blow as Yvain bore down on them. Elodie twisted to one side and grabbed the goblet of water. There was old magic everywhere. She couldn't just seize it as Lynette did. She needed its cooperation.

'Help me now,' she prayed to the water and the air and the stones, to the trees and the flowers, to the clouds above. 'If ever we were friends. We had a bargain once for Wren's safety and I need to save her now. Help me.'

She whispered into it, creating another charm until the water steamed and boiled. Without hesitation she flung it at the knight who reeled back for a moment and then, skin blistering, started forward again as if it hadn't hurt him at all.

It wasn't that it didn't do him harm. It was that he couldn't feel it. He couldn't feel anything. What had Lynette done?

Hedge witch magic could only do so much but it was all Elodie had. She couldn't free Yvain, not from so many enchantments woven over so many years. Maryn couldn't reach the Aurum any more than she could and that was worry enough.

But their danger was much more immediate as Yvain attacked again.

If only she had a sword. That would be something. He was much bigger and stronger than she was, but she was fast and skilled. She could hold him off for a little while, surely. Grabbing the platter from the table, she flung it at him.

Maryn tried to grab his arm and he flung her forward towards Elodie, right into the path of his sword.

Elodie launched herself forward to push Maryn away and her cousin cried out as she fell. It left Elodie entirely exposed and she knew in that moment she'd made her last mistake. He'd kill her. He wouldn't even know he was doing it. Yvain was gone from the eyes that fixed on her.

With a shout, a dark figure dived through the open door, a sword in his hand no more than a blur of light. He moved faster than should have been possible, light suffusing his skin and every movement lethal.

In a moment, he was between them, blocking Yvain's advance.

'Elodie!' Maryn gasped and her hands burst to incandescence as her lost magic wreathed her again. The light of the Aurum blazed through them both and for the first time Elodie saw fear enter Lynette's eyes.

'No, it's not possible!'

But it was. Everything had changed. Elodie felt only a vague echo of the magic she had once channelled but Maryn raised a shield and then turned the full force of her fury on the treacherous witch. She had been putting up with far too much for far too long, trying to keep Elodie safe. She had compromised herself. She had been betrayed and seen her city betrayed. Everything she believed in had been betrayed. Her fury was terrible to behold.

Elodie turned to the knights, hoping against hope that the spell on Yvain could be broken.

The man battling Yvain was pleading with him, begging him to stop, to listen, to stand down. And Elodie knew that voice.

It was impossible but she knew that voice. She would know him anywhere.

But Roland was dead. She had seen him in that in-between place, and known all that meant. How was he here?

And if he was a ghost risen to defend her – she winced as Yvain got in a brutal blow which drove Roland back, almost winding him – he was in an entirely physical form.

But how had the Aurum come with him? It wasn't in him, not more than in any other Paladin. And yet, he was here, her Paladin, her beloved! How?

Finn stepped through the doorway and she had her answer. If Roland glowed with the inner light of a Paladin, the boy was a beacon in human form. Everything in her, everything that she had ever learned and every instinct she had ever had about magic, wanted to drop to her knees before him.

Finn Ward. Finnian of Sidon...

It wasn't possible. He was a man. He wasn't of her lineage. He was Ilanthian.

But none of that seemed to matter anymore. The Aurum had chosen.

'*Hold,*' he said and the whole building trembled with his voice. '*You are my knights. You swore to serve. We fight the Nox with fire and flame, not each other. You made vows to me, and to the queen. So hold. I command it.*'

Both Yvain and Roland seemed to freeze, unable to stand against that command. They had both made vows to that power, after all. It held them to it now. Even Lynette's years of enchantments couldn't counter that.

'No,' Lynette snarled as she dragged herself up. 'He's mine. Not yours. We will be free of you. I will be free.'

She hurled herself at Elodie with curses on her lips. She

threw everything inside her, years of resentment and loathing, all the wild magic she had gathered and allowed to fester inside her, everything.

Roland moved without thinking, ready to sacrifice himself to defend Elodie. And helpless in the face of his own primary vows, bathed in the light of the Aurum, so did Yvain.

Instincts, perhaps, or some final moment of clarity, vows which were woven through their hearts and souls, made them move. They had sworn to serve Pelias as well, to defend the queen, to protect her. There was no withstanding it. Roland was an instant too late and that saved his life. But Yvain thrust himself fully into the path of his wife's magic. It tore through him as if he was no more than tissue paper.

Lynette's cry of rage became a scream of despair. She fell to his side cradling him, dragging him into her arms, but it was too late. She couldn't pull him back from destruction.

He stared up at her, confused still, but then his eyes filled with a terrible clarity as her spells, so many spells, unravelled around him.

'Lynette? What did you do?'

She pressed her hands to the wounds, trying to staunch the blood and stop the flow, trying to save him. But the magic she had gathered wasn't used for healing and the Aurum wouldn't help her.

Not even for Yvain, Elodie realised. It had always been unforgiving, cold and absolute. And now it forsook him as well.

Her breath caught in her throat.

'Don't... please... don't...' Lynette babbled desperately. 'All you had to do was take the sword when he offered it, love. All you had to do was bring me Nightbreaker. It would have been fine. It all would have been... This was never meant to happen... Please, Yvain...'

'Lynette,' the betrayal in his broken voice was almost too great to bear. 'You... you used me... You...'

273

A great sob of pain wracked her body. She pulled him closer but Yvain's eyes turned empty and then he went still. Lynette shook him once more, trying desperately to wake him, then threw back her head and screamed his name.

Roland, breathing hard, pulled Elodie into his arms and held her close. Tears were streaming down his face too. Yvain had been his friend, closer than a brother.

Roland held her, his hands shaking. Her Roland...

'You're alive,' she whispered in amazement, and saw something like a stab of guilt on his face. He was alive. Yvain, his friend, his brother-in-arms, was not. 'Roland... it's not your fault,' she tried to say, but the words wouldn't be enough. They would never be enough.

'I... I didn't know. I failed him.'

'We... we both did. But you're alive, my love. I thought I'd lost you forever.'

His hands tightened around her, pulling her close, and he pressed his forehead to hers as if trying to will her to see the vast ocean of his feelings for her. But she knew them. They were as her own and there was no way to speak of even a fraction of them right now. If the words existed, she couldn't bring them to mind, let alone give them voice. He was alive. That was all that mattered in this instant.

And an instant was all there was.

'Where's Wren?' Finn interrupted, his voice still rippling with the power he shouldn't have.

It was Maryn who answered, her eyes still burning. She bowed her head to him. 'Bright Aurum,' she began. 'We humbly petition—'

'I'm not going to ask again,' he growled and the danger in the situation made Roland stiffen, his arms tightening around Elodie in defence and making every hair on her skin stand up. They were still in danger. All of them. Wren most of all. The Aurum was angry. 'Where is she?'

'She's a prisoner too,' said Elodie as calmly as she could. How much was the Aurum and how much was still Finn? The Aurum wouldn't care about Wren. But it would be looking for the Nox. Only to destroy it and it didn't sound like that was Finn's intention. But that said... everything had changed. 'Leander has her. We don't know more than that but we will find her, Finn.'

Say his name, she thought. Remind him who he really is. And if he can't remember anymore? What then?

'The Sanctum,' Maryn said, her voice still shaking. 'They're going to go to the Sanctum. So he can crown her, remake her and claim both kingdoms.'

CHAPTER 45
ROLAND

Roland couldn't tear his eyes off Yvain. His friend. His brother-in-arms.

Enchanted by his witchkind wife, used and destroyed by her magic. Did he know? Had he guessed what Lynette was doing or what she had planned? Or was he so blinded by love that he had let it all pass him by?

But at the last, he had moved in defence of their queen. Because Yvain had once been the most honourable of them all and he had meant his vows with all his heart. In the final moment, he remembered that. He didn't deserve that end. It was wrong. It was so wrong.

'We have to move,' Elodie said, her voice betraying not a single emotion now. It didn't even tremble. Roland felt her put the horror of it all aside and take control of the situation.

Because she was the queen. And she had to.

'The city needs us. We must find the knights and rally them. We must protect our people. Grandmaster, I need you.'

A queen. A hedge witch. It didn't matter. She was always Elodie and she was always the one in charge.

'I have to find Wren,' said Finn and then he was gone, striding down the corridor and out of sight.

'What happened to him?' Maryn asked. She was not quite so well versed at hiding her shock as his Elodie.

'The Aurum filled him when we were in the College of Winter. I think Wren did it to save him from the power of the Nox but...' Roland sighed and raked one hand through his hair. It was damp with sweat and blood but what was that now?

'Wren did it?'

'Sidonia changed her. She's barely clinging on. She's trying, but – we may be too late already. I don't know what Leander's done to her since he captured her.'

Elodie swore under her breath and made for the door.

'What about her?' Maryn asked, nodding at Lynette, still sobbing over Yvain's body.

Elodie cast the woman a look which was half pity and half disdain. 'Lock her in. I'll deal with her later. Right now I need to find my daughter, before it's too late.'

'Our daughter,' Roland corrected her.

That stopped her in her tracks. She drew in a breath and a wavering smile passed over her lips. Just for a moment. It looked like relief. Then her face became regal once more and she nodded. 'Our daughter. And if Finn finds her first we may still lose her. The Aurum has no care for her at all. I don't know if even his love for her can withstand its power.'

'Elodie, your kingdom, your people... that must come first. You know that.'

She didn't want to hear that. Which was why it had to be Roland to say it to her.

They didn't make it as far as the Sanctum. Up ahead the sound of battle rang off the walls, and Roland took the lead. He was still the Grandmaster of the Knights of the Aurum, and a seasoned warrior. A couple of Ilanthian guards appeared, running headlong towards them without even seeing them until it was too late. He killed one and the other backed up, babbling about surrender and the light knew what.

'The knights got out,' he gasped. 'They're enraged... berserk... I've never seen anything like it. And there are things with them. Witchkind. And... and creatures... Nox defend us, such creatures...'

Good, Roland thought. That had to be good. And punched the guard in the face until he fell down and didn't stir again.

They followed the sounds of fighting, which was not the greatest move instinctively, but there would be greater defence for Elodie in numbers. When he glanced at her he saw that she had relieved the Ilanthian of his sword and held it with a practised hand. Maryn beside her bristled with magic. Having the Aurum back in the palace, even if it had sheathed itself in Finn's skin, was enough for the knights to become true Paladins again and the maidens to regain some semblance of their power. Even now, in the Sanctum, Roland suspected the Ilanthian guards had already learned that it was never wise to anger the Maidens of the Aurum.

The chamber ahead of them was a vast meeting hall, painted and gilded and tiled in marble. Now it was awash with blood.

'Grandmaster de Silvius!' Anselm shouted as he recognised them. 'The queen! Knights of Asteroth, people of Pelias, defend the queen!'

A sea of their people greeted them, patched together and armed hastily with whatever they could lay hands on. But they were Roland's knights, the palace guards and the remnants of the city watch, even the palace servants and several citizens of the lower city. At the sight of Elodie, they seemed to don their former selves. They hadn't surrendered easily, he saw that now.

Yvain might have ordered the knights to stand down, on Lynette's command, no doubt, but they had not gone without a fight. And now they were free to fight again.

And they had something to fight for. They all did.

Anselm and Olivier had found them and freed them, or brought them inside the palace walls, and another surprise was waiting as well, as witchkind took their place in among their ranks. Rebels and scholars and people from the lower city, some of them armed and some weaving frantic enchantments or calling on the elements around them to help.

'The city is safe. They've retreated up here but we can't get to them. The Sacrum is still in Ilanthian hands and we don't know about the Sanctum. They still have the regent, many of our nobles and some of the maidens as hostages and...'

'Have they now?' Maryn growled and suddenly the resemblance between her and her cousin was evident. 'We'll see about that. I need some of your people.'

Two figures joined them, small and slight and so terribly dangerous. Roland knew that as surely as he knew his own name.

Robin and Lark looked entirely innocent as they pushed their way through the force of fighters, but old magic coiled about them, stronger than ever, like leashed beasts ready to attack again.

'You came,' Roland said. 'My thanks.'

Lark smiled and four crows with bloodstained beaks and claws came to rest on her shoulders. 'We wouldn't have missed it for the world. Hedge witch,' she greeted Elodie with a tilt of her head. 'It is good to finally see you again.'

'Elodie,' Roland started to explain. 'They're witchkind children who helped us in—'

Elodie gave a stifled laugh. 'Oh, they aren't children, Roland.' And to his surprise she bowed to them. 'Old ones, my thanks for your aid freely given.'

Robin was grinning. 'We brought help. Roland asked so nicely.'

Roland surveyed the scene. There were vines climbing up the marble walls, and animals of all shapes and sizes. And other things, things he didn't have names for. Some had witchkind with them, directing them, some from the College of Winter and those who had lived hidden lives in Pelias, or who had lately found the old magic returning to their lives once more. Other things stalked the edges of the room and the corridors of the palace alone, wild and ungovernable. 'I think you mean you brought chaos.'

The boy shrugged. 'It's how we help. Order is very boring. We gave your people back their courage. And magic, the ones who wanted it. It's fun.' He grinned, showing all his teeth. 'We like you, Roland.'

Somehow that was more terrifying than anything he had ever heard. He glanced at Elodie, surprised to find her suppressing laughter.

'I see that. And he is very likeable, I agree. But now' – her tone sobered abruptly – 'I need to reach my daughter before the Nox takes her.'

'Oh,' said Lark and her gleeful little face fell. 'It might be far too late for that. The powers are meeting as we speak and they will tear each other apart. The old magic, our magic, is growing. It will not be constrained again and if it escapes, it might destroy those who would use it. She is the Nox, your Wren. Or part of it. Both she and the Aurum thrive on control of their own kind. The old magic does not. It will fight back.'

'Please,' Elodie whispered. To everyone's consternation, she dropped to her knees. 'Please help us.'

Lark gave a long-suffering sigh. 'Again? Very well, but we'll want a price.'

'Oh yes.' The gleam in Robin's eyes turned avaricious. 'There will definitely be a price.'

'I'll pay it,' Elodie said without hesitation.

'Are you sure? It could be a life. It could be a life for each of us.'

'Elodie!' Roland gasped, horrified.

'It won't matter if anything happens to Wren anyway. Please, whatever it is, I'll do it. Whatever you want.'

The twins just stared at her with that unwavering unnatural gaze. 'Not just you,' Robin said at last and Lark wrinkled her nose, so like a child it was impossible to say what they truly were. Creatures of magic, powers in their own right.

Roland should have seen it all along. And they wanted him as well. A life. Well, he'd always been prepared for that. But he was damned if he was kneeling.

'We need you,' he said at last. 'And if you need us, we're here. But first, please, help us save Wren and Finn.'

'That may be beyond our power,' Robin told him solemnly. 'I can make no bargain on that. Their fate is their own. And we will still demand our price whatever happens, Roland and Elodie. But we will try.'

CHAPTER 46
WREN

She sat on a throne. Wren was sure that wasn't right and she shouldn't be there, but she couldn't bring herself to move. Her body didn't want to obey her anymore.

The guards who had brought her here had carried her, slung like a sack of vegetables over their shoulders, laughing all the time. Pelias was theirs. They could do what they wanted.

Not to her, of course. Leander would have their heads. But to anyone else. They could treat the servants and the nobles as slaves and no one would care. They were drunk on their easy conquest.

Wren didn't even know how it had happened. Treachery, she understood that much. The knights had been ordered to stand down and then it was too late. They took the palace first, then the Sanctum, then the city. Or so it seemed.

But each time another report came in to Leander, he looked a little less smug.

Pelias, and Asteroth, was fighting back. And he was losing. At least there was that.

Drugged and bound in shadow-wrought steel, and with the power of light far beyond her reach now, there was nothing she could do. But at least she could see that somehow, in some way, he was losing.

She just prayed for the time to see it through.

There is no time left, the Nox whispered. *Give in now. I'll make us strong. It is coming. Perhaps we can survive the storm together.*

Wren clung to that last piece of her will, digging her nails into her palms, and willing herself to hold on.

Even the Nox would not be able to do anything with her body right now. And the knowledge of that was driving it to distraction and eating away its fragile grip on sanity. It was too far from the caves, deep in the realm of the Aurum. And she could feel its fear compelling it now.

'Enough!' Leander snarled, as some unfortunate underling slunk away having delivered some other piece of information. 'Reinforce the approaches. No one gets in. They'll be witness enough. Once she's crowned it won't matter anymore. There'll be nothing they can do.'

The vast cavern of the Sacrum was cold and dark, lit by braziers and candles which had been hauled in here in the absence of the Aurum. Because it really was gone. The hollow in the middle of the stone circle where it had burned was empty except for the throne Leander had ordered moved there. And Wren, of course. Captive, bound, helpless...

Just the way he wanted her.

She ought to be afraid, and some part of her was, desperately afraid. But there was nothing she could do. Not now. And the irony of it, that in its moment of triumph the Nox was as helpless as she was, made it a little easier to bear.

Across from her the remaining members of the regents' council knelt, Leander's witnesses, and hostages, prisoners like her, humbled now. Even Lady Ylena was on her knees, though she still held her head proudly erect and her eyes were fierce. She didn't deign to speak and Wren could see in the way she watched Leander that if she got the chance the old woman would attack him herself. She'd die, of course, but that didn't seem to matter either.

Laurence was there too, broken and exhausted, beaten for sport by Leander for the crime of daring to defy him. He still gazed at Wren as if, at any moment, she would save him, and she hated herself for somehow putting that hope in his eyes. She had no idea what she had done to put it there in the first place. She didn't have any such hope left herself.

They had lost. They had lost everything.

There was a scuffle as some of the Sisterhood of the Nox tried to make the whole thing more of a ritual or a ceremony, beginning a series of overlapping chants which called on the Nox and blessed the crown and the hand which held it.

Leander cursed and snatched the crown from them, marching across the open space to stand in front of Wren. The voices tapered off.

'Finally,' he said. 'Once this is done and we're wed, this whole farce will be over. You will submit to me and serve me. Just as the Nox served my forefathers. You'll see, Wren. We'll be happy. And Ilanthus will be strong. We will be like gods, you and I.'

Wren scowled at him, lifting her chin stubbornly and letting him see the full force of her contempt. She might not be able to move more than that, or speak, or wield any of the magic innate to her, but she would never give in.

We serve no man, the Nox hissed. *You are ours, Blood of Sidon, and we will make you crawl. We will have your blood and nothing else.*

Leander could hear it as clearly as she could. So could some of the others in the chamber. Was it her imagination or did his hands tremble against the black metal of the crown? If they did, he hid it a moment later. Leander heaved in a breath and controlled his fear, or his temper, she wasn't sure which.

She wasn't sure it mattered.

It was a weakness. That was something. It had to be.

'You served once and you will serve again,' Leander went on. 'You were made to be a tool, not a goddess. Crowning you in this place, the stronghold of your enemy where you are weakest, will make you whole. But this crown... this crown that Sidon used to bridle you once, that you hid from us... this will make you my creature and doing it here will hand us Asteroth as well. Both prophecies in one action. You will be my queen and serve me. Accept that. Both of you.'

'Never,' Wren ground out and the Nox joined her in a chorus. Even though saying that couldn't make it so, it still felt good. It was all she had left.

Leander sneered at her. 'I'll tell you to love me, Wren. To worship me. And you will. I'll wipe my cursed brother from your memory. Crowned by the blood of Sidon, by the power of the Nox's own blood. I claim you, Wren of Asteroth. You belong to me now.'

She wanted to spit in his face but that wasn't an option either.

Leander lowered the crown, its cool and heavy weight resting on her head. Her hair coiled and twisted like shadows, her skin shivered with cold and took on a sheen like diamonds. And then everything went dark.

Wren drew in a ragged breath and opened her eyes. The world was remade around her in othersight, blue and black shimmers that skimmed over the surfaces of things, of people, of the floor and the stones. It clung to the ceiling above her and she gripped the arms of the throne.

She was... whole. For the first time in centuries.

From far away the final pieces of the Nox rushed to join her and she opened herself willingly to welcome it.

CHAPTER 47

WREN

Dark flames sped out, encircling her as if lines of oil had been painted on the shining marble floor, filling the hollow which once held the Aurum. Wren heard a cry of dismay, a single voice almost broken with loss, and turned slowly, examining those people present.

Not the king of Ilanthus. Leander looked triumphant, his white-blond hair flowing back from a face so like that of his ancestor she couldn't tell which one he really was anymore.

But an old woman, dressed in finery but on her knees, wore an expression of anguish which gave Wren pause. She stared at her and then rose from the throne. Shadows coiled around her, whispering their sibilant song of praise as she moved across the space between them. Treacherous shadow kin who had sided with Leander over the Nox... oh, she would make them suffer too. The problem was they would only thank her for it. Flames followed her, dark and terrible, a blue-black light which illuminated the chamber of the Aurum in a new darklight of ancient magic. They licked around her feet and climbed the standing stones, to ripple across the polished marble of the ceiling.

Wren came to a halt in front of the lady regent of Asteroth and looked down on her.

She had been afraid of this woman once. She had loathed her. She had slandered Wren's father and driven him away.

'Bow to your queen, Asteroth,' Leander announced in a smugly triumphant voice. How he loved to make people grovel. 'Do her homage.'

Half of those present cowered, dropping their faces towards the floor around her. One after the other they bowed. All save Ylena, who, though she was still on her knees, still somehow held herself straight and tall.

'Great-Aunt Ylena,' Wren murmured, and reached out her hand. It was an offering of truce, far more than the regent was due now. But instead of taking it the old woman glared at it, repulsed. Slowly she dragged her aged eyes up to Wren's face.

'You are not my great-niece. You have no place here. Look what you're doing to our most holy place.'

Wren looked around her. The Sacrum was alive with shadows and otherlight. It was beautiful, a shifting, ever-moving kaleidoscope of darkness, aglow from within. Couldn't the old woman see that? The blue flashes of shadow kin eyes lit up the darkest corners, reflecting off polished marble, and lines like lightning shimmered in the air and tunnelled through the stone.

'Would you have cold and unfeeling light instead?' Wren asked.

'What would I have? I would have my queen of the line of Aelyn restored, our lost queen given back to us. I would have Asteroth free.'

'Instead you'll have the queen I've given you,' said Leander. 'More than any of you deserve.'

He pulled Wren away, schooling his features to something like devotion. All a lie, of course. Everything about him was a lie.

'My love, my goddess, my queen,' he intoned. 'Accept me as

yours now, your lord and king, and I will rule our lands with iron and with steel. I will be your champion and the strong arm to defend you.'

He sounded so smug. So self-assured.

The Nox and Wren both wanted to roll their eyes and refuse him but the press of metal on her throat and arms tightened, ready to compel her obedience. The crown felt heavy, the old crown of Ilanthus, the crown of the goddess queen.

Who had been lost to them.

Elodie wasn't the only lost queen, Wren realised. She frowned, struggling with that thought.

'I was a goddess,' she said. Or perhaps that was the Nox. 'And I was a queen. And...'

The rush of rage that flooded her stole her voice but the words carried on, shaking the stones around her. The fragile sanity she had managed to build around the Nox in Sidonia shattered.

And it was taken from me. Freedom was taken from me. The blood of my blood was weaponised against me. I was used, sent as an assassin, made into a monster...

Wren tried to catch her breath but it was too much. It was all too much. Such a being of power in such a fragile form... it wasn't right, it wasn't meant to be. She needed something to cling to. Someone, something... she needed...

I will be a monster no more.

She faced Leander and saw that he believed he had won. Even now. He thought that the crown would subdue the Nox, and control her.

But the Nox was no longer alone. Wren was with her, entwined with her. And she was not going to let that happen.

'I think not,' she said and the voice was her own. And yet it was more than just that. It throbbed and echoed with the greater force of the beyond, of the deepest darkness and the endless night. It was the endless void and the eternity of stars in that voice. 'You may serve, but you are not the one to command me. You never were.'

She took the Nox into herself and let it fill her. And at the same time, the Nox opened itself to her.

This was what they were meant to be. There was old magic in the stones here, flowing through the ground beneath them and spiralling up to this place of power. The Aurum might have claimed it, but it was not the only being that could reach it and manipulate it.

Once she had been part of that old magic. It had been split and broken, just as she had been split and broken. But now she was made whole. And it could be made whole as well.

Long ago, before the Aurum and the Nox, this had been a place of witchkind. Carlotta had died here, in this place, and she had been Wren's friend. She had given her a gift, a twist of straw in the shape of a bird.

'It'll help you remember who you are...'

The last trace of her friend's spirit still lingered here, in these stones, in this place of power, and Wren touched it now, reaching for it as if seeking a blessing.

And oh, she remembered.

The Nox remembered.

Something was still missing but it would not be long. She knew that, could feel it. All that she still needed was coming. Like a stormfront, like a rising tide, like the inexorable turn of the seasons...

The other part of her. Of the magic of this place. The light to her darkness.

Leander hesitated, a frown growing on his perfect brow, those pale eyebrows drawing together and his silver eyes clouding in doubt. 'Serve?' he echoed, in tones that almost rhymed it with slave.

Wren smiled at him, the coldest, most chilling smile that had ever found its place on her lips. 'Did you think you were fated to rule me, little king? The crown was made with blood and old magic. And perhaps had you used it earlier, it might even have worked. But not here. Not in the Sanctum, in the circle of ancient stones where the veil is thin. And this is above all a place of old magic. A place of power. Why else would the Aurum guard it so jealously? Your pet witch lied to you about the timing, about Wren weakening. But of course she did. She is witchkind and Wren is first and foremost witchkind as well,' she reminded him. '*We* are witchkind. We live free or die.'

The old magic surged up around her, the magic she'd touched in the forest, the magic which flowed in her veins as much as any darkness.

The shadow-wrought metal at her neck and wrists glowed with a fierce light, the darklight in them flaring brighter and brighter as she reformed them, changing them, just as she had seen Elodie do in the stone circle of the Seven Sisters, remaking them as she desired. Steel became silver, their innate magic hardened to diamonds, and they twisted themselves into new shapes. Nothing could bind her now, not made whole, not in this place of ancient power. The old magic in the land was loose again and now she drew on it as well, transforming those tools meant to enslave her into weapons of her own. Bands of pure power glowed in their place, focus points for that ancient magic. The metal moved, twisting itself around her skin, changing itself.

She drew all that magic into her and called on what she needed most. The missing part of her.

The door to the chamber exploded in a burst of blinding light and a man formed of light and flames stepped inside, a figure blazing in glory. Wren turned, hungry for him, and saw the look of blind hatred on his face.

Finn had come to find her. And so had the Aurum.

CHAPTER 48

FINN

Fire in his veins and thunder in his head drove Finn forward. The queen was safe, Roland was with her and the knights – *his* knights – were free, reclaiming the city. The Aurum had granted him all he had asked. He could feel the coiling press of magic coming through him, winding around him and pursuing him. It was in the earth and the air, in the stones of the walls and in the ground beneath his feet. It reverberated with his heart and it was joy, fierce and terrible.

Mine, the Aurum cried out inside him. *You are mine and always will be. My champion and my servant and my vessel, my strong right arm and my righteous heart.*

It was a song and an exultation and the power of that great and endless light flowed from him into all those around him. All over the city he could feel the knights regaining their strength and their courage, his people rising up and driving away their invaders. Battle was brief and glorious. He revelled in it, feeling the strength of *his people*, those he had sworn to protect and who in turn were sworn to him.

The pull of the Sacrum dragged at him. He needed to be there. That was his place, his duty and his destiny. He fought his way through the enemy without seeing them, his movements fluid and sure, his knights following him.

The other spirits of magic were gathering as well. He recognised them only as distant things. They were no threat to him. Not yet.

All but one.

The Nox was here. He could feel her now, a pull deep in his chest, as if he had been hooked through his ribcage and dragged towards her.

This was their fate, their moment.

He would confront her in his place of power and kill her. Finally, once and for all, he would be triumphant and the Nox, eternal enemy, opposite of all he stood for, would be no more. She would fall before him and he would have saved his people.

All of them.

He threw open the doors from the palace, light tearing them apart to make way for him, and stepped into the Sacrum.

She stood in the centre, while people knelt around her in abject surrender. She was dressed as a queen, and the dark crown on her head glimmered with its own light. Around her throat a choker of silver, crusted with diamonds, glittered, the metal crawling against her skin, alive with her dark magic. Similarly magically imbued metal crawled up and down her arms, twisting into long curved knives which covered her hands in a filigree of silver. The blades were viciously sharp, curving over the ends of her fingers, and as she turned to face him, the tips scraped against stone, with a line of sparks.

She faced him and he knew her.

His heart, treacherous and weak, almost came to a halt as Finn... Finn, not the Aurum... Finn recognised her.

Wren.

Because of course it was Wren.

For a moment something in him tore and he was just

himself again, the man who loved her, who had sacrificed every-thing for her and would continue to do so.

And then the fire rushed back, furious to be thwarted, to see her standing there, armed and waiting – the eternal enemy of the Aurum, the dark to its light – waiting for him in his place of power, and to have him pause.

No, he thought, no. Not mine. I'm not the Aurum.

But the Aurum didn't seem to agree.

You are a sworn Knight of the Aurum and I have bestowed my light on you, blessed you and made you whole. I have purged all darkness from you, just as you always wanted. You will obey. Or you will burn.

He was already burning. That was hardly a threat. He had been burning since the first moment he saw her.

'Wren,' he said.

She lifted her chin and gazed at him, with all the imperious-ness of a goddess. And she was still beautiful. She was every-thing he had ever wanted.

The sword in his hand was dark with shadow-wrought steel but it ignited as he raised it in salute, glowing like a hot iron in a fire.

'Brother,' said Leander. 'This is not your place, unless you are here to die. I am the king of Ilanthus now and you will never take my crown.'

Finn almost laughed. Not his place? Leander had no idea. As for the crown of Ilanthus, he didn't want it. He never had. He had only ever wanted one thing.

'I am here to serve the light, and I stand in the place of the Aurum. I made my vows here and I will carry them out as promised. Every vow I have ever made.'

The Aurum roared in the back of his brain and a shudder ran down his spine. It was pleased then. He wasn't sure if that was good or bad.

'No, this is your place,' Wren said, and her voice rippled

with power. He felt the light in him recoil from the darkness in her and for a moment he was frozen in shock. So much power. She was rooted in the energies of this place, her whole being linked to the Nox now, the roots of her power sunken in old magic, drawing on its strength. Even the Aurum seemed taken aback. She was still Wren, yes, but she was also so much more. 'And you are here to die. Both things can be true, prince of Sidon.' She glanced at Leander and the look was not kind. 'For both of you.'

'I'll kill him for you, lady,' Leander assured her. 'I'll stand as your champion and spill his blood, just as it should have been years ago. He was sworn to you first, given to you, and he should have died for you.'

'He has died for me, Leander,' she murmured. 'And will again. But you may proceed. You may stand as champion, if you will. Prove yourself to me as your brother did. Not as conqueror, or as king. As a man. If you kill him, perhaps I will reconsider your fate.'

The cold eagerness in her made Finn want to take a step back. She might still look like Wren, but she didn't sound like her, not anymore. Was he really too late?

She sank into her throne, still ringed by dark flames where the Aurum once burned, ensconced in its place of power. The Aurum growled at the sight but simmered low inside him, preserving its power for the battle ahead.

Show me your devotion then, Finnian Ward, it told him. *You gave up your name and your lineage for me once. You swore to serve me in every way. Now you must prove your loyalty. Now you must be my flame and my sword.*

Ironic, since the only sword he had now came from the stronghold of the Nox, and she looked on impassively as his brother drew his own blade, the royal sword of Ilanthus. Finn had almost died on Leander's sword too many times. He would have if not for Wren. The look of hunger Leander wore told him that this time, as before, no quarter would be given. His brother had everything to fight for, nothing left to lose. He had already won, in many ways. Wren was the Nox and they had taken Pelias. Asteroth was his and the Aurum was trapped. All he needed to do was beat Finn to hold onto it all.

And he'd done that before.

Finn's throat tightened, suddenly dry and choked with cobwebs of doubt. He couldn't beat Leander. He had never been able to best him in a fight. He had lost Wren, lost the kingdom he loved, and he was going to die. The surety of it weighed down on him with the shadows of this place, once bright and glorious and the source of all his hopes, now made dark and terrible.

'Finn... Prince Finnian...' He knew that voice. It came from the ragged group of prisoners. He looked that way to see Laurence Rayden there. Leander had been indulging the more bullying aspects of his nature on the boy. He bore marks of a savage beating, but his eyes shone with belief and when they turned on Finn, something unexpected sparked inside him. 'This is what she saw. She told me.'

Hestia... he had to be talking about Hestia. In the Sacrum of the Aurum, the princes of Sidon, watched by the Nox enthroned and crowned... how had she known?

Finn shook his head. He didn't want the crown. He certainly didn't want to fight Leander for it.

He was a Knight of the Aurum. He was a Paladin in its service. He held the last remnant of the bright power he served. He had no choice, no matter what the outcome might be.

If Leander would champion the Nox in an effort to win her favour, Finn had to meet him.

He hefted his sword in his hands and joined battle with Leander, a furious clash of blade on blade, giving up all that he was and all that he had been to the light he had sworn to serve.

CHAPTER 49
WREN

A wall of obsidian enclosed Wren, holding her like a statue. Not the magic Leander had tried to use to control her now but the raw power of the Nox.

She had thought they had reached some kind of compromise, this power and herself. Had it all been a lie? With the prospect of the blood of Sidon spilled on her behalf no matter what the outcome, and the possible destruction of the Aurum, the Nox clamped down on her as if made of iron.

Once it had been a choice, that sacrifice, that was what it had said in the caves. It had accepted Finn's body and his love. But with Leander's abuses, it wanted blood. Madness had taken it, and with it the desire for vengeance returned. The blood of Sidon had always betrayed the Nox in the end. And now it wanted to spill it. All of it. Every last drop.

That blood was far too close.

The Nox sank claws deep into Wren's heart, anchoring her in place and holding her there even as she tried to pull herself free. But her efforts were to no avail.

Finn moved in a fluid and lethal dance, he and Leander

joined in a way that defined both their lives and all their inter-actions. The princes of Sidon always killed each other. It was an integral part of their line.

It didn't have to be like that. She and Finn had discovered that. It could have been a sacrifice of desire and love instead. But once more they had chosen blood. Leander had chosen to kill for her. Every one of them, except for Finn, had chosen blood. They had chosen death.

Sidon had trapped the Nox and used her and forced her to do unspeakable things. And ever since then, his descendants had done the same. They had sacrificed their own to call her, to force her to comply. They had used her own desperate need for revenge against her.

They had chosen this, the Nox reasoned, as much as it could reason anymore. They had the option for love and passion and they chose to kill. They chose blood. Every single time.

And now madness had taken over, the Nox demanded it. She thrived on it. This was her vengeance and she hungered for the splatter of their blood. Once there had been a choice, but no longer. Blood was all that would satiate her now.

'Don't you see what they're doing?' Wren tried to ask the goddess, but her voice was small and unheard. 'It's the same cycle again. They're still using you. Leander is using you. It's a trap.'

But the Nox no longer listened to reason. She had been enslaved and used, made savage in service of a crown she hated, she had been broken by Elodie and scattered, banished to a life-less endless place. Now she was back she was clinging to Wren and would not give an inch in case it all happened again. For all her power, she was terrified.

The two men danced through shadows and dark-flame, illu-minated by otherlight. It ran across their skin and blazed in their eyes. The passion of the Nox and the Aurum reflected in them, robbing them of humanity. The more Finn relied on its strength, the more the Aurum ate away at what he truly was. The man in him was fading before Wren's eyes. He was becoming living fire and there was nothing she could do.

'Please, you have to make them stop.'

Blood of Sidon would be spilled here, in the chamber of the Aurum. It didn't even matter which one of the brothers it belonged to. Finn was preferable because that would hurt the Aurum itself but really...

The Nox didn't actually seem to care.

Wren had to stop them. Somehow, she had to put a halt to this.

'Wren? Princess?' The voice shook, wavering as the boy crawled towards her across the shining floor. Distracted by the battle, his guards had forgotten him. She turned her gaze on him and saw him quail. 'Goddess? What... what can I do?'

As he reached her side, he reached up and took her hand. His fingers were so cold, shaking, and yet still he took her hand. Something like clarity shimmered just within reach.

'Laurence...' she said and her voice sounded as if it was made of broken glass, even to her ears. He really was innocent. And so very broken. Leander had manipulated him, made him kill the mother he adored, and he was still trying to help. He was blood of Sidon as well, through his mother and her line, but like Finn, he was different.

No one else came near her. No one else dared.

She had promised Hestia she would protect him and she was doing an abysmal job of that. She wouldn't be surprised if Hestia came back from beyond the grave to punish her.

Beyond them the sound of Finn and Leander's battle changed tempo, the clash of their blades married with grunts and gasps. Finn had driven Leander back towards one of the great stones, but at the last minute the king of Ilanthus twisted away and caught Finn a glancing blow in the side. Wren's heart lurched and the Nox snarled.

Whoever wins I will make him ours, mindless and devoted. I will smother the light that remains. They will crawl...

It was so loud now, as if the goddess was hanging over her shoulder, snarling into her ear.

'Help me, Laurence,' Wren whispered.

He looked up at her. 'How?'

'Take off the crown.'

Finn was down on one knee, and as Leander pressed forward, he launched himself up in a flurry of movement which took his brother by surprise. Leander fell back, scrambling for balance, and Finn's face seemed to change. A ferocious expression burned across his features and Wren didn't know him anymore. She was going to lose him. One way or the other.

Unless she could put a stop to it.

Laurence pulled himself up against the throne. She could see the bruising all down the side of his face now, purple and yellow and enflamed. Another reason to hate Leander, as if she needed one. She lifted her hand and pressed the palm to his cheek. He flinched back from the blade that came with it and then stilled beneath her touch.

Is he ours? the Nox asked suddenly.

'Yes,' Wren said, 'he's ours. Blood of Sidon, blood of the goddess, and innocent of the crimes of his line... His mother was Hestia, your servant and my friend. And he's your child too. He has suffered and struggled, and tried to serve even though all around him abuse him. All the others have their own agenda. Even Finn. But not him. He alone is ours.'

The Nox gave a curious kind of purr and shadows twisted around the boy. He tried to pull back, tried to recoil, but he couldn't. These shadows didn't overpower him, or hurt him, though. Slowly the bruises vanished and his suspicious gaze grew round in wonder.

'Lady, let him go. He's just a child.' General Gaius stood before the throne. He looked haggard, but undefeated. There was blood pouring from a wound, turning his left side scarlet, but he still stood tall and proud.

'*Soldier of Ilanthus,*' she mused, and it wasn't Wren's voice this time, though she spoke. '*Most loyal general. Have you come to supplicate yourself?*'

She was losing control of herself. There wasn't much of Wren left. Tears stung her eyes again, threatened to spill down her face, and the Nox didn't even bother to blink them back.

'I will always serve you, lady, but release the boy. I swore to his mother I would protect him.'

The Nox smiled. '*So did I. And I have need of him.*'

Gaius looked anguished and then dropped to his knees. 'Take me instead. I'm not blood of Sidon but my line is noble, and we have served for generations, devotedly so, the goddess and our royal family. Please, lady... Haven't you spilled enough of his family's blood?'

His family? Didn't they even realise what the blood of Sidon was? Of course not.

'*My blood,*' she whispered harshly. '*My blood. Hasn't that been spilled enough?*'

Gaius looked confused, and his voice was no more than a whisper. 'Your blood?'

Wren turned her attention to Laurence again. '*You have a role in this. She must have seen that too, Hestia. Son of Sidon...*' For a moment all she could do was stare at his face, so young. If she got this wrong, if he wasn't fast enough, the Nox would kill him anyway. All she could do was pray...

'She told me...' Laurence whispered, his voice shaking.

'*Told you what?*'

He looked up into her eyes, his expression desperate and afraid. But she could see Hestia in him as well. Could see his mother's strength and determination. 'That when the moment came, I was to follow my heart. Trust myself. Do what was right...'

'Laurence, please...' and it was her own voice. It broke on a sob and the Nox rose up around her to finally smother her.

Laurence snatched the crown from her head. The Nox lashed out, the blades like lightning in the darkness. It was wild now, out of control, and the crown, the only thing suppressing it, vanished abruptly. She would kill him for his presumption, for siding with Wren over his goddess, or simply for who he was. For being within reach. He was Blood of Sidon and that was what she wanted after all. Spilling it would make her strong once more. She had promised to kill them all. Sons of Sidon, line of traitors and cruel monarchs, that blood flowed through his veins like a poison. She would take it and make it hers. She would tear him to shreds. She would...

'Wren!' Finn shouted. 'No!'

Something hard and cold slammed into her hands, knocking her blades aside. Laurence fell back with a desperate cry, holding the crown against his chest, and Gaius moved like the wind, pulling him out of the way and shielding him. The Nox's blades tore through the metal of the ancient dark sword Finn had wielded as if it was no more than paper, shattering it and scattering the pieces on the floor around her.

The sword Finn had thrown to protect Laurence, to protect them both, was destroyed in a burst of released magic and in that moment some kind of sense thundered back into Wren's mind. The crown was gone.

With a gasp of air which filled her lungs like fire, Wren surged to her feet. The blades disintegrated and the choker around her throat fell to pieces, scattering across the stone floor and vanishing in the black flames. The Nox gave a cry of thwarted rage as the insidious power it had wrapped around her shattered.

Wren looked for Finn, desperate to see where he was and

what had happened. He was unarmed now, helpless. He had given up his only chance in order to save Laurence, and to save her.

Leander kicked him full in the chest, sending him sprawling backwards. Finn rolled, tried to rise, but only made it as far as his knees.

CHAPTER 50

WREN

Finn stopped there on his knees before Leander, as if any further movement was too much, too difficult. He looked over at Wren and a smile passed over his mouth, just for a moment. Finn's smile, Finn's mouth.

Her heart trembled in her chest.

Oh he was still consumed by the Aurum, but that power had no reason to save an Ilanthian boy, or to keep Wren from killing him and compounding the Nox's power over her.

No, that was all Finn.

And now he was at his brother's mercy once again.

Leander took his time approaching him, his triumph assured now. He wielded the royal sword of Ilanthus like a toy, spinning it in his hands as if this was just a game or an exhibition match.

Strength seeped out of Wren's body with growing horror. She braced her arms on the throne, forcing herself to stay upright.

'I don't know why you bother, little brother,' he sneered. 'I always win. I always will. This has always been inevitable. This time we finish it.'

'No,' Wren cried. But there was nothing she could do now. She didn't have the power of the Nox at her fingertips and even if she did, it wouldn't cooperate with her. Finn had sacrificed his only defence to stop it, for her. Because even with all the power of the Aurum driving him, he would always sacrifice himself for her.

He couldn't help it.

She threw herself forward, but Gaius caught her. She didn't see where the general had come from. 'Don't look,' he whispered harshly.

Even he had given up. He was a general of Ilanthus, Leander's general, and he was trying to be kind to her at this last moment. It was almost too much to bear.

'Finn!' she screamed, trying to tear herself free. She couldn't see him, not around Gaius's broad chest, but she saw Leander.

He grinned at her. 'Be ready, my queen. This ends now. You and I will be one and all this fruitless struggle will come to an end. Time for my bastard brother to finally die.'

The sound of battle seeped into the Sanctum from outside but it seemed so distant and empty, echoing from a hundred miles away. All she could see was Leander's face and the sword. Wren shoved Gaius aside and this time he released her. Finn knelt while Leander bore down on him in a rush of movement and finality, his head bowed as if accepting all this, just waiting.

Her mind screamed, and she did what Elodie had always told her. She reached for the light with everything she had left in her.

It had to help him. It had to.

'Ward!' a great voice roared from the entrance to the Sacrum and something bright as the sun arced through the air. Finn reached out without looking and snatched Nightbreaker from the air. The sword was a line of fire in his hand, an extension of the fire in his heart. It belonged there. It had always belonged there.

With the simplest of movements, an almost casual twist, he brought the great sword of the Grandmaster of the Aurum in against his own chest as if praying over it and then thrust it upwards.

Straight into the body of King Leander of Ilanthus.

CHAPTER 51

FINN

For a moment it was almost as if nothing had happened. Leander still glared down at him, still held the royal sword of Ilanthus poised over him, ready to deal the death blow.

But no one moved. No one could. Finn felt a great rush of light flow through him, heard the Aurum's voice as if a choir sang in the back of his mind. He felt his body respond to it, vibrating from within with the sheer force of the power flowing through him. He was burned away by it, his very being scored from his veins, leaving him nothing but a speck of consciousness clinging to the edge of the world.

He rose slowly to his feet and Leander slid off Nightbreaker to crumple on the blood-slicked marble floor of the Sacrum. He still wore an expression of complete confusion.

The light of life, if it was truly light, had fled from Leander's eyes.

No one would miss him, Finn thought vaguely. How could they?

Around them everything had gone very still. The battle which had been about to spill in through the doors to the

Sacrum seemed to have stopped as the shockwave of what had just happened spread through the remaining Ilanthian ranks.

General Gaius was the first to recover. He dropped to one knee, head bowed.

'The king is dead. Long live the king. Men of Ilanthus, heed him and obey his word.'

No one moved. Finn turned to look over his shoulder, almost casually. 'Stand down,' he said in a voice that carried through the shocked silence. 'All of you. This is over.'

It only took a moment. Abruptly, everywhere, the Ilanthian army was dropping weapons and kneeling. The remaining knights and fighters of Asteroth milled between them in confusion, securing the prisoners and removing weapons from reach. But no one had any fight left in them now.

And it was, just as he had said in that voice that was not quite his anymore, over.

'Finn?' It was Elodie. There was blood on the white gown she wore, and she had a sword in her hand, along with a fierce light in her eyes. Maryn flanked her, magic still wreathing her hands and a look of murder on her normally sardonic face.

Finn... that was his name still, wasn't it? Maybe? And he was king now. King of Ilanthus. The Aurum gave a brief, humourless laugh, which came from his lips like that of a stranger.

He was going to tear that kingdom apart. Even if he didn't want to. Who there would accept him as king? A Knight of the Aurum, a Paladin, with the Aurum itself blazing inside his body. With Nightbreaker in his hands, there was no difference between him and the great light itself. They still thought he'd killed his father. Ilanthus would reject him and there would be civil war and it would be all his fault...

'Finnian Ward,' Roland's voice rumbled and he approached with some care. Roland had never been a fool, after all. He didn't use titles or royal names of great lineage. Finn had been his since he was a boy.

'Grandmaster,' he said, surprised to find that the voice still sounded like his own. 'Is the city secure?'

'It is,' Roland replied, still wary. 'The queen is safe.'

She wasn't. Not really. She was standing right there holding a sword and covered in blood. All of it belonging to other people, at least there was that. If anyone was going to keep Elodie safe, it would be Elodie, Finn thought absently.

The Aurum seemed to agree. It might not be best pleased with her still, but even the power of divine light saw her as a force to be reckoned with in her own right now. It was not about to try to command her again.

And then she too was moving, not towards him – she had no interest in him, or the Aurum, whatsoever – but towards the hollow where the Aurum had once burned. Towards a small and crumpled heap on the ground there, clad in shadow-colours and silver, her black hair spilling around her like ink.

Wren!

Something inside him snapped at the very thought of her. Of her, of the Nox, of whatever she was. Something he couldn't even define. Need and hunger and hatred and love, all tangled together, primal and overpowering.

Elodie gathered Wren in her arms, trying to wake her, to comfort her, reaching for a child who was no longer there. Finn could see that. Shadows burrowed through her body, wove their way through her hair. She was made of night and darkness, sprinkled with the stars and bathed in moonlight.

Finn stalked towards them, Nightbreaker held an extension of his arm, ready to put an end to it all, ready to kill her at last.

No, not Wren. He couldn't kill Wren. What was he thinking? What was he doing?

But the Nox had to die. It had been broken once and scattered, and exiled to the beyond, but not gone. He would finish it this time. Not a trace of it would remain, especially not that human form in which it had hidden the last part of itself.

You swore vows, my Paladin, the Aurum told him. *To cleave to the light, to serve me, to be my creature. And now you fulfil them. All of them. To fight the Nox, with flame and sword.*

'Finn? What are you doing?'

Anselm Tarryn and Olivier Arrenden blocked his way, still guarding Wren as they had sworn to do. They were knights and Paladins as well. They ought to serve, they ought to bow.

But they didn't.

'Stand aside, both of you,' he told them. Neither of them moved and he scowled at them. 'I won't tell you again.'

'We can't let you do this, Finn,' Anselm said calmly.

'And how will you stop me?'

They were armed, but exhausted from battle. Olivier raised his free hand and Finn saw the tracery of magic beneath his skin. Hardly a weapon, that. The Aurum had taken it from him once and it would again. It remembered the taste and the shape of it. Olivier had given it up willingly. He would beg to do so again.

'Please, Finn,' Anselm tried once more. 'Listen to us.'

'I'm hardly Finn anymore,' he warned them. 'I'm king of Ilanthus and the Aurum made flesh, and a thousand other contradictions. Get out of my way. I can end this, once and for all.'

'I'm sorry,' said Olivier. Two simple words and Finn didn't know what they meant until his friend reached out to press his hand against Finn's chest. It was so simple a gesture, and it didn't feel like a threat. It wasn't.

And yet...

A wave of something warm and comforting washed over him, healing energy which flooded him to his core and sent him reeling back as the Aurum tried to reassert its suddenly waning control. Olivier might have given up this form of old magic willingly as a child but he understood it better now, knew its worth and how to wield it. Knew when it was needed and what to do.

Finn's hand spasmed and he dropped Nightbreaker, Anselm kicking it deftly out of the way in a moment.

And just like that, the light of the Aurum fluttered back to something manageable and contained inside him. Finn blinked, trying to right his vision, as his flailing body was brought back under his own control.

Healed from that which he had never dreamed would be a threat to him.

'Olivier?' he whispered and strength left his body. He heard his friend swear softly as he tried to catch him and slow his fall.

'It's all right, I have you. You're going to be all right.'

Was he? Was Wren? He felt wrung out and lost. How must she be feeling? He tried to say her name, to ask how she was, when he heard someone cry out in alarm.

There was a commotion by the circle of the Aurum, the place where the throne had been moved to, where the flames had once danced. People scattered back from it again, former hostages and Ilanthians alike.

Lynette of Goalais stood there, her hair unbound and her eyes wild with grief and rage. Blood smeared her face and covered her once fine clothes. Like something from a tale of the darkest night, she held the crown in one hand and Nightbreaker in the other.

'Thank you,' she snarled. 'The last pieces of the Nox and the Aurum are all I need. I am witchkind and the old magic will at last be mine, restored and triumphant. We will live free, all of us, though it cost everything. You took my sisters, you took my Yvain... I am going to make you all pay.'

CHAPTER 52

WREN

It wasn't like sleep.

Wren was lost, helpless, trapped in an empty, brutal place. She was cold and hollow inside, like something had scoured out all that made her whole. And all she wanted to do was lie there, alone, at peace. It might hurt, but that was nothing to what she had felt, the agonies that awaited her if she woke. Better to be here. Better to remain lost.

There was no light in the beyond but no darkness either. If this was where the Nox had been trapped for twenty years no wonder it was insane.

'You must wake up,' said a small, solemn voice, so very gentle. She remembered it vaguely from somewhere. It sounded like the voice of a young boy, or maybe a girl, or maybe both.

'Why?' she whispered, and her voice rasped against a throat which felt like she had spent days just screaming. 'Haven't I done enough?'

There was laughter then. Not cruel, or mocking, but light, a sound of joy, like birdsong. Wren used to make a sound like that herself once, long ago, when she would run through the forest and she would hear it echoing back at her from the trees. It wasn't a sound of shadows or darkness. It had nothing to do with their whispers.

But she remembered it now. And it was the sound of magic.

'None of us can ever do enough, sister.' A small hand touched her face, wiping away tears she didn't know she was still crying.

Wren opened her eyes to see two children, a boy and a girl, with bright green eyes.

'You?' She knew them, somehow, perhaps from a dream or a distant memory. Something from when she was still so small, when Elodie had wrapped her up in her cloak and brought her to Cellandre, when they had first come to the tower in the forest, after that first night when the shadow kin had tried to take her away.

Elodie had gone to the trees and the forest itself and made a promise, an offering. And something had answered. She had made a bargain, but not with the darkwood. With something else.

'It's time to come home, little sister,' said Robin, his eyes so solemn. 'There's still work to do.'

'Finn needs you. Elodie needs you. And Roland...' Lark smiled brightly.

Robin and Lark... those weren't their names, she thought. Not really. But they were the names they had chosen here and now, in this place. The names they had given themselves.

'You know Roland?' Wren asked, bewildered. She didn't even know how she knew their names, but she did, as if they had always been there buried at the back of her memories, faces and voices that had slipped through the cracks and hidden there, lost to her until now, but so familiar, part of her.

Sister, they called her.

'He's a good man,' said Robin. 'A good father. We like him. You chose well.'

'I didn't choose...'

Lark tugged at her hand, trying to drag her somewhere. 'Of course you did. And we did. And Elodie did. Life is all about choices. You can't do that here. Now hurry, or we'll lose everything. The raw power unleashed will rip apart the fabric of the world. Lynette doesn't realise what she's doing. She thinks she's helping witchkind, but she isn't. She's going to destroy them all. Her heart is broken. So, I fear, is her mind.'

'Lynette,' Wren murmured, remembering. Her friend, she had thought, the woman who had helped her and cared for her but had been working against them all for her own ends. What had happened?

'She followed the wrong path,' Lark said. 'Trailing after her sisters, unthinking. We tried to guide her, to help her. We tried to help all of them but they wouldn't listen. We sent her Yvain, but even though she loved him as dearly as you love Finn, she used him and lost him in the using. She meant well but she is so very broken. And intentions do not excuse her actions.'

'She has the sword and the crown,' said Robin. 'No one else can stop her. She'll kill Finn.'

Finn... Wren recalled the murderous look in his eyes and her heart stuttered in her chest. But he was her lover as well, sweet and gentle, strong when she needed him to be strong, and so caring. He was everything.

She couldn't let anything else happen to Finn. She had caused him too much pain already. Even if it meant giving up any chance of a future, she would protect him. She had to.

'Take me back,' she told the twins.

A great rushing sound, like the tide turning in the midst of a tempest, or a forest caught in a hurricane, roared around her, a song of old magic and ancient powers, and Wren gave herself up to it.

CHAPTER 53
WREN

In the centre of the chamber of the Aurum, Lynette of Goalais brought Nightbreaker and the crown of the Nox together in a terrible clash of metal on metal, Aurum-forged and Shadow-wrought. The shockwave of power turned the air to honey, thick and cloying. Elodie held against it longer than most, still trying to shelter Wren, but even she couldn't stand alone against such raw power. Wren saw Olivier flinch and then fall without a sound, his face a stretched mask of agony. Beside him, Anselm tried to catch him and pull him to safety but had no clue what to do. Finn struggled to his feet but couldn't move forward, standing there like he had been turned to stone as the magic remaining in him was ripped out into the vortex swirling around the witchkind woman.

Maryn screamed as she fell, writhing, and others among the maidens dropped to the floor.

The magic pulled from them all flowed to Lynette, who stood in the centre of the maelstrom, her eyes white and unseeing, her head thrown back in agony and ecstasy, her mouth open. The blood smearing her face stood out like black lines.

'Stop!' Wren tried to shout. There was no trace of the twins here and no sense of their power. Perhaps they knew better than to put themselves in the path of whatever Lynette was doing. There was no one else. Anyone with power was already over-whelmed and the others... helpless to intervene. Roland and Gaius threw themselves at the woman only to be repelled by an unseen force that hurled them back across the floor.

Wren dragged herself to her feet, not even sure where she found the strength to do so. 'Lynette, you have to stop. This isn't going to do what you want. You aren't releasing the magic. You're stealing it. Taking it from everyone. You're killing them, all the witchkind.'

'I can bring him back, Wren. You can't begrudge me that. With this magic I can bring him back.'

Yvain... she was doing it for Yvain now. Not even for herself or her sisters anymore. Just him.

'Please, you need to think. You need to stop.'

'Need?' Lynette's voice was tortured with the power flowing through her. 'What do you know of need, princess? You never had need of anything. Our queen put your care above us all, above her kingdom, above witchkind, above everyone. She could have brought you to us from the first. We would have made you great. My sisters and I would have formed you into the goddess we needed. We would have joined you with the Aurum and made you magnificent. A goddess for all witchkind. But instead, she hid you and bent you to her own shape. I've had enough of waiting. I am the last of the three. My sisters failed but I did not. I gave up everything, even Yvain, to get here. I will not fail now. I will do this and bring him back.'

The draw of the magical vortex increased, pulling at Wren's heart and mind, dragging her forward now.

'Lynette, it's going to kill you.'

'Then I'll die,' she spat. 'It doesn't matter. He's only gone ahead of me. It isn't far...' The expression on her face faltered as she thought about that. Bring back her dead love. Bring back the man she'd betrayed and used. 'But even if I did, he'd never forgive me anyway, would he?' Lynette shook her head, her terrible decision made. 'Nothing else matters now. So I'll die. Don't you remember? We're witchkind, Wren, my dearest. We live free or we die.'

Agony lined her face, etched with Yvain's blood, but still she held on, crushing the crown and the sword together until they melted in her hands, one merging into the other in a white-hot maelstrom of light and darkness. Wind tore at Wren's hair, blinding her as it whipped over her face.

Old magic hummed in the air and tore at the ground beneath them. It roared from deep below the mountain and the walls of white marble shook. A crack fractured the ceiling, and now even those who were not witchkind fell under the onslaught of wild, unfettered magical power. Only Wren and Lynette were still standing and even as Wren reached her side, tried to reach out to the other woman, Lynette opened her eyes wide, far too wide. They were green and glowing, alive in a way no human eyes should ever be alive with otherness and strangeness, with something ancient that came from far beyond their world. Wren saw the moment that she gave way to panic, when she realised that there was no controlling whatever she had let into her. A powerful witch she might be, but she had hidden her power for so many years, using it only in small ways. She had enslaved the knight who loved her. She had turned Carlotta into her puppet, Wren saw that now, understood everything, and Lynette didn't have any regrets about doing that. About using a witchkind girl of little power as a tool. She was prepared to do whatever she had to, to achieve her end.

She would accept any cost. Even Yvain.

But she had not prepared for this. So much magic, so much power that had been constrained for far too long, the old magic tore her apart. Lynette opened her mouth to scream but no sound came out. There was nothing there to make a sound, nothing of the woman left within the shell hollowed out and used as a conduit by a power far more ancient and far more alien than the Aurum or the Nox, or even the twins.

Wren tried to grab her, but as her hands closed on the woman's arms – the woman who had been kind, who had looked after her in Knightsford and helped her navigate Pelias, the woman who had appeared to be her friend – the sense of loss and emptiness almost stole her breath.

Lynette had truly loved Yvain and she had sacrificed that love. She had used him because she felt she had no choice. She had broken him and that had broken her as well. But perhaps those who had set her on this suicide mission had never expected her to succeed where they did not. Her sisters had bound her with duty and vows and so much guilt and need, as well as untold enchantments of their own.

And they had not prepared her for the power of old magic.

Wren felt it now, running through her veins like acid, reaching into her mind to pull out every emotion as if it was a thing to be examined and cast aside. Wren felt it in her own body and mind, and in Lynette's as well, felt it ripping her apart piece by piece.

And then Lynette was gone. She seemed to just unravel in that power, right in front of Wren's eyes, disappearing beneath her touch like morning mist. All that remained behind was the echo of a desperate cry of betrayal and misery, reverberating through Wren's conscious mind as the old magic turned its attention on her instead. Something new, something other to examine, to play with, to pull apart.

'Wren!' It was Finn. His hand closed on her arm, strong and warm, as if he could pull her out of danger. 'Let it go.'

'I can't,' she told him. 'It will take all the witchkind, everyone with even a touch of magic in them, no matter how small, and it will unmake the world. That's what the twins meant. It's unbound, unfettered, with no understanding of our world, or of us. It's out of control and it's dangerous. I have to do this, Finn. I have to stop it.'

'Not you!' he yelled. He wrapped his arms around her, holding her close. His scent enveloped her and she almost sobbed with relief. 'Not *just* you. You can't do it alone, heart. Us. We can do it. The two of us.'

He was right, she couldn't do this alone. Even together they might not be strong enough.

But they had to try.

She had the will and the magical focus. He gave her all the strength he had, acting as her foundation and her rock.

Wren reached out. Not just for the light this time. She reached for the light and the darkness, for the dawn and the twilight, for the glints of hope and the shadows of despair. And she drew it all into herself.

All the green and glowing power, all the rising tides and falling stars, everything that swirled around her, all the magic of the witchkind past, present and future. She felt their cries and their sobs and tried to bring them comfort, to give them back hope and strength.

'It's all right,' she whispered, as all those magical senses turned to her in desperation. 'We're here. Hold on. It's going to be all right.'

Her mouth found his and she kissed him, branding his lips against her own as the power consumed them both and they fell into it together.

CHAPTER 54

ROLAND

Roland didn't know where he found the strength or the ability to move but something desperate and primal drove him. Elodie was only a step behind, her face pale, her hands trembling.

As they reached the spot where the two of them lay, still entwined together, Elodie sobbed, trying to gather Wren's limp form in her arms. 'What happened? Wren, please, love, please wake up.'

Finn stirred first, though he looked like even breathing was agony. He blinked slowly at them and for a moment Roland feared he'd lost his wits.

'Wren?' His lips seemed to stumble over her name and his voice sounded like it had been tortured to breaking. Roland helped him up carefully, but he just gazed at her still form. 'No.'

'There was so much magic,' Elodie whispered. 'She couldn't take it all in. Even Wren couldn't...'

'Oh, you would be very surprised at what she can do,' said a young voice behind them. Somehow it didn't sound young though. It was ancient. And wild. And oh, so powerful. More so than ever.

'Lark?' Roland whispered and the little girl from the forest smiled at him. There were flowers in her hair, living growing flowers, blossoming even as he watched. Robin stood beside her but his whole attention was fixed on Wren. His skin had taken on a mossy green tint that made him look even more wild and unnatural.

'Do something,' Elodie snapped, ever imperious.

Robin tilted his head to look at her. 'You kept her safe for us for so long, Elodie. We promised in Cellandre that we would protect her. Did you think we would forget?'

'I don't know what something like you thinks is *safe*, but this... this is not safe!'

'Hedge witch,' said the boy who was not a boy, 'can you not heal her yourself? That was always your gift. Not the Aurum, not all those charms, just healing. You were so very good at it when you set all else aside. Have you forgotten that as well?'

Hedge witch... Roland saw the expression change in Elodie's eyes, as if she had been slapped. And perhaps she had, and by the boy, no less.

'Try, Elodie,' said Lark. 'I believe in you.'

Healing, Roland had always been taught, was the hardest of all magics. And the most important. It was a blessing from the Aurum and yet the Aurum was gone. There was no sign of Nightbreaker, nor of the crown. No sign of the shadow kin or the flames. He couldn't even feel the touch of them in his heart. Not anymore.

'I don't... I don't know what to do...' Elodie whispered, and for the first time in his life he saw her look lost.

'Yes, you do,' he told her suddenly. 'You always do. Elodie, my love, heal her.'

Elodie hugged Wren to her, a mother with her only child, and kissed her head. She murmured something and Roland heard the soft sound resolve into a lullaby. She rocked Wren gently against her, and sang about driving the darkness away, and about sleeping softly, and about the morning that would come. It was the gentlest song, one so old that no one truly knew its source.

'*My child, my child,*' Elodie sang, '*my precious child, when you wake a new day will dawn.*'

Wren stirred and opened her eyes. Slowly Roland let out the breath he had been holding, the one threatening to make his lungs burst.

His daughter's eyes were no longer black and endless, no longer the darker mirror of his. They were green, and bright, and lit from within like sunlight streaming through new leaves in the forest.

'Elodie?' Wren murmured and held her even tighter. 'Don't let go, not yet. Please.'

'Never, my love. Never.'

'Where's Finn?'

'Here!' The word was pulled out of him as if by raw need. He reached out a shaking hand to take hers, pulled her fingers to his lips and kissed them.

'And Roland?' Wren asked. With her attention turned on him, Roland felt a world of love rising inside him. His daughter, no matter what had made her or why, no matter what she had become. She was his. Even if he had to share her with powers beyond his understanding.

'I'm here. No harm will come to you on my watch.'

Wren smiled. 'Thank you, Grandmaster... Father...'

Roland smiled. When he looked for the strange witchkind children who were not children at all, they had gone again, as silently as they had come.

CHAPTER 55

ROLAND

Finn took command of the forces of Ilanthus, ordering them out of the city and back to their ships. Frankly, Roland thought they were happy to go. There had been some delight at the prospect of war with Asteroth but that was gone now, with Leander dead along with many of their fellow soldiers. Reality was a harsh teacher. Gaius had not had the stomach for it to begin with, he confessed to Roland as they drew up the terms of a terrible stalemate they would now try to forge into a peace.

Laurence Rayden refused to leave Finn's side and Finn seemed to be fine with that, loath to let the boy out of his sight. He'd failed him too often, he said when Roland asked. Instead, Finn turned to the general of the Ilanthian forces.

'He's my only blood relative,' he told them as if that was that. Gaius nodded solemnly. 'Or will you take charge of him now, general? You have been as a father to him all these years.'

Gaius looked concerned and not a little ashamed. 'Not much of a father given what happened. Will you not bring him back to Sidonia with you, your majesty? He is, as you say, your blood.'

Finn scowled, and Roland realised that he'd instantly

thought of sacrifice, of Laurence being used as he himself would once have been used had things not worked out differently. 'I have no need of more bloodshed if that's your implication.'

Gaius gave him a level look and Roland had to suppress an urge to smile. This was not a man to be cowed. 'Then he is also your responsibility, as your only remaining family, your majesty. And you will be bringing him back to Sidonia with you.' It was not a question this time. He was making a deliberate point.

At the sound of that, Finn blanched. 'Back to Sidonia?'

'Your kingdom needs you.'

It seemed Finn had forgotten what killing Leander meant for him. Or just wished to forget, perhaps. Roland waited, ready to help if necessary. Finn was still like his own son.

As Gaius had explained it, Finn had been named heir on his return, lost that title when it appeared he'd killed his father thanks to Leander, but now, all of Ilanthus would bow before him.

Had it not occurred to him that he had defeated his brother in single combat, which was a time-honoured way of Ilanthian succession, and that had confirmed what Hestia had foretold? That Finn would be king of Ilanthus after all? Whether he wanted it or not.

'Very well,' he said at last, his tone more sober, perhaps a little defeated. 'Make ready to depart. I... I need to talk to Wren.'

The weight of those words was not lost on Roland. But what choice was there? Finn could not stay here, and without a king, Ilanthus would fall apart. The whole society revolved around someone of the line of Sidon wearing its crown. Finn and the Rayden boy were the only ones left.

'Roland?' Finn said at last and then seemed lost for words.

'I know,' he said. Because Finn needed to understand that someone still supported him as simply him. 'And I'm always here.'

It all took far too long to clear the Ilanthians from the city, and as Roland took in the full extent of the destruction, he realised that it was going to take an age to repair everything. As much as Ilanthus needed her king, Asteroth needed her queen.

He went to find Elodie.

The gates of the Sanctum were closed tight. Roland knocked as politely as he could in his impatience. Maryn opened them and gave him that familiar stubborn glare.

'Grandmaster?'

'I don't have time for this. Where is she?'

'The queen, you mean? Queen Aeryn of Asteroth? That queen?' She grinned wickedly. 'The *queen* is tending the injured. Her knights are with her. Well, Anselm. I'm not sure what Olivier is classed as now. He's almost as gifted a healer as she is, you know? A remarkable talent. His instincts are exceptional. And to think, he was almost squandered on knighthood.' She rolled her eyes at his glare and stepped aside. 'Are you expecting me to stop you?' she teased. 'Dear me, when Elodie told me to bring you right to her when you stopped politicking and wanted to talk. Whatever will I do?' Her laughter followed him as he went inside and he thought that this new light-hearted Maryn was potentially even more of a nightmare than before.

Elodie was sitting beside Ylena, who lay on a low cot-like bed, looking haggard, older than she ever had before. They were speaking softly to each other and Roland thought he heard apologies pass between them.

Not that Elodie was the only person Ylena owed apologies to. His own would be a long way down the list. But even so, he knew that the regent had only wanted to protect her niece and her kingdom. It had all gone horrifically wrong, but that was not entirely her fault. And she didn't seem quite so proud anymore.

'Elodie?'

She looked up at the sound of her name and smiled at him. It was as if the years fell away in that instant. She said a farewell to her aunt and joined him in the garden outside.

'Where's Wren?' she asked. 'Is she with Finn?'

'I'm leaving the two of them to come to terms with... well, whatever they have to do to come to terms with their situation in their own time. It doesn't seem fair.'

'Duty isn't fair,' she murmured.

'Yes, my queen.'

'Don't.' The word was harsh. 'Please,' she tried again, gentler now. 'Don't call me that. Don't make it all about that again. Please, Roland, love. I can't bear it.'

'Do you want to run away to the forest again? Because I think there will be a lot of people looking for you wherever you go. We need you, Elodie.'

'I don't care about them.'

'That's not true.' He knew her too well. Elodie cared about everyone. She always had done. To the detriment of her own hopes and dreams.

'I care about *you*.'

The words were a shock, but this time one that made his heart soar. A dizziness made him blink at her, surprised to hear it stated so boldly. 'And... and I you. Always.'

'I don't want to leave you again.'

'Do you have a reason to?'

She gave him a stern look. 'I am your queen, Grandmaster.'

Roland smiled. He couldn't help himself. It was not an expression that sat particularly comfortably on his stony face, but it felt right there, after so many years. 'That you are, Elodie. And my love. And the other part of my soul. Is that a reason to go away?'

'No,' she replied in a small voice.

'Is it a reason to stay instead?' He reached out to cup her face in his palm and she leaned in against him, closing her eyes for a moment, luxuriating in the caress. Her skin was so soft, and warm against the calluses of his fingers, fragile against his strength. And yet he also knew that was an illusion. There was no one stronger than Elodie. She was real and here, and his.

She moved quite suddenly and Roland was unprepared.

This time she kissed him, winding her arms around his neck so she could pull him close and hold him there as if she would never again let him go. Which was exactly where he wanted to be.

'Then stay with me, El,' he whispered, his lips still on hers as if he couldn't bear to be any further away from her. 'Now and forever.'

'Roland,' she told him, her voice gentler than he had ever heard it. 'We have so much lost time to make up for.'

CHAPTER 56

WREN

Wren was hiding. She couldn't face anyone right now.

Finn found her anyway, because he always did. He always would. She knew that with every beat of her heart. And the way it jumped into her throat when she heard his footsteps behind her.

She didn't have to look. She knew. Just knew.

His scent, the way he moved, even the slight hitch in his breath... she knew.

She leaned on the windowsill and stared off into the distance, out across the city and north to the edge of the great forest, a soft green line on the horizon. Her hair moved with the breeze, softly whispering against her skin. She had taken a knife to it the first chance she got, cutting it back to her jawline, and no one had dared to stop her. It still stirred with magic, but magic of a different kind now. The Nox was gone.

She didn't know what that meant.

Finn's hand came to rest on her shoulder, squeezing gently, carefully.

'I'll have to leave soon,' he said and she heard the way his throat tightened on the words, as if even his own body wanted to stop him saying them.

'We stood here before and you told me that,' she sighed. He was only going to the Ilanthian embassy in the city below them then. This time... this time...

He would be half the world away.

Perhaps he smiled. Perhaps he didn't. She couldn't bring herself to look. 'Wren, I...' His voice failed him. 'Please, look at me.'

They'd found him a change of clothes befitting a king. There was even a sleek band of gold on his head, gleaming against his brown hair. It was a practical crown, that of a soldier, or a knight. It suited him.

And she hated it.

'I can't go to Ilanthus with you.' She blurted out the words. 'I can't go back there.'

He flinched as if she had slapped him, but didn't pull away. Slowly, he let out his breath and then inhaled carefully before he tried to speak again. 'I know. I understand. I don't exactly want to go back there myself. There isn't anyone else and the kingdom is in chaos. The sisterhood is broken thanks to Oriole's actions and the army is demoralised thanks to Leander. There are already many nobles vying for position and saying things like we should be declaring an all-out war of vengeance against Asteroth, the College and anyone else in our way. It needs a firm hand, a calm mind.'

But why does it have to be you?

That was what she wanted to say. To scream it, to howl it. Like a child denied what she wanted. She bit her lower lip instead.

'I'll come back,' he said. 'I swear I'll come back.'

Wren just nodded and let the sting in her eyes distract her from the pain everywhere else. He couldn't promise that. They both knew it.

If he was king of Ilanthus he was never going to escape that. And she... she didn't even know what she was anymore. Not the Nox, thank all the powers for that.

But she wasn't quite herself either.

Wren threaded her fingers with his and brought his hand to her lips, running the lightest of kisses over the tops of his knuckles. He sucked in a breath and she felt his body react. In a moment, he would sweep her up into his arms and carry her off if she gave him even the slightest indication that she would let him.

She couldn't. She was losing him and the pain of that was intense. They could put off the recognition of that with sex, but eventually they would still have to face it, and it would be all the more difficult for that shared intimacy and attempted escape.

'I will never love anyone but you,' she told him. 'Wherever I am, whatever happens... no one but you. I'll wait. If you will truly come back...'

'Wren, my love, my heart, I promise—' She lifted her finger to his lips to silence him, a small surge of this new magic that flowed through her veins rippling against his skin.

'Don't make promises, Finn. It's too hard to keep them.'

He shook off the urge to be quiet she had tried to lay on him. She hadn't even been aware she was doing it. The magic flowing through her now was new and untried. But so very powerful. And so was Finn, it seemed.

He was not going to be silenced now. It was a testament to the power in him as well that he could do it. Did he realise? she wondered. That the old magic had marked him as well? Oh, most of it flowed in her veins now, because she had been created to hold power, a vessel for the Nox to one day fill. But in the end something far greater needed to be contained and she had offered herself up.

Finn Ward had been right there with her, with his forsaken

heritage, and his bloodline and his truest of hearts. And now, that Finn was no more. King Finnian of Ilanthus was needed elsewhere. He had to leave. But still he tried to make her a promise. More than a promise. A vow.

'I swear on the light and the dark, on all the old magic and the powers that live within us, I will find you again. I will dedicate myself to restoring peace to Ilanthus, find a way to build a secure future for my people and a ruler who will care as I care. And then I will find you again. Trust me, Wren. Believe me. No matter how long it takes, I will find you again.'

The air around them shivered and glowed. Somewhere, far off, she heard birdsong.

Wren smiled softly, unable to find an argument he would listen to. It was a nice dream.

And when he kissed her, touched her, made her sigh against him again, she prayed it was a dream that would come true. But she didn't believe it.

In the morning he would leave and so would she.

He would go with fanfare and ceremony. She would slip away in silence once she had explained herself to Elodie.

It had to be that way.

※

The twins were waiting for Wren on the road outside the lower city when she slipped away. Elodie had argued, of course. Told her not to be ridiculous, that she couldn't leave them, that they were family and that she needed to take her time to explore the changes in her. With the help of Elodie and the Maidens of the Aurum, she could come to terms with the power inside her and find a way to control it.

But it wasn't something to control. It just *was* and Wren had no desire to develop ways of using it. She was not there to serve the Aurum.

The Aurum was gone.

Roland was quieter, calmer. He had already lost Finn. His dark eyes watched her as she told them of her plans. When Elodie had finished ranting about headstrong children, and stupid adventures, and all the other things she had to say, Roland just enfolded Wren in his warm embrace and told her to stay safe, to keep in touch, and that if she ever needed anything, they would be there for her.

Elodie scowled at him and called him a fool. But when Wren left the room she heard the tears and the words of comfort he spoke. She forced herself to keep going.

'Hello, sister,' said Lark brightly. She was spinning colourful flowers out of nothing on the edge of the road, dotting them among the grass around the spot where Robin sat, his long legs stretched out in the sun. A soft breeze stirred the air around them, and there were butterflies perched on his head, his shoulders and all down his legs. As he moved they took off like a burst of flower petals.

'Are you going somewhere?' he asked, artlessly. He knew full well that she was leaving. And he probably knew where she was going, too.

'Cellandre,' she told them and started walking.

'Oh, good choice,' said Lark, dancing around her as they walked. Robin matched her pace for pace and gave the impression of someone much older than he looked.

They were creatures of old magic too, of course. Like her. They always had been. Wren felt like the child beside them, despite appearances.

'What about the others?' Robin asked.

'Roland and Elodie need to restore the kingdom to order. Maryn, Anselm and Olivier are working with the witchkind and the College to forge an agreement on their protection and future cooperation. Finn...' Her voice failed her.

'He's already gone back to Ilanthus,' Lark told her. 'The

ship sailed. He'll have good winds and calm seas all the way. We'll keep him safe, Wren.'

'Thank you.' What else could she say? Finn was gone. She didn't want to think about that. 'Why did you help?' she asked after a long pause. 'You didn't have to.'

'A long time ago,' said Robin, 'we were lost too. The dark-wood had us. We had gone astray in those shadows and they were feeding on us. And oh it was strong. Until you arrived in Cellandre. You pushed it back, you and Elodie, and rescued us. So we returned the favour, sister.'

'I'm not your sister.'

'You are now,' Lark replied with a laugh. 'Or will be. Something like that. There are always three of us, you see. Eventually. Linear time is tricky.'

'Lynette had two sisters,' she said. 'Alouette and Oriole. They were lost too and we found them.'

'They never really understood,' Robin replied. 'We tried to help them, tried to teach them, but... they thought everything was about them. But it wasn't.'

'They thought it would make them more than hedge witches,' Lark said, her voice suddenly heavy with sorrow. 'They always wanted to be more. And nothing was ever enough.'

Wren didn't quite know what to say to that so she kept walking.

Lynette had lost everything. She could have stopped, could have lived a life with Yvain and been happy. But she didn't. She couldn't.

That said, Wren was walking away from her family. And she had lost Finn.

'What are you going to do in Cellandre?' Robin asked after some time had passed.

'I'm going to be what I was always meant to be, a hedge witch.'

They exchanged a knowing glance she didn't want to think about. 'That's all?'

The old magic in her stirred and uncoiled, and seemed to laugh against her senses. She felt it in the land, in the wind, the small stream they crossed. She felt it inside her, a deep and abiding sense of rightness. It wasn't like the Nox. It didn't seek to control or overpower her. Nor was it like the Aurum demanding obedience and service.

It was part of her. And she was part of it. Just like the twins.

'What is more important than that?' she asked.

THE WITCH OF THE WOODS

If you asked anyone about the witch of the woods, they would say to stay away. It was just a known thing. No one strayed in the depths of Cellandre anyway because bad things had happened there. Villages had been wiped out, burned, the citizens slaughtered. Monsters had ranged there, shadow kin the size of which had never been seen anywhere else. There were darkwoods where bargains could be made and lives destroyed. Although since the Nox was gone no one seemed entirely sure what people might be bargaining with anymore. But old knowledge died hard.

The forest had changed since the witch had returned. She had calmed the trees and the old magic she brought with her had surely driven all the lingering darkness from it.

But you never knew. Especially not with witchkind.

The world was changing. That was also known. Witchkind were part of the government of Asteroth now, not just the maidens, but all kinds, the rebels and the College and all those hidden in between.

They had come out of exile, and revealed themselves again – healers and diviners, seers and growers, all kinds of workers of wonders who could ply their trade in the open now. It turned out that when the witchkind you encountered could actually help you, trade with you, and live alongside you, and were just normal people, everyone was much less suspicious about them.

The queen helped as well, of course. And so too did the knights. They sought out witchkind still, but not to hunt them down or expel them. Some even joined their ranks of the knights themselves and rose high among them.

Asteroth was changing.

The forest didn't change and never had, although it was greener and brighter, and awash with new life. The air sang with birdsong. It was eternally wild and sometimes still very dangerous.

Tales spread rapidly that if someone found themselves in trouble in the forest now, a woman might appear, slender as a young birch, with long hair as black as a raven's wing and eyes as green as spring itself. She set people back on the right path, healed the injured and returned the lost. She was gentle and kind and those who spoke of her did so with a wistful look in their eyes.

Others went in search of her, some driven by curiosity – who would return bemused and dizzy with tales of wonder – and others with more malice in their minds. No one spoke of them. They did not tend to return at all. Sometimes the laughter of children married with the sounds of birds, with rustling in the undergrowth, and with the sighing of the trees. It wasn't a threat. Not as such. But it was perhaps a warning.

There are many powers, the people who lived in the edges of the forest said. None of them are to be trifled with. None should be dismissed.

And a hedge witch should always be respected.

EPILOGUE
SEVERAL YEARS LATER

Wren had rebuilt the tower in the forest. It hadn't been an easy task but Robin had helped. Lark had just flitted from tree to tree, laughing at them. She often did that. Like a wild bird herself, filled with joy and unruly delight. Sometimes the two of them stayed with her, other times they were gone for weeks on end. There was no pattern to be followed and she accepted that they would go where they would, on a whim.

Once Wren had the tower back in some form of order and it felt more like home, she grew the thorn bushes up into a great barricade and spun the various wards throughout Cellandre. She could protect herself, and the twins, when they were there, could take care of themselves.

No one wandered this deeply into the forest anymore, not if they valued their safety, and she wanted to keep it that way.

Sometimes Elodie sent word, because nothing would stop Elodie, but she did that with magic. There wasn't time to tear herself away from her kingdom, or Roland, or the two precious children born to her just a few months ago.

Your brother and sister, she had said in her message and Wren had smiled. Robin and Lark had been completely absent since then, not even a sign of them in the breeze. They had always been captivated by Roland and Elodie, which made Wren wonder. She'd find out one day, she supposed.

Elodie had said the twins had once demanded a price for their help, a life each. Elodie and Roland had thought they meant a death but perhaps, Elodie wrote now, that had been a misunderstanding.

Whatever it was, it was a blessing and a gift to be accepted rather than questioned.

Suddenly Wren had more family than she would ever know what to do with.

And yet, she was mostly alone.

So when the horse wandered through the maze of her thorn hedge, and stopped by the lake to drink, she was surprised. It was a fine creature, wearing a saddle and bridle which had been crafted by a master. It wasn't elaborate or overly decorated though. Functional.

The saddlebags were not exactly full, but there were some belongings in them, again of good quality but nothing extravagant. Beautiful, in an understated way, and above all else practical.

The sword, however... that was a royal sword. She knew it.

Somewhere out there, lost in her forest, was a man of royal blood, but not one given to luxury or indolence. More like a soldier really. Or a knight.

Wren let out a weary sigh and went to look for him.

There were still places in the forest where the veil was thin. Once they had been darkwoods, and though the darkness had gone, they were still tricky. They could beguile the unwary and lead them astray without difficulty. They had a siren call, and whispered false promises, and it was far too easy to get turned around and trapped there if you didn't know what you were doing.

Finn was tangled in vines, his head on one side as if asleep, a soft smile on his lips. He wasn't even struggling, the fool. He'd given up.

Or perhaps he had never started trying to free himself in the first place and was just waiting. For her.

It must have been a while now for him to have fallen asleep.

Wren knelt down in front of him and pressed her fingertips to his temples. He wasn't hurt. Just dreaming, lost in the ripples of the music and the magic of the forest. And he looked still as handsome to her as he had when she first found him in similar circumstances so long ago. There was a harder edge to his features, age refining him a little more, but he was no less beautiful for that.

He wasn't wearing a crown now, and his clothes were simple enough. He wasn't even in armour, just well-worn travelling leathers.

'Whatever did you think you were doing?' she asked firmly.

His eyes opened, softly focused on her and he smiled his dreaming smile. 'Looking for you, of course.'

'That tends to involve less lying around in vegetation under a spell, Finn Ward.'

'And yet, I've found you. Just like before.'

'*I* found *you*.'

'Same difference.'

He tried to move towards her, no doubt to take her in his arms and kiss her, but the vines held fast. Irritation flickered over his features and he struggled a little more. They tightened, not letting go.

Wren grinned.

'I may have... um... miscalculated,' he admitted.

She raised an eyebrow. 'Do you think so? What are you doing here, Finn? Don't you have a kingdom to rule?'

'Ah, not anymore. Set up a council. Put Laurence in charge now he's old enough, with Gaius and some of the others to look after him, people we can trust. Abdicated.'

'Can you do that?'

He shrugged. 'Well, as king I could do pretty much what I wanted. So I did. And then I came to find you. Like I promised. I told you I would, Wren.'

The fierce joy that surged up inside her almost stole her wits. Wren frowned at him so she wouldn't show it too obviously but he wasn't fooled, she could tell.

'And how did you know where I was?'

'Stories started circulating about the witch of the woods, describing a woman of unsurpassed beauty, with long dark hair which moves by itself, here...? Who else was it going to be, heart? So I came to find you. Or let you find me, which seemed faster. I was right, wasn't I?'

He sounded ridiculously pleased with himself for a man trapped in a bespelled forest glade which had once been the most dangerous of darkwoods.

Wren sighed another long-suffering sigh.

'Am I always going to be saving you from this forest, Finn?'

'If you'll have me.'

Have him? Of course she would. Who else could she ever want? She leaned down to kiss him, taking her time while the vines held him in place and he groaned against her mouth, struggling just enough to get closer. He had always loved this, to surrender to her, to be hers alone. To let her take what he offered.

With a murmur, Wren told the vines to release him and Finn moved with languid relief, his hands sliding up her sides, burying themselves in her hair, his lips kissing her mouth, her jaw, her throat. Wren lay back on the forest's ferny floor, bathed in its dappled green-gold light, and they gave themselves up to the pleasure they had missed for far too long. He was here, he was hers again, and she was his, forever.

Somewhere in the distance she felt the old magic moving,

rising with their joy and surging with pleasure. It was free, and so was she. And this was how it was meant to be.

Just her and Finn and a whole future open ahead of them.

All around them, there was birdsong.

ELODIE'S LULLABY

My child, my child, my precious child,
When you wake a new day will dawn.
With birdsong, with birdsong.
When back the veil of night is drawn.

My child, my child, my precious child,
When you sleep the dark will bring you peace.
With birdsong, with birdsong.
And all our troubles soon will cease.

A LETTER FROM JESSICA

Dear reader,

I want to say a huge thank you for choosing to read *A Crown of Darkness*. If you did enjoy it, and want to keep up to date with all my latest releases, just sign up at the following link. Your email address will never be shared and you can unsubscribe at any time.

www.bookouture.com/jessica-thorne

A Crown of Darkness is the final part of Wren and Finn's tale, bringing everything full circle. I always knew they would never be happy ruling kingdoms or controlling other people's lives. I also wanted to give Elodie and Roland that happily-ever-after they so deserve. Robin and Lark were something of a surprise—I hadn't planned for them at all, which seems fitting—but what is writing without a few surprises along the way?

I hope you have enjoyed sharing this adventure with me and if you loved *A Crown of Darkness* I would be very grateful if you could write a review. I love hearing from my readers – you can get in touch through my social media or my website. I'd love to know what you think, see these characters and locations through your eyes, and of course, say hi.

Jessica Thorne

KEEP IN TOUCH WITH JESSICA

www.rflong.com/jessicathorne

facebook.com/JessThorneBooks

instagram.com/Jessthornebooks

ACKNOWLEDGEMENTS

These books have been something of an adventure for me. Writing them for release so close together meant we were able to interweave the story over several volumes, to look at it as an arc rather than individual parts, so thanks to everyone who made that possible.

As always thank you to my wonderful agent, Sallyanne Sweeney, and all at Mulcahy Sweeney Associates, my fantastic editor Natalie and everyone at Second Sky, my invaluable writing comrades of the Naughty Kitchen, and here in Ireland Sarah Rees Brennan, Catie Murphy and Susan Connolly. I can honestly say I would not have made it all the way through without you all.

I would also like to thank my friends, Kari Sperring, Kate Pearce and Jeevani Charika, for helping me pull these stories together and critiquing them. I did promise a happily-ever-after. Got there for most people, I think.

And finally thanks to my family, and especially to Pat. As ever, I couldn't do any of this without you.

PUBLISHING TEAM

Turning a manuscript into a book requires the efforts of many people. The publishing team at Bookouture would like to acknowledge everyone who contributed to this publication.

Audio
Alba Proko
Sinead O'Connor
Melissa Tran

Commercial
Lauren Morrissette
Hannah Richmond
Imogen Allport

Cover design
Mary Luna

Data and analysis
Mark Alder
Mohamed Bussuri

Editorial
Natalie Edwards
Charlotte Hegley

Printed in Great Britain
by Amazon

55796821R00202